1492
THE GATES
OF
HEAVEN

THE OTTOMAN EMPIRE TRILOGY

BEYAZIT AKMAN

kopernik

First published by Kopernik Inc.
®Beyazıt Akman 2018

Editor-in-Chief: Abdülkadir Özkan
Advisor: Prof. Halil Berktay
Series Editor: Dr. Yaşar Çolak
Director: Dr. Cengiz Şişman
Translated by: Peter Klempner
Design: Ali Kaya
Application: Sinopsis

Kopernik Publishing House
Kopernik Inc.
108 Olde Towne Avenue Unit: 308 Gaithersburg Maryland 20877 - USA
www.kopernikpublishing.com

Certification no: 35175
ISBN: 978-605-81098-1-0
First Edition: November 2018

Printed in ISTANBUL
Bilnet Matbaacılık ve Yayıncılık A.Ş.

ISTANBUL - LONDON - NEW YORK – WASHINGTON DC

1492 THE GATES OF HEAVEN

The Ottoman Empire Trilogy

BEYAZIT AKMAN

kopernik

BEYAZIT AKMAN: (1981) is a Turkish author of historical fiction, short stories, essays, scholar, book critic and professor of English literature. He earned his B.A. from Middle East Technical University of Ankara in 2003. He received his M.A. in English literature at Illinois State University, as a Fulbright Scholar in 2006, and completed his Ph.D. at the same university in 2012. For his doctoral degree, he focused on the image of Turks and Islam in Western discourse. He taught many courses at Illinois State on East-West discourse in the Department of English. In 2010, he was awarded the Smithsonian Baird Society Fellowship and conducted research at archives and libraries in Washington DC. He also taught courses on world and comparative literature as a visiting professor at State University of New York, Geneseo from 2012 to 2014. Akman has also been published many times in national and international peer-reviewed journals. He started writing historical fiction after years of archival research at university libraries in the United States. His first novel, *1453: The Conquest*, was an instant success when first published and became one of the bestselling novels for a first-time author in his native Turkey. It quickly became a contemporary classic and has been used as inspiration for many historical TV series, movies and novels, launching a new era of historical fiction in Turkey. Proving himself to be a top-notch historical fiction writer, he later wrote *1492: The Gates of Heaven*, which he describes as an ode to the lost Andalusian civilization. Recently, he published *1302: Othman Khan: The Birth of an Empire* in two volumes about the origins of the Ottoman Empire based on the most up-to-date research and scholarship about the Ottomans. Akman was awarded *The International Prize for Historical Fiction* and History in Fiction by the Writers' Association of Turkey. He has been invited to speak at international book fairs in Frankfurt, London and Istanbul. His latest work of nonfiction, *In Search of Lost History: East-West from Mehmed the Conqueror to Shakespeare*, dedicated to Edward Said, was published in 2017 by Kopernik Publishing. He is currently an assistant professor of English Literature at the Social Sciences University of Ankara. He is married with one daughter.

England

Holy Roman
Empire

France

Santiago de
Compostela

Castile
and Aragon

Toledo

Cordoba

Seville

Andalusia

Granada

Malaga

Sardinia

Pap
Sta

7

Avrupa Haritası, Piri Reis, Kitab-ı Bahriye
(16. yy. Sonuna Ait Bir Kopya) İstanbul Üniversitesi Kütüphanesi. No:6605
Map of Europe, Piri Reis, Kitab-ı Bahriye
(A Copy Belonging to the end of 16. Century) Library of Istanbul University . No:6605

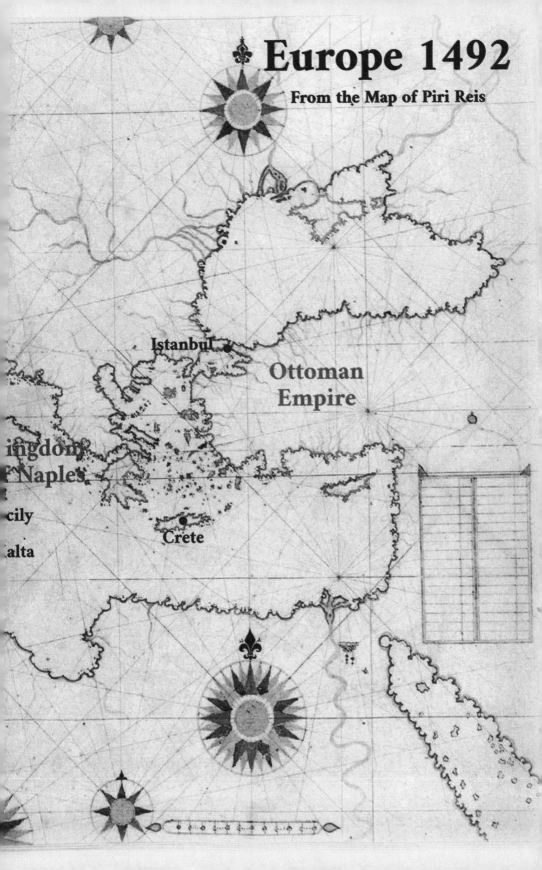

Dedicated to all oppressed people past and present.

God does not forbid you from those who do not fight you because of religion and do not drive you from your homes or from being righteous unto them and acting justly unto them. Indeed, God loves those who act justly.
AL-MUMTAHANAH SURAH, 8

And of His signs are the ships in the sea like mountains.
ASH-SHURAA SURAH, 32

It is the star of piercing brightness.
AT-TARIQ SURAH, 3

PROLOGUE
Aleph

RECONQUISTA
GRANADA, JANUARY 2, 1492

ariq ibn Ziyad.
Boabdil el Chico was looking behind from atop his horse with his mind drifting though the eight centuries that had come before. He looked at the scene in the colorful valley that stretched out from El Pucarra Hill, and if he were to give voice to the majestic name now passing through his mind, seizing his tongue, his palate, his lips, he feared his teeth would melt away. The retinue of his mother, viziers, and a few soldiers was so spindly a sight that he resembled more Don Quixote, attacking windmills with a wooden sword, than a king. Until the early hours of the morning he had been a sultan—the emir of Granada, the caliph, the only Muslim ruler of Andalusia. Now, however, his white turban weighed on his head like a tombstone, and the breeze blowing up the hill and ruffling his red cloak was just as heavy.

"Don't cry," his mother said.

There were tears falling down Boabdil's cheeks. He had earlier personally handed over the Alhambra, and his eyes were now as red as its walls. He had listened repeatedly to the dozens of commanders under his charge who had told him how their lives had passed before their eyes when they were about to die. Today, however, he remembered not his own life, but the eight hundred years of Andalusia's history. It was as if the accumulation of eight hundred years, the many voices of the millions of Muslims, Christians and Jews who had lived together in these lands for centuries and the spirit of the dozens of caliphs were now calling him to account from within himself.

He remembered that Tariq ibn Ziyad with seven thousand men had overtaken an army of a hundred thousand in 711. He turned his head. Half legend, half real, myriad stories he had heard about him came to mind. A ruler of Hispania of that earlier time, Visigothic King Roderic, was so self-assured of victory over Tariq that he had brought hundreds of mules along with his army. After his certain victory in battle, he would pile the Muslim soldiers on these mules to wind from city to city for his own amusement. On the battlefield, however, Tariq and his soldiers had brought such ferocity that the Visigoths would swear that soldiers rained down from the clouds for days. Upon the death of the king of Hispania and his tens of thousands of soldiers, not with mules, but upon galloping horses, Tariq advanced like a thunderbolt and captured Granada, Seville, Cordoba and Toledo one by one, up to the border with the Franks in the Pyrenees Mountains.

With seven thousand men, Tariq had established dominion in southwestern Europe that would last eight hundred years. How true it was that his name means shining star, the night visitor, a light.

Boabdil was now thinking that the horse on which he was sitting was not a black Arabian, but one of King Roderic's mules. And his name and the name of his father contrasted with the dignified name of the commander that he could not now bring himself to say. He had always found being called Boabdil artificial. It was as if he didn't deserve his true name, Abu Abdallah Muhammad XII, which the Spaniards could never quite get their tongues around. He was *Boabdil el Chico*—Little Abu Abdul. No one had or would mention his legacy, now trampled underfoot, alongside the name of the prophet in the long and splendidly titled history books.

He looked at the red roofs of Granada—the bright sunlight glinting off them. His retinue was also woefully peering out over the landscape. The glare off the metal roofs of the cathedrals, synagogues and mosque struck Boabdil's eyes so severely that it was as if even the buildings didn't want him to take in the sight anymore. They heard their own funeral prayers from the minarets and the church bells sounding their death knells rung in their ears. The chief rabbis had buried him long ago.

It was not only the city that Boabdil lost, it was everything that was beautiful in the name of humanity. Boabdil heaved a sorrowful sigh as if it were for a lost love as he gazed upon the faint glimmer of Granada. He looked out over the city for a long time like a young man taking one last look at his lover before leaving for good.

He caught a glimpse of the sparkling streams flowing from inside Andalusia's colorful gardens, not too hot nor too cold, but just right in the shade. From the angry Saharan Desert, Muslims from the dry land of North Africa found rain and greenery, mercy and abundance in this land. The rushing rivers, fertile plains and mountains with all kinds of plants were the most precious treasures for Muslims—of the Arabs, Berbers and the descendants of the Companions of the Prophet.

Andalusia was the Highest Gardens of Paradise on earth whose fragrant breezes embraced the faces of the People of the Book.

It was now a lost heaven. Its rivers were silver, earth musk, gardens silk and pebbles and stones were pearls.

It was where war and dance, music and enlightenment came together.

In Boabdil's eyes, the Cordoba Mosque was the Kaaba of the lovers of the arts— its architecture eternal with countless columns. It was as if for eight centuries the angels had appeared in its towering minarets and the prophets had met in its sanctuaries.

The wines of Andalusia were immaculate and its swords frighteningly sharp.

The fruits that no eye had seen, no tongue tasted, no creature had touched—pomegranate and orange trees and vineyards that the vast amount of agricultural knowledge had made possible—had withered and died.

It was as if nostalgia had been born for Andalusia, and romanticism had arisen for the place, where knights in pursuit of their love grew up and where princesses learned courtly romance. The legend of El Cid would be born here, and centuries later, Cervantes would create a new literature with stories of this land.

The sun would rise in Toledo and set in Cordoba.

Street lamps, windmills and flower-lined paths were devised in Andalusia, and paper and writing were given their deserved right.

In all of Europe, while the priests could not even read the prayer required for baptism, the Muslim peasants of Andalusia knew how to read and write, the Jewish merchants learned mathematics and there were Christian poets.

Ibn Rushd—Averroes to the Europeans—interpreted Aristotle inside the buildings, once so close, that Boabdil was now looking at from afar. Ibn Arabi conquered the hearts of these lands where Maimonides had learned the Torah.

It was not only that of Islam, but the common inheritance of all humanity wasting away.

Right next to Boabdil, and in a final effort to console him, his vizier, Yusuf ibn Kumasha said, "Don't worry, my Sultan. Great defeats are as important as great victories, so long as you don't give up your dignity."

Boabdil let out a heaving sigh. "Is there a defeat equal to mine?"

He knew well that his vizier was trying to give him solace. Only a few hours ago, neither his dignity nor pride remained. Had he not handed over the keys to the city to Ferdinand and Isabella, the king and queen of Castile and Aragon, bowing in front of them and kissing the hem of their gowns?

Everything had begun two and a half centuries ago—the pope

had proclaimed Iberia in need of crusaders, and then came King Ferdinand III of Castile and Leon. It started with Ferdinand III waging war on the dominion of Muslim cities.

It took all of two and a half centuries for the crusaders to take back the Iberian Peninsula, which Tariq ibn Ziyad conquered in twenty-five years.

Nobody, however, expected the Emirate of Granada to fall until the last moment. Granada had managed to remain protected from the rest of the country by the mountains to the north. Like the other Muslim emirs of recent centuries, Boabdil had engaged in all sorts of collaboration with Christian kings and queens, sometimes by paying them taxes and sometimes by giving his sons and daughters as ransom so he could escape. He was twice a hostage of the Christians, and twice free.

The last eight months of siege, however, was not only a siege on Boabdil, but also on Granada and Andalusia's Islamic civilization.

Christian armies had inundated the land every day as if carried by a flood. They were a swarm of locusts descending on Granada. The horsemen increasingly grew in number while ammunition, provisions and reinforcements came from the north.

With their marriage, King Ferdinand of Aragon and Queen Isabella of Castile vowed to complete the unification of Christian Iberia with Granada, and soon thereafter were readying to launch one of the greatest atrocities those lands had ever experienced in the Alhambra.

"I wish we had a few more soldiers, a little more ammunition. If only." Boabdil said.

His mother spoke again in rebuke. "The amount of soldiers cannot overcome a lack of piety!"

She's right, Boabdil thought. Had Tariq not won this land by entering into war outnumbered ten to one?

Another tear fell to the ground from the eye of the former emir of Granada.

"You couldn't fight like a man—don't cry like a woman!" his mother said.

Boabdil sighed heavily, turned his back to the city and set forth on his horse with his retinue from the mountain slope toward the coast. He again remembered Tariq while on the ships about to return to North Africa, feeling as if he was escaping on the ships Tariq had burned so that his soldiers couldn't return eight hundred years ago, and he was going to deplore it.

Boabdil looked out on Granada one last time. The only trace that would be left of him in these lands would be the name of this mountain where he now stood to the east of *Jabal Tariq*. Ten years later he would die wretchedly in the Maghreb, his children and grandchildren beggars.

The Spanish would call this place from where he gazed out at all he had lost as the *Puerto del Suspiro del Moro*—the Pass of the Moor's Sigh.

AUTO DA FÉ
MALAGA, AUGUST 3, 1492

The condemned man sighed and looked at the rope. There wasn't even a single knot in the rope between his inked fingers.

From a bird's-eye view, the plaza of Malaga's dockland on the southwestern tip of Spain looked like the setting of a play. Even though it was early in the morning, the square next to the realm's biggest harbor was getting crowded, and the people were waiting for the spectacle to begin on the stage rising in front of them. The clergy of the Inquisition had found and rounded up thousands of people from the surrounding towns and villages to make such a crowd.

The folk stood at the windows of the buildings surrounding the square, curious and waiting to be horrified. Some children had also climbed onto the roofs of the houses and up to tree branches and settled in there.

An insidious smile spread across the face of Cardinal Ximenes de Cisneros when he emerged onto the platform for the spectacle he had organized and saw the crowd. After all, the *auto da fé*—the twisted, principal vehicle of the showing of faith, as well as punishment—was to instill the spectators' hearts with fear of the power of the Church and the glory of Jesus Christ.

The platform in the north of the area, starting from the head of Paseo del Parque, was so high that it almost completely covered the walls of the buildings behind it. This scaffolding, fifty feet high, was built the day before to the confused looks of the people amid the din and clang of hammers, mallets and saws. The stairs came up the sides and there were two large thrones in the center of the platform with rows of chairs beside and behind them. The thrones were for Queen Isabella and Grand Inquisitor Torquemada, and the other chairs were for cardinals, senior administrators and leading priests.

There was another, narrower scaffold right in from of the platform, half as tall and with a dozen stakes rising from it, each six and a half feet tall and a hand's width around. Royal and Inquisition guards surrounded both platforms.

The deafening silence was broken by the sound of timpani, drums, trumpets and shawms. The priests appeared first carrying the fluttering flags of the Inquisition bearing the inscription *Justitia et Misericordia*. Their faces covered, they looked much taller than they were with their sharply pointed *capirotes*, and with their feet hidden by their vestments, one could imagine the priests were flying like specters instead of walking. The gigantic, serpentine procession slowly filling the gap between the crowd and the platform signaled that the *auto da fé* was about to begin. The musicians were followed by three monks, their arms covered in black cloth and each carrying a gigantic cross, followed by the condemned with their hands bound behind their backs.

These heretics were in a wretched state having endured hunger, torture and countless other atrocities. Most of them had sat in dark dungeons for days, weeks and some for months, and now once again seeing the sunlight, they struggled to open their eyes. The condemned wore yellow, sackcloth gowns called *sanbenitos* painted with a red St. Andrew's cross as symbols of disgrace, indicating they were convicted heretics. Some were carrying candles and other held ropes that could soon be passed over their heads and around their necks. Some of the ropes had one knot, some two and others, more striking, had no knots at all. There was a corpse in front of one of the stakes, half bone and half rotting flesh.

The executioners were wearing black hoods so that all that could be seen of their faces were their eye. They backed the heretics against the platform and tied the ropes hanging down from overhead to their ankles. Then they took the ropes from their hands and fixed them firmly around their necks. There were three knots in the rope the executioner had tied to one of the men's necks—a sign that he was to receive three hundred lashes. As for those who had no knots, they were those unlucky enough to not taste the whip.

After the Inquisition scribes, clergy, priests and cardinals had taken their places on the larger platform to the back, Grand Inquisitor Torquemada and Queen Isabella were finally sat on the thrones at the center. King Ferdinand, as always, had said he was too genteel to watch the *auto da fé* ceremony and had disappeared after concocting an excuse and telling the queen.

Cardinal Ximenes greeted Torquemada and Isabella and then gave a fiery opening speech in which he described the consequences for those who stray from the path of the Holy Church and from the teachings of Jesus Christ, all the while heaping scorn on the heretics for their transgressions. He spoke of the necessity of the *auto da fé* for the eternal salvation of sinners who squander the word of Christ and for the sake of their souls—that this is a gift to the servants of God. He finished his speech, adorning the end with Bible verses in Latin and the words of saints.

He then pointed to the executioners and started the ceremony.

There was a scribe sitting off to the side of the platform. With the beginning of the ceremony, Cardinal Ximenes began to read off the crimes of the heretics and the scribe dutifully recorded them on the papers passing in front of him, as he had years ago grown quite accustomed to transcribing the events of the ceremony. He dipped his quill in the ink and continued writing.

"Juan Frances, blacksmith, lives in Ronda, a resident of San

Mauber, France. He denied the existence of some saints. He came to the *auto* holding a candle and a rope. He was given two hundred lashes.

"Rebeco Sanchez, resident of Malaga. He claimed that marriage is much better than the celibate monastic life of the monastery and church. When told that what he said was contrary to the teachings of the Catholic Church, he persisted. He came to the *auto* with a candle. He agreed to pay forty gold ducats. He was exiled from Malaga for five years.

"Juan Tremino, resident of Almagro in Grenada. He collected information on people while claiming to be a clergyman from the Inquisition. He came to the *auto* with a candle and a rope. He will be an oarsman under the charge of Spanish captains for six years.

"Pedro Navarro, resident of Grenada, merchant. He has been proven to be a secret Mohammedan. His body was disinterred and burned at the *auto*."

The scribe remembered the teachings of Bernardus Comensis as he wrote these lines. *Mortui hæretici possunt excommunicari et possunt hæritici accusari post mortem ... et hoc usque ad quadraginta annos.—Heretics can be excommunicated when dead and heretics can be indicted after death ... and that up to forty years.*

Cardinal Ximenes read out the punishment for the next of the condemned and also recited the Bible verse that dictates such punishment, even though most didn't understand. The Latin was not easily understood amid the screams of those being tortured, and it mixed with their wailing and became some strange language.

"*Si quis in me non manserit mittetur foras sicut palmes et aruit et colligent eos et in ignem mittunt et ardent.*"—*If any one abides not in me, he is cast out as a branch and is withered, and men gather them and cast them into the fire and they are burned.*

The Inquisition scribe hesitated to write the crime and punishment of the next heretic. The man had been condemned to be burned alive. The scribe could easily see the ink on the man's fingertips even though he was ten yards away. Unlike the others, this heretic didn't show even the slightest bitterness even when the kindling under his feet was ignited. His head leaned against the stake—it was as if he saw a world that no one else could see, and he watched that beautiful world from an open window across from him.

The scribe had only just transcribed this man's Inquisition interrogation that morning. As if entranced, he could not pull his gaze away from the man's ink-stained fingertips. It was as if he forgot how to write entirely, and when the man started to burn, the scribe wondered whether the blue ink on his fingertips would mix with the red of the man's blood.

There were still three people in line to be burned alive.

ALEPH
MALAGA, THAT MORNING

The prisoner was laid out over the wooden board of the escalara. Flickering candles faintly illuminated the faces of the priests in the dark room. The scribe off to the side was seated next to a candle that shined on the paper in front of him, but his face remained in darkness.

One of the most important parts of the process was to place the prisoner's head placed lower than his feet. Cardinal Cisneros was infamous for implementing Grand Inquisitor Torquemada's *Dictatorium* word for word. It seemed he'd memorized the book and the interrogation methods it prescribed in fine detail. Guards came to both sides of the prisoners and tied his wrists to the sloped, wooden apparatus. They then tightened the ropes around his ankles.

Cisneros checked over the binding of the man's wrists and ankles and was confident they were tight. He looked at the ink stains on the prisoner's fingers with disgust.

"This is the biggest sign of heresy."

He would've snapped the man's long, thin fingers then and there if it weren't contrary to the laws of the Inquisition. He looked over the man's face. He didn't know what to do with his lack of response. He figured this was another heretic *converso*. He saw the New Christian converts who'd reverted to their Jewish traditions as no different that a dog returning to eat its own vomit. He satisfied himself with the thought that the man had no strength left to move after being held for days in the dungeon. The man's face was ashen and his eyes were sunken and dark.

It wasn't out of hunger or exhaustion, however, that the prisoner didn't respond. He'd heard of this room many times and knew well enough that resistance was of no use—he had to focus on not confessing no matter what happened. He had to concentrate all his energy on it. He knew the day before that he would be taken to this room when he wasn't given the usual wet, moldy bread for his daily meal. A prisoner could vomit during the interrogation, after all, and foul the room.

He'd reckoned that the few days he'd spent in the dungeon amid the smells of excrement, dried blood and damp would've made his nose insusceptible to it all, although the thick smell of urine in the room proved he was mistaken, and so he relaxed when they blocked his nostrils. The guards didn't do this for the prisoner's benefit, but because by only being able to breath through his mouth, the soon-to-begin interrogation would be much more effective.

"Bring the prongs," Cisneros ordered.

The prisoner shuddered when he saw the iron prongs covered in the filth of all the previous prisoners' spittle. He tried to move but the ropes cut into his wrists and ankles.

One of the guards squeezed his chin and opened his mouth as wide as it would go, then another shoved in the prongs and fit them in place. Then they put a piece of cloth over his face.

Everything was ready now and the guards had their eyes on the water bucket on the ground.

There were four other men in the room—three high officials seated at the long table draped in a black cloth in addition to the scribe recording all the details of the interrogation off to the side. They were a monk who was an observer from Torquemada's Suprema, one of Cardinal Cisneros' priests and a doctor. Cisneros looked over at the doctor after all the preparations had been made for the interrogation.

Seeing that it was his time, the doctor rose nonchalantly and walked over to the prisoner strapped to the wooden plank. He gave a cursory look over the man, then turned to Cisneros and nodded. "You can continue."

According to Torquemada's codes for the Inquisition, accused heretics must confess their crimes firmly and consciously and of their own volition, they should be able to hear what is said and be of sound mind. A confession could be considered invalid otherwise.

The priest stood up and started speaking, periodically glancing at the documents on the table. The scribe was recording everything he said.

"We of the Tribunal of the Holy Inquisition of the Kingdoms of Castile and Aragon—Cardinal Ximenes de Cisneros Archbishop of Toledo for the Holy Catholic Church, doctor of canon law Father Francisco Sanchez de la Fuente and I, licentiate of holy theology, Pedro Diaz de la Costaña—with authority from the Kingdoms of Castile, Leon and Aragon and Grand Inquisitor Tomas de Torquemada—"

He stopped and picked up the papers detailing the man's information and crimes and continued.

"It is said the accused, David ibn Nahmias Marrano, jeweler, of the town of Montalban in Toledo, who was baptized a Christian at the age of nineteen in 1481, and despite being a Catholic for over tens years, has continued to practice Jewish traditions and live according to the laws of Moses.

"According to the testimony given against him by the witness to the Holy Church in confession, the accused, David ibn Nahmias Marrano, refrains from word on Saturdays, has been seen lighting candles in his house on Fridays in observance with the Sabbath and was found to have manuscripts and books in Hebrew and Arabic in his house—"

The hatred on Cardinal Cisneros' face grew as Father Pedro Diaz de la Costaña read out the accusations.

"In addition, the accused built a printing press, the device coming from the Germans, in a secret place in the town of Montalban with his brother, Samuel ibn Nahmias, and in collaboration with heretic adherents to the Muhammadan religion in the old Emirate of Granada, printed and disseminated hundreds of Hebrew and Arabic texts, the Quran, teachings of the Talmud and Gemara, the heretic Averroes and his Aristotelian exegeses, the philosophies of the old Hellenic philosophers and the heretic Maimonides' books both in Hebrew and Arabic, all of which are forbidden by our Holy Church—"

Cardinal Cisneros was growing impatient for the list of accusations to end.

"The accused has denied all of the accusations for days, insists that for many years he has been a good Christian walking the path of Jesus Christ, and asserts that the allegations directed against him are slander. For this reason, it was decided that the torture used for even the most unrepentant heretics will continue on the *escalara*."

Cisneros looked at the guards sitting next to Father Diaz de la Costaña. This was the moment he'd been waiting for.

One of them put the end of a metal funnel into the mouth of the accused and another took a bucket of water from the ground and was readying to empty it into the man's mouth.

The young man's eyes shot wide open in terror.

Cisneros gave a sign and the guard slowly tipped the bucket. The water soaking into the cloth in the young man's mouth and blocked his throat. He was trying to swallow since he couldn't breath through his nose, but he convulsed helplessly as the water filled his throat. Hoping for quick release, David felt as if he was drowning while the guard continued to pour the water into his mouth. But the most important feature of the *escalara*, like the Inquisition's other torture devices, was to keep the accused alive while inflicting the most pain and without spilling a drop of blood. It was strictly forbidden to spill blood in an interrogation, as it evoked Jesus Christ's self-sacrifice for humanity.

"Say it!" shouted Cisneros. "Do you accept that you are a believer of the religion of Moses?

"Say it! Have you celebrated the Sabbath on Friday evenings? Have you attended the Jewish circumcision ceremonies?"

The guards set the bucket aside and removed the metal prongs and cloth from David's mouth so he could answer.

He was coughing and lifted his head as much as possible from where it lay as he tried with great pain to empty his lungs of the water. His pallid face had become bright red.

Cisneros looked at David in the face, waiting for an answer. He was gasping for breath. He didn't say a word and laid his head back.

Cisneros gave the sign and the guards replaced the prongs and cloth and began to pour the water again, although much faster this time.

David was convulsing in panic, flailing his hands and feet forward and back against the ropes in a futile attempt to save himself. He felt as though he was under the sea, crushed under tons of water, or that he'd been buried alive with the shovels thrown over him.

The *escalara* was the least bloody yet cruelest of the methods of torture Torquemada had discovered.

The feeling of drowning and the panic it elicited created both physical and mental fatigue. Cisneros knew well from experience that the majority of even the most unrepentant heretics sang like nightingales after the second round. After all, he'd delivered full lists of the names of even the most tight-lipped criminals to the Church. He grabbed a printed page of Hebrew text from the table and returned to the David as he lay prone.

"Say it! Did you write this?"

David looked at the paper and a smile spread across on his face to the stunned looks of those around him. His eyes were on the letter *aleph* at the top of the page, in red and larger than the rest of the black text. This sudden smile vanished just as quickly and the young man began to weep.

He was thinking of Esther.

His memories came back as he looked at the page, and his sorrow and suffering grew as the remembered. He remembered two weeks before when everything started, picturing all the details of the day.

Cisneros signaled the guards for the third time. The doctor at his side, however, protested this time.

"Aren't you going too fast? The man may die."

"Then this is a risk we'll take under warrant of the Church," Cisneros shot back.

The physician was about to continue, but Cisneros interrupted with an insinuating threat, "I've heard you're grandmother was a Jew, doctor. I wonder if that could be partly true."

The doctor silently returned to his place knowing that Cisneros could very easily deem him a heretic. It wouldn't have been the first time.

David was thinking of Esther and Davud the Brave—the man who'd started everything, the Turk whom he couldn't figure from where he'd came. His brother Samuel, Beatriz, Abdullah of Xativa and Zayd ibn Uthman all passed through his mind.

The guards began to pour the water into his mouth again.

VAV
CONSTANTINOPLE, FEBRUARY 1492

The calligrapher was out of breath when he approached the rowboat rocking like a cradle in the water on the Üsküdar coast. He was holding his leather bag hanging down from the shoulder of his caftan with both hands so its contents wouldn't jostle about too much. His writing sets were more precious to him than anything.

"I need to get across right away," He said as soon as he hopped in.

"Whoa, sir, Satan has a hand in all things done in haste," the boatman said.

"I'm late—very late!"

The boatman took his place in the center of the boat and grabbed hold of the oars with a grumble. The little boat set off on the shimmering water of the Bosporus as the sun rose higher in the sky. The silhouette of the city in front of the calligrapher was growing larger as they went—the Justice Pavilion in Topkapi Palace, Fatih Mosque and Galata Tower. Ships and boats of all sizes were shuttling between the two sides of the Bosporus, and sailing up the middle were mostly Venetian and Genoese galleys traveling to and from the Mediterranean and Black Sea.

The boat landed at the Sarayburnu pier and the calligrapher breathed out deeply.

"At last!"

He reached into his bag and realized that while in his haste to leave the house he had forgotten to bring any money. He looked at the pockets of his caftan and shirt. The boatman had begun to get suspicious.

"No?" he asked.

"I don't think I have any money," said the calligrapher, composing himself.

"I won't let you off this boat then. Are you joking with me, sir?"

The calligrapher rummaged through his bag one more time and stopped.

"I have an idea," he said.

"I want my money, mister. What is this idea?"

"Wait just a moment."

The calligrapher took out a blank page from his bag, put it on his knee and dipped his reed pen into the inkpot.

He drew a single letter in one motion that filled the page. He put his writing set back in his back and held out the paper to the bewildered boatman.

The man's eyes opened wide when he saw the paper.

"I've never seen such a beautiful *vav* in all my life!" he said.

He knew that such a large letter *vav* from a master calligrapher could fetch quite a sum.

"I believe this will cover our little trip," the calligrapher said as he quickly jumped up to the pier.

The calligrapher proceeded behind a royal janissary guard to the sultan's room in the palace. When they came to the door, the doorman told the sultan's personal janissary guard that no one was allowed in on special order from the sultan. The janissary stepped aside, and when the doorman saw the calligrapher he immediately opened the door. This order did not pertain to the calligrapher.

Sultan Bayezid was standing at the window as the man entered. He was wearing a dark blue caftan and a white turban sat atop his head. He was bent forward reading a letter he was holding and the sun was shining through the window onto the sultan's face.

The calligrapher approached and the sultan looked up and turned to face him.

There was a pained and distressed expression on his face. "It's bad news, my dear friend," he said.

"Is it from the spy in Iberia?"

The sultan nodded. "Apparently the situation has gotten much worse. It's time for action now."

The gates of Topkapi Palace—as tall as three men—were slowly closing when Hamdullah the Calligrapher left that evening. The line written on the arch the calligrapher passed under referred to the sultan who had built the palace.

Khan of Khans, the Shadow and Spirit of God in between People, Ruler of Earth, Lord of Two Lands and Two Seas, Roman Caesar Gazi Sultan Mehmet II bin Murad for Ever Victorious

NEW YORK
PRESENT DAY

The doors of the train closed quickly, leaving those pushed aside at the last moment waiting on the platform.

A young man looked impatiently out the window of the speeding New York subway train, watching for the sign of the coming station. It took a two-hour flight from Chicago to this city to see the man he was going to meet in half an hour. It all looked like a fast-running film from the window—the dark walls of the subway appeared and disappeared as the regularly spaced lights were replaced by darkness every two seconds. The stifling noise from the wheels on the tracks mixed with the sound of people talking all around him had become quite a racket.

The reflection of the crowd inside the train on the window made it look even more cinematic. There was a young Asian man holding onto the handrail, leaning over and explaining something to the girl in front of him. On the other side was a man in a suit with a leather briefcase who must have been a businessman, seated and reading the *Wall Street Journal* on his iPad. Next to him were two girls flipping around a map and trying to figure out where they were. Opposite them, a homeless man was sleeping, curled up on two seats. Even though everybody was crammed together, due to the man's odor, no one was making any effort to get to the empty space next to him.

The young man noticed his own reflection while he was looking at the reflections of everybody else in the window. He stared into his own blue eyes. His hair was still thinning and his beard had already gone quite gray. Despite having only entered his thirties, he wasn't surprised when his friends told him he looked more like he was in his forties. He turned away from his reflection, chastising himself for his vanity, and he began to browse through the daily newspapers on his Kindle. Jeff Bezos, the founder of Amazon, the world's biggest book site, and who has been described as the new Gutenberg, first entered the American market with the Kindle, and then the rest of the world. And it spread like wildfire faster than most people could have guessed. Now, everywhere—busses, planes, trains—everybody, young and old, was reading from thin tablets.

There was a headline in the *New York Post*—"Pastor Says Will Burn Quran" with the subheading, "The pastor said he is not backing down from burning a Quran, he has just put it off." The pastor was making his decisions according to the developments in the construction of a mosque in New York, but added that it isn't right to build this type of Islamic center in the city after September 11.

Another story—"Bloomberg Gives Historic Speech: Mayor Defends Mosque Near Ground Zero"—was about the city's Jewish mayor, Michael Bloomberg, who the previous day had made a poignant public appeal behind the Statue of Liberty in support of the building of the mosque.

When the train slowed with a painful screech of the breaks and he heard the announcement for Times Square, Beyazit knew it was time to get off and he tossed the Kindle into his bag. He rode up the escalator and then walked through a long underpass. He was dazzled by the sunlight when he finally got outside after the effect of the subway's square, white tiles, flat ceiling, moisture and acrid smell of urine. A sea of people met him when he stepped out onto the corner of 42nd Street and 7th Avenue. It was as if the entire world was meeting there. In times past all roads once led to Rome, then Baghdad, then Istanbul—now they all go to New York City.

He had been to the city many times before, and it was more crowd-ed every time.

He pulled the address out of his pocket and looked at the paper one more time at the corner of the Paramount building and ABC Studios. He still had a fifteen-minute walk to go.

He began to walk southwest from Broadway, mixing in with the river of diverse people. He could hear Jay Z and Alicia Keys' *Empire State of Mind* playing from some far-off place. He looked at the New York Times Building—the newspaper after which this part of Man-hattan had been named—and the gigantic letters on the skyscraper in *Englishtowne* font, itself practically having become a symbol of the press. The letters looked as if they had been printed in black ink on an old parchment on the façade.

Both sides of the street were lined with taller and shorter sky-scrapers—the Chrysler Building on the corner looked as if it had grown directly out of the concrete. The top of the building had seven terraced, steel arches, each one smaller than the one below, reminiscent of the horseshoe arches of Andalusia. The triangular glass on each arch that reflected the sunlight made it also resemble a crown. Beyazit thought that the ruler of this state—the Empire State—was perhaps this skyscraper. Manhattan's tallest building, the Empire State Building, however, was still further away, its mas-sive antenna seemingly wanting to get the news from around the world and spread it on the earth. It seemed as though the people waiting in line for the observation decks on the top floor wouldn't only see the New York skyline, but also the horizon stretching be-yond. The giant lighting rod at the tip of the skyscraper was daring lighting to strike.

Beyazit left behind the all-glass MTV Building, the Hard Rock Cafe, a few sex shops with risqué window displays, the not-quite-nude Naked Cowboy with a guitar and the Planet Hollywood that had famous actors like Sylvester Stallone and Arnold Schwarzeneg-ger attend its opening years before. He knew he was coming to

Times Square when he saw the brightly lit, LED Coca-Cola sign. One of the two most domineering buildings amid the sea of people had a 3-D sign made up of a hundred thousand little neon lamps, like the other hundreds of gigantic advertisements around. Across from the Coca-Cola bottle was a gigantic advertisement for Budweiser with its yellow lights constantly in motion. These companies were all vying to attract customers with their electro-kinetic lights on the corner of Broadway and 7th Avenue. The square was as big as two stadiums. On one side there was a Virgin sign with each letter constantly changing color, McDonald's and its golden arches famous the world over and a flashing Toshiba sign. On the other side of the square, there was an American Eagle sign, white on blue in heavy contrast. There was a large American flag hanging from one of the buildings. Sony, Samsung and all the companies that had brought forth these technological wonders made it seem as if all the peoples of the world met here on these screens hanging on the walls of these stores. "CIA Water Torture Scandal" flashed in huge letters across one of the HD screens. Waterboarding people in interrogations to make them talk had come up again.

There was such energy in the square that it seemed like it was the earth's transformer center and that the entire world's electricity flowed from here. Stock market values flowed across the curved Nasdaq screen while a line about the Israeli-Palestinian conflict ran in the news band below it. The crowds were too busy endlessly taking pictures or having their pictures taken to notice the news or the stock market. Two out of every three people either had a digital camera or were posing for their iPhones. Hungry people were milling around the counters of the mobile Sabret Hotdog stand, although unlike Beyazit, they obviously didn't know that its name means be patient.

Beyazit realized he was nearing the shop he was looking for when he came to 47th Street, and he turned left off Broadway. It was only five blocks away, about three hundred yards. He felt lonely as the crowds thinned out. He heard a strange silence from where he had just come—the racket had ceased and he felt cold between the concrete and the buildings rising up to the gray sky. A gigantic rat popped up from a storm drain and disappeared into a parking lot. There's no doubt that New York's rats are well fed.

Beyazit stopped when he saw the small, modest jeweler on the corner. He looked at the address on the door and then looked at the address on the piece of paper he had. It had *Al-Andalus Jewelry* on its shop window.

He had found the man he was looking for—David Marrano.

Beyazit sat in a chair in front of the counter in the little jewelry store and smiled as he stirred his tea in a familiar, slim-waited Turkish glass.

"I didn't know you could find these glasses in America," he said. "I turned Illinois upside down and I couldn't even find a pair."

The saucer was even white with little red designs as is so often seen in Turkish cafes.

The man sitting in a wheelchair on the other side of the counter who must have been over ninety took a sip from his tea and smiled.

"My grandson brought them from Turkey," he said. "I was always explaining it to them, and when they saw them when they went and visited Istanbul, they snatched up a set for me. I can't drink tea from any other glass. Turkish culture and Sephardic culture are really similar after all."

The Sephardim was the name of the Jews of Andalusia.

Beyazit saw David Marrano take a long look into his glass. Despite the man's age, and if he didn't take into account the wheelchair, he looked remarkably healthy—his face twenty years younger. The man's hair was completely gray, but his head as full as if he were twenty. Generally speaking, time had been generous to this man even though his face and hands were thin with spots left from age. "These cups remind me of my childhood in Istanbul, and those red and white striped arches of Andalusia."

"Do you remember your years in Istanbul?" Beyazit asked.

"I mostly remember my childhood and the Bosporus. The horns from the ships still ring in my ears." He paused for a moment in reflection. "Maybe I only remember the best parts of my childhood. Being a kid is always the best, isn't it?"

Beyazit looked at the jewelry in the display case on the walls, all fitted with precious stones—diamonds, rubies and emeralds. It had quite a rich inventory for such a small shop. There were also items displayed on the walls—a quadrant, an astrolabe—which one would more likely expect to see in Professor Fuat Sezgin's museums.

He was also trying not to take notice of the burley man in a black suit next to David Marrano, although Beyazit didn't quite understand whether the man was a merchant or Marrano's security. There were also old wall clocks hanging on the wall and ticking away behind the old man. All of them showed a different time, their pendulums swinging back and forth. Most of the clocks, their pendulums, hour and minute hands, and cases were plated with either gold or silver. There were two framed texts hanging right in the middle of the clocks, one in Hebrew and one in Arabic. Beyazit wondered what was written on the pages, but he didn't ask.

"So, when was the last time you were in Turkey?"

"It was the eve of World War II, I guess," David Marrano said. "My father had just finished his two-year military service. Then the dark days started in the '30s and '40s when there were riots in western Anatolia against the Jews there. Fascism, that disease that erupted in Eastern Europe at the beginning of the century, wasn't over yet. With influence from the British, the Greeks acted as if they had just learned that they were Greeks, and naturally, the Turks responded against it. And again, those left in between it all was us—the Sephardim. The Wealth Tax applied to non-Muslims in 1942 really hurt us deeply."

The old man continued looking at his guest's face. The hundred years Marrano had seen were hiding in the depths of his dark eyes.

"Don't let me calling fascism a sickness surprise you. I'm not against nationalism, but what happened to the Ottomans was a game well played by imperialist Europeans. They destroyed the Ottoman Empire's multicultural society. Otherwise, love for one's homeland and nationalism is sacred. Imperialists also divided countries like India and Pakistan with this game.

"After what was committed against the Jews in Germany, my father also immigrated to the New World, to New York, like so many others who fled as far away as possible. The Turks respected him because he was religious, even though they called him a prude. Even in the military, he performed his worship several times a day and kept kosher. There were still doubts about our future, though. I went to school and college in America and I married an American here."

"I suppose there're similarities between Muslim and Jewish dietary restrictions, aren't there?"

"Of course. People put Judaism and Christianity side by side with a false perception and place them against Islam, but Jews and Muslims are much closer to each other. Once you add the Sephardic customs from Istanbul to this mix, there's nothing else left but nuances. Ottoman culture fed our culture—wood carving, synagogues, our choirs of *maftirim*."

"Have you ever gone back to Turkey?"

"I went for work when I worked at the World Bank. I gave thirty years to that institution. I was chairman of a commission that provided funding for aid to developing countries—Congo, Mali, Niger and Sudan in Africa; Bolivia, Colombia and Brazil in Latin America; and Czechoslovakia, Lithuania and Yugoslavia in Eastern Europe."

Marrano shook his head and wrinkled his face. "But I've experienced the breakdown of many ideas. The European countries that absorbed the blood of these countries for years—Britain, France, Spain, Portugal—these states are the first responsible for the blood that is still being spilled in those developing countries, but they've disappeared when it comes to helping businesses join the projects that would develop those countries. They talk big in their parliaments, but when we come calling they pretend to be in an endless economic crisis. And look, we were able to collect important funding from Turkey to help some countries in North Africa.

"I had the chance to meet a lot of senior managers in Turkey due to my position at the World Bank."

"So did you start at the United Nations after you left the World Bank?"

"Yeah, I was hoping there might've been something I could change. I was there for five years. It took me less than half an hour to walk from here to the United Nations building. But I was blacklisted when I prepared reports on behalf of Palestine. We came to the conclusion concerning the Mavi Marmara incident that Israel should apologize to the humanitarian foundation and pay due compensations. The imperative came from Israel. They asked for my resignation the following week."

The old man leaned forward in his wheelchair and looked at his legs. "This damn thing's also a present from that administration. I was at an international demonstration in Palestine against the Israeli occupation when I was young. Israeli soldiers opened fire and a bullet hit me right in my spine. I've been condemned to this chair for over forty years."

Marrano leaned forward again. "Look, we are a people that has been condemned to a life of exile on earth for centuries and we've experienced massacres throughout history. Having our own land is our most sacred right, but it should be done with respect to the rights of Palestinians. If we oppress Palestinians, how are we any different from the Nazis or the Catholic Inquisition? An Israeli leader who kills Palestinians is no different than a Nazi killing Jews. People shouldn't think that Jews and Zionists are the same. We're not! I've never seen myself as one of those Zionist, Israeli fanatics.

America should solve this problem independently, without being influenced from anywhere."

Marrano jabbed his index finger at some unseen thing. "But the point that the administration in Israel doesn't understand, or rather what it wants to forget, is that today Jews have tremendous fortune all over the world—many architects and developers in this city are Jews—and even today if Jews can read the Torah and Talmud and speak Hebrew to their hearts' content, it's because of the contribution, help and support from Islamic civilizations. There wouldn't be Judaism today if it weren't for Andalusia first and then the Ottomans. Jews owe their existence today to Muslims in times past."

Marrano paused for a while and crossed his arms. Then, his voice furious, he said, "And while the golden age of Andalusian Judaism was about to end, when our people were being uprooted in Europe, an Ottoman sultan, a Muslim ruler, eventually opened the gates of heaven to us."

Marrano smiled as if his anger had melted away. He leaned toward the young writer.

"Your late father named you after an Ottoman sultan."

"It's interesting that you mention the names," Beyazit said with a little smile. "You have the same thing, too. But I always thought Marrano was an insult. Why'd you choose to use it?"

"David ibn Nahmias Marrano," the old man said, "was my great, great, great—I don't know how many greats I have to put to go back five hundred years—he was my great grandfather. At that time, yes, some say that Marrano was an insult, but I've never taken offence, and I've always been happy with it."

He put his hands on the case and looked at the young man again. "Alright, let me explain his story. I know that you've researched this topic for years and that you believe in names.

"This story needs to be told, Beyazit. What I'm going to share with you is one of the biggest hidden treasures of history and one of the greatest tragedies experienced after the Holocaust. Turkey,

Israel and the world need to hear this story now more than ever. It's a lesson in humanity the Ottomans taught five centuries ago.

"You'll have to wait a little while to see the main heroes of the story, but it'll be worth it.

"Don't say that you weren't warned, though—you should be careful when explaining this history, because they'll call you a Mason or a Jew simply because you tell it. You'll have friends and enemies from both sides.

Beyazit smiled as if he was unconcerned with the warning. "Let them read my novels *1453: The Conquest* and *Othman Khan*," he said.

David Marrano then pointed at the two texts on the wall. "Do you remember these?"

Beyazit looked at the Hebrew and Arabic texts. "Are these—?" he said, trailing off.

Marrano nodded and started to tell the story.

Beyazit began to see a five hundred year story while Marrano was speaking, as if he had entered a tunnel to the past, with the scenes slowly laid out in front of him, following the chain of events.

There was a big crowd passing by outside yelling, "No mosque at Ground Zero! Muslims go back to Arabia!"

BOOK ONE
David and Davud 1492

1

Sultan Bayezid looked through the narrow window at the sun that was showing itself in its full glory. He'd forgotten that he shouldn't stare at this glowing orb of fire for too long.

He found it strange. Could the sun really be gazed upon for so long?

He was dazzled and had to squint, but it seemed the sun wanted to show itself to him today—that it was dancing for the sultan's gaze.

Bayezid wasn't wearing his turban or boots. He felt like he was naked even though he was wearing a brilliant white shirt that hung down past his knees and a pair of pants of the same color underneath.

He turned around and looked at the simple room. There was an unassuming rug on the wooden floor, a mattress in one corner and a reading stand in another.

The bed looked unruffled. So he hadn't gotten up yet. Had he come here last night to sleep? But it was still the day and the sun was wonderful.

He was hungry—very hungry actually. How long had it been since he had some trotter soup? A week? A month? A year? He couldn't remember.

He was craving trotter soup so much that he could smell the garlic and feel its tinge in his nose. He remembered his youth in Amasya. What days those were. Both he and his friends together, one day a huge kebab, trotter soup, pilaf with braised meat, and a different dessert at each meal—baklava, rice pudding or syrupy cake.

But how had he come to this room? What had happened to those days?

"Call me the head cook!" he yelled.

He paced back and forth from one side of the room to the other for a while and then stopped. He couldn't stand it.

This inner struggle he had started against himself was going to finish today and he was going to put an end to this torture. How many years had it been—ten, twenty? He would have trotter soup made and he was going to sit down with it.

The head cook was busy fulfilling the sultan's order, so Bayezid sat behind the reading stand and tried to read a couple lines from the Arabic book laying open on it.

"And, when Moses said to his people: 'O my people, indeed you have wronged yourselves by your taking of the calf. So repent to your Creator and kill yourselves. That is best for you in the sight of your Creator.' Then He accepted your repentance—indeed, He is the Acceptor of repentance, the Merciful."

The sultan read the line, *"So repent to your Creator and kill yourselves,"* and recalled why he was in this room.

He rose to his feet again and looked outside. The sun had gone, and in its place was a crescent moon. It was still light out, but now with the strange, silvery shining of the crescent moon. The crescent moon looked like a palm leaf with graceful folds and was so bright that he shaded his eyes with his hand.

He turned back around and saw that Sheikh Hamdullah had seated himself on the divan in the corner. How had he not seen him earlier? Bayezid had lost himself while reading—maybe he had come in then.

There was a knock on the door and servants entered carrying the sultan's trotter soup.

The servants placed a low table on the rug, on top of that a silver tray, and then the piping hot soup and a spoon. It was exactly how the sultan liked it, with lots of vinegar and garlic.

As soon as the servants left, Sultan Bayezid knelt down at the table and took a deep smell of the wafting aroma. The best cook in the empire had prepared the soup so wonderfully that he had even garnished it with butter in the form of a rose.

Bayezid remembered that he hadn't encountered such wonderful soup in quite a long time. He took the spoon in his right hand and was about to dig in, but he stopped.

He looked at Sheikh Hamdullah. It seemed Hamdullah was angry and glaring at him.

He remembered the verse again. *Repent to you Creator and kill yourselves!*

He looked at the soup.

Then what Hamdullah had told him while they were still in Amasya rang in his ear. *He who cannot handle soup, can rule neither himself nor the world. You will not pass on only one spoonful of soup. Satan enters into man through one's blood. One judges oneself starting from a single spoonful.*

He had repented years ago for nothing haram to enter his life, not only for himself, but to intercede in the habits he and all of all his good friends had acquired in their youth. It was then when he had begun to scrutinize his eating and drinking habits and his personal discipline.

But he couldn't stand it any longer. He couldn't only have one spoonful of this soup.

He dipped the spoon in and pulled out a heaping spoonful.

But he couldn't go any further.

You're a great sultan—if you can't handle soup, what good are you to your sultanate?

He didn't know if this was in his head or if it was coming from Sheikh Hamdullah still sitting across from him. In his youth, in the years he took lessons from Hamdullah, what the master had taught him would echo in his head even when he was alone—it was as if he was having a conversation with him while he practiced his letters.

He emptied his spoon again into the bowl and slammed the spoon down onto the silver tray. He was angry.

"Oh the Flesh!" roared Bayezid. "Here's the soup you so desired, the one you've been aching for. If you want to, here it is, eat it!"

The sultan hadn't yet closed his mouth, and from between his lips, a blind, shadowy, jet-black creature appeared like a weasel from its den. The animal attacked the soup so violently that the entire bowl was empty after it writhed around the bowl a few times. It leaped back onto Bayezid's body and tried to get inside the sultan's mouth, but Bayezid immediately stood up and trampled the animal.

Sheikh Hamdullah also rose and kicked the animal that was convulsing on the ground.

Hamdullah covered its lifeless body with a white sheet that looked like a shroud. Sultan Bayezid, dripping with blood and sweat, pulled the white sheet from his head and sat up in bed.

He was gasping for breath—he didn't know how exhausting a dream could be. Beads of sweat were forming on his forehead. When it was morning, Hamdullah would be the first to interpret this dream.

He got up from bed and milled around the room. The sacred book he had been reading before he had gone to sleep was still there on the reading stand opened to the *al-Baqarah* surah, verse fifty-four.

Repent to your Creator and kill yourselves.

He looked out the window from his room—one of the hundreds of windows at Topkapi Palace. The crescent moon shining down on the Bosporus created a magnificent reflection on its waters accompanied by a star.

The view reminded the sultan of his younger, stormy days in Amasya. He lost himself in it. His was such a great fight. Not with others, though, with himself. He had struggled so hard with his own devils.

He pulled himself together and turned around. Today was going to be long. There was a special Divan meeting waiting for important decisions from him. He decided it was best to not sleep any longer, did his ablutions and sat back down at the reading stand.

2

Sheikh Hamdullah was sitting on the edge of the divan by the reading stand. He was also the general secretary to the Divan in addition to being a master calligrapher. The sultan still hadn't arrived. Hamdullah looked at the two guests sitting on the couch against the semicircular wall off in the far corner. The two guests had half a dozen top-level diplomats around them along with Shaykh ul-Islam Ahmed Efendi. Each one of them was showy in their caftans, robes and grandiose headpieces, but none attracted as much attention as these two extraordinary visitors to the Divan.

They were easily separated from the dozen high-ranking Ottoman councilors, not because they where not members of the Imperial Council—the *Divan-i Hümayun*—or their credentials, but by their clothes. Chief Rabbi Moshe Kapsali was wearing a shimmering, straight-collard, purple silk robe, a black gown and *tefillin* wrapped around a silk turban. Next to him was the Orthodox patriarch. The gold *encolpion* with images of the Virgin Mary and Jesus hanging from his neck and his headgear—what the Greeks call a *klobuk*—with its long veil hanging down and covering his neck and shoulders, were drawing attention.

Hamdullah listed off the attendees of the Divan in turn from the paper he had prepared. Right next to where the sultan was separated from the rest was Grand Vizier Yakup Pasha sitting in the shaykh ul-Islam's shadow, next to the vizier were the Anatolian and Rumelian governors-general, the janissary agha next to them and, finally, next to him, Captain of the Sea Admiral Kemal Reis. This elite group was followed by the head sergeant, the treasurer, the chamberlain of the doorkeepers, scribes of stations large and small, interpreters and other senior officials.

According to Hamdullah, the youngest member of the Divan was Kemal Reis, whom he guessed was somewhere between twenty-five and thirty. This former pirate had only a few years ago had a death warrant on his head. Now, however, with a turn of fortune and history, he sat at the highest echelons of the empire.

Hamdullah was surprised when Grand Vizier Yakup Pasha had come to the morning prayer at the Hagia Sophia the previous day and told him that the sultan would attend today's meeting of the Divan. When he saw the extraordinary guests of the day, however, he was sure there was going to be a different agenda to be considered. He had thought that Sultan Bayezid intended to do away with one of his deceased father Mehmed's reforms when the grand vizier first informed him, as sultans had presided over all the meetings of the Divan before Mehmed the Conqueror's time. One day, a peasant had barged into the meeting in a clamor, and in front of the great conqueror of the Eastern Roman Empire, waved his arms and petitioned, *Tell me who of you is the sultan. I have something to say!* while the theologians, scholars and diplomats were all stuck staring at each other. Mehmed had decided that he would no longer attend the Divan after this, which had cast such a shadow on the dignity of the empire.

It crossed his mind while Hamdullah thought of this story how much Sultan Bayezid didn't resemble his father. The first thing Bayezid had done as soon as he ascended to the throne was to return all the monastery land that Mehmed had seized back to its owners. He tried to measuredly do away with his father's reforms that he saw as too liberal—the reforms the people had grown tired of and that had negatively affected them—and he strengthened the ties between the state and the people. Over the past ten years Bayezid had been sitting on the throne, there were those who when comparing him to his father called the new sultan a puritan and also those who blamed him for being too peaceful and not acting as ambitiously as his predecessor. After the rapid conquests by the sword, as Hamdullah saw it, Bayezid was trying to focus on spiritual conquests and was striving to make the land he had gained with science and culture flourish—otherwise his father's gains would be meaningless.

Everyone stood up upon Bayezid's appearance at the sultan's door.

As always, Bayezid had a humble manner with his head down, and he greeted the members of the Divan with his hand over his heart. Bayezid sat on the throne. He was wearing a quilted, white turban he had designed himself in accordance with the regulations, a close-fitting green robe, a fur-lined violet caftan, yellow leather boots and a belt of the same color. The Chinese cloud patterns on his robe, crescent motif on his caftan and his embroidered shirt had an unobtrusive elegance.

The sultan took his seat and the Divan began to debate the first item on the agenda.

Yakup Pasha took the floor after reading the third vizier's order of the day.

"Sir, as you know, hundreds of people passed away in the great earthquake in Edirne, and the number of wounded and crippled is also very high. We are sending physicians and medical supplies there, but when the catastrophe is great, it takes just as much strength to wrap the wound. By God's grace we will overcome this difficulty. God is great—he gave us this punishment and we will endure it."

Sultan Bayezid, as was his practice, listened to what was said first, then gave his own opinion with all his clarity. He would never approve of such extreme fatalism as that of Yakup Pasha.

"God is great, master Vizier, you speak correctly. God is both the Punisher and the Creator of Good. God is both the Enrich- er and the Self-Sufficient—whom it distresses, to whom wealth, wealth gives, sometimes it restricts, sometimes it opens outward. But will we attribute the punishment to God and not seek a crime in ourselves? Repeatedly saying that God is great, so will we wait for a physician to descend from the heavens? There is no argument, and a big hospital will be built in Edirne. Send however many con- struction foremen, architects and excavators are needed. Here, call- ing this an opportunity, perfect, let us establish the most developed hospital in the realm in a short time. Moreover, the people who are suffering will see that the city is being determinedly rebuilt and will recover."

The court scribes were noting down the sultans orders, starting to prepare the drafts of the firmans they would produce the next day.

Sheikh Hamdullah had been with the sultan since he was a prince in Amasya. He took the floor next. Hamdullah was a man of the empire respected by the ulema and the scholars at the ma- drasahs.

"If His Majesty the Sultan permits, let us not merely turn away from this hospital that will be built and leave it underdeveloped. Let us build a large madrasah next to it that will educate the phy- sicians and caregivers who will work in that hospital. Let us fill the library with ibn Sina, Galen and Hippocrates. Let us send out scholars from the Sahn-i Seman Madrasah that your late father had built and raise up the ulema there. With your kind permission, let us found a robust school for spiritual sciences and mental matters, which we feel a lack of in Edirne, and even Constantinople. Let us try to cure these bizarre things that the Omnipotent God sent to us as an example—the lovesick, the weak-minded and those who harm themselves—let us cure them as our elders wrote, with the sound of water, with music, with affection and with myriad other activities."

As Hamdullah always did after speaking, he said, "God knows best," and turned his head to his lectern.

Sultan Bayezid had listened interestedly to the proposal. "You speak the truth," he said, gently nodding his head. He turned to Grand Vizier Yakup Pasha. "You heard the hodja. I don't need to add anything. I give the court announcer full authority from this palace for the construction. The hodja will give you the necessary details."

"At your command," said Yakup Pasha as he signaled to the court scribes.

"What's next on the agenda?"

Yakup Pasha turned to Second Vizier Ayas Bey. When Ayas Bey realized that his turn had come, he looked at Shaykh ul-Islam Ahmed Efendi with a bored look on his face. The other members of the Divan looked him over for a while.

The vizier started to speak, "There's a man called Old Man One Hand. Word has it that he troubles the Turkmen nomads in southern and central Anatolia. He raves that he's the Mahdi and ascribes the disasters that befall the empire such as earthquakes and floods to the coming of Doomsday."

Everyone in the Divan winced when they heard the word Mahdi, foremost the shaykh ul-Islam. This was only one of the countless charlatans who had been declaring themselves the Mahdi recently. Be that as it may, these men's supporters were suddenly growing like a snowball rolling down a hill.

"He says the Apocalypse will come in the year 900 of the Hijri and he's deceiving these poor people into following him and building his flock."

"This is not the first Mahdi we've run across, master Vizier." Bayezid said. "They collect followers quickly and they disperse just as fast. What makes you so worried?"

"You're right, Sir," said Ayas Bey. "But this time it's a little different. Old Man One Hand and his followers blame you for the disasters in the empire and he's inciting the people against you. Furthermore—"

"Furthermore what, master Vizier? Say it, why don't you."

"Furthermore, he claims you're intruding on Jem Sultan's rights and that God does not accept this injustice and is damning your sultanate.

Murmuring began in the Divan as soon as he said the name of Jem Sultan. Sultan Bayezid had grown so weary from fighting with his brother who had claimed the throne for more than ten years that he would not suffer the utterance of his name unless he found himself forced to do so.

Bayezid grumbled and drew in an angry breath. "Tell Governor Hadim Ali Pasha, let him take care of this. Let me know if the problem gets bigger. Have him find and summon this man and let him speak gently. Let him tell this man that if he doesn't give up the case he will bear the necessary consequences. Let him do the intimidating."

The viziers nodded in agreement with the decision. Everyone was of the same mind that the sultan's decision was the most apt step to take for this matter.

The room fell silent for quite a while before the sultan turned to his viziers. "Is there any news from my brother? How is his health?" he asked.

Nobody was expecting these questions. The Divan was taken aback that Bayezid would still embrace and inquire about his brother all these years later despite Jem having created so many problems and opposition when he staked his claim to the empire and challenged his older brother for years on end.

Yakup Pasha answered right away. "Nothing has changed, Sir. We hear that he is comfortable at the Vatican. We get reports on it every day."

Sultan Bayezid had appointed his best spies in all the European empires and regularly received reports from all of them, as he didn't trust any of the French kings and knew very well that the pope played both sides. Bayezid insisted on keeping records of which prince Jem Sultan ate with and on which day and which king he had met with—he collected intelligence on everything.

The sultan then asked about Jem Sultan's mother—his step-mother—who had taken refuge with the Mamluks in Egypt. "And what about Valide Hanim and her daughter?"

"We have just recently sent out her annual subsistence, Sir. We hear she's doing quite well."

"Write another letter, send the news and tell them that this is their place and let them know that they can live here without any harm coming to them."

No matter how many times Sultan Bayezid had called Jem's mother to the capital, he hadn't been able to convince her to come. It was still mentioned even years later that the mother of a prince could not live in exile abroad. Bayezid had years earlier given up summoning his brother to the empire when Jem Sultan had proposed to split the realm in two. He had no intention of offering his brother something that was not his—the empire's single ruler, authority and ideology that their father Mehmed had created with his blood and intellect.

The sultan continued with the agenda without prolonging the previous topic any further. "What's the next issue?"

They covered that the king of France wanted to send an ambassador, the attacks of the Knight of Rhodes in the Mediterranean, renewing agreements with Venice, other matters of foreign affairs and the members' appointments. Then all eyes fell on Chief Rabbi Moshe Kapsali.

It was time for the Divan to take up its main issue for this meeting.

Kapsali looked at the sultan.

"Come now Rabbi, we're listening," Bayezid said.

Kapsali rose to his feet, nodded, and began to speak.

3

"Very honorable, generous, and dignified Sultan Bayezid, son of Mehmed, always victorious, and dear sirs, I greet you all with humility. I present my deepest gratitude to the esteemed padishah for accepting me in his presence and seeing me worthy of being on his council. As the spiritual leader and representative of all Jews in the Exalted State from which—from the time of your late father Sultan Mehmed the Conqueror—we have known freedoms, increasing right to life, the right to conduct trade, the right to land ownership and many more humanistic freedoms, that you have allowed the Jewish people to own homes and have not oppressed our rights, no matter how much we thank you and we bow our heads, it is not nearly enough."

Kapsali hesitated after his words so full of praise. The members of the Divan could easily see the strain on the old, pious man's face and that he was distressed.

"I'm a man out of sorts here in front of you today. I am the representative of an oppressed people subjected to the most inconceivable killings and torture not even deemed proper to be inflicted on those in hell, the voice of an oppressed people forced to endure the cruelest tyrants, to suffer the worst persecution and greatest barbarism the land has ever seen. As you all know, the Catholic king and queen of Hispania, Ferdinand and Isabella, swore an oath to wipe their realm clean of any trace of the Jewish and Muslim people as soon as they invaded beautiful Granada this past month. That land where Muslims, Christians and Jews had lived arm in arm in peace and drank pomegranate juice from one another's cups. It's obvious that the intoxication of victory created from their having put an end to an eight hundred-year Islamic empire has made them both quite giddy. They've now set upon the Jews after having created so much trouble for your fellow Muslims. Not a day goes by that I do not receive a cry for help or a beseechment for salvation."

The attention and sorrow of the members of the Divan grew as Kapsali spoke. The old, pious man swallowed the lump in his throat and continued with his appeal. He took out a few pieces of paper from the leather bag he'd brought with him.

"Here are a few of these cries, dear sirs," he said, and began reading/

"My dear friend Moshe, I am sending you my house key. Save this for me, as I no longer have a home in this land. The Inquisition said my wife was a witch and burned her alive, it said my son was a secret Jew and tortured him to death in his interrogation, and my only daughter has become a whore in the hands of the Catholic knights. As I write you these lines, which I will entrust to a friend on his way to Italy as I hide in the seclusion of desolation, I know they will be my last. While you are reading this, I and hundreds of other Jews, just as we cannot live peacefully in this land, neither will we be able to rest in peace below it. Our ashes are scattered all over Hispania, they are thrown into the fields and they are poured into the pigsties."

Kapsali's eyes were filling with tears as he moved on to another letter:

"We write to you, Moshe Kapsali, we write to you, living on the other side of the Mediterranean, in Constantinople, because the world no longer hears us. No civilization along the Mediterranean, no king, no ruler is opening his door to us. Those who have fled to France are sold as slaves. The kings of the Germans send mariners who pledge to save us after we give them all our belongings. They take us out to the middle of the sea on their ships, toss hundreds of people overboard and then return to Spain, fill their ships with people and again toss them to the bottom of the sea. We write to you because we hear that everyone lives freely in the lands of the Great

Turk, no matter language, creed or origin. We write to you because we know that people from all religions are rich, merchants, free and are ruled with justice and live with all the rights they could desire. We write to you, Moshe Kapsali, because we do not have anyone else. We are begging you, Kapsali, because we know that you know the Great Turk and that you can ask for help from him in our name."

Sultan Bayezid already knew of all this from what was described in the letter he received a few days earlier from his spy in Spain, Davud the Brave. Davud had told him about the aims of the Catholic Church and explained in great detail all of the plans Ferdinand and Isabella had begun to make for the non-Christians. The sultan, however, wanted the members of the Divan to hear firsthand of those experiencing this torture, so he personally invited Moshe Kapsali to the Divan, as he was a friend of his late father.

Kapsali continued. "Is it only the Jews who are subject to this oppression? No sirs, unfortunately it is not. The Jewish people, like a whipping boy, we may be willing to bear all the sins of Europe, to be held responsible for the Plague, to be blamed for poor harvests and the fecklessness of wicked rulers. But no, the suffering are not only Jews, but also your fellow Muslims, dear sirs. Here is one of them."

Kapsali asked the sultan's permission and called in a man who had been waiting at the door to the Divan. In entered a frail, dark-skinned Berber with sunken cheeks whose exhausted black eyes had retreated further behind his dark lashes. Speaking Arabic, Sultan Bayezid asked the man to introduce himself. The man, haggard in appearance, stood in silence for a while before he began to speak.

"I am a soldier of the last ruler of Granada, Abu Abdallah Muhammad XII. We were promised that the Catholics would not harm us when he surrendered the city to Ferdinand and Isabella and left us behind. According to the agreement our leader made, our mosques were not to be touched, we were to be permitted to worship and our lives in the city were to be left unmolested. But the very next day they started to use the mosques for their pigs and accosted the women. Now they say that they'll force us either to be

Catholic or to leave the country, just as they did to the Jews. They hinted that they would come for the Muslims straggling behind after casting the Jews out."

Every word of Andalusia was like a sledgehammer striking iron in the middle of the hall.

"And here I am in front of you," the wretched man said. "Do something before it's too late. There's already no Islamic empire in Andalusia. At the least, give a helping hand to those left behind. If you don't, no one will."

The Andalusian started to cough in pain. He pulled out a handkerchief and covered his mouth as he left the room. He had said what he had come to say anyway.

The chief rabbi took his seat.

The members of the Divan all sat in silence.

Sultan Bayezid turned to the patriarch, the spiritual leader of the empire's Christians. "Patriarch, how do you explain what these Catholics do? Is there room for this in their religion?"

"No, never, Great Sultan, it's impossible," the patriarch said. "You also know Christian philosophy quite well, and as you know, when you are slapped, you turn the other cheek. Our Lord Jesus Christ, his entire life suffering torture and hardships, never once stooped to tyranny and never turned away from trying to persuade the people. These Catholics—Ferdinand, Isabella, and their religious leader Torquemada—are very clearly heretics. There is no way to legitimize what they do."

"Very well, sirs," the sultan said at the conclusion of the meeting. "We'll think on this issue and make a decision befitting of the Exalted State."

The calligrapher Hamdullah was looking at the Captain of the Sea Kemal Reis from the corner of his eye as he recorded the final minutes of the meeting. The captain was sitting confidently and had been listening to what was said. Hamdullah sensed Kemal Reis would do his utmost to rise up if he were amid the Andalusian campaign.

Hamdullah wouldn't be mistaken.

4

"We must handle this secretly and with as little fanfare as possible," Bayezid said.

Hamdullah, who always listened to his ideas; Captain of the Sea Kemal Reis, to whom he would soon give an important duty; two of his senior viziers; and Chief Rabbi Kapsali were all by his side. Bayezid would retire to his private quarters after the Divan meeting.

He turned to his viziers. "You listened to the men—these poor souls. The sons of Osman can't remain silent to this. All the same, we can't declare all out war on the Spanish Kingdoms. Whatever we do, we must to it secretly."

War between the Ottomans and the Spanish Kingdoms would mean going to battle with the world's largest Catholic power. Notwithstanding, Sultan Bayezid dared to think that his ever-expanding fleet could take on the Spanish fleet. The problem, however, was that the pope would take any attack on a Catholic power as a direct assault on the Vatican. In such a case, holding Bayezid's brother, the pope could support Jem to be the new sultan, and he would create enemies out of nothing, both inside and out, making the issue all the trickier.

His viziers were also of the same mind. This required a special tasking.

The sultan approached Kemal Reis and looked him in his sea-blue eyes. "Captain," he said, "gather you old, trusted men and a small fleet of three to five ships. You will comport yourselves as soldiers. Go with these men to the Port of Malaga, gather as many Jews and Muslims as possible and bring them to our lands."

Kemal Reis didn't wait to respond. "As you command, Sultan."

The master seaman had already decided whom he needed to take with him for this assignment. He would gather his friends one by one, the old Mediterranean pirates along whom he had broad-sided and boarded ships and fought together elbow to elbow before he had accepted his duty for the empire three years ago.

Yakup Pasha spoke up from among the viziers. "There is, however, a problem, Sir. How many people could small galleys possibly hold?"

"I've thought about that as well," Bayezid said. "Call the chief of the shipyard to me at once, I must speak with him."

Chief Rabbi Kapsali had remained silent up until this moment, but he now approached the sultan with his head bowed. He looked as though he was waiting for permission to speak. Sultan Bayezid gave Kapsali the sign he was waiting.

"Sultan, there is one man in the Andalusian Jewish community who is very important to us. I met this young man's father and uncle while visiting Europe in the time of your late father. They always spoke of your father with gratitude."

The chief rabbi began to explain to the sultan about this man—David Marrano.

Bayezid listen to his friend Kapsali and to himself—*God give common sense to Ferdinand and Isabella. How can these people be such fools that they can so bloodthirstily discard and sacrifice the wealth and riches of their own kingdoms?*

5

David Marrano was looking at the white, arched columns of the Church of Santa Maria la Blanca. He was quite fond of going to Sunday Mass at the church in the Jewish quarter in the city's southwest, nearly surrounded by Toledo's Catholic neighborhoods. The church was built nearly three hundred years ago in the twelfth century, at the end of the Golden Age, as a synagogue. He thought that at that time it had evoked much more of its own essence. David believed while amid the congregation of one hundred to one hundred fifty people all singing *Ave Maria* under the direction of Cardinal Ximenes de Cisneros that it was a projection of the church's history. He had developed a game of looking over the walls to rid himself of the troubles he experienced when singing a hymn he didn't believe.

His brother Samuel was standing at his side. He jabbed him with his elbow and whispered angrily, "Don't start looking around again!" His eyes were on the priest who was facing the congregation.

Even though they were in the back row, David's tall frame could easily attract attention, and Samuel detested it.

"You're going to get us in trouble again!"

David smiled and continued to gaze at the walls while his brother was having a fit. A synagogue until a century ago, this house of worship was one of the most beautiful, noble and elegant structures in the city at the time. Even though Jews had been pushed into specific neighborhoods and had been forced from time to time to wear yellow patches on their shirts as a badge of disgrace, Toledo had never been as oppressive and overbearing as it was now. Even though this tolerance couldn't compare to what it was under Muslim rule three centuries ago when Jews, Christians and Muslims lived side by side, the Christian King Alfonso VIII of Castile was tolerant enough to have a synagogue built for the Jews of the city. Like the rest of the building, the horseshoe arches that rose above the dozens of white, hexagonal columns had been influenced by the Islamic architecture of the Mudejars and the Almohad. The capitals of the columns, brown and carved with pinecone and other plant motifs, were also from this tradition. The dozens of arches inside the church undoubtedly emulated those in the Great Mosque of Cordoba. David had earlier heard that this synagogue—which was built after the Christians captured Toledo after four hundred years of Muslim rule—was built on the ruins of an even older mosque.

Whether or not these rumors were true, this synagogue, built in an Islamic style, and now a church, reminded him of his father who had been forced to convert to Catholicism decades ago during pogroms against the city's Jews. And so the Christians contemptuously called the Jews who had converted *marrano*.

Samuel was singing a hymn and elbowing David to him to warn him.

No matter how much he struggled, David was only as Christian as the Santa Maria la Blanca was a church. There was a large cross with a crucified Jesus hanging from it behind the altar with a statue of the Madonna holding the baby Jesus in her lap directly below it—so this was indeed a Catholic church. Although, when compared to the other churches in Western Europe, there were neither the common, pointed Gothic roofs nor colorful stained-glass windows depicting scenes from the Bible, which gave it a transitory atmosphere, and it still retained that character devoid of such depictions after it was converted into a church. Its belfry, patched onto the synagogue when it became a church, also seemed to be smirking from above.

This time Samuel stomped down hard on this brother's foot.

The pain in his foot seemed to wake David from his daydream and he turned his head forward, immediately catching Cardinal Cisneros' eye.

"That bastard's been watching you for an hour!" whispered Samuel between his teeth.

Indeed, Cisneros had lifted the hymnal in both hands and was looking in their direction. He had no idea how long the priest had been looking at them, but he hastily moved to show that he was reading the text as soon as he realized the situation and tried to sing the hymn more clearly. He had worked very hard to memorize the Latin hymn just as Catholics try to fully learn the traditions of the Stations of the Cross, confession and specific prayers. If he made even the slightest mistake, it could create conflict and suspicion about his Christianity. It was perhaps the last thing David had to worry about, though, compared to the work he had begun.

He was involved in the same work one Sunday when he came to Toledo instead of going to the church in his own town of Montalban. It was Esther, though, who he really worried about, and he wondered whether he would be able to see her that day.

The *brit milah* ceremony for Esther's newborn brother was happening right after the Mass, and David had already grown impatient.

6

The young man knew his wife had come home, not by the squeaking of the stairs, but from the smell of warm, fresh bread wafting through the house. The best bread in the empire came from the bakeries in Constantinople.

He rocked the cradle holding their baby, who looked ready to do anything but sleep, and smiled.

"Momma's home, little Filiz."

He put his finger to the baby's face and wiggled it. The little girl's dark brown eyes looked just like her mother's, and they darted around from side to side. Filiz wrapped her little hand around her father's finger and tried to stick it into her mouth. They were in the corner of a spacious lounge on the second floor of a wooden house. The young man had placed a handwritten book aside on the divan and was trying to rock the baby to sleep on the other. The light from the rising sun was streaming through the window beside them. The view from the window was like a painting with the city square and the Hagia Sophia, its minarets piercing the blue sky.

He was happier now that he could read his book to his heart's content, more so than from smelling the bread and knowing he would sate his hunger or that his wife would finally get the baby to sleep.

A young woman was standing at the top of the stairs. "You couldn't make her sleep again, could you?" she scolded.

There was a cloth hanging around here bosom holding the loaf of bread she had just bought at the baker with the other women from the neighborhood. The man's head cocked to one side like every time she got angry. When she wasn't home, he and his baby were more like a mischievous brother and sister than father and daughter.

The woman placed her cloak embroidered with tulips that she wore outside on a wooden hangar.

"Elif, darling, she didn't sleep. What can I do?" her husband said as he stood up.

He went over to his wife and looked at the cloth with black deer figures on it lying on the white floor. Elif grabbed the bread and walked passed her husband.

"There's no bread or anything else for you," she said, only half joking. "You know she gets cranky when she doesn't sleep. You just played with her and didn't put her to sleep, didn't you?"

Whenever she would leave them two, he would keep the baby's attention, making funny faces instead of putting her to sleep. The woman went to the kitchen off the other side of the room and put the bread on the counter. She went to the other side and stirred the cinders beneath the clay pot that she had prepared before she had left the house. The songs from the birds perched on the plum tree in the yard were floating through the kitchen window.

"The fire's gone out. Wonderful!" Elif was actually angry now.

Her husband immediately came running to the kitchen. "No, I swear, I tried not to forget," he said, knowing it was his fault, but still feeling the need to defend himself like a naughty child.

His wife was busy stoking the bottom of the oven as he unfolded the cloth, leaned over and smelled the warm bread. He took a deep breath. "Oh, it's excellent!"

His wife turned around and leaned her head to the side, this time with love and compassion. She knew quite well that if he loved one thing more than eating freshly baked bread, it was smelling it.

He would hunch over the bread like a hungry wolf every time she brought a loaf back from the bakery and would take in a deep whiff.

"Don't you dare eat it," Elif said. She walked back to their baby in the sitting room. "Close it back up, don't let it get cold. The food still has a while to cook."

He begrudgingly heeded his wife, wrapped the bread back in the cloth and went to the sitting room. He looked at her from the other side of the room while she held the baby. Even though Elif had given birth seven months ago, he still thought she was as full of grace and beauty as the day they married two years before. The lacework she had done herself hung down from the edge of her pistachio green veil. She unbuttoned her red dress, removed one of her plump breasts and brought the baby to it. The man wished he were there instead of his daughter. He loved his wife's plump breasts, but not as much as her thin waist and wide hips. He thought her legs were as proud as the magnificent, ivory-colored columns of ancient Greek temples. He was looking at his wife as if he wanted to wind his way between those columns again.

He sidled up behind her, grabbed her waist and unwound her veil. Elif smiled and reclined her head slightly. "Don't you see that I'm feeding the baby, darling? Not now."

"I didn't do anything," he said.

He buried his face in her dark brown hair. It was as if it had the smell of opium and he lost himself in it like an addict. He pressed his body firmly against his wife and slid his hands down to her hips.

"Not now," she said, again, and went off to the other side of the room where she sat on the floor beneath a miniature hanging on the wall that she had painted. The sunlight streaming in through the window on the other side of the room shined directly in her face and she turned away.

The man smiled. "Would it be so bad if she had a brother or sister? They could play together."

"Of course, that's easy for you to say," Elif snapped. "You either close yourself up in the room and bury yourself in books or don't come back from the palace for hours. You only know how to care for the baby when you want to."

He came to his wife again like a disobedient child. Then the call to prayer began.

"Come on, do your ablutions and pray," his wife said. "We'll eat afterward."

He looked at his wife. "Afterward?" he said, moping like a child.

He likened his wife's face to the moon as in the poems he read and her eyelashes, each one a crescent, which made the ministers jealous of him. Elif was embarrassed and lowered her head while the baby continued to nurse.

The sunlight on her face grew more intense and shone into her husband's eyes so he couldn't see. It grew increasingly white, widened and enveloped the entire room. Then it got smaller and smaller and smaller like the light receding behind at the mouth of a cave. It became a single point in the middle of the darkness and then disappeared. The jet-black, impenetrable darkness stayed for a while.

Davud opened his eyes and sat up in bed.

He was dripping with sweat and his hair was a tangled mess. His heart was thumping in his chest and he was panting for breath as if he'd just fully exerted himself. He looked at the walls of the tiny, dark room of the monastery where he lived in Spain. There was an old, wooden table full of books with one chair beside his bed and a window with wooden shutters. A cross was hanging on the wall above the bed. He smelled the bread baking at the monastery every morning.

He leaned his head forward. "Why, God?" he said in despair. "Why?"

He reckoned from the birdsongs outside that he'd woken up late—it was already dawn. He put on his tunic and got out of bed with the hope that he would today receive the news he'd been waiting years to hear.

7

"It'll mean the end of our work if we even get close to the Jewish quarter," Samuel said. He was anxious.

The two men had set out on the road after the sermon. They pressed their backs against a wall in an opening in the Jewish neighborhood between its narrowest street and Santo Tome Avenue, waiting for a group of passers-by to disappear from sight.

"There's nothing to worry about. You're getting anxious over nothing. And there aren't any priests or monks around."

"Who's afraid of priests?" Samuel shot back. His brother's cool headedness was driving him crazy. "Jews are more eager to sell out their fellow Jews than Christians are to their own."

David knew there was a certain truth to what Samuel was saying. Many people, both innocent or not, had been branded and tried as heretics since the first inauguration of the Inquisition court in Toledo ten years ago, and it was believed that most of the witnesses to their crimes were Jews. According to the rules of the court, anybody could make an accusation and their identity would never be revealed, so it was never certain who the witnesses were.

David looked down the main street and saw there was no one suspicious around, so he and his brother set back out on their way. They made their way quickly and soon came up to Reyes Catolicos

Avenue. They saw the large Monastery of San Juan de los Reyes, which was still under construction, and veered off onto a side street.

"You'd think there's no other place left for a monetary," Samuel said. "They're blighting this great city, building this monetary right in the middle of the Jewish neighborhood. And it's so big, too."

Queen Isabella had personally given the original order for the monastery's construction, intending it to be one of the largest Christian buildings in all of Spain, not just Toledo. It had been under construction for nearly fifteen years, having started in 1477. They would have aroused suspicion even being on the street had a monk doing an inspection seen them. The Inquisition considered Jewish converts to Christianity showing back up in Jewish neighborhoods as evidence of them only converting to save themselves but still practicing Judaism, which was a crime of the highest degree.

David, however, was neither thinking about the monastery nor about being caught. He was only thinking about whether or not Esther would be cold to him, and it kept running through his mind as they went.

"Would it be alright if we didn't go to the ceremony?" Samuel asked, even though he could guess what the answer would be.

David shot a glance at his brother.

"I mean, what I'm saying is if it's worth the risk."

"We already had to come to town to do the negotiating for the paper," David said.

"The Muslim quarter is on the other edge of the city—we could've also handled our business without coming to this Jewish neighborhood."

Samuel was silent for a while, but then started back up, "You're still trying to see that girl, aren't you?"

"I have things to talk about with Isaac Abarbanel," David said, although not very convincingly.

"Do you really think the kingdom's top financier would really come here?"

"You know he's close with Abraham de Silva," David said, referring to Esther's father.

"Ah, so you're not going to the house for Esther, then?"

David looked away from his brother without responding, and Samuel didn't persist with it.

"Would you shut up please, Samuel. I have business with Isaac Abarbanel."

"Don't worry, he won't come, you're just fretting over nothing."

They were both relieved when they saw the Synagogue of El Transito—the largest in the region—as they were close to the house. The city's Jews who were in good condition lived in the houses with yards right behind the synagogue. Esther's family— the de Silvas—lived in one of the beautiful houses overlooking the Tagus River.

Samuel hastily pounded on the door, looking around from side to side to make sure no one saw them.

"Open up, open up, we're here!" he said just loud enough to get their attention but without raising his voice too much. David was right behind him.

The de Silvas' neighbor's oldest son Yehuda opened the door. He didn't look too happy to see them. He stuck his head out the door to take a look around and motioned for David and Samuel to enter.

"Have they started yet?" asked Samuel.

"They're about to start now," Yehuda whispered. "We thought everyone had come," he said, making it clear that he was surprised to see them.

"Communion went really long. The church was more packed today than usual. People who believe in Christ are increasing every day."

"Or those who are afraid," David said. He could see that Yehuda was uncomfortable.

They entered the big sitting room and took their places next to the dozen people there and prepared to watch the *brit milah* ceremony in which little Yosef Hamon would be circumcised. All the distinguished Jews of the region were there—the Nassis, Yosef Caro, Abraham Zacuto and their families. David was scanning the room for Esther.

Everybody was gathered in a circle around two chairs. One chair was for the spirit of Elijah the Prophet whom they believed to be a witness to the ceremony. The other was for the *sandek*—the man who would hold the baby during circumcision. David was taken aback to see Isaac Abarbanel sitting in the chair. He knew Esther's father was one of the wealthiest Jews in the city, but no matter how much he hoped for it, he really didn't expect to see Señor Abarbanel—who was one of King Ferdinand's head advisors.

Samuel started twiddling his fingers. David quietly slapped down his brother's index finger. "Don't even think about it!"

Samuel had developed a strange habit of touching the nose of every person he met ever since he saw an Inquisition knight slice of his father's nose—and not surprisingly, the habit had come to cause him unnecessary trouble.

Meanwhile, a newly married couple brought the baby forth while reciting prayers. As was customary, a newly wed couple would become the child's godparents, and their carrying the baby was a *segula*—a beneficial charm—in hopes that they, too, would soon conceive. David finally saw Esther behind the couple moving timidly toward the *sandek*.

The girl's lily-white dress contrasted under her black hair and against her dark eyes, and it seemed the sky-blue sash was there to spite her thin waist. As always, David's heart started to pound when he saw Esther's hair bound at the back with a scarf. Despite being unmarried, Esther covered her head with a white scarf with blue fringe along its edges in accordance with the customs of modesty, or *tzeniut*, so her dark hair wouldn't attract too much attention, although David was never afraid of wondering. The silver *hamsa* amulet hanging from her neck flashed in everyone's eyes as it reflected the candlelight from around the room. Also known as the

Hand of Merriam—Moses's sister—or the Hand of Fatima to Muslims—it was believed that the eye in the palm of the amulet guarded against the evil eye and that the five fingers symbolized the Torah. David had never seen Esther without it.

He realized that she had noticed him when his eyes came to her golden-skinned face. David's clothes also set him apart from the rest of the group in a way. Unlike the men around him, he wasn't wearing a blue-striped, white *tallit* shawl around his shoulders or *kippah* on his head. Esther's face, so full of smiles until then, fell flat as soon as she saw him, once again shattering the hope that David always carried with him. It was as if Esther sensed he had come from Sunday Mass. David looked at the newly wed couple carrying the baby and imagined it was him and Esther instead. This was something he had dreamed of countless times.

The *sandek* took the baby in his arms and the *mohel* began the prayer to start the ceremony.

And it happened again as soon as the prayer started—momentarily relieving him of his disappointment. David first saw the Hebrew sentences, appearing in backward writing, then turning into phrases, words and letters. It was like they were being printed on an imaginary page in front of him—*bet, aleph, resh, qoph* and *vav*. David was cautious to think about the arrangement of the letters, calculating how much space would be left at the end of the line, just has he always did when he heard a Hebrew text. The letters in the continuing line were in red ink and suspended in the air, then black-inked words lined up from behind one after another, but as in a mirror reflection in David's eyes, and they gained their true meaning when they came into communion with the page.

The moment didn't last long, however. From across the room he saw Yehuda stop. Even worse, Esther went straight over to him. Whether it was a coincidence or a conscious move, David didn't like the look so full of delight on Yehuda's face. Everyone in the neighborhood had known for ages that Yehuda had always wanted to marry Esther, living just next door. Yehuda carefully straightened the *tallit* on his shoulders, one side of which had shifted a bit.

Everyone began to pray with joy when the baby started to cry. Samuel, however, was starving and growing impatient for the food at the end of the ceremony. A pounding came at the door. Nobody was expecting any more guests.

One of the guests screamed out in terror as if he'd just seen the Devil.

"Inquisition guards!"

All eyes turned to David and Samuel. Everyone was thinking that the two brothers would be led out of the house with death sentences if the priests saw them.

"They brought all their trouble along with them," Yehuda hissed, his voiced dripping with animosity.

8

The janissary peaked out from the wall he was hiding behind at the man wandering around in the middle of the ruins. Was it this monk, just a stone's throw away from him, the empire's most secret, and yet still most famous spy whose name he had heard for years? Was he really the man who dispatched a king in Paris, who saved the life of a prince in Budapest—a ghost who roamed through all Europe's kingdoms and sent reports back to Sultan Bayezid?

The janissary spent almost two days on horseback nearly without stopping to get from Granada to the ruins of Medina Azahara, three miles north of Cordoba. He thought it would be a good idea to watch the man for a while until he came to the meeting point to see whether or not he was the right person. The foothills of the Sierra Morena gave way to the sprawling ruins, surrounded by empty land—a ghost town in the middle of nowhere. There was no one other than the janissary and the monk in the vast valley. The janissary thought over the orders he had received again. He knew he would come across a monk, but he thought the man in front of him—a little over six feet tall and very thin—looked frail and gaunt given his height. It was hard to believe that this man was the spy otherwise known as Davud the Brave. It was doubtful he was even a Turk.

The monk was walking around a large, rectangular, stone pit that must have once been a pool. "It'll stop today," he thought. "Hopefully I'll get the news today saying I will go back to my land, my country, my home."

He ran his hand along the ruined wall to his side—it still had some essence of the old palace. Centuries of wind and rain had shattered the walls and dislodged the stones from their mortar. Countless unknown people from unknown places had run their fingers along these walls as they moldered away. The ruins were the color of desert sand and standing in the middle of immense green, giving silent, parched screams of their former owners' names to the sky. So little was left of the Muslims who had come from the golden-yellow land of Arabia, through the deserts of North Africa, and on to this lush continent.

Davud thought about Caliph Abdur Rahman III and Zahra. Legend had it that the caliph was destroyed by the untimely death of his favorite concubine, her last request being that he build this city. It took ten years to complete and he named it after her. The people in the city were expecting a palace and had no idea that years later one of the land's grandest and most magnificent palace complexes would rise up. Abdur Rahman didn't only build a palace complex—he built an entire surrounding city, as well. There were hundreds of horseshoe arches, porticos, domes rising above colonnades, courtyards as big as the buildings themselves, royal apartments, special housing for the servants, libraries for scholars and splendid meeting halls to receive the ambassadors who came from the four corners of the known world, all spread over four hundred acres. The madrasah where students from Europe came in droves to study resembled the Mosque of Cordoba. Davud stood at the edge of the pool and imagined it as the depictions of it he had seen in dozens of books he had come across. Some of these inky pools were made from marble from Constantinople, and had various animals—lions, deer, crocodiles, dragons, kites, ducks and hawks—in the middle with water shooting from their mouths, all surrounded by multi-colored flower gardens. Davud felt as if he could smell these long-withered flower gardens. There were wood carvings with Arabic verses in *Kufic* script amid the red and sand-colored arches embellished with emeralds, rubies, marbles and pearls perched upon columns, some of whose capitals were plated completely with gold.

Davud hadn't only chosen this spot as the meeting point for the man from the Ottoman Embassy in the Granada Emirate because it was far from any prying eyes, these ruins also held an eerie connection to his own past. Just as Abdur Rahman and Zahra were separated, so too was he from Elif. He looked over the stones that had come from Constantinople, and once again it ran through his mind—"It will end today. I'll get the news for me to come home today."

9

"Father Cisneros, how pleasing to see you among us," said Abraham de Silva as the host of the gathering. He owed the peace in the city throughout his life to maintaining good graces with the Catholic clergy. Cisneros folded his hands and, composing himself to hide his anxiety, Abraham tried to figure out why the priest had come.

The cardinal looked around fondly so that Abraham de Silva, who was perhaps fifteen years his senior, would show him respect. He was wearing a white, woolen tunic that draped to his feet under a black cloak of the same abundance and length that covered his shoulders and chest, typical of the Dominican order. His cowl and vestment of the same black also made Cisneros appear as if he were taller and broader than he actually was. Like all Catholic clergy, his tonsure was bare—completely shaven, with only a ring of hair left surrounding his pate. Cisneros, the tufts of hair around his head like a crown, now had a boastful look as he faced Abraham.

"There are those around here who say they have seen Christian apostates returning to Judaism," Cisneros said, looking Abraham de Silva in the eye.

Two church guards were walking around the house and basement floors while the two men were talking.

"Well, when I came to the respectable de Silva family's house, I thought I should ask him in person whether he's seen such apostasy recently."

That his hands were hidden, folded inside the wide sleeves of his tunic, added even more to the cardinal's ethereal air. He tried to wander around and look at the faces of the guests in the house in an attempt to read their eyes. The slightest wrong movement could give him the sign he was expecting to find.

"I thought, though," he continued, "Abraham de Silva does not want to be an enemy to our sacred Church, to risk all his assets, his life, his future." He looked over at de Silva's daughter. "He would not want to endanger his children's future. If he saw such a perversion, he would immediately inform us himself."

Abraham de Silva recognized Cisneros' underhanded threat. The lightest punishment for anyone who lied to the Church, hid a heretic or even saw such a perversion and did not notify the Church was the seizure of all their property, and the worst was certain death. This, however, was not the first confrontation de Silva had experienced with the Catholic clergy.

"Good Father, they thought right," he said, fortifying his voice so as not to show his fears. "As you see, there are only those of our own religion among us, and we perform our holy *brit milah* ceremony for us alone. We don't have such people around us."

Looking at Cisneros, de Silva knew he didn't believe a word he had said. The contemptuousness in the cardinal's eyes was frightening. The rest of the crowd was deathly silent as if everyone had frozen in place.

Cisneros slowly walked across the room to the bookshelf and began leafing through the pages of the books. The bookcase covered the entire wall, about two people tall and ten paces long.

"You have a great fortune," Cisneros said. "All of these are handwritten books. Such things alone should be enough for a family to live for a lifetime."

He stopped in front of one of the shelves and began to flip through the pages of a book with a red, leather cover.

"Do you have any Hebrew or Arabic texts among them?" he asked, turning once again to de Silva.

De Silva smiled in a show that he wouldn't fall for such a simple ruse. "Dear Father, you know that those books were banned years ago and they came and collected all that there were."

Cisneros was about to put the book back on the shelf and turn back to the group when he noticed a circular line running from under the bookshelf into the sitting room. Having found what he was looking for, he turned around, arrogant and pleased with himself, and looked over the distressed faces in the room.

"So you thought you could deceive me?"

De Silva had no chance to say anything before Cisneros pushed the bookshelf aside with all his strength and flung open the hidden door. He stormed in, certain he would find what he was looking for, but his certainty quickly turned to anger. There was nothing in the tiny room other than a couple worthless cups, a chest and cobwebs. Having finished searching the house, the guards stood over the door above the dumbfounded cardinal.

"We couldn't find anybody," one of them said.

Cisneros' face, and even more so the top of his bald head, was red with rage.

"Why do you have this secret room?!" Cisneros roared.

"The owner of the house, my grandfather, had it made ten years ago when the city was in revolt, dear Father," said de Silva, trying to be as calm as he could. "I've just left it and I've never had need to use it."

Cisneros climbed out of the room and, nearly nose to nose with de Silva, seething.

"I don't know what kind of game your playing, but you'll pay a heavy price!" At that moment, Isaac Abarbanel appeared from behind de Silva. He gave Cisneros a penetrating glare.

"There is no price to pay," he said. "I'll extend your greetings to his excellency the King."

Cisneros flung his head back. "We'll see about that!" he said as he followed the guards out of the house.

Certain that they had gone, everyone gathered in the house, who had seemingly been holding their breath the entire time, took a deep sigh of relief. De Silva and two others went down to the secret room and opened the lid of a chest in the corner. One of the men leaned over and pushed down on the false bottom, revealing David and Samuel staring terrified from the bottom of a narrow stairwell.

David thought that they were found and were going to be captured, but was relieved when he saw the blue and white dress Esther was wearing enter the stairwell. She approached David holding a handle in the darkness. "Are you happy? You nearly gave all of us a death sentence."

David looked at her, his face lined with sorrow and dejection. He didn't say anything.

"You endanger our lives, as if turning from our religion, acting like the Christians who act against us, going to their churches, praying like them, dressing like them and living like them weren't already enough!"

Samuel was standing behind David and couldn't hold himself back any longer. "We didn't want to choose this life. And we're just as Jewish as the rest of you."

"Oh yes, you're just as Jewish as us and just as Christian as them—God knows what you really believe!"

Samuel was ready to retort but David motioned for him to keep silent.

Abraham de Silva approached his daughter from behind, having heard the terse exchange. He put his hand on her shoulder.

"You've gone a little too far, Esther. Please forgive my daughter, my boy," he said. "These are troubled times and, as you well know, the Church is putting as much pressure on us as it can."

Esther knew she had gone to far and regretted saying what she did to David as soon as she had said it. She knew of David's feelings for her, but there was no way she could accept the idea of marrying a convert.

David looked at de Silva and shook his head as if to say it was all right.

De Silva looked at Samuel. "Come on then, let's go up and eat."

David and Esther remained behind while Samuel and de Silva climbed the stairs. She was about to leave through the darkness, but David grabbed her hand from behind.

"You don't know, Esther," he said. "Nothing is as you know it."

"What don't I know?" Esther asked, surprised.

In despair, all David could say was, "I can't say."

"I know what I need to!" Esther said, pulling her hand away and going to climb the stairs.

David stayed in the darkness of the room for a bit longer.

"I can't tell you for your own safety," he finally said. Esther had already climbed up and left the room.

10

"I still can't believe you touched Abarbanel's nose," David said.

Samuel was snickering. "What can I do? It's not my hand."

He had had this obsession with touching the noses of new people he met ever since he was a child.

"Anyway, did you at least get what you wanted from him?" Samuel asked.

David looked very pleased. "He promised he would give more than I expect," he said. "Abdullah is next on the list now."

"Have you gone mad?!" Abdullah of Xativa said, waving his hands. "I swear, where am I going to find that much paper in a week?"

David had been trying to convince the bookseller for nearly half an hour. Adbullah was a merchant who had moved to Toledo from Xativa—Spain's center of paper production Muslims had established a long time ago. They were in a small shop on the Plaza de Zocodover next to Alcazar Fortress in the northwest of the city.

Abdullah and his apprentice were sorting the stacks of books and placing them on the shelves. David was following him on his heels while trying to convince him.

"This job is different than everything else, old friend. I know you can find it if you want to. It's really important to me."

Abdullah looked distressed. He pulled a crumpled handkerchief out of his pocket and wiped the sweat from forehead.

David was pleading. "I'll pay whatever you want."

"Moving and distributing that much paper—it all takes time. And moreover, the Church is constantly breathing down our necks, night and day. It's nearly impossible to make a sale of this much paper without them catching wind of it. It's difficult and risky."

David looked at Samuel milling around in front of the door and shook his head. "There's no hope."

He turned back to the bookseller. "Abdullah, you can find a way. If you can't do it, no one can."

David knew very well that Abdullah's connections in Xativa and the paper warehouses in the city were wealthier than anybody else.

The apprentice dropped a book he was handing to his master.

"God damn it!" Abdullah snapped, and slapped the back of the boy's head.

He picked the book up from the ground and inspected its corners. "You're lucky it has a strong cover and nothing happened. Get that stupid look off your face and hand over the one with the brown cover."

David pressed one more time. "What do you say? There's no chance?"

Abdullah looked down from the book in his hand to the ground and then at David. "For the love of God what're you going to do with that much paper?"

"Forget about that. It's better for you if you don't know."

Abdullah looked like he was trying to read what was going through David's head. "You're up to something again, I know, but let me see." He took a deep breath as if he knew he would regret it. "It'll be expensive—paper is no cheap thing."

David nodded readily as if that was the response he was waiting for.

Right then Samuel ran through the door. "Psst!"

When they looked outside they saw a group of priests in black vestments passing slowly in front of the shop.

"All's clear, they're gone," Samuel said, taking one more look to make sure.

"I'm going to want all the money in advance," Abdullah said. "You see how we'll suffer."

"One-third now and two-thirds when the paper gets to Montalban," David said.

"Oh, we're also bringing the paper to Montalban, are we? That's a two-hour journey from wherever you look."

"How about half in advance and the other half when the paper's in our hand?"

Abdullah smiled. "All right, it's a deal." He looked back over at his apprentice and slapped him over the head again. "Don't stack them so high. Go on and get our guests a pomegranate sherbet."

The apprentice ran off to get the drinks, rubbing his sore head.

11

The janissary and the monk met face to face in the corner of a ruined room, a third of its ceiling having withstood the test of time above the few arches still standing.

The janissary looked the monk in the eyes. "*A posse ad esse*"— *From possibility to actuality.* There was something frightening in the man's blue eyes.

"*A fronte praecipitium a tergo lupi*"—*A precipice in front, wolves behind*— responded the monk coldly.

The janissary continued, seeing that the first part of the secret interchange in Latin was correct. "*Ad eundum quo nemo ante iit*"—*To go where no one has gone before.*

The monk quickly responded, "*Accipere quam facere praestat injuriam*"—*It is better to suffer an injustice than to do an injustice.*

Hearing that the second part of the interchange was correct, the janissary figured there was nothing left to do but deliver the letter. He was perplexed. He had expected a more well built man, a giant even.

"Why were you hiding behind that wall for half an hour?" Davud asked, finally switching back to Turkish.

"What hiding?"

"It was for half an hour. I'm saying, why did you watch me from behind that far wall?"

The janissary couldn't immediately get anything out through his surprise. "How'd you know I was waiting there? There's no way you could've seen me."

Davud cracked a smile. "What, did you think that because I'm a monk I'm blind?"

"Still though, it was impossible for you to see me."

"I most likely could've picked up the scent of the fragrance you put on in Granada from a mile away." Davud turned around and walked toward the still intact balcony of the building and looked into the distance as if he was gazing off from the edge of a cliff. "The smell of the manure from the horse you tied up is even wafting around."

The janissary was dumbfounded and quite embarrassed. He had been sent because he was one of the embassy's most resourceful and skilled men.

"Still, there's no way you could've known where the smells were coming from," the janissary said.

Davud looked over at the janissary again. He pointed to the wall were the janissary had been hiding. "The wind is blowing from the southwest, up from Granada from where you came." He was growing tired of these questions and approached the janissary. "Need I say more?"

The janissary looked over the man across from him and saw that despite his young age, his hair and beard had already started to grey.

"The letter," Davud said.

The janissary opened the leather bag hanging from his waist, pulled out a sealed letter and handed it to the man. He still wasn't able to shake off his surprise.

Davud took it from his hand. "By the way, you need to work on your Latin. If it weren't me you were looking for and someone else had intercepted you instead, they would've understood right away who you were from your accent."

The janissary by now couldn't say a word.

"You should be going already," said Davud, filling the janissary's silence.

The janissary turned to walk away, dejected, like a soldier unable to fulfill his duty. Although on the way back to his horse, he turned and asked, "Is it true what happened in Genoa?" He couldn't hold back his curiosity. He should learn of this at the very least. "I mean, did you really escape and kill a dozen fully equipped and armored Venetian knights?" He had heard this story and others about Davud the Brave so many times in Granada that they had become legends.

Davud walked back over to the balcony. "I don't know what they told you, but my time in Genoa was years ago. I'm not that man anymore." He looked off in the distance. "You should know, if you don't go right know your life will be in danger."

The janissary came to his side and looked out at the horizon. "Why's that? Is someone coming? I don't see anything." He blocked the sun from his eyes and tried to see off into the distance, but there was nothing other than the endless green expanse.

"You don't know how to look," Davud said, his voice growing sharper. "Go already!"

12

"You definitely need to see this," Mark said.

He was taking David to the back of the carpentry workshop. David sneezed again as he walked past the large worktable in the middle of the shop. David liked the strong smell of wood and lumber, but the sawdust was getting to him. The tip of his nose had turned red and his eyes were watering from sneezing nonstop. Everywhere—the floor, the worktable—was covered in layers of sawdust.

"Please excuse the mess, my friend," Mark said. "I've been doing work outside. And when I am in the shop I'm dealing with you and this tool."

The workshop looked like it was in ruins. David noticed that all the sets of tools on the walls were out of place—chisels, saws, gouges, hammers and other implements were scattered over the worktable and across the floor.

"I'm tired of explaining to everyone who comes in and asks what it is," Mark said, pulling away a curtain to reveal a wooden contraption around eight feet high, about just as long and a little over three feet wide. "I keep it covered."

"It's better anyway, the fewer people who know," David said.

It wasn't surprising that Mark had kept the printing press covered because he was sick of having to explain it to people, and not that he was afraid. Mark was the last person the Church would suspect of anything. He had a *limpieza de sangre*—a certificate showing his purity of Christian blood for the Old Christians with no recent Jewish or Muslim ancestors, a direct Catholic line. These people held a special place for the Church.

The H-shaped printing press looked like a gigantic chair with a larger seat than back. Mark walked behind it and stood across from David.

"Now, look at these gears," he said, pulling the pencil from behind his ear and beginning to turn the screws of the wooden rollers—two hand widths in diameter. They started turning down the threads in the middle of the large H.

He looked at David and smiled. "Do you see it? The screws go down one by one."

"So, there's two successive screws."

"Exactly," Mark said, returning the pencil to his ear.

"So what's this for?"

"It's so the cylinder turns faster and makes printing easier." He smiled. "I noticed it when I accidentally bored two rows of holes in the cylinder."

David noticed something else strange about the contraption and was slightly confused. "It's good, but the printing plate is twice as long as it needs to be."

Mark smiled again and went back behind the other side of the big H.

"This is the main thing I wanted to show you, actually."

He pulled out the printing plate on a system of rails over the large worktable and under the roller.

"When you're going to print, you push the paper under the roller by turning the arm here. You lift the press up after half of the page is printed, this arm turns again, and this time you push the other half of the page under the roller."

David was delighted. "So you print two pages before you have to change the printing plate."

"Exactly."

This was a lot different than the contraption he had worked with for years that the Germans who had come to Zaragoza had taught him how to use.

"When can we get this set up in Montalban?" David asked.

"That's easy, but there's something else that worries me," Mark said as he walked away from the press.

There was a carving of Jesus on a crucifix hanging on the wall that he had done and varnished himself. He looked up at the carving as if he was going to say something but couldn't—as if his earlier gayety and excitement had melted away.

"Why're you worried, Mark?"

"I don't know, there's something strange."

David looked at his friend the carpenter—he didn't understand a thing. Mark turned back to David—he looked concerned.

"Well, I was saying that I found a new job outside and I'm really busy right now."

"Yeah?"

"I got the job from the Church. It pays quite well. You know there's no way I could turn it down."

"Naturally, you need to be able to support your mother. She needs it."

Mark had never met his father and had been looking after his mother ever since he was a child.

"Sure, but—they're having me make abhorrent things. Contraptions you've never seen—apparatuses, pulleys, wooden beds. I see these contraptions in my dreams and I've woken up every night from nightmares. I'm worried for you, my friend. The man called Torquemada sends new orders and new projects to the Church nearly every week. Sometimes even the highest cardinals struggle to do what they want and they can't make sense of what's going on."

David walked over and put his hand on his friend's shoulder. "Don't think about it and leave those things to me. We've been dealing with these people for centuries. We can't even say that man's name correctly and he can't do anything to us."

"Don't take him lightly, David. What I've heard about him would make a person go mad."

"Alright," David said. "You leave the worrying to me and you can finish this contraption as soon as possible, sound good?"

Mark dropped his head. "Alright then." He knew his friend would persist anyway. David had talked with him for weeks about making a new printing press, spending days with him to explain the drafts he'd drawn for its design.

"Don't say you weren't warned."

David left the workshop and Mark picked up a board and set back to work. A shadow passed in front of the door right behind him as soon as David had left. The carpenter threw down what he was holding and ran outside, but there was no one following David. Mark could have sworn he'd seen someone following him. He figured he must've been mistaken and went back inside.

Outside the shop, a man hiding in a passageway off to the side popped his head back out and began to quietly follow after David.

David was going to experience the greatest suffering in an insidious torture device that Mark had yet to make. But today, neither of the two friends had any idea of this.

13

Grand Inquisitor Tomas Torquemada and his regiment were heading toward Granada from the Council of the Suprema. The last Muslim kingdom in Iberia had already fallen in Granada and the look of pride on Torquemada's face could be seen from a mile away. He was going to hold a large ceremony in the Alhambra and put into place the last stage of the plan he'd been calculating for months.

He saw a Franciscan monk on horseback while passing the ruins of the Medina Azahara and ordered his retinue to halt. Inquisition guards selected from the old knights made up the majority of the more than two-dozen strong regiment. As always, Lucas was at the head of the guards just behind Torquemada. The knight was a brutish, enormous man—he wore a pig-faced bascinet with a perforated, conical visor and two horns rising from the top. Even the sight of Lucas' helmet was frightening and drove people to flee as far from him as they could. The knights of the Santa Hermandad were the boldest in the kingdom. Isabella had given them to Torquemada as a small gift and Lucas led the charge under the Grand Inquisitor. Torquemada stood out in the middle of his retinue—a mitre with golden embroidery on his head, a luxurious cassock and a satin stole with crosses emblazoned on its ends. The horsemen in front of and behind the knights of the Santa Hemandad were in groups of three, in full armor and heavily armed. The clergy had recently been increasing their security due to their concerns over their own safety. Torquemada ordered his assistant to call out for the mounted monk in a black cassock to halt.

Davud heard the command in Spanish and immediately dismounted. He bowed in front of the retinue and greeted the Grand Inquisitor.

Succumbing to his curiosity, the janissary, who was still behind the ruins, watched the scene from a distance, this time making sure he was fully hidden. He reckoned this was the only way to see if what was said about Davud the Brave was true. If what he'd heard were true, Davud would have no trouble at all evading all these knights, like a hot knife through butter. Unfortunately though, there was no way he could hear what the monk and Torquemada's retinue were saying from how far away he was.

"What are you doing here so early in the morning?" Torquemada asked. Torquemada had never liked the Franciscans, which for centuries had been in discord with the Vatican and any other central authority. He thought they had always run counter to the Church—either manipulating the people in opposition to the teachings of Jesus or preparing a plan for revolt against the bishopric. And he likewise didn't take kindly to this Franciscan monk in a brown cloak.

"Your Excellency, we beseech to find God every morning," the monk said.

"Haven't you yet found God?" Torquemada scoffed.

"We find him anew every day, every hour and we thank him again. We see him again and again in the green of the grass, the blue of the sky and the blackness of the earth. We find God in the chirping of the birds, in the rabbits' hop and on the wings of eagles."

Torquemada bristled at the monk's pertness. He puckered his face and gave Lucas the order, "Search this man!"

He didn't think they would actually find anything on the simple monk, but rather wanted the guards to provoke him into resisting.

Davud showed no sign of fear or agitation. Lucas immediately dismounted and began to look over Davud, breathing disquieting heaves through the holes in his pig-faced helmet. Davud simply stood still, waiting for the knight to discharge his task.

The janissary was still hiding behind a wall in the ruins—"Ha, here it is, he'll finish them now," he thought. Although it wouldn't be quite that easy to overcome Torquemada's special guards, this was Davud the Brave after all. The janissary was thoroughly excited that he would witness firsthand the talents of the famous spy.

On the contrary, though, Davud raised his arms to the side, making it easy for the knight to search him. Lucas, meanwhile, was suspicious—Davud's shoulders were much too wide and sturdy for a monk—and he continued to prod him, trying to incite some reaction. He was ready to draw his sword at the monk's slightest protest. Lucas felt something on Davud's chest and looked up at Torquemada in triumph. He reached into Davud's cloak and pulled out the letter.

"But, how can this be?!" the janissary muttered to himself. "How could he allow them to find the letter?" Was this not Davud—the Davud? He wondered if he had delivered the letter to the wrong person. If he thought he had a chance against more than two-dozen soldiers, the janissary would have already sprung to attack to retrieve the letter.

Torquemada was still on his horse and took the letter from the guard with his silk-gloved hands, looking at the monk with disgust as he broke the letter's red wax seal. He was impatient to find what scheme the monk was up to and was ready to give the order to arrest him.

He unrolled the parchment and began reading. The janissary broke out in a sweat. "It's all over! His identity's been revealed and everything's ruined."

As Torquemada came to the end of the letter, his expression turned from impatient victory to increasing bewilderment, venom and hatred.

"What is this?!" he growled at the monk.

"It's a list of books the church in Montoro wants reproduced," said Davud, as calm as he had been since the beginning of this inter-action. "I received it just a while ago from a vicar and I'm bringing it to the monastery."

The Grand Inquisitor crumpled up the parchment and threw it at Davud's face. "I know you're up to something—my instincts have never failed me." He gestured to his men. "Arrest him!"

Davud had not expected things to go this far. He knew that the cardinals had grown quite aggressive of late, but not so much that a single monk in the countryside would be considered a threat. Lucas took the monk's hands and tied them with rope behind his back— Davud began to think about what was going to happen. Of all the scenarios that ran through his head, none ended well. He knew well that release was nearly impossible after arrest by the Inquisition.

14

Then a voice came, "On what right?"

Davud turned his head along with everyone in the expeditionary regiment toward where the voice had come and saw Father Paulo approaching on horseback. Paulo was the archbishop at the monastery where Davud lived. Father Paulo also wore a fine woolen, brown and hooded habit specific to the Franciscans. He was in his sixties, his beard was nearly completely white and his face was chiseled with the type of wrinkles only time can etch. His moustache and beard completely hid his mouth.

Torquemada raised his head in disdain, as if he'd just seen an old enemy, when he saw Father Paulo.

Father Paulo bowed slightly to Torquemada and his retinue in greeting. "May the grace of our Lord Jesus Christ be with you, your Excellency—but on what right are you arresting this monk Daniel?" Father Paulo said, using the name he'd known Davud as since they first met.

"This has nothing to do with you, Father," said Torquemada.

"This monk is a member of our order and, as you know, any injustice done unto him is an injustice to us all," Father Paulo said. "If there's an offence, it's of course my duty to personally deliver the wrongdoer to you. But as far as I can see, Daniel hasn't done anything other than carry this list of book I had requested of him."

Torquemada knew Father Paulo was right. If they were to challenge and arrest him without cause, it was clear the Franciscans
would rise up and foment unrest in the city.

"There's something on this man," Torquemada said, his anger
rising. "Something I've not been able to find yet."

"What kind of a thing, your Excellency? Something in defiance
of you? Has he lied? Has he been aggressive? I'm his keeper—for
years he's been by my side and I've never seen any sort of mischief
from him." Father Paulo looked over at the monk.

Torquemada spoke despairingly although still finding great
benefaction, "Release him." Lucas untied Davud's hands. He was
staring the monk in the eyes from behind his pig-nosed visor. He
had grown exceedingly suspicious of this monk.

Torquemada looked at the monk, who was rubbing his wrists
from where the rope had cut in. "We'll see you later." He turned to
Father Paulo. "And you before him!" He then ordered his men to
proceed.

"I don't understand a thing," the janissary said to himself in his
hiding place. He was quite confused.

Davud picked up the crumpled parchment from the ground and
tucked it into the rope belt around his waist as Grand Inquisitor
Torquemada and his guards set off toward Granada. "It will end
today," he thought. "Today I'll be saved from all this absurdity."

Father Paulo and Davud were on their way atop their mules to
the Monastery of San Jeronimo.

"I can't understand these men any longer," said Father Paulo. "There's no limit to their malice and ambition. And not only
against non-Christians—they deem all ill treatment even of their
fellow Christians to be proper. If Jesus Christ were alive now, just
as he would raise the dead, he would surely send the living down
even deeper."

"Quite so, but how'd you know I was here, Father?" Davud asked.

"I know that you visit the ruins from time to time. I was certain you were here when I didn't see you at the monastery." Father Paulo's voice deepened as spoke. "I heard yesterday that the Grand Inquisitor and his dogs were heading for Granada, and I know very well that Torquemada wouldn't leave a Franciscan monk alone."

The wind was blowing the old man's white beard back as they rode.

"It seems you've known the Grand Inquisitor for quite some time," Davud said.

Father Paulo smiled. "We were sacristans at the same church when we were children."

Davud wasn't expecting that. "You were there together with Grand Inquisitor Torquemada?"

"It was a long time ago, Daniel." It seemed the father didn't want to speak of what he preferred not to remember and he fell silent and then changed the subject. "So did you get this list of books you mentioned, then?"

Davud showed him the crumpled parchment in his belt. He was growing more impatient to read the letter—which he'd assumed was his order to return home.

The roof of the monastery came into view in front of them.

15

Abdullah of Xativa was struggling to talk to Zayd ibn Uthman while he was chasing after him. He'd worked with Zayd for many years at Xativa's largest paper mill, which Zayd owned. Zayd was the third generation in his family to produce paper in Xativa, and some said it went back as far as to when the city was under Muslim rule. His paper mill met the needs of almost all of Europe, not just Iberia. He even had business partners in Venice, Milan and Amsterdam.

"Come on Zayd, let's sit comfortably and talk," Abdullah said through his panting. They were standing next to a watermill beside the Albaida River. The gigantic waterwheel gushed out water so loudly as it turned that Adbullah had to shout.

"I'm always thinking about it," Zayd said. "Does the name of this river mean *the white one* because paper's been made here for centuries, or is it just a coincidence?"

Abdullah never understood more than half of what this man said whenever they met. He was looking forward to returning to his little shop in Toledo as soon as he made the necessary agreements.

"I think it's a coincidence," he said, wanting to return to the topic he'd been trying to explain for the past fifteen minutes.

Zayd looked astonished. "Nothing's a coincidence, my dear friend." He looked again at the mill, jotted down some notes on the plaque he was holding and then went to enter the building.

"What're you going to do, who are you going to sell this much paper to," he asked Abdullah as he followed after.

Relieved to be away from the gushing water outside, Abdullah soon realized that with the thundering of the trip hammers inside the mill—each as large as a person—he had no other option than to yell if he wanted to get on with Zayd. Half a dozen trip hammers in rows pounded away at wet rags, rendering them into pulp. The hammers were relentless, moving with the power of the mill. Some of the workers in groups of threes and fives were emptying new rags into the troughs the hammers were pounding.

"There's a Jewish man," Abdullah said to Zayd, who was standing in front of him and checking on the troughs. "He'll give an advance of one-fifth."

Zayd smiled and looked at his old friend. "If you say one-fifth, you'd definitely take half of it."

Abdullah promptly objected. "No way, I wouldn't, I swear to God!"

Zayd frowned at what Abdullah had said. "You never give up that habit of swearing to God."

Abdullah was an incorrigible man to talk with, and Zayd sighed, as if to say it would be harder for him to straighten himself out after this time.

"I can't ever understand," Zayd continued. "How's it that someone like you, who's so busy with books morning and night, who lives and breathes them, never even learns the bits of knowledge on the pages of those beautiful books you wander around surrounded by and knows no business sense or ethics?" He scratched something down on the paper he was holding. "But you aren't the only one. Where are those day—life's now full of porters carrying loads of books on their backs."

"What fault of ours have you seen so far, man?" said Abdullah.

The paper merchant knew Abdullah was cross, but he also knew it would be short lived—he was aware that so long as Abdullah's work was done, there wouldn't be any resentment. Meanwhile, two people passed in front of Abdullah and emptied the troughs into a container. The rags had been well reduced to pulp.

"Oh, come on, don't frown," Zayd said, slapping him on the shoulder. "Can't I ever tease you a bit? We've been working together for so many years, Abdullah."

The two men then went a little further and came up to a wooden vat that looked like a giant basin. One person stood in the vat full of water and pulp, stirring the mixture with a rod longer than he was tall, while another drew a paper frame through the slurry. Water drained from the screen on the backside of the frame when it was removed from the water, leaving behind a thin, rectangular sheet of white paper paste. A third worker then took these sheets and placed them in a stack a little further away.

Abdullah had kept on talking, "This paper's going to be sent to Montalban later."

"So, when the Church asks us whom we sold all this paper to, what're we going to say? You know they keep watch over all our sales. There'll be a problem if we sell this much paper to anybody else other than the monasteries."

"I worked that out, too. I'll say we're going to take it to my warehouse in Toledo. It'll be to my disadvantage every time it's transported from here piece by piece, after all."

Zayd noticed while he had been listening to Abdullah that the worker in front of him had dipped the paper frame into the vat incorrectly.

"Not like that, son—you're doing it wrong," he told him. He handed his notes and pencil off to Abdullah and rolled up his sleeves. He took the frame from the boy and showed him how to do it. "Like this, see? You dip in the frame and make a semi-circular motion, and then when you take it out you have to lift it straight up." He pulled the frame full of paper paste up and lightly shook it from side to side to get the water out. "If you don't do this, it won't disperse evenly and one side of the sheet will be thick and the other will be thin. Here you go."

He gave the frame back to the boy and turned back to Abdullah. "He's new to this work—he still has to learn. You don't get it at the first go."

Abdullah thought if this had been his own apprentice, he would have slapped him upside the head.

A little later, two workers took the pile of wet paper to the half-pillars at the far end of the mill. They put the pile in a press and, turning its large arm, forced more water out of the sheets in the vice.

Two other workers then carried the sheets to a counter off to the side with smaller turning wheels. One took the pile of sheets and hung them one by one on a string of sinew for them to dry.

"The only thing for animals to do in papermaking is to be string," Zayd said, cracking a smile. "There're still people who use a hundred twenty animals to make one book. What a waste."

Zayd took one of the sheets from the pile and held it up from its corners to the sunlight shining through the mill's windows, looking to see whether or not the white sheet had any defect.

"Look," he said. "This is what I call a sheet of paper! Thank God." He hung it back on the line having done his daily check and satisfied with its quality.

"There's one more thing," said Abdullah, playing the last card up his sleeve. "The paper's also going to be used for copies of the Quran."

He'd finally gotten Zayd's attention.

Adbullah was going to go on, but Zayd looked at him and said, "Alright."

The work was dangerous—it could cost him his paper mill, and even more so, his life—but Zayd didn't care in the least. What pleased him most was having the sheets of paper he produced used for the Quran. Abdullah didn't have to say anything else.

He looked at Abdullah and said, "Alright, you've won. I'll sell you as much paper as you want."

While Abdullah was enjoying himself and was all smiles, the paper that Zayd had just hung on the line had begun to dry quickly from the sun, and a faint watermark started to appear. This sign—having passed through the frame screen onto the still-wet paper—showed its place of manufacture.

While Zayd and Abdullah discussed the other details of the deal, it didn't cross their minds that this mark could identify them to the Inquisition and cost them both their lives.

The watermark on all the drying sheets was nothing more than a simple crescent pointing upward.

16

David was seated on a stool. He took one of the steel bars as thick as a finger from the worktable and placed it into the vice. He slid the magnifying glass on the table in front of him and placed the tracings he had earlier made on transparent paper from the pages of the *Arba'ah Turim* on top of the steel. He meticulously placed each line of letters on the long and thin, square metal bar.

He took the thinnest of the files from those of all sizes and thicknesses hanging on the opposite wall and sat down at the table to begin working away at the edges of the metal. He could see the fine details of the letters more easily with the magnifying glass, occasionally bringing the edge of the metal rod that was slowly starting to take shape up to his eye. He blew on it to clear off the shavings and continued to file away at the characters that were starting to take shape.

This specific letter was four times larger than the others—it would be used at the beginning of the book. David preferred the first letter of the first page and those at the beginning of every chapter to be like this. He also had to make at least seven versions of each letter. Some of the letters were wider and some were thinner so the end of the lines weren't left empty—a trick he'd learned from the Germans in Zaragoza, in addition to all the other subtleties and finesse of his work.

He grooved and filed as the letter took shape and then blew away the metal shavings again after smoothing out the protrusions. He warmed the metal rod over a candle flame and then wiped it clean with a cloth. It was essential that no metal dust remained in the crevices of the characters. Even the smallest particle would appear as a small dot on the page and would damage the quality of the print. He tested each letter afterward, dipping them into ink and pressing them by hand onto a small piece of paper.

He smiled when he saw the new letter on the paper—one would think he had seen Esther. When he was satisfied that the letter was flawless, he went to the forge to harden it, going back and forth between holding the steel rod with a pair of tongs over the embers in the hearth and quenching it in water. Finally, he left it in water to cool.

He also made a mold so he could replicate the letter over and over again. For this, he went back to the worktable and pounded the steel letter into a palm-sized piece of copper. David had always thought the color of copper resembled the oranges often seen in Granada's gardens. He pulled away the steel rod, revealing a perfect imprint in the copper.

For the third step, he started reproducing the letters by pressing the mold into a two-chambered box. He went back to the forge, and with a small ladle, took the inky, mottled mixture of molten lead, tin and antimony and poured it into the mold that he had prepared earlier. When he opened the wooden box, the letter, having quickly cooled, dropped from the mold down to the table. He ladled out more of the molten metal and repeated the process again and again.

He picked up the final letter from the table and, thinking of Esther, tossed the *aleph* in with the dozens of others. The *alephs* had a particular leaden shine to them.

One after another—*aleph, bet, kaph, nun*—all the letters of the Hebrew alphabet formed their own piles.

Everything was now ready.

17

Davud checked the outside of his room in the monastery again to make sure no one was around, then entered and locked the door behind him.

He pulled a bucket filled to the rim with water in front of him and sat down on the bed to read the letter Torquemada had crumpled earlier. He unrolled the parchment and laid it out backside up to allow it to flatten. Holding the sheet with a list of prayers from the Bible and books in Latin from the top and bottom, he let out a quick, "Come one, *bismillah*," and slowly submerged the parchment into the water and pulled it back out just as carefully.

The Latin writing on the parchment started to run and spread across the velum parchment, which was becoming soft and pliable.

He sunk the sheet into the water again and removed it. The ink was completely gone after the third time, having mixed in with the water. He left the parchment for the water to drain and then continued with the process, which he'd done countless times before—sitting at the table he held the sheet over a burning candle, careful not to burn it.

He grew increasingly more impatient as the parchment began to slowly dry, excited to read the news for him return home. He circled the parchment over the flame to dry it out completely, and as it did, faint Arabic script began to appear where there had earlier been Latin lines. Over the flame of the candle, the letters began to become words and the words turned into sentences. The secret text was coming into view more strongly where there once was the list of Latin books. Even though the lines were faint, they appeared just enough for him to make them out, and he began reading the Ottoman text.

As soon as he started to read the letter, however, he realized something was wrong.

The letter was not a summons, and was furthermore far from the message he was expecting—something of heading to the port in Malaga and boarding a ship. He was to return home, but there was a condition he would never have expected.

Disappointed and dejected, he began to read his latest assignment.

18

July 5, 1492

Bismillah ar-Rahman ar-Rahim

In the name of God, the way to the garden of blessings,

May God honor and grant peace to our prophet Mohammad, the Messenger of God

From Khan of Khans, the Shadow and Spirit between God and man, Ruler of the Earth, Master of the Two Lands and Two Seas, Emperor of the East and West, Guardian of the People of the Book, the Dust from the Prophet Muhammad's feet, the Khan Saint Bayezid son of Mehmed son of Murad Forever Victorious,

Peace be to Davud son of Mahmud who continues the holy war amid the sweet-smelling flowers and shining streets of Andalusia, the legacy of Tariq ibn Ziyad on the far end of the lands of the French.

The path without fear and without danger is the work of His mercy. The provisions of the traveler are the fruits of his wisdom. It is He, the Judge, who teaches the name of Adam, who made language and writing possible.

It is He, the All-Knowing, who gave knowledge to Solomon who spoke with the birds, son of David who melted iron. It is He, the Absolute Ruler, who made them caliphs over the earth. It is He, the Owner of All, who gave dominion to David—it is He, the Self-Sufficient, who tested Solomon with riches.

We received your letter regarding how you have wandered through the French kingdoms for years and have witnessed firsthand the wars between the Italian city states, the battles between the French and the English, the unification of the Kingdoms of Castile and Aragon, and the many recent events more closely related to the Exalted State, and having been active in these affairs in accordance with the benefits of our supreme state and the gains of mankind, God's orders and the teachings of the Prophet, invigorating your duty according to the obligations of jihad in line with the principle of enjoining good and forbidding wrong, and that how you, like your late father Mahmud Efendi, after every discharge from the capital, desire to be relieved of your duty and return to your own lands, the degree to which you want to return to the warm hearth of home and how you can no longer stand your longing for a hot soup—we discussed it and came to a decision.

It is your most natural right and, of course, our desire for you to return to your country, to breath its air, to reap the crops in Anatolian soil, to be in the queen of cities, to lead a life worthy of the victories you have experienced and sustained. However, as you also mentioned in detail in your letter, the fall of the Emirate of Granada—the apple of Tariq's eye, who now dwells in paradise, the far end of the Occident, the Crescent's salute to the ocean—has saddened us all. The rule of the Catholics Ferdinand and Isabella is tyrannical, despotic and savage—a kingdom devoid of enlightenment, lacking humanity and void of compassion that tortures non-Christians, drives them from their houses and land, and forces them to convert—we have learned all of this with regret and embarrassment for humanity, we understand, and have asked for compassion from God Almighty.

It is our desire that, as it looks as though this is the last island of justice on earth, when returning to these lands, with this right, all of the peoples of the non-Christian communities living there, those writhing in the clutches of all the sundry, peculiar methods of interrogation of the Inquisition, and above all, the legacy of Tariq, Abd al-Rahman, and al-Hakam and the people of the book—worthy of Moses, David, and Solomon—reckoning our exalted book mentions Abraham 69 times, Ishmael 12 times, Isaac 15 times,

Aaron 20 times, David 16 times, Solomon 17 times, and Moses 136 times—let not the Jewish community, which respects these prophets and shows faithfulness, be deprived.

There is no doubt in the possibility that a servant carry this great people on his back. Strong and steady is God. Nonetheless and howbeit, it is quite necessary to save the humanity of the one who cannot save the people and, through the saving of humanity, the people will be born anew. Humanity is culture, it is legacy, it is knowledge—it is the minds that meet in the lines from the filter of centuries. It is precisely for this reason that a very valued man of God, loved by my people and a leader of one of the non-Muslim communities, our friend, Chief Rabbi Moshe Kapsali Efendi, has requested from us that the individual named David ibn Nahmias Marrano, a notable of Andalusia's cultural legacy, along with those who can be regarded as carrying the enlightenment of the culture of coexistence of the Islamic empire that lasted there for seven centuries be snatched from the dragon's mouth, so to say, in the depths of hell and be brought with you to the Exalted State. Our prayers and endeavors are to this end—that when you arrive at the port in Malaga, with Providence, you will find one of the empire's mighty sea captains who I will personally enlist, Kemal Reis, and the fleet under his charge, who will transport you and the Jewish and Muslim victims.

We believe and pray that our fleet, like Noah's Arc, will wrest these writhing, poor souls from the apocalypse in the heart of oppression. You will then be honored and remembered as few men on earth are.

Our origin and ancestry are noble, we are full of grace and favor, our justice will be decorated with time. No one will see cruelty from our armies and our swords will not touch the hair of one's head, let alone even hurt a fly. May our domain be prosperous with justice. His are the most beautiful attributes—He is the Enricher, Justice, the Forgiver. He is the Conqueror, He is the Ever-Living, He is the Self-Sustaining. Without His want, not a leaf would fall nor a speck play in the breeze. Do not embarrass God.

May the patience of David, the knowledge of Solomon and the love of Muhammad be with you. Knowledge belongs to those who believe and victory to those who persevere.

19

"Who is this David?"

Davud was sitting up straight on the edge of his bed, awestruck and looking to the southeast. He sat with his head hung, looking at the ground with his hands on his knees. He said *Allahu Akbar* under his breath, bent forward and read, moving his lips slightly. He straightened himself, continuing to mutter and bent forward once more, this time his chest nearly touching his knees. He repeated the motion again and then straightened up. He recited that all worship is done for God and for God's sake—he prayed to Abraham and Muhammad—he sent his compliments to all Muslims and, after imploring for happiness for himself and his family in this world and the hereafter, he turned his head to both sides and saluted the two *kiraman katibin* and finished his prayers.

He nearly paid the price of revealing his identity by sitting on the floor and prostrating with his forehead on the ground during the years he was in Venice, putting his life at risk and laying bare the secrets of the empire. An Italian who knew that those who pray regularly have swelling on their left foot where the metatarsus and peroneus bones meet and a mark left on their foreheads almost proved the he was Muslim. Since that day, Davud only prayed on the ground occasionally so as not to leave these signs. This was at least better than the times he was forced to worship with his eyes in a crowd.

"Who is this David?" he thought again.

This question was running through his head the entire time he was doing his prayers. He set the letter alight over the candle as soon as he'd read it, his hope of returning home going up in smoke along with it and falling as ash. He understood that the sultan was addressing him personally from the turns of phrase in the letter and from the *Riq'ah* script, that Sheikh Hamdullah had written it. He stopped his prayers to get over his anger, but he couldn't concentrate on his devotions for even a minute.

This time more than ever, when he started his prayers, he imagined being on a flying carpet like what he read about years earlier in the *One Thousand and One Nights*, going to the Kaaba in Mecca, and making an entreaty to God. Davud had always thought this magical flying carpet resembled a prayer rug—a metaphor for passing by the problems on earth, salvation from the tumult of life, an ascension to the heavens, to the universe of meaning from the material world. But this letter today, far from offering him deliverance from where he found himself, instead pulled him to the ground as if he were riveted and sealed in the soil.

Somehow, he couldn't shake the question from his head. It gnawed at his mind like a wolf and left him preoccupied.

"Who is this goddamn David?!"

BOOK TWO
The Alhambra Decree

20

"*anto monta, monta tanto—Isabel como Fenando! Viva España!*"
The crowd surrounding Queen Isabella and King Ferdinand cheered in unison as the monarchs passed through the Crimson Towers Gate of the Alhambra Palace. The retinue of the Kingdoms of Castile and Aragon of noblemen, barons, lords, knights and high officials of the Church—cardinals, priests and clergy—lined the way dotted with the flower gardens and pomegranate trees of the Alhambra on a steep hill at the base of the Sierra Nevada. Everybody was celebrating the victory of the great Spanish Kingdom while the king and queen made their way past the pomp of their retinue to the Red Palace in the heart of Granada.

"*They amount to the same, to the same they amount! Isabella and Ferdinand! Long live Spain!*"

As Queen Isabella of Castile proceeded with a lofty air on her white horse, she was pleased that, as always, her name was said first. Years earlier, the most important condition for her marriage to King Ferdinand of Aragon to unify the fragmented kingdoms was that the authority would not pass through the king, but come from the queen. Her horse, with a harness and bridle decorated with precious stones, was a nose ahead of the king—and although the revelatory shouts of the people about the crown had been reckoned to the finest detail to show the equality between king and queen, they had taken shape on Isabella's orders.

The gusts of wind blowing against her as she wended her way to the palace, however, made her uncomfortable—she felt something disquieting.

The wind blowing up the hill of the Alhambra rustled the queen's chestnut hair and caressed her face—her white lace *mantilla* that fell from her head to her shoulders also played gently in the breeze. Her corset pushed up her breasts with the top unclasped, her bosom framed by the square neckline of her red, brocade shirt embroidered with silver. Her tight, iron-clasped corset squeezed her waist thin, and as it widened beneath, her skirts extended to cover her horse's back and body. Her vertical collar circled her neck and rose to her ears—and looking straight out from in front of it gave the queen an even more triumphant air. Her slit sleeves, hanging three feet down from her shoulders looked longer than she was tall and the glittering gold cross on her necklace gave her an ethereal quality. Following after her was Grand Inquisitor Torquemada, leaving no sign unseen that the full power of the Church was firmly behind Isabella.

She tried to ignore the wind and, to soak in the pleasure of this glorious victory, Isabella glanced over at the king, Ferdinand, who was one year her junior. Ferdinand was familiar with the look of power and pleasure in Isabella's blue eyes—he thought his queen was driven by success and had designs on mischief. If it weren't for the crown atop his wide, pointed, red velvet hat, he would've doubted that he was a king. The shouts of *Isabella and Ferdinand amount to one* were all a charade to him, nothing more than a proclamation to friend and foe that this country is not only ruled by a woman, but that it also has a king. Luck smiled on him years ago when he came as a husband to Castile—the largest kingdom in Hispania—and he snatched up his chance to crown his small kingdom in greater Hispania. He understood before long, though, that the queen would take all the strings from his hands one by one. He had no other choice but to bow his head in despair. It served his purposes at any rate. He had long ago grown tired of the cheers and fanfare and had started thinking about the day when he could celebrate with some concubine or princess remaining from the Granada Emirate. When it emerged that he would wed the nineteen-year-old Isabella, the first think that came to his mind was whether or not he would have to give up the palace pleasures he enjoyed with the women, and sometimes the men. However, as it helped to keep him far from the work of the realm, Isabella never spoke against his fondness for women and men—so long as he didn't forget to fulfill his duty as a husband. Wanting to whet his appetite, Ferdinand lowered his eyes to the queen's breasts, half visible above her neckline.

The king and queen came to a halt when they arrived at the Alhambra's Vineyard Gate. The two dismounted, stepping onto their attendants' backs before reaching the ground and walked toward the Court of the Myrtles. To her misfortune, while passing through the crown gate, the queen's skirts caught on a some twisted metal left from the recent battles and sacking, leaving a tear in her dress half a yard long. Isabella's religious belief and practice of assigning overloaded meaning to signs in life made this incident worrisome, as if the palace were denying her entry. She angrily unsnagged her dress and continued on her way.

The queen came to the head of the pool in the middle of the courtyard and looked around for a while. Despite the weeks of war and battles, and now amid the grandiose traveling retinue, she stood there looking proudly into the water as still and clear as a mirror. It was as if she'd started to take in the magical symmetry and enchanting geometry of the Alhambra, of whose renown she had herd for many years. Her reflection was so beautiful that, like Narcissus, she thought she could stare into this water for the rest of her life. This thought didn't last long, though, looking around and noticing that the surrounding architecture outdid her own beauty many times over. The palace's finely carved walls, moldings, eaves and ceilings, its richly decorated single, double, triple and quadruple columns, and the tiles covered with hundreds of geometric designs left no doubt who the beauty was.

Then she saw the diminutive reflection of her husband in the water of the pool—his rail-thin legs clad in skin-tight breeches extending from below his abundant, thick fur coat. His lechery reflected unrestrained, Ferdinand tried to draw attention to his penis bulging in his snug breeches. Then from the left, she saw the figure of Torquemada—from whose side she had not left since childhood—slowly appearing in the reflection. He was wearing a black cowl and habit over a simple tunic. She understood what the Grand Inquisitor was going to tell her and was trying to find the right time.

She looked at her reflection once more. The woman she saw was the queen who had put an end to the eight centuries of Islamic rule over Iberia. The moment she had dreamed of since her childhood and throughout her spiritual guidance under Torquemada had now been realized with great, Catholic Spain.

The queen signaled for the retinue not to follow, and she, the king, Torquemada and her closest guards continued together on to one of the Alhambra's countless other courtyards. She looked at the carved white walls and the dome above the tambour, which altogether looked like a white wedding gown. This was the Ambassadors' Hall. The sunlight streaming through the nine windows opening out from the ten-foot-thick walls struck such interesting angles and the filtered light created a mystic aura inside—there was no doubt that the ambassadors who came from every corner of Europe felt themselves to be in heaven's waiting room. Isabella spread her arms as if to bathe in the sunlight, her sleeves turning in the air.

Then she ran quickly between dozens of columns, their arches passing overhead, each an artistic wonder, and entered the Court of the Lions—possibly the palace's most famous courtyard. In the middle of the surrounding porticoes with pairs of columns was a fountain in the shape of a bowl on top of the backs of twelve lions with water spurting from their mouths. The fountain was encircled by a pool that carried the water through four graceful channels to the surrounding chambers, dividing the main area into four parts. Isabella felt as though she was walking through a dream when she saw the lions. As with the other rooms and courtyards, however, her pleasure was short-lived, like a dream turning into a nightmare. To her it looked as though what the lions carried on their backs was not water, but fiery slag—the pleasantly flowing water that had refreshed listeners for years pounded in her ears like a creeping wave of lava. She feared that the stone lions would now come to life and pounce on her.

Furious, she then passed through the next courtyard and found herself in the Hall of the Two Sisters. Bewildered, Ferdinand followed behind her. The hall was so named after the large, twin marble flagstones in the floor and its walls were adorned with carvings of the most beautiful Andalusian calligraphy. Now like a roving drunk, Isabella knew that this was the rulers' private chamber—in the heart of the Alhambra. The queen looked at Ferdinand, feeling as though she was walking about in the most private area of the palace. The king looked around, understanding what was wanted of him and, seeing that no one else was around, he approached her. The queen pushed Ferdinand onto his back on the table behind him inlaid with mother of pearl. She jumped onto the table without care for her layers of skirts and dress and—after standing for a moment and looking around—she then straddled Ferdinand's loins. She flung off her undergarments from beneath her dress into a corner and Ferdinand assumed the position she was waiting for—his head hanging back off the edge of the table. Isabella ground quickly back and forth and up and down, the cross around her neck flinging from side to side—she looked around at the horseshoe arches, giving her an unwanted feeling of being a shy bride on her wedding night. More so than having her way with Ferdinand, it felt as if she were violating the Alhambra.

The Alhambra was finally hers—it should be hers.

It was like the carved writings of dozens of caliphs and emirs carved on the walls were spinning around—she was looking through their eyes—Emir ibn Nasr, Caliph Yusuf, Sultan Abdallah Muhammad.

This was the final nail in the coffin of the Granada Emirate.

This was the deliverance of the great, united Spain.

Whether she wanted it or not, the distinguishing feature of Granada, this palace—Muslims' betrothal—was finally hers.

As she looked around at the walls, the queen saw Torquemada appear from behind the intricately carved door to the courtyard. Rather than showing any shame, Isabella ground harder and with more delight, looking the Grand Inquisitor in the eye as she rode back and forth.

Tomas de Torquemada praised God that she wasn't desirous of women, unlike how her deceased brother Enrique was of men. It was no care of his that Ferdinand and Isabella were first cousins. He would not say a word to the queen today. The time had come to move on to the last stage of his flawlessly running plan and he had no intention of making any misstep that would impede him from this. Isabella knew his feelings in this regard and she would always use what leverage she held until the very end.

The grand Islamic emirate had already fallen and the land of Tariq was now hers.

The Jews were next in line.

21

"Come on, faster, hurry up!" said the man hastily, pushing the Moor in front of him. Having lived a life on the open seas, the sun had deeply burned the captain's face, his once light skin having become ruddy. His bobbed hair had gone nearly completely grey and despite having just entered his forties, he put off quite a youthful air. As it was now, however, his quickness and unstoppable nature made this mad captain appear much younger than he was in the eyes of the Moor who was sweeping his way through. The Castilian and Aragonese soldiers were running to and fro while the two men could be easily picked out from among the Granadans fleeing out of fear, both tall, one paler and one darker.

"Why are we in a hurry? Where are we going?" the Moor asked again.

This expert cartographer, Pedro Alonso Niño, grew even more angry as the man in front of him continued to scuffle along as he tried to walk quickly amid the chaos following the war through the narrow streets and high-walled gardens of the city, where in some places the buildings had been reduced to ruins. The black smoke rising into the sky became even more evident and the commotion more chaotic the closer the two got to the Plaza de Bib Rambla. Niño couldn't understand what this man wanted from him, but he couldn't say a thing. Queen Isabella had freed him from bondage only half an hour earlier to work under her command.

Pedro Alonso Niño believed in fate. He believed, but he'd never experienced the fickleness of fate as much as today. He didn't know while thinking for the past two hours whether he should be sad or pleased. While he was one of the Granada Emirate's leading cartographers, having spent his life at the tables in the palace stacked with piles of maps, atlases, octants, rulers and compasses, now that the city had passed into Isabella and Ferdinand's hands, he, like most of the scholars at the palace, would be put to service for the Spanish Kingdom. Then, as he waited for death to come in a dungeon, suddenly this sea captain appeared who had had requested Queen Isabella put him under his command.

"Stop, stop!" yelled the captain behind him. He went down over one of the city's countless fountains and drank thirstily. Niño looked over the man—his ordinary jacket, the frilly cuffs of his filthy white shirt protruding from his coat sleeves and his snug breeches. He thought how impossible it was to understand the Spanish—how could such tight breeches even be comfortable? Why had they stopped here and put themselves into such a tight squeeze?

"I've been thirsty," the captain said, reaching his mouth under the stream of water, "all day," and then went back for another gulp.

Niño watched in slight revulsion as the captain slurped up water from his hands and then went straight in with his mouth, water streaming down his face and chin, lapping it up like a greedy animal. The man's collar, chest and sleeves were all soaking wet. Niño read the Arabic inscription on the fountain above the stream of water and the name of the sultan who had it made above that. *Abu Abdallah*, it started, running to the left, but the rest of the inscription had been broken off. The captain moved to the other side and Niño picked up the broken piece from the ground—*Muhammad*. Abu Abdallah Muhammad, Granada's last emir.

"Unlucky Boabdil," he thought wistfully.

"Come on, we're late!" the captain said, grabbing and tugging at Niño's arm, the broken part of the fountain falling to the ground and, this time, shattering to pieces. Niño reckoned he wouldn't like this captain at all. Without doubt, Boabdil truly was unlucky.

The two arrived at the Library of Generalife, or *Jannat al-Arif*, in the Plaza de Bib Rambla.

"Oh no!" said the captain, biting his fist. "Are we late? No, no, we've made it, there's no way we could be late!"

There were a few cardinals walking about the library along with dozens of priests and monks. The priests went in and came out with their arms full of books and then loaded them onto a horse cart normally used to carry manure. Even worse, Inquisition guards were also milling around.

"What? What're they doing?!" Niño said. "Where are they taking those book?"

"Forget about it. Now's not the time for talking, we need to go in."

The captain looked around and tried to figure out whom the top-ranking cardinal was. "You wait here," he told Niño, and went over to a cardinal in a black cassock with red piping and a scarlet biretta on his head whom he had easily picked out from the others.

Niño watched in astonishment from a distance. The cardinal opposite the captain first wove his hands as if to say no, then waved over to the nearby guards and ordered for them to take him away, but the captain pulled out some papers from his pocket and showed them to the cardinal. The cardinal carefully looked them over and then looked up at the captain—despairingly nodding toward the entrance. The captain then turned to Niño and waved for him to follow. Niño felt the cardinal glower at him as he passed.

The captain and Niño squeezed through the priests into the library and, turning to Niño, the captain said, "Now it's your turn, let's see your cunning."

He was taken aback again when he saw the books scattered across the floor and being pulled from the shelves like teeth from a jaw. He looked from side to side bewildered and asked, "What're they going to do with these book?"

"We don't have time for this now. Come on, where're the maps?"

Seeing that he had no other choice, he composed himself and as if his memory flooded back, he motioned toward the corridor on the right. "The geography section should be on this side."

They went through a long corridor with Niño in the lead and the captain behind him, passing by side rooms—some completely emptied and some still full of books. Then they stopped.

Niño pointed at the room they stopped in front of. "It should be here."

"So what're you waiting for?" said the captain, and pushed him through the entrance.

Niño reluctantly scanned over the shelves covering the walls. The captain pulled another paper from his pocket and started listing off names.

"Try to find al-Idrisi first. This is the most important one."

Niño reached up and pulled out a book from the third shelf up in the stack on the left. "That's it, al-Idrisi," said the captain. Niño bristled at his pronunciation.

The captain had no mind to care what Niño thought. He held the book—two or three times bigger than the others—to his chest as if he had just found gold and began hastily flipping through its pages.

"Fantastic!" His eyes beamed as he turned the pages and saw all sorts of maps. He couldn't read Arabic, but he could identify all the oceans, seas and continents.

He looked back at Niño.

"So now," he looked back down to his list, "Ma... Ma... mun's atlas?"

The captain had started to look like a complete fool to Niño.

"You must mean al-Ma'mun—a caliph in the ninth century. He didn't make the atlas, he ordered his cartographers to make it." He begrudgingly threw the book to the captain. "It's a collection of all the atlases in his time and it compares their latitudes and longitudes."

The captain couldn't hold the gigantic book any longer and carried it to the table in the middle of the room and started flipping through al-Ma'mun's Map of the World.

"For the love of Christ—these are exquisite!" He was now see-ing drawings he had never come face to face with before, and even though he didn't quite understand them, he was sure he'd never run across such calculations before in his life.

"What else do you want?"

The captain struggled to pronounce the names—al-Biruni, al-Zuhri and several others.

Niño looked over all of the shelves again and again. "Those ar-en't here," he said, pointing at the empty shelves, "They must have taken them."

A group of priests then entered the room and started clearing out the shelves.

"It's time you two go," one of the priests said, more a threat than a request.

"We were going already," the captain said, and taking the two books, he and Niño left the library.

Niño was looking at the priests.

"What're they going to do with these book, captain? For the love of God, tell me. Where are they taking them?"

"You'll understand soon," the captain said, evading the question. He was thinking about which libraries they were going to next. The Library of Muhammad V, Yusuf I's private library with hundreds of pieces and the Granada naval library were only just a few. The captain felt he was going to die of excitement the more he thought about the books in his hands and the ones he was going to get.

Niño was about to ask if he should go, but the captain cut him off.

"Our work's only just begun!"

Niño's mind was on the fate of the piles of books being loaded onto the horse cart, hopeless about what was to come next, while the captain was thinking he was opening the lid to a massive trea-sure chest. He reckoned he was now ready for the open ocean.

Christopher Columbus had found the maps that would change the world. Now he had to find the Pinzon brothers in Palos.

22

The priest of the Zaragoza cathedral guessed it must be something out of the ordinary when he two royal, mounted guards appear in the distance, but he still couldn't believe his eyes when he unrolled the parchment in his hands and started to read the royal edict.

King Ferdinand and Queen Isabella, by the grace of God, King and Queen of Castile, Leon, Aragon and other dominions of the crown—to prince Juan, the dukes, marquees, counts, the holy orders and their priors, the lords of the Castles, knights and all Jewish men and women of all ages and anyone else this letter concerns—salutations and grace unto you.

It is well known that in our dominion there exists wicked Christians who have Judaized and have committed apostasy against our Holy Catholic faith, the majority cause of this being relations between Jews and Christians. Therefore, in the year one thousand four hundred and eighty, we ordered that the Jews be separated from the cities and towns of our domains and that they be assigned separate quarters, hoping that with this separation the existing situation would be remedied and we ordered that the Inquisition be established in these domains—

Two small children were running around barefoot and chasing each other in the city square in Burgos on Sunday morning, and when they saw a crowd start to gather around a priest, they squeezed in among them and, craning their necks, tried to understand what the priest was reading from the sheet he was holding.

—and in the term of twelve years it has functioned and the Inquisition has found many wicked and guilty people, we are informed by the Inquisition and others that the great harm done to Christians persists because of interactions with the Jews, and in turn these Jews try with all means to subvert the Holy Catholic faith and try to lure faithful Christians away from their beliefs.

These wicked Jews have instructed these Christians in the ceremonies and beliefs of their laws, circumcising their sons and giving them books for their prayers, and declaring to them the days of fasting, and gathering them to teach them the history of their laws, informing them when their are the festivities of Passover and how to observe it, giving them unleavened bread and ceremonially prepared meats, and giving instruction on the things from which they should abstain in relation to food and other things required for the observance of the laws of Moses, convincing them to the full extent that no other law or truth exists outside of this with the wicked books they print on the Devil's new contraption. And thus it is made clear based on the confessions from these Jews as well as from those they have perverted that it has resulted in great harm and detriment to the Holy Catholic faith—

After singing *Ave Maria* at the Mass in the cathedral of Seville in the southwest, the priest continued reading from the same edict to the puzzled looks from the congregation.

—and as we knew the true remedy for these injuries and difficulties lay in severing all communication between the aforementioned Jews and the Christians and dispatching them from all our dominion, we contented ourselves in ordering the said Jews from all the cities and towns and other places of Andalusia where it appeared they had done major damage, and believing that this would be sufficient so that in these and other cities and towns and places in our reigns and possessions would be effective and they would cease to commit the aforesaid. And because we have been informed that none of this, nor the justices done for some of the said Jews found most culpable for the abovementioned crimes and transgressions against the Holy Catholic faith have been a complete remedy to obviate and correct these crimes and offenses. And it appears that every day the Jews increase in continuing their evil and harmful objective to the Christian faith and religion where they live and converse; and

because there is nothing to offend more than our holy belief, which God has protected until the present day and as to those who have been influenced, it is the duty of the Holy Mother Church to repair and decrease this situation to its previous state, due to the fragility of the human being, it could occur that we could succumb to the diabolical temptation that continually fights against us, so that, if the main cause being the so-called Jews, if they are not converted, they must be expelled from the Kingdom. Owing that when a detestable and powerful crime is committed by some members of a group it is reasonable that the group should be dissolved or annihilated and the minors and elders be punished one for the other and those who pervert those who are good and honest living in the cities and the towns and by their contact can harm others should be expelled from amid the people and even if for minor causes that are injurious to the Republic and more so for the greater and dangerous and contagious crimes such as this.—

Meanwhile, the bishop of the city read the same lines in a large courtyard of the old Mosque of Cordoba—the largest Islamic sanctuary in Andalusia, which had been converted into a church. In another city of the kingdom, Davud hopelessly hung his head at the foot of the arches of an old mosque as if he had been waiting for such a pronouncement for a long time.

—Therefore, with the council and advice of eminent men and knights of our reign and with that from other people of conscience and knowledge of our Supreme Council and after much deliberation, it is agreed to dictate that all the Jews and Jewesses should abandon our kingdoms and that they never be permitted to return. We further order in this edict that the Jews and Jewesses of all ages who reside in our dominions or territories depart with their sons and daughters, servants and familiars, both grand and lesser folk of all ages, by the end of July of this year and not dare to return to our lands and not so much as take a step to trespass in any manner. Any Jew who does not accept this edict and is found in our dominions or returns will incur the punishment of death and confiscation of their belongings. And we have ordered that no person in our reign, without import of social status, including nobles, hide or keep or defend a Jew or Jewess whether publicly or secretly from the end of July and the subsequent months in their homes or elsewhere in our region

upon risk of punishment of losing their manors, fortresses and their heredi-
tary privileges and assets. ...

We give and grant permission to the previously mentioned Jews and Jewesses
to carry with them their property and belongings out of our regions, by sea
or by land, excluding gold and silver, or minted coins or other articles pro-
hibited by the laws or our reign.—

At the Synagogue of El Transito in Toledo's Jewish quarter, Abraham de Dilva and Isaac Abarbanel swallowed hard and looked at each
other in horror as if they had seen the Devil while the two Inquisition
guards assigned to the chief rabbi forced them to listen to the edict.

—Thus we order all councilors, magistrates, knights, guards, officials, good
men of the city of Burgos and other cities and towns of our reign and domin-
ions, and all of our vassals and people to respect and obey this letter and all
contained within it to give the kind of assistance and help necessary for its
execution, subject to punishment by our sovereign grace and confiscation of
all belongings and property to our royal house, and that this be notified to all
and that no one feigns ignorance of it, we order that this edict be proclaimed
in all the plazas and meeting places in all the cities and in all the principal
cities and all the towns of the diocese, and be done so by the herald in pres-
ence of the public notary, and that neither one nor the other do contrary to
what has been defined, subject to punishment by our sovereign grace and the
annulment of their offices and confiscation of their assets for those who act
in contradiction.

And we order that evidence be provided to the court in the form of signed
testimony specifying the manner in which this edict is carried out to this end.
Given in this city of Granada on the XXXI day of March in the year of our
Lord Jesus Christ one thousand four hundred and ninety two.

Signed I, the King, and I, the Queen, and Juan de Coloma secretary of the
King and Queen who has written it upon order of their Majesties.

Grand Inquisitor Tomas Torquemada had an insidious smile on
his face as he held the edict that Queen Isabella had signed while he
stood in the Hall of the Sisters, where a few weeks before Jewish
poets had recited praise of the caliph. Now everyone was either
going to become Christian and leave this land.

23

Columbus was panting atop his mule and wiped the beads of sweat building up on his forehead with a piece of cloth. He looked as though it was he and not his mule who'd done the carrying on the two-week journey from Granada to this place. He knew he'd arrived at Palos when he saw the mountainside and the city's pier full of ships and he took a deep breath of relief. Maybe if the beast he was riding had been a horse it wouldn't have been as exhausted, but the orders from the Church were very clear—horses were only for the royal family and their retinue and Church officials. Although he had not abided by this order in the past and had surreptitiously ridden horses, he had no desire to push his luck now lest he run into the fanatical priests of the Inquisition. At a time like this when fate was laughing at him for the first time in his life, he couldn't allow for things to go even worse.

Rather than from setting out on the rode on a mule, however, he was exhausted because the journey was on land. He was in love with the sea like every man of Genoa born and raised on the water—it wasn't the sea that made these men sick, but dry land. Even though he was the son of a wool weaver, Columbus had spent his childhood watching the admirals, sailors and deckhands anchored of Corsica, and he took the first chance he had to join them on the sea. Now, however, he was forty-odd years old and had yet to ever command a fleet let alone captain a full crew, and thus he'd come to Palos for this reason. He had to find Martin Alonso Pinzon and his brothers—the Pinzon brothers.

He rode his mule from the outskirts of town toward the pier.

The olives in the groves gleamed in the sun's rays, shining like little bits of copper from the trees in the valley. Many of the people from the small port city of Palos in the southwest of Spain, had given up farming for seafaring. Palos was the main place of residence for the Spanish seamen who tacked along the Mediterranean and who more recently set out for the African coast.

Columbus noticed something extraordinary as he passed through the city square—it was teeming with an unusual amount of Dominican friars and, in addition to that, there was a strange silence at the pier. The sailor hopped off his mule and tied it up in front of a building next to the pier. He went into the building—a mix of taverns and restaurants frequented by customs officials and sailors who came to fill their bellies and have a cold drink.

He guzzled down a bowl of pomegranate juice—a gift the Arabs had brought with them to Spain—and then asked the tavern keeper where he might find Martin Alonso Pinzon. The man continued with his work as if he hadn't heard a word, so Columbus asked again, louder this time.

"Hey, I'm asking you where can I find the Pinzons!"

This time the tavern keeper came up to Columbus quickly from behind the bar and, before the sailor understood what was happening, pulled out a thick cleaver.

"If you say that name one more time I'll cut your tongue out!"

Columbus got the lump in his throat. He was taken aback at what he was going through. He nodded his head in fear and understanding as the tavern keeper pulled the knife from his throat.

He checked his neck where the clever had been pressing and said to himself, "For Christ's sake, I was just trying to find an old friend, that's all."

A man sitting next to him turned and whispered, "How do you know Martin?"

"He repaired my caravel a few years back," Columbus said, catching the man out of the corner of his eye. He went on whispering, "Do you know where he is?"

"We don't much like the people the round heads brought here to be spoken of."

Columbus didn't understand. "Round heads?"

"Be quiet, man! The ones brought to the Inquisition."

He realized round heads was the term the people in Palos had come up with for the Dominican friars due to their shaven heads, but he still just got more confused.

"Did they bring Martin to the Inquisition?"

"Him and his brothers."

"On what charge?"

"There's say the Pinzons are secret Muslims."

"The Pinzon brothers—Muslims?!" Columbus couldn't believe what he was hearing—he'd made a two-week journey from Granada for a group of Inquisition criminals.

"What claim is there that they're Muslim, then?"

"They were seen always washing their arms and hands and washing up too often. There's also apparently Arabic writing and numbers on their sailing instruments."

Columbus laughed in exasperation. "Everyone's known well for a long time that the Arabs invented those instruments and that they've got Arabic numbers on them!"

The man answered with the same sardonic expression on his face. "I don't very much think the round heads've got that detail."

A shiver ran down Columbus' spine. There was no way of sailing the ocean without the Pinzon brothers. The only man he knew in Palos and the only one he trusted to captain a ship was Martin Alonso and, moreover, he needed the man's caravels and the men under his command. He clenched his fists, took off his sailor's hat and scratched his head—he couldn't get out of this somehow.

Although as he thought, new ideas started coming to mind.

Columbus composed himself again and, laughing to himself, thought maybe this was another twist of fortune. Martin possibly being in the hands of the Inquisition could also be useful for his endeavors—perhaps it would be cheaper than he thought to work out a deal with the most famous shipbuilder and outfitter in Palos.

He turned back to the man next to him. "So, where did they take the Pinzon brothers?"

"Where they take everybody, to La Rabida Friary. You know that place?"

An impish grin spread across Columbus' face—he personally knew the prior. Fortune certainly was smiling on him, and opening doors along the way.

24

Columbus and a Dominican friar walked through the dark cellars of La Rabida Friary. Columbus looked at the damp walls and noticed the dried blood and vomit as the light from the friar's torch danced on the interior of the corridors. He covered his nose with his arm to ward off the intense reeking of the place. The two passed people groaning behind the bars, some lying on the ground, others pressed up against the irons begging for forgiveness and groping at his waistcoat.

A friar standing in front of one of the dungeons furthest down looked though his jangling ring of keys until he found the right one and unlocked the door. A man was sitting in a corner of the small cell, his head in his hands and his knees pulled up to his chest. He was motionless, as if knowing that talking or screaming here would be of no use to anything, his head hung in resignation to his fate.

"Martin Alonso Pinzon, today is your lucky day. Our Lord Jesus Christ must've taken pity on you," the friar said.

Martin slowly raised his head. He looked at the two men in the doorway, the lines of his nose, lips and bones of his chin were pronounced on his dark, thickly stubbled face. He tried to reckon what was happening, like after waking up from a nightmare. His dark eyes under his black brow had a hardness to them as if they would bore holes through the cell walls.

The friar turned to Columbus. "You have half an hour."

He walked into the cell and the friar closed and locked the door behind him.

"Do you still not understand? There's nothing to be worried about! When we keep go west, we'll arrive in China in a few weeks and then on to India."

He had introduced himself to Pinzon as soon as he entered the cell, and the captain from Palos, whose memory was stronger than he had anticipated, immediately recognized the man from Genoa. He even remembered what Columbus hadn't—that the Genoese sailor had disappeared without paying him his debt of five thousand maravedi coins. That money could buy a caravel, and with his business connections, Pinzon could've even built a carrack with that amount of money. After all, he was one of the most renowned shipwrights in all of Iberia.

"After we do what I'm explaining to you, it won't be five thousand marevedis, but an unfathomable amount that we'll earn, my friend!" Columbus said, and dove into explaining his plan as fast as possible.

Pinzon was a good judge of character having had hundreds of men under his command both at the shipyard and on countless voyages as a captain and, as such, he knew that trusting this man would not bring any favor. He sensed there was some inconsistency in what he was explaining. Columbus was trying to persuade him, repeating the same thing over and over, and Pinzon had a woeful feeling that, as he found himself in a cell, he had no other choice than to get on with this man.

"Didn't you always say it, Martin?" Columbus continued. "That the ocean can be overcome and the lands on the other side can be reached? How many times have you told me about the maps on your shelves, the journeys beyond the ocean that the Moors—I can't remember their names now—wrote about in their history books, about your ancestors' successes centuries before, and that it can be done again with enough ships and crew? And on top of that, I've found the maps we'll need!"

Pinzon knew he was talking about the books like those by al-Idrisi and al-Masudi, but he grabbed Columbus by the collar when he mentioned his ancestors.

"Quiet, man! Did you come to rescue me or to send me to burn at the stake?"

The last thing Pinzon wanted echoing through the friary was that his family was related to the Marinid dynasty of Morocco. He could trace his ancestry as far back as Abu Zayyan Muhammad III, but it wasn't something that would make his life easier to bring to mind again here where he was accused of being a secret Muslim.

Columbus smirked—even the man's strength, standing at nearly a head taller than him, wasn't enough to scare him.

"I was wondering," Columbus said. "Is it true? Are you really—?"

He couldn't finish the question—Pinzon had tightened his grip on Columbus' collar and spun him against the wall, knocking the wind out of him.

He let Columbus go, hopeless, and walked to the other side of the cell.

Columbus coughed a few times and composed himself. "I can't believe you! I came to give you freedom and you attack me! Be a little more sensible, Martin."

"Look," Pinzon said. "Your calculations are all over the place. Yes, I know the ocean has been crossed before, but I've never claimed they arrived in China or India."

"If you want, we can talk about this when we leave. I need you— your ships and your men." Columbus walked up to him and looked around. "It looks like you need me, too."

Pinzon sighed in dismay—Columbus was right.

"And so what about my brothers, the men under my command? We can't do any of this without that crew."

"I don't know which of them I can save, but with this letter we can gather a crew large enough for three ships."

Columbus showed him the letter of permission Isabella and Ferdinand had given him in Granada. With it, he was authorized to employ ninety men—enough for three ships. Columbus figured that since no one would agree to the madness he was talking about, his solution was to use the sailors and prisoners in the dungeon as crewmen. Most of them weren't guilty of being secret Jews or Muslims, anyway.

"So who will be in charge of the fleet?" Pinzon asked.

"I will, of course."

Pinzon furrowed his brow and Columbus immediately added, "But whatever you say along the way will be. You're the captain— you and your brothers."

The door to the dungeon opened while Pinzon was thinking.

"Your time's up," snapped the friar.

Columbus looked at Pinzon. "So, we have a deal?"

25

Davud arrived at the inn at the entrance to the town of Villa del Rio, hopped off his mule—which had just made a days-long journey—and tied it to a post along with the half a dozen horses already there. Villa del Rio was a one-day journey from Cordoba and three days from Toledo. The signboard at the entrance to the inn said *Los Gallos de Pelea*, and just above it there was a carving of two roosters facing each other for the majority of the folk who were illiterate. It was an odd name—The Fighting Cocks Inn.

Two men came stumbling out drunk under the sign while Davud was looking at it. When one of the men saw a monk in front them, he tried to pull himself together and make the sign of the cross.

"Forgive me, Father," he slurred, drool dripping from one side of his mouth and a smile cracking on the other—but, as standing was already too difficult, he couldn't quite make the sign of the cross correctly. He looked even more ridiculous as he tried to stifle his laughter, only to outdo himself as he missed one of the steps leading down and fell prone to the ground. His friend took hold of his foot the best he could and dragged him away.

It was already quite dark out, and Davud was going to fill his belly and spend the night at this Fighting Cocks Inn. He thought that maybe it wasn't such a good idea to stay here when he walked into the tavern, but he was tired and he didn't want to waste time looking for another place.

As soon as he entered he scanned the building and its interior—an instinct he had gained over the years. There was a counter with men lined up at it on the other end of the room where the tavern keeper was filling up their wooden cups with wine. There were rooms up one flight the stairs on both sides of the counter. The top floor completely covered the mezzanine where women were leaning against the banister and trying to excite the men below. Some had their breasts out, some had slits in their dresses open to the waist and still others were sauntering around in their undergarments. Men were standing by some of them, haggling over prices while their hands groped at their breasts and hips.

There was a kitchen at the back behind the counter and women carrying trays and jugs were serving the rowdy bunch eating and drinking at the tables in the middle of the tavern. But the real racket was coming from the men standing in a circle on the left side of the room, everybody trying to peek through the small, open spaces between all of their shoulders. Davud finally got why the inn was called the Fighting Cocks. Feathers were flying in the middle of the crowd, the little creatures tearing each other to shreds, their wings flapping, all mixed with the cheers of the men who had put wagers down on the fight.

He counted twelve swords in total between those on the mezzanine, at the surrounding tables and at the counter in front of him. He saw knife handles tucked into the belts of all the five men in a group at the second table from the back on the right. What drew Davud's attention most, however, were the two men with swords and tall boots haggling with the women on the mezzanine. Both the quality of the men's blades and the leather of their boots were signs that these could be Castilian knights.

He went to the quietest corner with the least people and furthest away from the cockfight—and when he sat down and started to eat the chicken he'd ordered, he felt some of his exhaustion begin to subside. He also requested that his mule be given fodder. He lost his appetite, though, listening to the cockfight from the other side of the room while he ate his chicken. He had guessed as much, but he couldn't eat beef because they neither cooked it properly nor bled the animal well during slaughter—so blood would continue to flow through the half-cooked meat on the plate. He had grown accustomed to everything after so many years on foreign soil, but he could never seem to fill his stomach.

"Did you lose your way, Brother?" said a voice cackling behind him.

The cockfight had ended and the crowd had all dispersed to their tables, save for a group of three men standing over Davud—one was monstrous, twice as big as the other two quite diminutive men. The enormous man who'd spoken spit on the ground and grinned at the other two. His two front teeth were missing and the others were a sickly yellow and dark.

Davud didn't even lift his head and tried to eat another piece of the chicken from the plate in front of him.

"Hey, we're talking to you!" another one of the men piped up.

Davud lifted his full tankard of water to his mouth, trying to quench his thirst.

The three men pulled up stools and sat down at his table.

The brute was the first to speak. "You deaf, Brother?" and sidled up next to him, nearly cheek to cheek. Feeling the man's hot, putrid breath on his face made Davud's stomach turn. He wrinkled his face and turned away.

This time one of the other men shoved his shoulder. "Come on, speak up why don't you!" He turned back to his friends. "So he's deaf and mute." Although he couldn't help thinking that the monk's shoulder he'd just shoved was more muscular and harder than he would've expected. Davud reckoned the man had gathered as much and looked up at them for the first time. The way he looked in his cassock and the cowl falling over his shoulders always gave a false impression of the muscles hiding under his tunic.

The man on the left, like the other before, also shoved his shoulder. "So what order you from, Brother?"

"He's from the dog-licker order," said the other little man, bursting out in laughter with his friends. "His head's not shaved—what kind of order is that?" the brute laughed, patting Davud's head.

"You touch me again and I'll break your hand," Davud said. The confidence and authority in his voice surprised them. The three men all looked at each other for a moment and then started laughing again.

One of the smaller men imitated Davud's look and voice. "If you touch my shoulder again I'll break your hand."

Still laughing, his rotten teeth flashing, "I'm touching you!" the brute said—and as he was about to lay a hand on him, without moving anything other than his left arm, Davud grabbed the man's hand, twisted it back and broke it all in one movement before he had any idea of what had happened.

"My hand!" the man screamed and fell to the floor. One of the smaller men opposite him was about to lay into him, but Davud brought his hands together and elbowed the man in the face. He also fell to the floor. The smallest man pulled a knife from his belt and planted himself opposite Davud. He was shaking with fear, but was also fixing to get even for his friends. All the people around had turned to watch them, holding their breaths for the end.

Davud stood up and waited for the man to make a move with his knife. The man waved his little blade at Davud's heart. He grabbed hold of the man's knife hand, pulled him toward himself and head-butted him in the nose. The man fell to his knees, his nose broken and with blood pouring down his face.

Right then, Davud felt the sharp points of swords outstretched from both sides—it was the two knights he'd noticed on the top floor when he'd first entered. He hung his head, regretting that he wasn't able to pass through this town and avoid this inn.

Davud left the Fighting Cock Inn, disappearing from sight atop one of the horses of the men he'd sent to the ground and taking the others as reserves. The crowd in the tavern stood and looked in stunned silence at the five men on the floor. The knights' swords were sticking straight out of their bodies.

While he was riding as fast as possible toward Toledo, he had a sneaking suspicion that David would bring much more trouble to him—his fear and anxiety had lessened, although he was looking at difficult choices on the horizon.

26

The young woman was bent over a low desk, painting the last details of the miniature as it all slowly started coming together. She dipped her brush into the colors on her palette next to the painting—ash grey, slate grey and silver—and pressed the fine brush to the sheet with care. The paint laid flesh over a skeleton, spreading over the faint lines and breathing life into the body, bringing the small creature on the edge of the sheet to life.

"It's a rabbit!" said the young man. He was sitting cross-legged next to the woman, going back and forth between reading the manuscript on his lap and watching his wife add detail to her work. He always watched her paint with great admiration and he was delighted as she bent down her swan-like neck and tilted her head from side to side to get different perspectives. Her hand holding the brush looked like a little paw and her eyes whirled over the sheet with the wonderment of a baby's.

"It's not a rabbit, it's a baby rabbit," she said.

He laughed at the distinction she made between the two as if they were two different animals.

"It doesn't look so much like a kit to me, although I could hardly tell it was a rabbit."

He liked nettling his wife, which annoyed her, and she always took what he said seriously and would shoot him a dirty look.

"You're blind. It's a rabbit!"

The two were sitting in the workroom in their house. It was spacious with walls of a deep, woody brown, one of which was completely covered with books on shelves. The embroidered, crimson rug from Isparta livened up the room, and just above it on the center of the ceiling was a handmade star decoration. Next to the man sitting at the foot of the bookcase was a globe his father had left him, and behind that hanging on the wall were maps and several pieces of calligraphy. Miniatures the woman had painted hung on the opposite wall. She was sitting under the window and rays of sunlight lit up her worktable.

The man put away the manuscript he'd been reading, stood up and went over to his wife. He bent down and looked at the miniature again, this time in the sunlight.

"Are you sure this is a rabbit. Oh, sorry. A *baby* rabbit?" he said, knowing he would make her angry.

"Would you just get out already," she said, more annoyed, and elbowed him in the leg. He grunted and rubbed his leg.

"Is that what color baby rabbits are?"

She was quite mad now and looked up at him. "My rabbits are this color. Do you have something to say?"

He looked over the entire painting with amazement and pride—he actually did know how talented his wife was. There was a woman and man turned away from each other at the center of the painting. Behind them was a light orange obelisk and erect, yellow, twisting serpents, giving away that it was Constantinople. There were rows of pink mountains in the background with glinting orange highlights. But the most attention-drawing part of the painting was just above the man—the *Simurgh*, or phoenix, with three tails and its wings spread open—and explaining the tale, the birds that dared not follow it—an owl on top of ruins, a little further off a splendid and many-colored parrot, lost at the very top amid white and lavender Chinese-style clouds and flying away from the *Simurgh* an eagle, and of course, unable to pass up the flowers, a nightingale in the gardens below.

The man wondered why the *Simurgh*—which, according to the legend never alighted on the ground and was the ruler of the birds—was flying over the male figure. The female figure was facing the young rabbit the woman was working on.

"Why is the woman looking away from the man?"

"She must be mad at something, but I don't know at what."

The man thought about the melancholy he sensed in the painting for a while and looked over its details again and again.

"The woman and the man both look quite sad," he said. The expressions his wife had put on the faces of her figures were so clear it was impossible not to take notice of them. The mottling of the predominant colors on them also reduced their intensity.

"Nakkash Efendi says I have to work a little more on facial expressions."

She was taking lessons from Baba Nakkash, who was eighty years old and among the chief artisans in the empire.

"I think you need to work a little more on rabbits," he laughed. This time, she shot up and chased him out of the room.

"I'll show you a rabbit," she yelled after him.

A rabbit jumped up from where it had been munching on grass, looked around and hopped off. Davud was sitting against the base of a tree, his eyes welling up as he watched the rabbit. He leaned an arm on his knee and stared off hopelessly into the distance. His horse continued to graze, tied to the same tree. The orange hues of the setting sun in the valley he found himself in spread out across the horizon and the far-off mountains and sky looked as if they'd been painted with unusual colors like those in his wife's miniatures.

"Elif," he said. He leaned his head back against the tree, his lips moving as if they were independent from the rest of him. His head was as heavy and lifeless as a dead man's.

"Elif," he said again. It had been so many years. "I miss you so much, Elif. I miss you so much."

27

Burak Reis looked out at the horizon from the forecastle of his fast-moving, light galiot, barely breathing. He squinted his eagle eyes—his shadow from the sun behind him hitting the sea along with the silhouette of the ship made the famous, twenty-five-year-old pirate appear as a giant. He would have, however, rather wanted to have been on a brigantine at the least, and not this small galiot for the battle he was about to enter. The boys of nine and ten next to him still had tears running down their cheeks.

He stood upright and motionless, spite emanating from his face, and gave the order when he saw three specks on the horizon that were barely visible. His powerful voice echoed as strong as thunder shaking down from the sky.

"Hard windward!"

It was like the fury and malice in his voice came from the dark clouds above, enough to overturn the sea.

As soon as Mute Yusuf heard the order, he swung from rope to rope like an acrobat and relayed the command to the yardmen. The deep knife scar that ran from below his left eye down to his chin had the same curve as the sails he was swinging over. The riggers repositioned the sails ninety degrees windward, whirling and clanging the ropes and blocks.

Hajji Mustafa, already in his eighties, was right behind Burak Reis. He turned his compass around in his hand and murmured to himself, "Not bad—Now this's very good—Look this is all wrong," as he read the wind and course, trying to calculate the speed. Burak Reis never set sail without him. Hajji Mustafa's piloting was always the same.

Helmsman Yunus couldn't see anything on the horizon from the quarterdeck but shifted course on the captain's command. "That old man surely knows something," he said.

Despite the lookout at the top of the ship having better eyes than everybody in the fleet, when Burak Reis was angry he would stand at the ship's bow and peer out at his target, and at these moments, he knew better than all of them. Helmsman Yunus also wanted to take revenge for the pilgrims at least as much as the captain did.

Perched in the crow's nest at the highest point of the ship, the lookout boy was trying to see five or ten miles away, holding the mast with one hand and shielding his eyes from the glint of the water with the other, wondering what Burak Reis had seen. There was no trace of the Saint John, which he'd been looking for in the endless blue for three hours.

Far under him, just below in the lower deck was Overseer Mikhail running his hand over his beard and bellowing, "Stroke together, stroke together!" He was trying to make the oarsmen row faster by pacing between the rows of galley slaves ordered two by two on each side of the ship. "Come on you damn infidels! Faster, faster!"

The galley slaves gripped their oars with more resentment with every word, rising as their oars hit the water and then thrusting their chests to their poles, and sitting back down with a thud. Most of the slaves were convicted prisoners who knew that the Turks didn't constantly use whips like the Venetians and Spaniards, and especially since they'd get a share of the plundered booty, they churned their oars more fervidly. But this morning, the blunder of the Knights Hospitallers of Saint John enraged even Overseer

Mikhail so that he hung his whip that he had not touched for years on the broadside of the galley.

Burak Reis' galiot was now advancing on the sea like a snake with the power of the oars and the support of the wind, its bow churning up white froth. The captain was still looking ahead from the forecastle. His tawny hair glistening under the sun and the glimmer of the sea shining in the blacks of his eyes, it was as if the young man was not on a ship, but rather a part of nature, a sculpture under the golden sun from the blue of the sea, distilled in that place.

The lookout on the topmast began yelling, "Northwest! Northwest! Thirty-five degrees!" pointing from one side to the direction he was shouting. The thirty sailors and forty warriors on the ship all looked at once, hanging over the balustrades or leaping on the ropes beside them and peering out in the direction the boy was pointing to.

They could easily pick out two crusader galleys and an Ottoman caravel off the starboard bow in the direction that Burak Reis had shown about half an hour ago. The galleys were sailing diagonally toward each other, the red crosses on their pure-white sails and the flags on their standards streaming in the wind.

Rattler Hajji checked the dagger in his belt—his saber hung on his left and his dagger on his right. A warrior to his side grasped hold of the hilt of his cutlass and another set aside the whetstone he had been using to sharpen his axe for the past hour.

"I didn't reckon they'd be that big," Rattler said.

"Hey mate, what're you afraid of, Rattler?" the ship's merchant, Big Ahmed, said with a chuckle that spread to the surrounding crew and fighters. Rattler's little snowball of a Maltese terrier didn't leave his side, keeping watch over its master, its tiny, pink tongue dangling from its mouth.

Turning his back, Rattler said, "Why don't you shut your trap and let's see what these damn bastards are up to before we let loose the hound of the Seven Sleepers."

"Enough already, I'm willing to fight ten knights, but keep that filthy fleabag away from me!" Big Ahmed said. Like the others, he was trying to figure out how many knights were on these two fully equipped galleys that were growing bigger than any of them imagined as they drew nearer.

The two crusader galleys were both nearly twice as long and twice as tall than Ottoman galleys. They had attacked an Ottoman caravel loaded with pilgrims that was setting sail for the Hejaz in the early morning at the opening to the harbor in Alexandria in the southern Mediterranean, and finding the ship without any defenses, they slaughtered many of the elderly men and woman, as well as the children, captured the young men to be galley slaves and sent the young women off to the slave markets in the Peloponnese. Most of the elderly who were too old to row or be much use for any work were thrown into the sea.

Burak Reis knew that the Knights Hospitallers of Rhodes were said to often attack Ottoman ships and villages, sailing up and down the coast of the old Menteshe Beylik. He changed course and set off toward Rhodes to find the crusaders as soon as he heard that a ship of pilgrims had been attacked.

The captain put a hand on the shoulder of the boy next to him. "Is this your ship?" The boy's father had been thrown overboard into the sea, his mother raped by three knights on the deck of the ship, all in front of his eyes—he looked up with bloodshot eyes.

He nodded. "Yes."

Burak Reis motioned Mute Yusuf over and the yardman took the boy from the captain.

"Come on, then. We're going with you to the lower deck. And don't come up again until I come get you." He put the boy in a cask in the hold and warned him again, "No matter how much the ship rocks, no matter how loud it gets, you don't come out."

The child barely ever talked as if he had swallowed his little tongue—he was afraid of Mute Yusuf, who was a large man, and the scar on his face didn't help—but he swore that he would do as he was told, no matter what, and ducked down into the cask.

"What's it now, Yusuf? You start babysitting?" Big Ahmed snickered. Rattler also gave him a teasing smirk.

Mute Yusuf glared at the merchant and took his place again on the forecastle deck.

With the captain's order to prepare for battle, the pirates spread sand over the deck so they wouldn't slip in the blood that would soon be spilt and hung thick mats over the bulwarks to protect against cannon strikes. On Gunner Topal's orders, a man on each end took cannonballs from the armory, wrapped them in canvas and set them on deck. They poured water on the deck to protect against sparks and hung wet canvas over the door to the powder hold.

The man in charge of keeping time at sea with the hourglass and also the mid-deck sergeant, Boatswain Mahmud, turned to the pirate to his side.

"What do you reckon Blind Ali? Think we're sunk this time?"

All on board were taken aback by the colossal galleys in front of them and the rows of more than three hundred knights and mercenaries lined up on their decks. The knights' armor gleamed in the sun, blinding Burak Reis' men.

"The bastards got a mirror in our faces, but it won't do nothing. That's it." Blind Ali had gotten his name from his reputation of shooting arrows with his eyes closed and hitting his targets at six hundred paces. "These pricks are up against someone there own size now!" he sniffed, flipping around and stringing his bow in a trice—which even a wrestler couldn't bend. He drew an arrow from the quiver over his shoulder and set it to the bowstring. He was trying to make out the highest-ranking commanders on the ships, knowing that the knights would soon be in range.

Pierro Navarro—the fiercest of the Knights of Rhodes—was standing on the bridge of the lead galley and laughed when he saw the Ottoman galiot approaching at such speed. The famous knight was in full armor, holding his helmet under his arm.

"I thought today had been profitable enough," he said in Italian to his assistant. "But look at that little fish swimming straight into our mouth!"

When viewed from a distance, Burak Reis' galiot truly did look like a minnow swimming as fast as it could into the mouth of a shark.

Far and away from attacking ships carrying the Knights of Rhodes, most would turn tail and flee the red crosses emblazoned on their sails. The entire Mediterranean knew that these men were nothing to trifle with—these ships carried the finest knights and mariners of Italy, all born and raised at sea.

Putting on his helmet, Navarro gave the order to his master sergeant, "Prepare the men for battle!"

The captain of the second galley—the knight Helion de Golon—received the signal from the lead ship and ordered the batteries to port. Like Navarro, de Golon was also one of Grand Master of the Order of Rhodes Pierre d'Aubusson's best men, and he confidently watched the small galiot on its approach. Under his feet were two hundred galley slaves, one hundred on each side, straining at their oars under the cracks of whips. There were five men on each oar seated side by side—most of them were prisoners from Ottoman and African lands and they realized that something was wrong. Each one was shackled around the ankle with the chains passing through metal rings on the walls. Yasin was a tall and slender young man who had until the previous evening dreamed of being a pilgrim. He labored at his oar, his back exposed for hours to the lashing whip, which shredded his skin and left deep gashes. That was the cost of life, however—when he grasped the oar with all his might he could be spared the whip. He wept heavily while he labored away with all the strength he could muster. There was no time for him to pity himself for what had happened or to mourn the dead.

Burak Reis turned to Blind Ali as soon as the galleys were within range of his men's arrows. The head archer received the signal he was waiting for and, along with the dozen men he had posted along the starboard bulwark, yelled out *ya Haqq* and the arrows began to fly. The first arrow Blind Ali shot caught the squire next to Pierro Navarro in the cheek. His armor would have saved him from a mortal wound if the arrow had been only one finger higher or lower, but the man was instead now writhing on the deck, screaming in pain.

Blind Ali's men were all master marksmen, and they targeted many of the knights on the lead galley were targeted with the first volley since they wouldn't have been expecting such an attack. Burak Reis knew well what it meant to attack the two large crusader galleys with his small ship, and was aware that he had to use all his skill—he had no choice other than a surprise attack and he had charged Blind Ali with taking aim at the knight on the lead galley. He was going to attack the quickly approaching second galley while those on the lead ship recovered from the disorder and confusion. Blind Ali and his men had indeed already inflicted considerable casualties on that ship in a very short time. What was always a shock to their adversaries, however, was that Ali's men's aim became more precise as the waves swept under the small ship and it descended form the crest. After a while, as Burak Reis had hoped, not a soul could be seen on either of the two decks.

"Smart asses—they've cleared out!" Rattler yelled. "They ducked a little too late, but I'll give it to the bastards, they're cowering now. Look old man, don't say I didn't tell you. If these shits capture us alive after this they're not going to make us knights, that's for sure! It's up to them!"

Everybody was used to Rattler talking nonsense and whatever came to his head, Burak Reis most of all. Nobody except for Big Ahmed would ever answer him, but they all knew he was just putting words to what was already going through all the crewmen's minds.

Now it was time to move on to the second phase of the plan.

Then, five columns suddenly rose from the sea three hundred feet in front of them. The second galley had fired its cannons before completely broadsiding its enemy.

"They fired before they were in range! They're all over themselves, those idiots!" Rattler cackled.

Gunner Topal was at the far end of the deck waiting behind three cannons with a fire iron in his hand, its end smoldering. He had one eye on Burak Reis and the other on the galley and his firing range. The captain looked at him as if telling him to wait. The artillerymen in front of him were also keeping an eye on his face—each was holding a fire iron, waiting behind a cannon while others prepared the cannonballs for the next volley.

With the look the captain gave Mute Yusuf and Helmsman Yunus, he turned the ship and laid the stern alongside the furthest galley. The captain knew the galley was trying to broadside his ship so it could drown it in cannon fire, and he was working to avoid that at all costs. And so he was left no choice but to make very subtle calculations of the wind, the direction of the current, his own ship's speed and the movements of the galley directly in front of him that was constantly trying to turn broadside.

The first shot had to be precise in order to launch a firm attack on the far galley—otherwise the men on the galley would be able to pile up enough ammunition for the cannons on the quarterdeck to get off a full second round. The galley also had four times as many cannons as Burak Reis' small ship.

Burak Reis nodded to Topal when he felt they were close enough, "Now!"

Already itching for action, Topal set his burning fire iron to the three cannons in front of him. The barrels recoiled as they fired and the pirates watched enrapt as the cannonballs hurled toward the enemy galley's quarterdeck. The first cannonball plunged into the water, shooting up a large column of water, but the other two smashed into the galley's stern. Burak Reis signaled to Mute Yusuf and Helmsman Yunus as he had before, this time to turn the ship twenty degrees starboard. Topal then fired three cannons from portside, letting fly three cannonballs toward the same deck of the galley and splintering the stern.

While the pirates were cheering that fortune was smiling on them, a thundering crash came from starboard and a large break opened in the port bow. The splintered bulwark flew like knives and arrows, striking the nearby pirates—piercing one's eye, lodging into another's arm and lancing yet another's belly. A second cannonball struck right where Helmsman Yunus was standing and blew off his foot. There were heavily wounded pirates lying everywhere.

"Oh fuck!" Rattler yelled. "The bastards have cannons on the caravel!" His mates who knew that he never swore like this unless it was absolutely warranted understood immediately the severity of their situation.

There were half a dozen cannons staring them down from the portside of the caravel heading straight for starboard.

"I've never seen a cannon on a merchant ship!" Big Ahmed said.

"That's the infidel mind," Rattler hissed. "Don't ever take them lightly. They'll do whatever they can with their scheming. They'll pinch the drawers off your ass before you can look and see what happened!"

Mute Yusuf knew that the captain's plans had all been turned on their head. None of them would've guessed the crusaders would've been so calculating to move some of their cannons to the Ottoman caravel they had seized.

Gunner Topal yelled out, "Captain, we don't have much time! They're reloading!"

Moreover, Helion de Golon's galley was now off their portside and the gunners were preparing the guns. The men on the galley under Navarro's command had by now shaken off their initial shock from the surprise barrage of arrow and had turned the bow toward the pirates' galiot.

If Burak Reis didn't act fast, he'd end up going down with his crew. He also had a chance—it would be worse to be captured alive than to die fighting the crusaders.

Burak Reis felt they were being squeezed between the galley and the caravel. He shouted out the order, "Tack lee! Back the oars!" and due to the ship's small size and the deftness of its captain, it was just able to manage the maneuver. The bow of the small galiot swept past the galley's portside bow, almost colliding with it. The fuses on the cannons had by now been readied again and the captain gave the order to fire—they were set alight and three cannonballs blew away the galley's bow and ricocheted into the air. The cannonballs fell back down in an instant and tore through more than two-dozen knights, raining down body parts over the deck.

The captain gave a second order and brought his ship around to the galley's portside, screening his vessel off from any fire that could come from the caravel—it couldn't fire without the risk of hitting its fellow galleys. But de Golon had been trying to broadside the galiot since the beginning of the battle, and now he finally had—a dozen cannons sticking out from his galley's gun ports let fire and tore through the hull of the small ship. Burak Reis had reckoned this would happen and had ordered all the pirates and galley slaves to the other side of the ship, which rocked up the broadside to withstand the cannon fire and also reduced the casualties.

But be that as it may, the ship would go down if that side took one more round of cannon fire—it had already started to take on water.

The captain paid this no mind and gave Topal the signal. The head gunner ordered the guns facing the galley to be filled with chains and pieces of iron. The pirates were elated seeing this and started shouting out in joy, "By God! By God!"—they knew that after this sort of fire they would throw down the planks to board.

"All men to the planks!" roared the captain.

"Ha! That's more like it," Rattler laughed. "I've been bored to death."

Their ship came broadside to broadside with the galley and the pirates wasted no time swarming it, scaling the side with grappling hooks and ropes and flying up and over the ladders. Some of the more strapping and daring men felt no need for any of these and tried to jump straight across or, after plunging into the see and taking a few strokes, attempted to climb straight up the hull of the crusader's galley. They were unyielding and bearing down on the knights.

The bulwarks of the galley were so much higher and there were so many more knights, though, that it made boarding almost impossible. The knights hacked through the pirates with their renowned swords as they threw themselves toward the crusaders—slicing away as if harvesting wheat, with severed arms, legs, heads and ears flying in every direction. Some of the crew on the galley grabbed pikes and skewered the Turks charging from five yards off.

Navarro's galley had now gently come abreast the small ship and fired its cannons with a thundering boom. Burak Reis knew the danger of approaching from behind—he would lose the battle if he didn't do something at once. One of the cannonballs from Navarro's galley struck the forecastle deck, and there, amid the navigating instruments, blew the pilot Hajji Mustafa to pieces.

"This isn't boding well at all, mate!" Rattler barked.

Burak Reis would've never set sail without Hajji Mustafa—he was his eyes, his ears, his wisdom, his heart. The eighty-year-old man still didn't listen despite all of the captain's warnings and entered the skirmish with a cutlass in one hand and a pointed compass in the other.

The captain couldn't hold himself back any longer—he drew his sword and emerged from the shroud of the topgallant mast and leapt at the mountain of nights with a cry, "By God!"

Rattler called out, "The captain's jumped over! Come on, you old pirates! The captain's jumped!" The pirates boiled over all at once with this call and followed after their captain, driving forward with ever more rancor and tenacity. Some swung from the ropes, some from the topmast and others from the bowsprit, one after another, their swords drawn and flashing. Before long, Mute Yusuf, Rattler, Blind Ali and Big Ahmed had all taken their places alongside Burak Reis. The veteran pirates formed a small circle, there backs to each other, cutting down the knights around them and widening the circle around them as they went with the men coming from the galiot opening the way. The knights on the galley watched in astonishment as the pirates jumped aboard the ship like horses to their deaths and ran ahead, their swords over head, opening the way for their mates to follow. A knight quickly ran his sword through a pirate, but was then taken down from behind.

The cutlass Burak Reis was brandishing might as well have been a penknife with the speed he wielded it—with every flash an armored knight collapsed to the deck or fell overboard and sunk like a stone to the seafloor. Most of the pirates were bare-chested and nude to the waist, so when the fell overboard, they swam back to the galley, scaled its sides and entered back into battle.

"You damn bastards, attacking unarmed, defenseless, lonely pilgrims is easy! Come on at us if you have the balls for it!" Rattler yelled, working himself up even more and fighting fiercer as he did so. He went from knight to knight, running them through the belly with his sword as he lopped off their arms and caved in their heads with the ax in his other hand.

"Shut up, Rattler, you lout!" Big Ahmed yelled, half serious and half joking. "Don't get all smug as if we're beating these bastards. I can't feel my arm anymore—I'll take out ten more men, then I'll see how I feel about taking myself out!"

"There's nowhere to lie down, Little Ahmed! If you die, I'll kill you myself with my own hands! Don't think I'll let you die before you pay me back your debts!" Rattler shouted back.

The tide was turning.

Mute Yusuf entered the galley slave deck on the enemy ship and found himself outnumbered by the overseers three to one. As it was in every battle, the galley slaves were made to lie beneath their benches and were kept under watch so they couldn't aid the enemy and would have their heads cut off if they were to peek up. Mute Yusuf easily ducked under the chain mace the first overseer was expertly spinning over his head, and as soon as he righted himself, stuck the man in the throat with his sword and cast him to the ground. The two other descended on him together instead of taking him on one at a time. He parried the blow from the overseer on his right and countered, but he knight on his left was about to strike. Right then, young Yasin, who had been lying under his bench, grabbed hold of the knight's foot, throwing him off balance and he fell down. Mute Yusuf didn't miss this opportunity and head-butted the helmet of the still-standing knight. The helmet caved in as if it were empty and the knight in all his armor collapsed to the floor from the blow. Without wasting any time, Mute Yusuf took his sword and drove it through the back of the man's neck.

Now freed from their chains, the slaves wanted vengeance for the misery they'd suffered for years, and like wolfhounds released from their tethers, they ran topside and leapt on the knights. Some of them fought with the weapons they found lying on the deck while others laid straight into the knights with their bare hands. One of the slaves who had rowed on Helion de Golon's ship for fifteen years was so seething with rage that he didn't only slaughter the knights coming at him with the ax he had taken, he hacked them to pieces, tore out some of their hearts and drank their blood.

"Good God Almighty, the man's gone mad!" Rattler said, watching the man out of the corner of his eye while he made good room for himself in this battle of changing fortunes.

"How nice, Rattler. Looks like you've found a friend, mate!" Big Ahmed was quite enjoying himself now.

Burak Reis had cut down many of the Knights Hospitaller's senior knights, Helion de Golon foremost among them.

The galley slaves spread over the ship and its control had now fallen to the pirates—both its rudder and rigging. The crew and knights who were captured alive were immediately taken below deck and put in chains at the oars.

Pierro Navarro knew that de Golon's galley had been lost when he saw the crusader flag torn to shreds and cast away. The pirates had to now draw up the planks from their ship and prepare the galley for battle with Navarro—their galiot was lost already and was going to sink—and they all boarded the crusader galley. Mute Yusuf hadn't forgotten and went below deck to retrieve the boy he'd hidden and took him to the galley.

Burak Reis seized his advantage, and using his cunning, caught the wind and had already run abreast of Navarro's ship. The first thing Burak Reis would do when he took over a ship was to have the galley slaves whip the knights he seated in their place. Then, with Mute Yusuf's deft adjustments to the sails and Helmsman Yunus' ingenuity, they circled the ship around and attacked the stern of Navarro's galley. The galley was now weighed down with nearly twice as many men, both dead and alive, and was taking on more water, and with his ship running lower than Navarro's, Burak Reis knew exactly how to attack the ship.

Before Navarro knew what was happening, Burak Reis' galley slammed and lodged into the stern with a thundering crash, its ten-foot bowsprit penetrating to the fifth row of rowers' benches.

"Ha, old man, now isn't that suggestive—and a little obscene! You've rammed our rod straight up the crusaders' ass!" Rattler howled, with all the pirates joining in.

Topal fired the five cannons he'd loaded at the bow and reduced the stern of the crusader's ship to it framing.

After this shock, it was quite easy for the pirates to swarm over the ship and capture the knights and crew, including Pierro Navarro. The knights on the withdrawing Ottoman caravel surrendered immediately after the horror of what they saw.

"North! Due north!" the lookout shouted down from the crow's nest as loud as he could, pointing at the three ships heading straight for Burak Reis.

"Don't let these be more crusader reinforcements from Rhodes, old man," Big Ahmed said.

Burak Reis peered out at the horizon, and for the first time a smile spread across his face.

"No, these are some old pirate hands. Some true salts."

He recognized the famous sailor's galley even though it was five miles off. It was the Blue Lion.

Kemal Reis was on his way.

28

Burak Reis hadn't seen Kemal Reis for three years. "So, now you're saying we'll pull out of Constantinople, tack through the Aegean all swarming with crusaders, Venetians and Genoese pirates, and then slip passed the Knights Hospitallers on Rhodes and change course to the southern Mediterranean, and then continue on our way as if the orders of knights on Crete and the islands off the Peloponnese don't keep a sharp lookout."

Burak stopped to take a breath and Kemal Reis continued listening with a self-assured look on his face, indifferent to what the famous pirate was saying.

"And then if we're still alive, we'll wave to those hellish Knights Hospitallers passing by in the dozens of miles around Malta, and just continue on hard off to Andalusia. And I didn't even mention the pirates on Sicily or the butchers on Corsica and in Venice. Leave all them to the side—there's still the three-decked galleons off the Spanish coast that have some seventy cannons firing fifty-five pound balls!"

The two were on Kemal Reis' galley—blue and maroon with pistachio green yards—with a crew of thirty-five men, one hundred soldiers and two hundred galley slaves. The ship—the Blue Lion—had a large, carved wooden lion on its bow. Burak Reis had saluted the Ottoman admiral, firing three cannons, as soon as he saw Kemal Reis' squadron of three galiots and two galleys, with Kemal Reis responding in kind and the two met up in the waters off the southwestern Anatolian coast. Burak Reis took a rowboat to Kemal Reis' galley straight away and the two embraced each other heartily on their reunion after so long. Then Kemal Reis dove into explaining the orders from Sultan Bayezid. The two friends spoke in the admiral's gilded quarters for more than an hour.

Kemal Reis continued to listen to Burak with a smile on his face.

"Come on, we'll really do all of these things? Docked at the Malaga port unscathed? So what'll the Spanish and Portuguese ships be doing there, fishing? No—the men'll be at the cannons, and they won't be firing salutes. They most likely won't let us even land at he pier with the cannons they have at the port!

"So, tell me if I understand right, old man. If we make it through all these dangers, then we take the poor Jews there and bring them to Constantinople, is that it?"

Even though Burak Reis was a year and a half older than Kemal Reis, he still called him old man out of respect.

Kemal Reis smiled. "And you would tell me I've grown accustomed to the comforts of the palace, Burak. But now that I take a look, apparently you're the one who's gotten soft. I wouldn't think you were so scared of some heathen armies."

"So what would you do, old man? We can't get support from the great Exalted State. There're storms in front of us, maelstroms behind, Venetians to our right, the Genoese on our left, sharks below us and swords waiting for our heads. A man gets more wary after staring into Azrael's eyes all day and night. We on the sea don't sleep in the feather beds of the palace."

Kemal Reis had been a fellow pirate with Burak on the Mediterranean until three years ago, bringing down the European pirates who gave no peace to the Anatolian coasts and villages there as well as the pilgrims on the route from the Aegean to the Mediterranean. With the invitation from Sultan Bayezid, however, Kemal Reis considered service to the empire to be a binding duty and he became head of the navy in the capital. Burak Reis, however, thought military discipline wasn't for him and that his place was among the intrepid seamen. He had continued sailing up and down the waters off the Aydin and Menteshe coasts for half his life with his crew—the yardman Mute Yusuf, Helmsman Yunus, the merchant Big Ahmed, and of course, Hajji Rattler and pilot Hajji Mustafa.

"You're still going on about three years ago, Burak Agha. Your little galiot's gone under and these two crusader galleys need a good amount of repairs. If we don't serve the empire, who will? The time when war was only on land is over. We need a massive, unified force to stand against Venice and the Spanish in the Mediterranean."

Rattler and Big Ahmed entered, bringing Pierro Navarro and the other senior crew taken prisoner to Burak Reis. He had ordered that the other prisoners be made comfortable.

Rattler pushed Navarro forward. "Ha, this little shit, captain of two galleys—more like captain of my cock." He shut up when he saw Kemal Reis glare at him and Big Ahmed elbowed his side.

"Sorry, old man," he said, directing himself to Kemal Reis. "We pirate hands aren't so used to protocol. I beg your pardon."

Burak Reis looked at the knight standing opposite him as straight as a board—there wasn't the least look of regret in the man's face. "So what of yours do you trust so much that you're still all puffed up like a guinea fowl?" he asked in Italian.

"I am aide to Grand Master d'Aubusson of the Order of Saint John's Hospitallers on Rhodes," he said defiantly. "You'll pay dearly for attacking crusader ships, and torturing or killing me will only make it worse!"

Rattler didn't understand a thing the man said, but he could guess from the way the knight held his head upright and his mouth hanging in indifference. He slapped him over the head. "Go on and talk like a man, mate! You'd think the bastard's the pope himself instead of a crusader knight!"

Burak turned back to Kemal. "You see, old man, it's always the same story. These men are both evil and powerful. It's no crime to these men when they attack pilgrims of no harm to anybody who're only engaged in devotion and then run them through. It is for us, though."

"You think I don't know this, Agha?" Kemal Reis had been spending most of his life battling these knaves ever since he'd become admiral of the navy.

Burak looked back to address Navarro. "First of all, don't be afraid, we're not going to torture you. Unlike you, we don't consider it such a great feat to attack defenseless people, torture them to death, abuse them, throw the elderly and children into the sea or lash slaves until their backs are torn and streaming blood. But, I doubt I can be so compassionate concerning your death."

Navarro swallowed hard and shot back. "If you kill me, d'Aubusson will take revenge on you for it. He would moreover consider it cause for war against the Ottoman Empire, agree that Sultan Bayezid's sovereignty is invalid and proclaim his brother Jem as the new Ottoman sultan! Then your sultan will be nothing more than just a pitiful member of the dynasty. You think about the rest!"

This drove Kemal Reis to rise to his feet. It felt as if the sun had gone and a cold breeze picked up. Everyone knew the troubles Jem had caused while under the protection of all the kings in Europe for years.

He turned to his old friend. "Look Agha, the encounter you had today and battles up to now have been under your leadership. What happens to the galley slaves and other chattel is up to you and the ships you've won now belong to you and your crew." He looked at the men standing around. "However, what this prick just said was an affront to the great padishah and the grant empire I've devoted my life to, so it concerns me. I'll buy this man's salvation from my own treasure, no matter how many *akche* of silver—he's free."

Burak knew what they were going to do and, no matter what he did, he was aware that he wouldn't be able to stop Kemal. He made the motion for Rattler and Big Ahmed to unchain the man's wrists and ankles—and there, under the confused looks of the pirates and Kemal Reis' crew, although no more so than the look on Pierro Navarro's own face, the man was set free on the deck.

Kemal Reis stepped in front of Navarro. "Give this man a sword," he said to the pirates. One took his scimitar from his belt and handed it to the knight.

"No, that won't do," Kemal said. "He's not accustomed to that kind. Bring him one of the knights' own swords, he'll be able to use that more comfortably."

The pirates milled about looking around while the knight waited, worrying about what would happen, and as soon as they found it, they brought it forth. Navarro was uncertain and took back his sword with hesitation.

Kemal Reis returned to Italian. "You're a free man now. It's my sworn duty to kill you for what you've just said against the empire and the sultan. The Exalted State doesn't bargain with marauders. But know this—my word, the sultan's word, my signature, is his edict. Let all the people here on this galley bear witness—if you defeat me, no one will lay a hand on you and you will return freely to your trash heap on Rhodes."

He then turned to Burak Reis and the common Turkish of the empire said, "If I die, you'll wrap me in this big, white sail and throw me into the sea as is custom." He pointed to the topgallant sail. "I don't give my blessings for anyone to lay a hand on this man, Agha." His voice was as clear and vehement as they'd ever heard it.

Having no other choice, Burak Reis nodded.

Kemal Reis ordered everyone around to make room.

"*Bismillah*"—in the name of God—he said, drawing his sword with his eye on the knight.

Navarro knew very well that the Ottomans kept their word and that, above all, a promise from a dignitary from the capital had the power of a firman. He was a master swordsman of the Order of

Saint John and he would much enjoy slicing this Ottoman admiral's head from his body. Now, however, he saw the courage in the man's eyes opposite him—he hadn't ever expected him to be so brave—and he couldn't even find the strength to hold his sword, let alone wield it. The knight had never been wounded in battle and had always come out unscathed. He looked around him. Kemal Reis—tall and slender—looked to him like a giant.

He was tall and burly himself, but he saw a darkness in Kemal Reis' blue eyes that he had never seen before in any storm at sea—the look on the admiral's face was as hard as stone, more powerful than an angry sea.

Kemal Reis let out a roar, "Come on mate and attack! What're you then, d'Aubusson's cur?"

The knight having mentioned Jem Sultan and threatening Sultan Bayezid had enraged him.

At long last, Navarro threw down his sword and fell to his knees weeping and incoherently begging for mercy in Italian. The crew standing around couldn't believe what they were seeing—a renowned Knight of Saint John like that.

Kemal Reis reluctantly placed his sword back in its sheath as if a small victory had been stolen from him and then took a seat.

"Take this man to the oars," he said to his men. "Put an oarsmen of our own on each side of him."

Burak Reis smiled when the two met up later. "You haven't changed at all, old man! Your love of service is going to kill me."

"Regulations are everything, Agha. Have you ever suffered from being favorable? It'll never come to an end."

Kemal Reis stood up as if it were time to go. "So tell me. Are you in on the Andalusia campaign or not?"

Burak Reis stood up and the men embraced. "You're wrong if you think you'll set sail on this adventure without me, old man. Of course I'm in. There's just one other thing on my mind. How many people can these galleys hold? They'll already be full with oarsmen and soldiers. Let's say we squeeze in a hundred people into each of them—that means that according to what you've said, there's thousands of people fleeing Spain."

"I've thought about that. Or, more to the truth, Sultan Bayezid has thought about that. You leave that part to us and you'll understand when we set off from Constantinople in a week and meet up off of Crete."

"Alright, then. But there's one more thing." Burak Reis' face went pale and his eyes misted up—he was thinking of Hajji Mustafa. "My pilot was killed, you know that." Kemal also knew Hajji Mustafa well and he was deeply saddened that he'd died in the battle. "I've never set sail without him. We need someone like him, someone who can hold the Mediterranean in the palm of their hand like a tiny lake, someone who reads the stars like a compass, someone who can pilot night and day. Don't get me wrong, there must be a hundred pilots under the navy's command, but Hajji Mustafa was something else. We'd be going to Andalusia with our eyes closed if he were alive."

Kemal Reis gave a chuckle and turned and yelled up to the upper deck. "Ahmed!"

His fellow old salt's laughter got to Burak Reis, even if just a little bit.

The two men were looking at the forecastle, waiting for the men to come. The sun was shining on the ship's bow and Burak Reis squinted to make out the young man coming from the other side. The sunlight glinting from behind the boy made it almost impossible to make out his face. The young man came up to them, a quadrant in his mouth, maps tucked under his arm and holding a quill.

"What's the matter, Uncle, why're you taking my time?"

Kemal Reis put his hand on the boy's shoulder and looked over at Burak Reis. "Agha, I'd like you to meet my brother Hajji Mehmed's boy. He's my pilot, and for the capital, too. This boy doesn't get seasick, he gets landsick—he says he gets nauseas whenever he goes on dry land."

Burak Reis believed unconditionally that Kemal completely trusted the boy. He put his hand over his heart and, bowing slightly, gave the boy a pirate salute.

"Peace be with you, lad. They call me Burak Reis."

The boy saluted him even though his hands were full and took the quadrant out of his mouth. "And peace be with you. They call me Ahmed Muhiddin of Karaman, or Piri for short."

Burak recalled that he'd heard this name before.

BOOK THREE
Fire and Water

29

The *consejo de la Suprema y General Inquisición*—or the *Suprema*—was the center of the Inquisition, based in Seville at the cathedral in the center of the city, which had long ago been converted at the beginning of the thirteenth century from the Almohad Mosque—one of Europe's largest houses of worship. They had planned for its dome to rival that of the Haghia Sophia in Constantinople when the mosque was transformed into a cathedral.

The Inquisition's special guards surrounded the area around the complex, as if its thick, castle-like walls and frightening Gothic architecture weren't already enough. Knights from the Orders of Calatrava, Montesa, Alcantara, Santiago and Santa Hermandad made up this special guard. Not even a bird could land on the Suprema's grounds. Moreover, there was a distinct restlessness among the guard this day, as six of the cardinals in Spain and Grand Inquisitor Torquemada were holding one of their routine meetings inside.

Sunlight filtered into the meeting hall through the horseshoe-shaped windows in the thick walls, streaming curved shafts of light throughout the room, although not enough to really penetrate the darkness. The torches on the walls and the candlesticks in the middle of the table overlain with a red cloth were just enough so the cardinals could make out what was written on the sheets in front of them. The cardinals seated around the rectangular table were passing around the books Torquemada had brought. Even though they didn't know either of the languages, they could easily tell which ones were written in Arabic and which were in Hebrew.

"There's something I don't understand," Cardinal Mendoza said from the right corner of the table. "Why did they put these dots at the tops of the pages?" He pointed to the ink spots between the lines on the edges of the letters.

"Maybe it's some kind of code," the cardinal across from him said. They had never come across any manuscript with these kinds of dots.

"No," Torquemada said, standing at the head of the table. "This is the product of the German's instrument, that work of Satan." His nostrils flared when he was angry and the creases in his face grew deeper. His bulbous nose projecting from his flat face seemed to become more pronounced at such times. Wearing a white tunic and a black, cowled cassock of coarse wool, Torquemada stood out from the cardinals in their red, velvet cassocks and red birettas.

A murmur started to grow among the cardinals as soon as they heard this reference to printing.

"We've recently heard that it's reached as far as Italy and France," one cardinal said. "We've just now learned that it's come to Spain."

"We found this devil's instrument in Zaragoza last year and destroyed it," Torquemada said, looking over their faces.

"And moreover, most of the books they're printing in Latin are Bibles," Mendoza said. The Suprema had been quick to oppose the reading of the Bible by the common folk—those who didn't have the necessary knowledge to understand it—and had monopolized the production and distribution of the Gospels to their own monasteries.

"What types of books are these?" another asked.

Torquemada answered, his voicing growing ever more ill tempered. "The texts of the holy books of the Jews and the Muhammadans, chapters from the Talmud and Torah, and stories about the life of that impostor Muhammad."

"So how'd you get your hands on these?" one cardinal asked.

"The Inquisition guards found them in the Jewish and Muslim quarters in Salamanca, Valladolid and Avila."

"But most were found in Toledo," Cardinal Ximenes added. "That's why we believe the center of operations is somewhere there."

"Do you know who's doing it?" one asked.

"There's no information about the publisher, a name or an address in any of the seized books. As far as we can tell, though, these books aren't only in Spain, they're also sent to other cities like Venice and Amsterdam.

"And how, then, will you confirm the publisher's identity?" Mendoza asked.

"It's obvious that this kind of work takes more than one person—a carpenter to build the press, a paper merchant, a binder and a smith to make the letters."

"There's dozens of these types of people in Toledo. How'll we find who's doing it?"

Not believing what was being said, another cardinal spoke up as if he were thinking out loud, "They all need to be interrogated."

Torquemada stood silently and looked around the table. The cardinals could tell from his face that this suggestion had already been put into practice.

"A great many innocent people will suffer," one said from across the table.

"It's up to God to decide who is innocent and who's guilty," Torquemada said. "But we've found a way to speed this work along. We've brought a book hunter from Malaga, and he's already on the trail of these printed books."

Torquemada and Cisneros looked confidently at each other. Having wrested the port city of Malaga from the Muslims a few years earlier, the book hunters there had turned up hundreds of Arabic and Hebrew texts every day and had gotten to know their new profession well in a short time.

These book hunters would go from mosque to mosque and synagogue to synagogue, sometimes even house to house, finding and burning banned books. Some of the book hunters had gotten so proficient at their jobs that they could tell which printing press and which paper merchant's paper was used as if they had handed it to them themselves.

The book hunter Torquemada had brought from Malaga was the best in his trade. Santiago had been in the business for a while already.

Index Librorum Prohibitorum

First we started burning books, then people.

We were burning people to save their souls and to ease their eternal suffering. Christ our Lord and Savior knows best. No one could guarantee that every soul we set light to would be completely forgiven. And so we wouldn't be forced to burn more people, we had to destroy their books that would have poisoned the souls of others. As the leader of the Inquisition, Torquemada's rules on this subject were clear enough to not leave any room for doubt. The second paragraph of the fourteenth article of the Inquisition's Directorium fully dictates the details of the punishments for people according to the degree of their crimes and the destruction of books that detract from the path of God and from the teachings of our Lord and Savior Jesus Christ and that have harmed the way of life of clean and noble Christians and clouded their minds. All we monks and priests had to do was apply the rules. The decision maker and final conclusion was the Holy Inquisition.

Before, though, my duty was only to write down the proceedings. I was a simple Inquisition scribe.

At a simple wooden table in a corner dedicated to me, the ink from my quill recorded all the details throughout the interrogations. We first wrote on parchments made of animal skin, and then we began to use the paper invented by the Mohammedans in Xativa, as paper could be made much faster and cost less than parchment. I now understand when I think about these lines, the most ironic moments of my life were that the torture inflicted upon the Mohemmedans in the interrogation rooms was recorded on this, their own paper. I remember one instance of a Mohammedan paper merchant who had tried to poison the minds of Christians with the teachings of his own religion, writing down his interrogation on paper our Holy Church had bought from him. An inquisition torturer made a miscalculation and the arm of the man drawn over the rack was pulled from his body. The spurting blood covered the paper and erased everything I'd written and, trusting my memory, I had to write it all again. Don't every disregard the power of my memory—the acts of writing and reading have given me the ability to memorize some books from beginning to end, line to line.

The paper that one Muhammadan in the Kingdom of Castile fabricated, then another Muhammadan merchant sold to the Church, and then over which the blood of still another Muhammadan spilled was perhaps the starting point of all of my drama. I wouldn't say that I saw and felt everything at that moment ten years ago. The one thing I am saying is my life had become a mystery in these moments when I went into all later interrogations—several questions rung in my head that I couldn't answer—but still, I simply avoided these questions and went on with my work. What is interesting is that I used to perform my work doggedly and faithfully to suppress these questions.

But there's a story behind what started everything, the first spark of which lit the fire and led to my present, lamentable situation. It is meaningful, indeed, that I call it a fire.

It started with Grand Inquisitor Torquemada's right-hand man, Cardinal Cisneros, placing me in what at the very beginning was a very exciting assignment. Stepping out of the putrid torture chambers and getting some fresh air, even if for only a little while, I was going to travel to different times and different books. There's no doubt this was more pleasant and breezy than keeping the records of the people who would burn.

My new assignment was to identify banned books and ensure they were destroyed.

When we took Granada, on Torquemada's orders, we were to find and destroy the books and manuscripts of heretical beliefs that ran counter to the teachings of our Lord Jesus Christ and that were taught to innocent people to poison their minds. The part of the work that interested me, though, was that I was to identify the books that posed a threat in the large cities on the edges of the Kingdom of Castile such as Toledo, Cordoba and Seville, and prepare the Index Liborum Prohibitorum—the list of books that must be burned—by finding them and classifying those of a heretical nature.

My work was easy at first. I would go with the two assistants given to me to the buildings in the city that had books, to the Muhammadans' old madrasahs, the shelves in the old mosques and other libraries, perusing the books and collecting the ones written in Arabic to study them back in the scriptorium at monastery. So many Arabic books had been destroyed already that we avoided having to deal with a great many of them. Then they added Hebrew, as well. Now we were out on the hunt for copies of the Talmud and Torah. We had grown accustomed to this for a few years, as we were at no lack for manpower—there were priests and monks everywhere. One of the most sensible ways to save oneself from the claws of the Inquisition and live a reliably calm existence was life at a church or monastery—of course, there are those who are weak to the guiles of women and they pay a certain price for this type of life.

But then things change, and a great abundance of books started to appear all at once. We couldn't reckon where they'd come from. There were books in every building we went to, in every house we suspected, as if they were flowers sprouting in spring. We couldn't reckon whose handwriting they were, how they were produced or which scribes could write that fast. Most of these texts were in Hebrew and Arabic and they contained works that had been long banned, like those by Maimonides, Averroes and ibn Arabi. Then we realized that these weren't manuscripts, but the product of that devil's contrivance that had come from the German kingdoms not so long ago. We had heard of this contraption for quite some time, but had never seen its products.

They looked like normal, handwritten books from the outside—it was impossible for someone not intimately acquainted with books to distinguish them. But when the book hunters, the masters of this craft like us, looked at them, the details that showed that they'd come out one by one from a printing machine showed themselves—there were dots of ink on the pages, some letters were darker, some fainter and the lines on some pages were askew.

When we were suddenly faced with this onslaught of hundreds of book like a swarm of bees, it was obvious that we wouldn't we able to destroy them all at one go. If we burned ten books, we would find a hundred more the next day in various places in the city in the houses of secretly worshipping Jews and Muslims.

I started reading a copy of each of these books, most of the texts in Hebrew and Arabic, and concentrated on the ones I needed to scrutinize, as it was a more accomplishable task to take up five books than to try to destroy a hundred. If we could determine which books were more damaging, then we could eliminate them more easily. Notwithstanding, Torquemada and Talavara would later also hunt down those hundred books, but my life was sufficient for the bedevilment of a few.

Here I'll take refuge in the four books that, like the four legs of a table, constitute the trivet of the library of the meaning of humanity while thinking on the ideas and pages that pass through my mind. I give thought to these four thinkers in the final moments of my life—the four philosophers who have never left the first lines of the Index Librorum Prohibitorum— Aristotle, ibn Rushd, ibn Arabi and Maimonides.

31

The sunlight from the window fell on the right side of the elderly calligrapher who was kneeling on a red cushion in one of the quietest rooms in Topkapi Palace as he gave his full attention to the sheet of paper in front of him. Although all the rooms in this part of the palace were serene and peaceful, as if all the sounds on earth avoided them out of respect, the old man had specifically been invited to this room today.

Another man, who looked comparably quite young, was sitting at his teacher's knee and holding the master's inkpot.

The calligrapher gently dipped his narrow, four-inch reed pen into the inkpot his student was holding. The tip of the pen rested on the raw silk strands stuffed in the inkpot, drawing up the jet-black ink when they met, like a lover drawing a kiss from a long-departed beloved. The pen drank up the ink like a Bedouin in the Sahara who, after going days without water, now drank thirstily from an oasis. The ink quickly soaked into the pen's pores and ran up the hair-thin slit from the tip—a dance of old, practiced lovers.

He removed the pen from the inkwell and brought it over his drawn up knee. Resting on his knee was a leather pad with a yellowish piece of paper he had just cut to size on top of it. *"Bismillah"—in the name of God—*he mumbled, touching the pen to the top corner of the paper and pulling it away.

Despite his age of sixty, the calligrapher's eyes were sharp, and he felt he could see the ink spread from pore to pore on the paper. He raised his head and looked over at his student dutifully watching from his side. The student noticed a faint smile beneath his teacher's snow-white beard. His teacher was pleased—the ink was the consistency he wanted and the reed pen was well cut.

"Everything starts with a point," Hamdullah the Calligrapher said. "It's the points that give meaning to both letters and numbers. A number cannot be without zero and a letter cannot be without a point. And both of them here are this point."

After he finished talking, he went to the top right for the first line and, with a top-down motion, he wrote the sultan of the letters. First he made its head and then its body, all with the hand strokes of a master, never taking his hand from the paper.

His student looked with admiration at the *elif* taking shape on the paper. This was the most beautiful way to write an *elif*—such a simple letter, but could possess such deep expression.

"A point creates this *elif*, and *elif* creates all the other letters."

The student had first learned his master's philosophy on *elif* twenty years before in Amasya, in the days of his first lessons. Hamdullah was in love with this letter, and he would say something new about it in each of his explanations, still inspiring his student after nearly a quarter century.

"Every *elif* is a heart. The point transforms into an *elif*, whereas *elif* gives rise to the other letters. As letters turn into words, words into sentences, sentences into lines and lines into books, the point shows the law of the heart at every stage, the way from sameness to the profusion of the multitude. In the essence of every line is a word, in the essence of every word is a letter, in the essence of every letter is an *elif* and in the essence of every *elif* is a point. The beginning of the multiplicity in the One, and this Oneness lays in the essence of the pen. It is the transformation of this One in different forms that's called the heart. Strands make a fabric and fabric a shirt, stones make a wall and walls a building, drops make the sea, specks make matter, minutes make the hour and hours transform into days—it's all of this that gives evidence for this great law."

The student listened respectfully to his teacher, who stopped to take a breath from time to time while continuing to write. He was dazzled by the dance of the letters as they appeared on the paper one after another—*ha, lam, mim, dal, sin.* He'd been practicing calligraphy for nearly a quarter century but still felt that he could never write even one letter as beautifully. He gave thanks once again that he could witness firsthand his master's ingenuity.

Hamdullah dipped his pen in the ink again and continued. "So, if a point is *elif,* is *elif* not a point? Does a line not return to a word, a word to a letter and a letter to a point? Of course they do. Everything searches for its essence, finds its essence and returns to its essence. This is what they call *return.* Humankind starts with a body and later coalesces with a soul, life passes and, of course, ends, then the body returns to its essence and reverts to soil. And what about the soul? What is its essence?"

Hamdullah held his breath once more and continued from where he'd been writing. The student marveled that there was not the slightest tremor in his teacher's hand despite his advanced age.

The calligrapher paused after making an *elif* in the middle of the line. "Do you know that story? When the Almighty created the reed pen, the *elif* was the first to prostrate to Him. Everlasting God said, *You were the first to praise me, and for this, I will keep you upright for eternity.* It is because of this, they say, that *elif* is the sultan of all the letters—as the others descend and rise, the *elif* always stands upright.

Hamdullah lifted his head from the page again and looked at his student. "Would one who praises God bow to another? Would he who knows mercy and punishment from Him beg from another? The most upright, sensible and indestructible people of the earth are those who bow the most in front of God. The *elif* is humankind. It's such a letter that God the Creator honored Adam by starting his name with it, and also with His Majesty Ahmed. The noble name of the exalted Abraham also begins with this *elif* in the lead with divine Arabic letters."

Hamdullah finished speaking and dipped his reed into the inkpot again. His student once again held it out for him. He was going to write the name of God—Allah the Manifest and Conspicuous—again beginning with the upright *elif*.

"Then they say that *elif* is the light. The Uncreated created it from light, as they say. He had everything written one by one in the Book of Fate, and with that, explained creation and the universe. *Elif* wondered to every point of the universe and around the world several times telling of the whole fate of humankind, and then closed the book. This is why one who understands the *elif* understands the letters, and he who understands the letters first knows himself and then understands creation and the universe. Man learns what he doesn't know through writing. Hence, there is always enlightenment at the end of a piece of writing because its essence is the Light. It's the Light that teaches man what he doesn't know through the reed pen."

Hamdullah had come to the end of the line. Bayezid fell into the past as the reed went in and out of the inkpot. The lines and the inkpot now evoked vague recollections of his youth that he'd almost completely forgotten. He hadn't always been such a dutiful student who obeyed his master. On the contrary, he'd been quite the rebel, never listening and self-absorbed. Hamdullah had to try very hard to put him on the good path.

What days those were—the years he was in Amasya in his youth while he was still a prince. He thought of the night that had changed his life.

32

Müeyyedzade Abdurrahman took another glass and poured more wine from the jug as he joyfully recited a couplet.

"O cup bearer, pour such a wine of love
That intoxicates the sea with one drop"

Müeyyedzade Abdurrahman was one of Prince Bayezid's best friends for pleasure and enjoyment, and his heart could never pass up a gathering. Although Bayezid wasn't into drinking, he also didn't mind being with his friends who were. Abdurrahman would get drunk and take great pleasure in reciting poems and asking riddles in verse. Now at the prince's villa, this young man—a son of one of the wealthy families of Amasya—was seated right next to the prince, enjoying himself with the sounds of the various suits the musicians in the other corner of the room were playing one after another. These weren't only the best musicians in the city, but the most talented in all the empire. The strains from the tambur, qanun, rebab and many other lutes and viols added to the gayety of the prince and his guests. The smiles and love songs from the women among the musicians excited the young men listening.

Prince Bayezid laughed. "Seems like he's nice and flying again."

All the others laughed along with him. Müeyyedzade Abdurrahman, Hizirpashazade Mahmud next to him, Shavur the Lame and Hamzabeyzade Mustafa across from him were all Bayezid's closest friends.

"It's not for nothing," Hamzabeyzade Mustafa said. "When a man gets drunk his head gets light as a feather. It gets so light that it escapes the earth and flies around the heavens and taunts the starts."

Mustafa took a walnut and fig sweet from a plate and shoved it in his mouth.

"What better to describe intoxicating beauty than through wine drunkenness," Mahmud said. He was the youngest among them, knew Persian as if it were his native language and could solve the most difficult algorithmic problems without pen and paper. "They both come washing over you all at once and make your head swim." He took another sip from the wine glass brought specially from the Grand Bazaar in Constantinople.

"But you've done it!" Mustafa burst out laughing.

"Pour me from wine's ruby lips perpetual drunkenness
If I'm but a tramp, with grace, make me a king, o sultan

"Wine's trouble—it's got no effect after a few glass, and then when it does, it constantly elicits the call of nature, so to speak. And what about my darling gum opium? After the first chew it makes a man forget his troubles and tribulations and brings joy," said Abdurrahman, who also wasn't averse to opium from time to time.

"And what about later?" Bayezid asked. "It all brings false happiness like material pleasures. And those feelings melt away just as fast. Then your stomach hurts, you're nauseas, you puke, and you always have a headache the next day, don't you? Then you chase after it. Is there no point to the poet's words—

"Opium and drink, what great misery
That push a man to weakness and frenzy
The hash smoker cannot hide his secret
The wine drinker thinks his words are silv'ry"

Mahmud recited complementary verse for the prince—

"As comes their pleasure, it's splitting to hear
And as goes their pleasure comes times of fear
There is nothing left of you, let's posit,
What misery the title of addict"

"What gives, gentlemen, really? A statute banning opium and wine's been added to the law books, don't you know," Shavur said. "Opium's bad like this, wine's bad like that. They say don't drink, but are we offending anyone?"

"Well done, Shavur!" Abdurrahman said. "Wine's left you lame, but it's still your friend!"

Shavur had gotten blind drunk at a tavern two years before and fallen down the stairs, losing a leg as a result.

"Hey, look here! What fault does wine have?" Shavur said. "The ignorant chide me for only having one leg. So what if I only have one, I've got two hands. You all get it!"

Bayezid and his friends cracked up and gave another hearty cheers. Shavur had really been drinking quite a lot more in the past few years. Until he'd overdone it, he'd been a qadi in quite a few provinces. His knowledge of Islamic jurisprudence was impeccable.

Mahmud spoke up as the musicians continued with another piece. "I was in Kastamonu last month and the people there really love your brother Jem Chelebi. An inn opened right across from Nasrullah in the city square and the people go there and talk non-stop."

Bayezid's face sank when heard his brother's name.

"What would you know, Mahmud?" Abdurrahman shot back, knowing what would happen. "If Jem plants a tree, Prince Bayezid plants a forest. If Jem builds a wall, Prince Bayezid builds a palace. If he built that inn, our man here would build a caravanserai!"

Bayezid smiled. "You speak the truth. I've heard of that inn, and I'll have a new, larger place built. But my brother's governor of that county, so he's knows everything going on in Kastamonu. There's no way I'd be able to build anything there right now. If God grants it, though, and I become sultan, the entire empire will be full of caravanserais and hospitals, not just Kastamonu. God willing."

"Do it, sir, do it—but no more of that God stuff at the table. The man upstairs wouldn't listen to princes or anyone else and it wouldn't be any good for us," Shavur said.

"Good Lord, do him a favor!" Mahmud said.

"Hey! What'd I say—what're you saying?"

They all fell apart laughing again.

Shavur perked back up. "Hey, make a hospital for the lovers, too. Springtime's come and the lovesick are wondering around dejected. Let them listen to these ditties and have some fun. What else left is there?

"Free your wild curls to gather on your cheek

As when the days of spring come, love will reign"

"Or just give them wine," Abdurrahman said, "and watch how they find their beloveds in the last drop!"

33

Pao of Athens was anxiously rowing his boat through the darkness of the night. He looked to the right and left of his little boat at Iron Mikhail and Diogenes the Butcher—both grumbling. He was fed up and tired of transporting these two brutish Greek knights and their friends from Chios to the Ottoman coves. Pao was the first boatman the Greeks, some orders of knights and a few groups of Venetians and Genoese living on Chios, Samos and other islands had called on to take them to the nearby Ottoman shores when they got bored or when they were looking for provisions or entertainment. Although the men paid him handsomely, Pao would've much rather lived a peaceful life, fishing and earning less than putting himself in such needlessly dangerous situations.

Diogenes turned to Pao from the right side of the boat and said, "Come on you doddering fisherman, row faster!" He went to take another swig from his jug of wine and, realizing it was empty, hurled it at the fisherman. Pao ducked his head to the side and the jug plopped into the sea.

And so it had begun again—it was only a matter of time before these drunkards would get him into trouble. Pao reckoned that that these men would be lost to the hands of the villagers or that the locals would think he was also a brigand. He continued to row faster, not making a sound and looking from side to side. There were a few ships watching him in the darkness. They were all leeches, according to Pao—raiders and old knights who never found success on crusade and then later settled on the Aegean islands. And now these two would most likely deceive some poor villager, steal a year's worth of wheat or set fire to a peasant's house.

"Kostas found a Circassian girl the other day in Seferihisar, you've got to see her," Mikhail, with his constant, stupid smile, mumbled over to Diogenes. "The girl's so beautiful that our boy Kostas went in for it when they were still on the boat. The girl did give that bear quite a fight, though. Kostas still has scratch marks on his face. This Circassian girl was thrashing around under him—tearing at his hair for dear life, biting his wrists to the bone—but he gave her a good wallop and she fainted right off—she couldn't have been more than fourteen. Our boy never wastes his time! He already had his way with her all unconscious before they'd even got to the island!"

They both burst out laughing.

Diogenes composed himself. "I don't like it like that. Let them struggle as much as they want, I want to look into their eyes, alive and kicking. I like it when those little chicks thrash around under me."

This made them fall apart in laughter again.

"I can't see our ship anymore," Mikhail said, turning around and looking out behind Pao. There was no moon that night and they couldn't see a hundred yards in any direction. The raiders from the small galley carrying around a dozen men that had set off from Chios and anchored at Seferihisar had put down in five rowboats and quietly headed for the Ottoman cove. The remaining crew had been waiting for an hour back on the galley for the boats to return with sacks of provisions and slaves.

Iron Mikhail's face dropped. "What's that group called—the Chelbs? They annoy me something fierce."

"Chelebis," Pao said without thinking. He regretted it as soon as he opened his mouth, but he couldn't stop himself. Mikhail and Diogenes glared at him.

"I'd toss your head in the water right now if it didn't mean that I'd have to row on the way back!" Mikhail spat at him. "Our boys were caught in a village across from Mytelene on Lesbos—none of them survived."

The Chelebis were the defenders the villagers had set up against the coming raiders.

"I heard about them, too. Some say it was ten men, some say a hundred—sharp shooting archers, master swordsmen, soldiers attacking with a scimitar in each hand, apparently. I think they're exaggerating. It was probably a dozen young Turks on an adventure."

Mikhail nodded.

"You're right, Dio. We heard from the fishermen, too, that this cove isn't guarded."

This was the main reason they'd chosen Seferihisar.

"Forget about them for now and think about the feast we'll have not too long from now." The two men returned their good spirits.

"We've arrived, sir," Pao said, landing the boat onshore. Diogenes and Mikhail peered out in front of them and could just make out a couple houses amid the trees up from the beach.

Mikhail immediately jumped into the surf and whispered to the other boats, "Everyone be quiet, be quiet!" The water came up to his knees and the tip of the scabbard hanging from his left side dipped into the waves.

The others also jumped into the surf and started to slowly creep toward the woods. Pao brought his bought ashore and sat down to wait along with the other boatmen. It wouldn't be long before the brigands showed back up with young girls over their shoulders and sacks of grain slung over the backs. A few villagers would come running after them before they even knew what had happened, but it would be too late—most of the men would be killed in their sleep, or for every one of them there were five raiders, tying up the girls and boys straight away and taking them off as slaves. They preferred them to be young since it was both easier to carry them and they would fetch a better price at the slave markets.

Diogenes the Butcher took out his two, trusty axes that he always carried while he approached the trees. It was his skill and brutality with these axes that had lent him his nickname. He knew that Seferihisar was a tiny village on this cove and that there were a few houses just up from the shore. Even though the villagers here made a living on fishing and olive oil and there wouldn't be any wheat to be found, the Butcher's mouth watered the more he thought about the village girls and their legendary beauty. He looked at Mikhail walking next to him and the nearly dozen others. Mikhail had drawn his sword and was walking cautiously. He always talked endlessly about his exploits in the battles he fought against the Muslim knights in Jerusalem, and the men were confident being around him. They didn't really believe his stories at first, but once Mikhail had gotten into an argument with three expert knights and they saw him slice through two of them like he was chopping vegetables.

The group stood still when they came up to a midsized house with two stories that was set a little off from the others. Diogenes called five of the men over to him and whispered for them to go in and subdue the people inside and then give the signal to the rest of them from the top floor when everything was ready. He was never one to take unnecessary risks. He would first rummage around with his men and then continue on with the hunt for people.

Diogenes waited with two men behind a tree at one side of the house while Mikhail and two others were posted behind a thick tree on the other side.

The largest of the men in the raiding party shouldered open the door and the group stormed in brandishing their swords, axes and maces. Screams started to come from inside after not too long—the men outside were still waiting for the signal. The Butcher was starting to worry, but then a window opened and one of the raiders appeared. The men outside were about to rush inside, but then the man tumbled lifeless out of the second-story window. There was large ax in his back, its handle sticking up into the air.

Then one of the men came running out from the door and shouting, "It's the Chelebis, the Chelebis!" only to be skewered through the forehead by an archer on a black horse who came out of the darkness like a bolt of lighting and disappeared just as fast.

"It's a trap!" Mikhail gasped.

He grabbed his sword with both hands and started moving toward where the horseman had disappeared into the trees. He ordered his men to flank him. Diogenes and his men were barging into the house on the other side.

He couldn't believe what he saw inside—one of the men was laying on the floor with his skull smashed to pieces while another still lay dying with blood gushing from his belly and a third was collapsed on the stairs, gasping in pain as he stared at his severed arm on the floor. It looked like a slaughterhouse.

"In the name of Christ!" Diogenes yelled. "How many are you, you sons of bitches!? I'll hack you to pieces myself, limb from limb! Show your damn yourselves!"

The sound of one man's footsteps came from the top of the stairs. Someone was slowly making their way down from upstairs. The two men with Diogenes gulped, grasped their swords tighter and waited, ready to attack. The Butcher raised his two axes and waited at the bottom of the stairs.

Outside, Mikhail and his men were walking through the trees in darkness with their swords up and ready. Nobody could see anything around, and Mikhail knew that this silence wasn't a good sign at all.

Back in the house, it seemed like it was no ordinary man descending the stairs, but a giant, and with each thudding footstep the waiting raiders' hearts began to quicken. The man slowly appeared to Diogenes as he came down the stairs—first black boots, then a white belt around his waist, then a muscular chest and long neck behind his white shirt that was hanging open, and his black, unbuttoned vest. There was an ax in one of his hands, its tip still dripping with blood, and in the other a yataghan that was just as bloody.

Diogenes looked at the man's large handlebar moustache, his two mountainous eyebrows that met in the middle and his fiery eyes.

The man stopped on the landing in the middle of the stairs. "They call me Big Chelebi," he said, more a growl than a statement. "But jackals like you who torment the oppressed also call me Azrael."

Diogenes and his to men immediately set upon the Chelebi—the two men rushing him like rabid dogs.

Mikhail heard the whistling of an arrow, getting closer in an instant and felling the man to his right before he knew what had happened. Mikhail saw him on the ground with an arrow sticking straight out him. The man on his left took off for the shore yelling, "I'm not sticking around for anymore death!"

"You imbecile!" Mikhail yelled right before an arrow caught the man in the back and brought him down. "If you're men, show yourselves! Fight like men, face to face!"

A man on a black horse then emerged from the trees in front of Iron Mikhail. Mikhail stood holding up his sword as the man looked him up and down.

"Is it a man or a dog that kidnaps young children and sells them into slavery?!" the shadowy figure on the black horse roared.

Mikhail was taken aback by the youth in the man voice—it was clear he was no more than twenty or twenty-five. The shadowy man shoved his bow into his quiver and leapt to the ground in one swift movement. He pulled his sword from his belt and headed toward Mikhail. "Show it and let's see what you're made of!" Mikhail waved his sword at the young man, trusting his years of expertise that he would easily take him down.

The Chelebi stepped over the bodies of the two raiders he'd just cut down from the landing and squared up to Diogenes. The Butcher flinched having just seen his two most expert men slaughtered, but he was still sure of himself. It wasn't many the man who came up against his two axes and remained in one piece.

"Two axes can't be used at once," the Chelebi said harshly. "You'll take a while to chose which one to use while your adversary gets the upper hand."

The two men started to slowly circle each other like two wild-cats.

"Think now. You have two axes and I have an axe and a sword. Whose favor do you think that's in?"

Diogenes reckoned the man was trying to mess with his head and was looking for the moment to strike when he was confused. Without waiting, he swung his axes at the Chelebi, first from the right then from the left. He wielded his axes expertly and they whistled through the air. Despite his size, however, the Chelebi moved so fast that he parried the first blow with his sword and the second with his ax and continued off to his side.

"Two axes are always better," Diogenes growled, this time aiming for the Chelebi's face and swinging his axes one after the other, driving the Chelebi into a corner.

The young Chelebi evaded Mikhail's attack with a nimble swing of his sword the old knight didn't expect from him. He spun around and swung his sword from where he had staved off the advance straight at Mikhail's face. The knight was able to duck at the last moment owing to his years of experience what would have otherwise been a deadly strike, and the young Chelebi's sword lodged into a tree. Immediately seeing his chance, Mikhail quickly lunged with his sword at his foe's stomach. Pulling it from the tree and escaping from the corner.

In the house, the Chelebi fended of Diogenes' first ax blow with his yataghan sabre and the second with his own ax. He saw his chance and struck Diogenes in the face in a flash, splitting his cheek in two and striking his wrist with such force that he severed his hand while Diogenes fell awkwardly to the floor. Diogenes lay there staring at his wrist spurting blood next to the hand still clutching the ax.

"Wrong answer, " the Chelebi said. "A sword beats an ax."

Meanwhile, the young Chelebi outside had nimbly evaded the strike from Mikhail's blade as he brought his own down on the old knight's wrist. Mikhail's hand fell to the ground with his sword. Blood gushed from the stump on the end of his arm as Mikhail stared at his severed hand as if in a nightmare.

The Chelebi walked out of the house unscathed, and seeing this, the villagers slowly emerged from where they had been hiding in the trees. The Chelebi walked over to his young counterpart and looked back at Mikhail lying on the ground next to his severed hand. The villages gathered around, praising the two men, "God bless you! May God grant you your every desire!"

Mikhail lifted his head and struggled to speak. "Where're the rest of you? How many of you are there?"

"What others, you fool!" one of the villagers said. "They're father and son and they never work with anyone else. They call them Big Chelebi and Little Chelebi—you picked on the wrong village."

Mikhail forgot about his missing right hand once he realized that two locals had defeated a dozen knights and raiders. They'd taken the Chelebi's bait.

Big Chelebi noticed a red cross on Mikhail's tunic smeared with blood and grime, and his face flushed with rage.

"Tell me why you carry that cross? Are you a knight?"

The villagers stopped smiling when they heard the question and everyone backed up against a tree, looking at the man on the floor, his wrist still oozing blood.

"What do you think?!" Mikhail spat at him, suppressing the pain. "And from the line of the old Knights Templar at that!"

Little Chelebi looked at his father, but before he had time to say anything, Big Chelebi picked up a cudgel and smashed in Mikhail's face. His face caved in with the cudgel stuck and sticking into the air.

The villagers had already subdued the raiders at the boats by the time the Chelebis got to the beach.

"What're we going to do to their galley" Little Chelebi asked.

Big Chelebi had been looking out to sea since he had gotten to the shoreline. His eyes had adjusted to the darkness and he could make out the galley and its surroundings.

"Don't you worry about that, son. I'd say the admiral already knows."

There was a fleet of half a dozen ships around the galley that had come from Chios. The Chelebi recognized the blue of Kemal Reis' ship and the snarling lion on its bowsprit. Its rowboats were already on their way to shore.

34

"I don't know about that, Captain, it's been a long time," Big Chelebi said. "I can't even dip a toe into the surf."

The Chelebi and Kemal Reis were walking barefoot in the sand beneath the shining sun while soothing waves lapped at the shore. Kemal Reis had been talking about the campaign to Spain for the last half hour, explaining at length that Burak Reis would also be joining them.

"I need you, you know that," Kemal Reis said. "Beyond Crete it's all a den of jackals—Venetians, Genoese, crusaders, Sicilian pirates, Corsican knights and then finally the Spanish and Portuguese fleets. I need all the top sailors and fighters I've known throughout my life for this campaign, Chelebi. It would be very difficult without you and your men. Tzachas, Karamürsel—you need to find them all and come with me." They stopped and stood still for a while. "You were my best fighter, you know that."

Big Chelebi and his son had been pirates under Kemal Reis' command for years on the Mediterranean. When the Knights Hospitallers had slaughtered Big Chelebi's wife on his home island of Lesbos, where they had hidden during a battle at see, he had vowed to never again set off for sea and swore an oath that he would club in a crusader's head whenever he saw one. This is why he had just smashed in Mikhail's head—otherwise he would've left the man to his fate living with one hand.

Big Chelebi had killed hundreds of knights with Kemal Reis on the Aegean and Mediterranean, and it was only by seeing their blood that he could escape his grief. He wouldn't go to sea again and would instead continue his life with his son at his side on the shores of Lesbos and the Aegean, defending the vulnerable villagers from knights and raiders.

Big Chelebi looked out over the sea, turning silver in the distance. The darkness had well begun to fade.

"Being at sea took my wife from me." He got a knot in his throat and his eyes teared up as he spoke.

Kemal Reis saw the tears welling up in the mountain of a man's eyes, like black rainclouds ready to open up and burst forth over his slopes.

Big Chelebi struggled to continue, "I don't reckon I could do it again. I don't think I could set out to sea again. Captain, tell me to take on an army by myself on dry land and I'd go running barefoot and empty handed, but don't ask me to set off to sea again with my son. Who else would protect these villagers?" He bowed his head. "Forgive me."

Kemal Reis heard the resolve in his voice and understood.

Kemal Reis set off with his fleet for Constantinople while the sun was rising over the hills, leaving behind the knight's galley as spoils for the Chelebis and the villagers.

The father and son watched from the golden shore as the fleet turned into a single point in the distance. Neither of them said a word.

35

Torquemada was quietly standing off from the large, wooden table in the Council Hall and listening to those speaking inside, rubbing the cross on the chain around his neck inquisitively. There was one visitor in the room set aside in the Alhambra for the guests of the king and queen who didn't please Torquemada. The Grand Inquisitor could only see the jester in the room from the doorway, but he could hear everything.

The bells on the corners of the dwarf's floppy cap jingled as he brayed and hopped back and forth like a donkey, his head waving around. Even without his buffoonery, the jester's appearance, his cap, checkered vest, tattered trousers and pointed shoes—one missing a tip—was enough to tickle one to laughter.

"It's a donkey!" Ferdinand said and giggled. He was sitting next to Isabella in the hall, its walls and ceiling covered in velvet and wooden ornaments. The jester was brought in to amuse him while the queen discussed politics. The dwarf was busy imitating animals for the king to guess. He folded his hands into his chest and started flapping his elbows up and down, moving his head back and forth.

De Silva's old friend Isaac Abarbanel had been pleading beside the jester for half an hour, trying to get the king and queen's attention. The old man was in complete contrast to the jester, making him appear even older with his white beard, kippah and flowing, black robe.

"I implore you, your Royal Highness," he continued. "We've lived here for centuries. This is our motherland, our home. I implore you to think over your decision once more. We Jews bring no harm to the great Spanish kingdoms and are for its benefit actually. It's been like this for centuries."

"It's a chicken!" Ferdinand laughed. He looked over at Isabella and Abarbanel as if waiting for congratulations. The jester clapped his hands and shot his head back and forth.

"Do the next one, do the next one," Ferdinand demanded, and the jester bade his command.

Isabella was listening thoughtfully to Abarbanel, although she looked bored. Abarbanel was the wealthiest Jew in the land and the kingdom's top financier and tax collector for the big cities. He always occupied a special place in Isabella's opinion, and she never doubted his loyalty to her.

"Even during the siege of Granada, when the army was in need of equipment and food, did we not put nearly a million marevedis into the kingdom's treasury?" Abarbanel said, more forlorn. "We're the land's wealthiest merchants, the businessmen who pay the most taxes, the best doctors, the most knowledgeable scholars—you know this well—and we're always in service to you, the Catholics. And this will continue as it is. The absence of Jews is no gain for great Spain, but an irreparable loss."

Isabella thought there was some merit to what he was saying. She had three personal doctors at the palace and all three of them were Jewish. She knew quite well that Jews were experienced and useful in diplomacy due to the many languages they spoke. The treasury was also mostly filled with the taxes they had collected. Isabella, however, truly believed that the Jews would convert to Catholicism instead of leaving the country and all these problems would thus be resolved.

"We of course hold your services in high esteem," the queen said, "but you also know that there is no obstacle to continuing these services as Catholics. The Church believes that our taking

Granada and putting an end to the eight hundred years of Muslim rule was a great harbinger—a harbinger of forming a great Catholic union—and we also find this to be right." She stopped for a moment as if to allude to something and then continued. "What you need to do, though, is very simple."

Abarbanel found it ridiculous, and worse, infuriating that the queen sincerely thought that her demand for Jews to convert would be just as easy for them as it was for her to change dresses. He knew that Isabella had always been a fanatical and deeply believing Catholic, but had never thought she could be this ludicrous.

Ferdinand jumped up. "It's an elephant!" The jester had his arm hanging from his nose and wiggling around, sometimes sticking both arms out from his mouth like tusks. Sometimes he wobbled and swayed to lose his balance and fall to the floor, but would spring back up on his feet and do it again.

"Your Royal Highness, you know that your demand for us to convert is not such a simple thing. And even if I were to accept it, hundreds of thousands of Jews would oppose it. Also, if we do convert, the Inquisition would become the rightful owner of all of our property, possessions and souls. You've already personally witnessed their arbitrary treatment by Catholic knaves in some cities."

Abarbanel had paid thousands of maravedis countless times for the release of innocent Jews arrested by the Inquisition—paying the kingdom ransom on his own accord for countless people and saving their lives.

"Dear Abarbanel, do you think it was easy for us to make this decision?" Isabella said. "In truth, it's not even a decision that we have made. This is what our Lord Jesus Christ commands of us."

She began to recite a verse from Proverbs, "*The king's heart is in the hand of the Lord, as the rivers of water—He turneth it whithersoever he will.*"

The man in his misery realized there was no other choice when he heard Isabella recite the verse she had learned from Torquemada. Abarbanel had reckoned there was a material purpose behind the *Edict of Expulsion* and that he would be able to save his fellow Jews' lives by paying the ransoms, as he'd done for years.

He took a step toward the king and queen. "Permit me, let me mobilize all the Jews in the land, I'll collect money, I'll transfer most of my wealth to the Holy treasury, and also—" He paused. "Let me put forth ten thousand gold ducats in your service for the further enlargement of the Spanish Kingdom." It was twice the amount he had earlier calculated in his head.

Hearing the amount, the jester—still at Abarbanel's side—stopped his animal imitations and plunked himself down on the ground and lifted his head up at the man.

King Ferdinand also stopped laughing at the game and turned to look at Abarbanel. He waved the jester away—ten thousand gold ducats was no small amount. The jester plodded out of the room like a child at the end of playtime.

Isabella was about to speak when Ferdinand cut in, "Thirty thousand." That was millions of maravedi. "If you give thirty thousand gold ducats, maybe we can find a solution to your problems and we could think over our decision.

"Just think what we could do with that money!" he whispered to the queen.

Abarbanel was dumbfounded by the amount he'd reckoned as enough suddenly increasing to almost an impossible figure and beads of cold sweat started running down his back. He took out a handkerchief from his pocket and wiped away the sweat form his forehead. He was having difficulty swallowing. Thirty thousand gold ducats was nearly equal to the fortunes of hundreds of wealthy Jews, and it wasn't easy money to collect. It was worth trying, though, considering that the continued existence of all the Jews in Spain was riding on this money. Abarbanel breathed easier with this last thought—if nothing else, he could buy the Jews their existence in return for a ransom.

Isabella was aware that such a source of revenue was significant given that the exchequer had been emptied to a great extent with the siege of Granada. She wouldn't have to give up the Jewish merchants or the doctors of whom she was so fond. Both Ferdinand and Abarbanel were looking at her, and she was about to accept the offer. The fate of the more than eight centuries of a Jewish presence in Iberia rested on Isabella's lips, and they were in the shape of the beginning of an assent.

At that moment, Torquemada flung open the door he'd been waiting behind and came roaring into the hall like a lion free of its chains, his cassock and cloak flailing behind him. He held the cross around his neck up to the king and queen. "Do you know what you've done?!" He turned his fiery eyes to Abarbanel with full wrath.

He turned back to Ferdinand and Isabella. "Judas also betrayed our Lord and Savior Jesus Christ for thirty pieces of silver! Thirty pieces of silver cut down the Son of God, and you're doing the same for thirty thousand gold ducats! Know this. If you accept this offer, I will resign all my duties and I'll refer your treachery to God Almighty!"

His face, normally paler than most, was now glowing with rage. He turned his back and was storming out when he abruptly turned back around, waving the cross in his hand at the king and queen. "Be aware of what you're bargaining for!" Where once there had been thought of gold, now the hall resounded with the thundering tension of a sledgehammer.

Torquemada then turned and left, and Isabella, as if to atone for her guilt, turned to the old man, lifted her head and looked down her nose. "Our decision is final, Abarbanel. I suggest you and your fellow Jews gather in the merciful arms of Christ and that you not deny God's compassion."

Abarbanel bowed his head in a cold sweat. His only hope had just gone up in smoke and he thought there was nothing more that could be done. Perhaps the stories were true—1492 was the very Doomsday mentioned in the Torah.

But if that were the case, where was the Messiah?

36

Elif... elif... elif...

And then another. And then another. And then another.

Prince Bayezid had forgotten how many *elifs* he'd written today. He grew more impatient with every letter he wrote and, as his impatience increased, so did the misshapenness of the *elifs* from his hand. *First you will practice the letters*, Sheikh Hamdullah had said. *You'll start with a single letter. You won't move on to another letter until you write that one in perfect Naskh! Don't waste ink—that ink will clean you!*

But how many will I write, how will I know that it's perfect, how hard can it be to write a single letter? Bayezid had said. There were still dozens of questions niggling at his mind. Hamdullah had smiled. *Don't worry—when the letter is ready, it will let you know.*

Bayezid had thought that after perhaps three, maybe five *elifs*, he would be able to perfectly imitate the letter in the example script that Hamdullah had put before him. Practice meant to imitate and implement, and practicing letters was work for the day.

The prince's villa in Amasya got sunlight from the left, as Hamdullah had cautioned him, and his knees had sunk into a cushion at the base of the window.

Once again he sat on his left side and the paper was on the board on his right knee as Hamdullah had showed him, and with pen to paper, he wrote another *elif*. It seemed as if it would turn out right this time. After a dozen pieces of paper, perhaps even a thousand *elifs*, he was still unable to write a letter that appeared perfect on the line. He was never able to arrest his agitation or his temper. As he couldn't even write one letter, he couldn't help but think how he'd write twenty-eight different ones.

How could it be so difficult to only write one *elif*? Was it not all together just a single line drawn from top to bottom? *Touch the edge of the reed to the paper and pull from top down. Lean it softly left and don't forget the head of the letter. Could there be such a thing as a headless man? What about a headless realm? Well Prince, so there can't be a headless elif!*

Bayezid's mind wandered from Handullah's words to his friends at the bacchanalia—he thought of Müeyyadzade Abdurrahman, Hizirpashazade Mahmud, Hamzabeyzade Mustafa and the others. How did he end up in this mangle of letters? How could this great prince be shut up in a room of the villa—would he be forced to re-peat this same single letter from morning to night?

His temper flared. He tore up the paper of *elifs* and tossed the shreds to the floor. He snapped his reed pen in two and threw it against the wall. He kicked the inkpot from the floor with such force that it shattered into pieces against the wall and the black ink began to gently ooze out over the red carpet. *This ink will wash your soul*, Hamdullah had said.

It had all started just one week ago at of one the gatherings of pleasure and entertainment that the prince loved so much. Bayezid was in this same room still in daylight hours, and he and his friends were wending through a labyrinth of food and drink.

"Cheers!" Abdurrahman said, raising his glass. A half-dozen people were reclined on cushions cross-legged along the walls of the most ornate room in the villa, lifting their glasses to the musi-cians who'd been playing lively strains for the past three hours. A large, woven rug covered the floor with a few low tables inlaid with mother of pearl, and on them dishes of feta cheese, cherries, nuts and dried fruit. On the wall behind the musicians hung a dazzlingly ornamented quiver holding a bow and arrows.

Bayezid's friends had the servants wandering around to refill their glasses and continued their conversations, sipping their wine. It was no secret that some of Bayezid's friends drank wine like some aristocrats did then.

The musicians nimbly sounded their harp, tambour and rebab while the frame drums and tambourines kept the beat. Young dancing girls gyrated—their silk and satin dresses showing off their unrestrained bodies and making the onlookers' hearts skip a beat. Their twirling movements were like flames driving the audience to sweat.

A noise struck up at the door. "I hope nothing's wrong, what's going on?" one said. Everyone was looking at the door. It opened with a boom and there stood Sheikh Hamdullah. Two servants had ahold of him from both sides, trying to restrain him. His eyes were furious and his fists were squeezed tight.

The music and the dancers stopped and froze in place. Everybody's eyes were on Hamdullah. The sultan in Constantinople had specially assigned him to give his son lessons, but nobody ever listened to Hamdullah.

His burning eyes were on the prince in the middle of the gathering.

Bayezid spoke up after a moment, albeit it timidly, "What's the matter, Hamdullah, sir? To what do we owe this visit?"

Hamdullah shot back, "And you ask this with no shame?!" Then he added as if forced, "your Highness the Prince."

Bayezid answered without budging—reclining on a divan, his arms stretched out along its back. "What wrong of ours have you seen, dear Sheikh? We aren't hurting anybody. We're just enjoying ourselves."

"You're greatest wrong is to yourself! Isn't that enough? And this is no way of enjoyment! We have a calligraphy lesson now. That's why I came."

Bayezid burst into laughter hearing this. "God bless you. That's your trouble?"

The others smiled and continued drinking their wine.

"I guess I forgot there was a lesson today. We'll do it tomorrow, Hamdullah, sir."

"Impossible," Hamdullah said. "I have business tomorrow. I set aside my day today for you—the lesson will be today. I can't deal with you every day!"

Bayezid was starting to lose his patience. "Don't you see, Hamdullah, sir, I have guests."

Müeyyedzade Abdurrahman piped up, "For shame, Hamdullah, sir. Is enjoyment also a sin now? Is it written in the Book that gaiety is a sin? We're not going to be the ones to give up all worldly things like those Christian monks!"

"Good God Almighty!" Hamdullah said and turned his head, his eyes catching the quiver hanging on the wall—red velvet with golden brocade—and he got an idea.

"I'll give you some fun," he said. "But first we're going to make a deal."

The guests looked back and forth at each other and then over at Bayezid. Everyone felt something new and fun was about to start and they were bursting with excitement. Bayezid looked up at Hamdullah without saying a word.

"I've heard the Prince is a great archer. He and I will each shoot an arrow and you all will be the spectators. Whoever shoots an arrow the farthest wins."

Bayezid rolled over laughing again. The others also could barely contain themselves after hearing this challenge. Only Abdurrahman seemed to be unpleased with the proposition. The prince didn't want to miss the opportunity and replied, seeing that his laughter hadn't changed Hamdullah's mind.

"If I win, you'll never bother me again and you'll send word to my dear father in Constantinople that my lessons and everything else are going wonderfully. Deal?"

"Deal, consider it done," Hamdullah said. "If I win, though, you'll stop these gatherings this very day and you'll dunk your head into the water in the horse trough outside and collect yourself. Then you'll sit down with me and start your lesson."

Bayezid was so certain he'd be able to beat Hamdullah that he was barely listening to him. "Alright," he said.

Abdurrahman grabbed Bayezid's wrist as if to tell him to sit a while longer. Bayezid wouldn't have listened anyway.

"Now then, let's get this done with and then we'll have all the time in the world," he said impatiently, walking over to the other side of the room and swiping the quiver off the wall.

The guests all gathered in the grounds behind the villa, waiting in suspense for what was going to happen. All the prince's friends were giggling, except for Abdurrahman. Some had come out holding their glasses of wine—even the musicians had joined them out of curiosity, leaving their instruments behind.

Bayezid had an uneasy confidence because of Hamdullah. The young prince had no shortage of archery practice under his belt and he imagined he'd win this challenge from the calligrapher and go back to the merriment inside.

The prince walked to the center of the grounds and extended the quiver to Hamdullah. "The Prince's precedence," Hamdullah said graciously.

Bayezid bowed his head politely. He pulled the bow out of the quiver, bent it over his knee and quickly strung it up. The best Ottoman bows were notoriously difficult to string, but the ease with which he did it was evidence of Bayezid's mastery. The prince's biceps tensed and bulged while he was stringing the bow to the point where it looked as if his sleeves would tear open.

The bow was ready and Bayezid removed an arrow and took aim over the expansive grounds. He gripped the arrow and placed his feet just like a master archer.

He released his index and middle fingers and the arrow shot into the sky, flying in an arc and falling back to the ground out of sight.

"Hey, would you look at that!" Mustafa shouted. "That's at least fifteen hundred paces!"

At a thousand two hundred fifty yards, shy of a mile, it was an average shot. One of the servants ran to where the arrow had fallen and waved back to the group in the distance.

Bayezid unstrung the bow and turned to Hamdullah. "Your our turn." Like all the others, Bayezid also thought there was no way Hamdullah would be able to string the bow.

Hamdullah took the bow, bent it over his knee and strung it with the same ease as the prince had done. This was the first thing that quieted the rabble's delighted laughter, turning it into a low murmur.

Hamdullah nonchalantly chose an arrow and fitted it to the bow, then turned to where Bayezid had just shot. He drew the arrow to his right chest and whispered just loud enough for those standing nearby to hear, "God is Truth!" He let the arrow fly as his lips were closing, it pounced into the air like a wildcat and soared off toward the horizon.

The prince and the rest of the crowds' mouths hung open in amazement. The arrow flew over the servant next to the one Bayezid had shot and fell out of sight about five hundred yards farther away.

"My God, how?!" is all Mustafa could muster to say.

A second servant went running to where the arrow had fallen. The servant passed the other standing by Bayezid's arrow, continuing for another half that distance before stopping and waving his hand.

"That's nearly nineteen hundred paces!" Mustafa said.

Everyone's faces fell in dismay—except for Hamdullah.

Hamdullah turned to Bayezid, who was staring at him dumbfounded. "Exactly why do you think you call me sheikh, my boy?"

Müeyyedzadde Abdurrahman came up to Bayezid. "That's what I was going to tell you, Prince. This man's a sheikh of archery—he's trained archers for years."

Bayezid broke out in a cold sweat. "Damn it, now you tell me!" he snapped, defeated. He hadn't known that Hamdullah came from an order of archers and was called sheikh because of his mastery of archery, not from his scholarship on jurisprudence. He couldn't figure out whether he should regret the deal he'd made or pity himself.

"Come on now, the fun's over!" Hamdullah said, reminding the prince of the conditions of their deal. "Everybody out! The prince and I have a little work to do at the watering trough!"

It had been a week since that day.

Bayezid had been growing angrier with himself with each passing day and with each calligraphy lesson. He saw the black ink spreading out over the rug and realized he couldn't take it anymore. He was going to call for his friends this very day and they would go to all the taverns in the city and live it up. He was an importance prince and he wouldn't be cowed by a calligrapher his whole life. He'd kept his word for a week now—wasn't that enough?

Shreds of paper were scattered behind him as he flung open the door on his way out.

Each shred had dozens of the letter *elif* scrawled across them, all laying around a broken reed pen.

37

Qitmir was running across the deck of the ship with its little, pink tongue flapping around.

"Come here, damn it, you fleabag!" Big Ahmed yelled, chasing after the little snowball of a Maltese.

The galley had just been repaired from topmast to keel and the little dog was scampering about, jumping up on the bulwark then taking off across the deck, running under the sails and between the pirates legs, managing to stay at least a good ten feet in front of the merchant chasing behind. About the size of a small cannonball, the dog darted from one hole to another like a little rat, with hefty Big Ahmed crashing into the beams and crewmen. His face had gone red and sweat was pouring from his forehead and chest. They were just about to make their second go-round of the galley.

"You little shit, when I catch you you're going to be shark food! Then you'll see what it's like, you little rat!"

The dog rounded the mainmast and jumped off his chest into Rattler's arms.

"Why're you torturing this tiny thing, Little Ahmed? Go pick on something your own size!" Rattle chided.

"That little son of a bitch broke open the grain sacks again and knocked around all the pots and pans in the galley! I'm going to snap that little beast's neck this time!" he said, reaching out for the fluff ball.

Rattler turned away and kept the dog out of Ahmed's reach.

"Yeah, well you never feed it. Would it be so bad to give him a little piece of meat?!"

"Oh, so now it's your dog for me to feed is it, Rattler? I've got my hands full with work. There're three hundred thirty people on this ship—yardmen, riggers, oarsmen, carpenters, galley slaves and soldiers—you aware of that?!"

Qitmir was panting in Rattler's arms, his entire body heaving with each little breath.

"Oh, and what would happen if you fed him? Would it really mean one less chickpea for those three hundred thirty men?"

"That's not even the problem. I can't agonize over whether this animal's hungry or not—I don't have any time! It's yours, you feed him!"

Meanwhile, Yasin, the lookout up the mainmast in the crow's nest, yelled out, "Port, forty degrees!" Yasin had begged Burak Reis to take him on board when he had saved him from crusaders, and then shortly began working on the ship.

The two men stopped arguing and turned to look along with the rest of the pirates.

Burak Reis and Mute Yusuf stood up at the stern and looked out at the horizon. Burak Reis had anchored his galley—painted red with yellow bands, which he'd named the Crescent of Victory—and was waiting to the northwest of the island of Naxos, fifty miles off Crete and the islands off the Peloponnese, just as Kemal Reis had told him to do two weeks earlier. A galley painted in green and two galiots were anchored just off from the Crescent of Victory. The galleys had been beautifully repaired—their keels and bulwarks put in tiptop shape and the sails replaced, along with the three masts and booms. All on the galley thought that every ship that had appeared in the distance across the sunlight glinting off the sea had been the Blue Lion.

"Those're Venetians with goods heading for Constantinople," Burak Reis said.

"Captain," Boatswain Mahmud said, "I want to go on the hunt! What would happen if we attacked and had a little fun of it? Damn it, I've started growing moss from sitting here." His leg hadn't even healed yet from the battle three weeks earlier.

"Bully, Boatswain!" Burak Reis said. "One of your legs still doesn't quite hold you up quite right and you're still looking for adventure! We have orders to stay here and wait for the old man. I don't know about the rest." He looked back out at the horizon. "And these buggers are taking goods to the city anyway—let them be on their way, the poor bastards."

"Come on captain, let's raise a little shit. Old habits die hard, right? You're letting them through easy, but they wouldn't suffer our ships if they saw them. And as for being under the old man's orders, well, that's something else."

Helmsman Yunus yelled out from behind, "Boatswain! Quit flapping your gums off to the captain. Go on and fill your maw up with some sand and learn how to pass the time!"

Some of the bumbling boatswain's mates in charge of keeping the time would turn over the hourglasses before the tops had completely emptied, ring the bell and confuse everybody. The pirates would also needle the boatswains about this no matter whether they were in charge of keeping the time or not.

The pirates all grumbled and sat back down. Some of them leaned back against the bulwarks with their legs out to nap, some sharpened their cutlasses and swords, and some others leaned on the gunwales and looked out over the horizon.

"What do you say Blind Ali," Big Ahmed said, coming up to him, "would Kemal Reis back out of this? I mean, it wouldn't be wrong if he did. There're crusaders, Venetians, Spanish, Portuguese—I've seen those bastards' galleons once, they're more floating islands than ships. Let's say we have fifty cannons, they have a hundred. And if we have three masts, then they have five. Next to that our galley looks like a rowboat. Look how much time's already gone by. I don't think they're going to come."

Blind Ali was sitting with his quiver and a pile of arrows in front of him, checking each one of their shafts and feathers. He looked up. "You're wrong Ahmed. Seems you don't know Kemal Reis. He'd take a dinghy and row all way to Spain by himself if he had to. He'll put as many people as he can on the boats and then go back to Constantinople. I've never seen a more faithful and courageous man as Kemal Reis—or Burak Reis, for that matter."

Then they heard three cannon shots in the distance.

"They're coming, they're coming! Off the bow!" Yasin yelled down.

Everyone on board jumped up and looked out over the bow at Kemal Reis' Blue Lion with a colossal galley on each side and a galiot behind each of them. The Blue Lion was just in front of the rest of the squadron all coming broadside by broadside and nearing quickly.

They all started to shout, "Cheers for the Captain! Praise God! Lord be!"

"Where did he find these ships?" one said, pointing to the two large galleys just behind the Blue Lion.

Burak Reis returned the salute with three cannon shots. The ships' masts grew taller as they got closer, rising like minarets.

The men on Kemal Reis' ship and the pirates with Burak Reis were now all chanting together, "Haul the bowlines!"

They were finally ready to set out. Mute Yusuf climbed to the mainsails, Helmsman Yunus manned the wheel, the yardmen took their places atop the foremast and jiggermast, and the galley slaves gripped their oars tightly. The Muslim galley slaves gave a shout of *Bismillah* and readied their oars.

Kemal Reis' ship and the others all turned west. His squadron would first head to the Peloponnese, then Sicily, and then cruise around Sardinia before heading to the Malaga port in Spain. The campaign was underway.

The pirates kept shouting with excitement, "Haul the bowlines!"

38

The town of Montalban was a small, quiet and calm place where everybody knew one another—an hour by horseback from Toledo. Davud was riding his horse to a house on the northwestern edge of town along with the townsfolk who'd gathered in front of him.

The priest of the town church was looking at him from afar and trying to figure out who this monk was. Davud bowed his head to him and then turned his head forward right away so as not to receive any unwanted attention from the priest.

Three men were working in David's workshop, which wasn't much bigger than a haystack.

David closed the frame around the text from the other side of the press after one of the workers covered the lines well with an inkpad. Then the paper was fitted in place and slid under the large press with the rail system Mark had devised. Finally, David turned the long bar with his full weight, bringing the press down and back up. One of the other workers slid another sheet in to be pressed and David turned the handle again.

A man waiting at the edge of the press carefully removed the sheets and hung them on a string to dry. There were hundreds of pages hanging from strings around the workshop, covering the entire interior and creating labyrinthine corridors. Hundreds of printed pages were stacked in rows along the base of the walls, waiting to be bound into dozens of books at another secret workshop. Stacks of rolled up pages as tall as a person also stuck out in rows from place to place, with names written on them in Hebrew such as ibn Arabi, ibn Rushd and ben Maimon.

Samuel appeared in the workshop's door right when David was about to press another page. "Close the door quick, there's a monk coming!" His voice was full of dread and shaking. He grabbed his brother's arm and pulled David into the front room, passing between and beneath all of the hanging pages and closing the door behind him. Then he pounded his fist against the door—the signal for the workers inside to bolt it shut in case of emergency.

David looked at his brother, bewildered. "What business does a monk have here? Dou you think they've found out? Did someone rat us out?"

In the front part of the work shop where they now were was where they made silver jewelry that they sold in the shops in Toledo. There was a small stove off to the side, a hammer and anvil in the middle, a large worktable and tools of all sizes for twisting and bending hung on the walls.

"I don't know," Samuel said. "Come on, wipe off your hands, they're covered in ink!"

"Damn it!" David said, picking up a cloth from the floor and scrubbing at his fingers. The soap he'd made of ash, animal fat and hot water would take the ink off, but he'd forgotten it in the back room—and it was much too late to get it now.

One of the townsfolk running in front of Davud came through the door. "David, there's a monk who wants to see you."

David and Samuel looked at each other and swallowed hard, readying themselves for the calamity they were about to face. They stared from the darkness of the room through the sunlight filling the doorway. They could hear the monk dismount and start walking toward the door.

They waited in silence as they saw the man appear in the doorway, a silhouette from the sunlight behind him.

"Which of you is David?" the figure said.

David and Samuel looked at each other as if they didn't know what to say. The townsman inside didn't say anything.

David could make out the figure's face as he entered and relaxed when he saw that the man's head wasn't shaven—he wasn't Dominican at least. The monk's face had a comforting and trustworthy expression that David couldn't immediately make sense of. He was still a monk, though, and only three steps away from the printing press where he'd been making books in Hebrew, so he could only take so much comfort from it.

David finally spoke up after a while, "I'm he."

Davud took another step forward and looked over the young man who was only slightly shorter than himself.

"David *ibn Nahmias Marrano*?" Davud said—there could be dozens of men named David in this town.

"The very same," David said, timidly and obediently.

Davud turned to the townsman and gave him a look to leave, which he did hastily. He then looked over at Samuel with the same meaning.

"He's my brother," David said. "Whatever you're going to say to me, you can say in front of him." David was firm.

Davud nodded slightly.

He looked at the two brothers again and locked on David's eyes. "Get yourself together." He spoke with the shortness of an order more than a request. "We're leaving."

"Where?" David asked, confused.

"To Constantinople."

39

"I'm not going anywhere," David said, turning his back. He went and sat down on a stool at the worktable and started filing a ring. Nothing Davud had said had had any effect.

"And how am I to believe you. Are you a monk or a Turk, are you telling the truth or are you lying? How am I supposed to know? Maybe this is the Inquisition's knew game, maybe you're a spy form the Church!"

He didn't look at Davud as he spoke, flipping around and angrily filing away at the silver ring.

"Don't you understand?" Davud said. "If you stay here, the Inquisition will be the end for all of you. All Jews will be forced to leave the city in a few months. The *Edict of Expulsion* was read out a month ago already!"

David was thinking about Esther and her family.

"That doesn't concern me. I'm a Christian," he said, hiding his thoughts, although not believing it himself.

"That's even worse, then. The Inquisition can take you away at any moment. If you were Jewish, they wouldn't touch you, but they've found a remedy for this now, too. Either everyone will agree to be baptized as Catholics or they'll be forced to leave the land. The New Christians will always live their lives under the watch of the Inquisition and having to prove they're faithful Catholics. You'll wake up every morning afraid and wondering which of your friends has informed on you, which of your enemies has made erroneous confessions to the Church about you!"

David looked at the man persistently trying to persuade him and pursed his lips. "You've forgotten that we've been living with that fear for years already."

Davud looked hopelessly over at Samuel for help. Samuel, though, was pacing around the shop in thought. He didn't know what to think, let alone what to say.

Davud wouldn't be able to return to the capital without this man—his name was written on the sultan's order. Every time David rebuffed him, Davud felt his own return home slipping further from reach, and he was forcing himself to stay calm and repress his anger.

"And why me? There's tens of thousands of Jews and New Christians here. Why me and not them?"

"Ottoman ships will be at the Malaga port in a few weeks and they're going to take everyone who wants back to the empire. I've been charged to take you safely to those ships. Someone in Constantinople must care for you very much. I'll explain on the way. Thousands of people are already on their way, and just as many are on the road to Portugal."

David lowered his head, still steadfast, and turned the ring around in his fingers. "You've come all this way and you've apparently done quite a bit to find me, but I don't want to take any more of your time. You'd better head off for those ships as soon as possible."

"You don't understand, man! You need to come with me!" Davud pounded his fist down on the worktable, sending all the tools on it flying.

"I don't want to intrude on your conversation, but a priest is coming," Samuel said, his voice shaking.

"Oh, is it a priest or is it an Ottoman vizier out there? God knows!" David said.

Davud had one eye on the door bolted shut behind him. "Don't open your mouths and leave everything to me."

Samuel had been sidling up to Davud and, thinking he'd found his chance, reached out to grab his nose. As a reflex, Davud shot up and grabbed his fingers just an inch away—Samuel had never seen anybody able to grab his fingers so fast.

"He feels compelled to grab the nose of any new person he meets," David said. "He's been like that since he was a kid, but he means nothing by it."

"Dear Brother," the priest said as he entered. "How nice to see you here. I was going to say for you to stop by the church, but you passed right on by." He had the explicit tone of an inquisitor in his voice. Davud could tell he was from the Dominican order from his white tunic and black, cowled vestment. The shaved crown of his head made it even more apparent. It was also obvious that this man would report anything out of the ordinary to Torquemada.

Davud responded very calmly in Latin. "*Deo duce, Dei plena sunt omnia*"—*God as our guide, all things are full of God.*

The priest was taken aback, as it seemed that Latin was this monk's native language. He nodded his head. "*Oui*," he said. He couldn't pronounce Latin half as well as this monk.

Davud put his hand on the priest's should and turned him toward the door.

"*Deo adjuvante, non timendum. Si Deus nobiscum quis contra nos*"— *With God's help, nothing need be feared. If God is with us, who shall be against us?*

Davud could see the priest felt put upon while he spoke, so he continued in Castilian so as to not further embarrass the man.

"Father, there's a new church being built in Toledo that's about to open for services and we need some gold and silver engravings. They told us that this jeweler is quite good. I need to give him the instructions and leave at once."

"But I've been told nothing of this," the priest said. "Would I not need to be informed first?"

Davud put on a kind face. "Everyone's a little too busy these days due to the edict from the Alhambra, so the chain of communication could have a fault. We'll be more careful next time, Father."

Davud gave the priest's shoulder a light squeeze. "Until next time, Father. Now, if you'll allow, I need to finish my business and get going."

"Nice act," David said after the priest had left. "Don't know how you did it, but I haven't changed my mind."

Davud sighed and pointed at the back door. "What're you printing behind that?"

Samuel and David looked at each other in shock—they didn't know what to say.

"What printing?" Samuel said.

"Where're you getting that we're printing anything?" David added.

"Both of your eyes shot over to the door as soon as the priest came in. You did the same thing when I came in." He pointed at David's hands. "You could also see the ink stains on your hands from ten yards away."

David quickly tried to hide his hands behind his back as he walked to the front door and pushed it open. "I don't know what you're talking about. Go already before you bring anymore attention to me!"

Samuel walked over to his brother and looked back at Davud as if to tell him to leave. Samuel was holding a hammer and his brother a file. Davud looked at the two brothers hopelessly once more and walked outside.

There was no way a hammer and file would have stopped Davud the Brave, but there was no reason to force them to go to Constantinople. It was clear these two men didn't grasp the grave danger of the barbarity in Spain.

It was only a matter of time before the book hunters would discover their printing press.

Averroista

It began with Aristotle—it was his writings that set in motion the chain of events that would upend my whole life.

Or Averroes—who the Muhammadans call ibn Rushd in their language—because without ibn Rushd, we wouldn't know Aristotle, and without Aristotle there would've been no reason to know ibn Rushd.

His name was pronounced Aven Rusht in the languages in Hispania and then spread throughout the Latin-speaking world as Averroes, and after three centuries the name was not odd in the least—I even thought these were two different philosophers at first. Many banned books have passed before me—in Arabic, Hebrew and Latin—both handwritten and printed with that Devil's contraption, all with at least twenty different versions of his name, and it was quite a while before I realized they were all the same man—Filius Rosadis, Ibn-Rusid, Ben-Raxid, Ibn-Ros-din, Ibn-Rushchod, Den-Resched, Aben-Rassad, Aben-Rois, Avenrosdy, Adveryos, Benroist and many more.

Thank the good Lord Jesus Christ that these two men had fewer epithets than names. There was only one—in Arabic, Aristotle is al-Mualim al-Azim, or the Great Teacher. Ibn Rushd was also known as the Commentator in both Latin and Hebrew. Sometimes they were both called the Teacher or the Great Philosopher, but one couldn't know whether what was written was the philosophy of Aristotle as explained by ibn Rushd, or if it was his own philosophy or, as it were, by Aristotle himself, ibn Sina, al-Farabi, or Aflatoun—the Muhammadans' name for Plato—who'd all come before.

My introduction to ibn Rushd, however, was rather odd, as it was neither through the language of ancient Greece nor Arabic. None of the hundreds of works by Aristotle and Plato I've seen were in Greek—and these most likely haven't survived to our day. Most of these books were either in Arabic or translated from Arabic into Hebrew. I, for one, was introduced to Metaphysics with the Great Commentary in Latin. Let those who believe the Tower of Babel was in Mesopotamia, near the center of the world in Jerusalem, come and look at the enchanting libraries in Andalusia.

With my appointment by Cardinal Cisneros, we continued to identify and destroy the heretical books throughout the kingdom. The job grew, as well, with Torquemada also appointing me to go find a printing press.

I would shut myself in my small room in the monastery and leaf through the books from the libraries that our holy monks found to be objectionable. Just like how many priests and monks had done at the beginning, I thought every book in Arabic that came to me was the Quran, full of all the Muhammadans' false teachings, and threw them in the pile of books to be burned. I was able to quickly get through the books that had piled up around me like many Towers of Babel, as I saw they were written in Arabic as I leafed through their pages. The same was true for the Hebrew manuscripts and books. In fact, there was no need for monks like us to know either Arabic or Hebrew to do this work—even the ignorant who could neither read nor write could recognize these language's letters and be employed for their destruction. This wasn't often the case, particularly when going out on the hunt for Arabic and Hebrew books—these people were not used for this.

The books in Latin, however, were a thorn in the flesh.

Cardinal Cisneros has specified that the only thing written or published in Latin should be the Bible, and even this, done at the monasteries given authority to reproduce the Holy Book, should be under tight control. As in past centuries, we sometimes banned the reproduction of the Bible. The number of people who can read is quite small, and Cisneros believes *those who read the Bible should be the clergy, otherwise it would be a deadly sin for those who read it and interpret it as they see fit. The single entity in charge of, responsible for and authorized to explain the Father, the Son and the Holy Spirit, and how people need to live is the Church, and individuals reading and trying to understand religious texts on their own could be grounds for heresy. I believed and observed this principle throughout my entire life. What need would there be for the Holy Church or us, the educated clergy, if everyone who found themselves with a Bible could read it? There was no way someone without the proper education could understand the Bible.*

Then, however, the Vatican again began to reproduce the Bible and the Latin writings on it under pressure from some liberal heretics in Padua.

Sadly, not all were the Bible, and neither were all the others in Latin on the teachings of Jesus Christ. I only understood the tragedy and comedy of it years later, that we burned thousands of Bibles written in Arabic, thinking they were heretical books, and spared just as many a Quran and book mentioning the teachings of the Muhammadans for the simple fact they were written in Latin.

It's possible I was about to save one of these books in Latin at one of these moments in my small room at the monastery, thinking it was the Bible. It was my top priority to determine the heretics' books—it was Cardinal Cisneros who would decide whether these Bibles would be burned or not, as having too many stray Bibles around was not acceptable.

I was closing a book when Aristotle's name on one of the pages caught my eye. The book was large and very thick—picking up, moving, sifting through and classifying these books was a tiring task. I hefted it back onto the lectern in front of my chair and carefully looked at the first page. I was acquainted with Aristotle, as the Church had banned some, but not all, of his writing for being polytheistic and against its teachings. I didn't understand him, though, like many of the people who opposed this Greek philosopher, and even the few times I read him secretly as I tried to understand, I was taken by my conscience and fled the library.

The Holy Church was right. Faith is only through the heart and the soul. The world of man, nature, the universe, the sun rising in the morn-

ing, the moon at night, falling rain, the greening of the trees, a person from the seed of man, the body from soil, blossoming flowers, the swelling of the oceans, the fallen woman and the thousands of varieties of animals—in short, creation. It was a futile and perverse endeavor to try to understand existence and all the causes and consequences lying behind it. To be a good Christian, all we must do is accept the teachings of the Church and live by them. It was necessary to accept that one would not understand the beginning and end of anything or the cause of the mind or what it is. There was no need for logic and faith to coincide. The science they call rationalism at best would drive man away from Christ. The Vatican was certainly just in its excommunication of the Parisian Bishop in the past century, Siger of Brabant, and Peter Abelard and his hundreds of advocates a century before for their teaching of Aristotle, reason and logic. Even though Abelard had fallen in love with Heloïse—the niece of a cannon of Notre Dame—whisked her off to birth their child and secretly married her, and was duly castrated, teaching Aristotle was a much graver sin. Contrary to what Abelard claimed, it's unnecessary to understand a thing in order to believe in it—this is a philosophy that threatens faith.

While emulating Abelard and imagining the beauty of Heloïse like all the other clergy who'd never experienced any kind of physical love or lust, however, the pages I started to read drew an entirely different picture for me.

I wasn't aware at that moment that I was reading one of the Commentator's most important works on the Great Teacher. It was ibn Rushd. I only learned of this much later. But it was as if this philosopher—born and raised in Cordoba, just a few day's ride away—had called out to me despite all my objections to think about what I was looking at before me and to see all sides. Later on, the Arabic books I saw by ibn Sina, al-Kindi, Husayn ibn Ishaq and al-Zahrawi along with their countless Latin translations ran rampant in my mind and came together as they stared back at me. My mind roiled as I turned the pages, trying to find my way as if I was wandering amid the maze of this city's al-Hakim garden walls, trying to find my way—both striving for the exit and taking pleasure from it. Ibn Rushd's words told me to be calm as I felt my belief, the greatest treasure in my heart, falling away. He spoke to me as if saying my understanding, my belief, was strengthening, that whereas belief and logic appear separate, they are one—their roads look divergent, but the Truth is one.

This is how I began to understand what ibn Rushd had called the Double Truth a century before my time.

I felt I was traversing through layers of earth to the center of the world and on to the beginning of creation as I turned the yellowed pages of this gigantic book. What kind of being was God, how did He create the world, are the heavens endless, what was the beginning of existence like, what is death—is there life after death, is there a hereafter—what can the rules of logic and the laws of nature tell us, can man find God through his own wisdom without religious texts or revelation, does thinking and contemplating harm belief or does it fortify faith? That's all to say, can philosophy and reason overlap with faith and belief?

There's no conflict between reason and belief, according to ibn Rushd. On the contrary he says, it's a religious obligation for people to question what they believe and reflect on what they see. Ibn Rushd relates dozens of verses on this from the sacred book of the Muhammadans like, O people of insight, take heed—So will you not then take heed?—they are deaf, dumb and blind, so they cannot be mindful. By using the mind and the senses to observe and understand creation, ibn Rushd believed that man could come closer to God. The ability to use syllogisms that God bestowed on man, to evaluate by only using the mind, is a treasure, and because of this, all of creation and time can be taught through a sacred book of three or five hundred pages. Failing that, using the example of the Holy Book, he says that if all the oceans were ink and the trees pens, the pen of God would not be enough to scratch out a word.

This philosopher and scholar argues that no action on Earth is spontaneous, there is a reason for every outcome and that creation exists within these laws of the natural sciences, also emphasizing that the task of thinking man is to investigate these outcomes. It points to how the rain falls, how the sun rises, the phases of the moon, the passing of the seasons, how a person grows, how living things operate and the answers to a great *number of questions—but also that what knowledge gives and its answers, at all times, is a Creator, a First Being that has no need for cause, a First Mind that encompasses the laws of natural things, alchemy and life.*

Following Plato, Aristotle also places at the center of his philosophy the all-encompassing Mind as the First Power, or the First Exigency, outside of space and beyond the concept of time. The problem is that the Church finds it extremely contrary to Catholic teaching that what Aristotle sometimes calls the laws of nature and its systems are rendered as precluding God Almighty and our Lord Jesus Christ as if binding God to the laws of the natural sciences. Ibn Rushd, however, explains that revelation and reason point to the same truth, and this is what he calls the Double Truth.

As the philosopher's theoretical sciences are universal and esoteric, when they're split, universal knowledge itself is separated into the areas of dialectic, fallacy and metaphysics. While the universal sciences examine existence in general, the esoteric sciences concentrate on the qualities of matter. These are also divided into the natural sciences that concern the changes in nature and mathematics as the study of qualities abstracted from matter. What interested ibn Rushd, however, were the rules of metaphysics and how the laws of the natural sciences coincide with mathematics. For example, without mathematics, we wouldn't be able to understand that there is a cause for every object on earth, and when we follow them back to their source, there is ultimately a need for a First Cause that requires no source of its own—it is precisely because of mathematics that we can understand things like the number of planets and their movements along with the sun and the moon.

What's interesting is that centuries before ibn Rushd, similar thinkers such as ibn Sina and al-Farabi were at times accused of heresy. As such, in his writings, ibn Rushd mentions many Muhammadan scholars who place reason before religion and criticizes them harshly. As for the limits of man's will, he speaks of three schools—the Mutalizites who argue that man is completely free, the Hanbali who argue for fate and that all things come form the hand of God, and the Asharites, who fall somewhere in the middle of the other two—and criticizes each of them by using reason from various perspectives.

I later came across and was lost in amazement with these and similar concepts in *Summa Theologica* and *De Unitate Intellectus contra Averroistas*—On the Unity of Intellect, against the Averroists—the masterpieces by Saint Thomas Aquinas, one of the leading men of the Holy Church. Perhaps this is why Dante referred to Aristotle in his *Divine Comedy* as *il maestro di color che sanno*—the master of men who know—and afforded respect to ibn Rushd as *Averoìs che 'l gran comento feo*—Averroes who wrote the grand commentary.

It perplexed me that, despite the rules of logic and genius that prepossess man's reason, ibn Rushd supported Aristotle's views that there cannot be a beginning or end to the world and that it is as eternal as God, and that the resurrection of the body is in the vineyards and gardens and not as we understand it as life after death as explained in the tales in the sacred books. Saint Thomas Aquinas also said of man's metaphysical existence in his *Summa* that the world had a beginning to existence as an object of faith, but not of demonstration or science—*mundum incoepisse est credibile, non autem demonstrabile vel scibile*. He expounds that philosophers' mission is to explain in real terms to people the answers to questions such as what life after death is and where the soul goes. He further believes that only scholars of these fields should explore such questions, as it shakes the folk's beliefs when they're shared with the common people.

In the end, for both Aristotle and ibn Rushd, *finis vitae est finis vitae*—the end of life is the end of life. They say one need not expect much from the body after death. The permanence of concepts such as Wisdom, Spirit and Singular Power took primacy for both.

It was a mid-afternoon when I finished the Great Commentary, and I was thoroughly confused. I was both grateful to ibn Rushd for showing me completely different doors and a new horizon, and angry that he afflicted some of that which I held to be certain truth. I was also overwhelmed with a terrific sense of guilt that I'd read Aristotle and a Muhammadan scholar with so much interest. I made up my mind that very afternoon. I snatched up Aristotle's Metaphysics, leaving the other Arabic and Hebrew books to be destroyed behind, and walked from the monastery to a valley down the way where I set fire to it on a rocky outcrop.

The heretical thoughts I had would be lost one by one as the ink that poisoned my mind was cleansed in fire as each page went up in flames. As ibn Rushd and Aristotle's words swirled up in smoke, so too would the ridiculous ideas in my mind drift away. I hoped to be rid of it—burning it myself to ensure I never picked it up again and not leaving anything to chance.

I didn't know, however, that I was mistaken and wouldn't find respite from these thoughts gnawing at my mind, as every time a read philosophy, I'd look for these thinkers' ideas in the Arabic, Hebrew and Latin books I took up. I never dreamt at those moments when my rage grew that the fire of my fury would be assuaged as I burned more books. I continuously found and burned ibn Rushd's Tahafut al-Tahafut, or Incoherence of the Incoherence—and Jawami' kitab ma ba'd al-tabi'a in Arabic, its Catalan version Compendio de Metafisica of the Latin translation Epitome Averrois in Librum Metaphysicae—ibn Rushd's Short Commentary on the Metaphysics—and many, many others, but could not ever set one to the flame without reading it first.

I understood much later that on that day when I burned the book on the rocks that I surrendered my past to the flames. Every book I burned thereafter was only fuel for the fire. As ibn Rushd said, man must face creation in the end. I was only to delay this a little longer.

I still had to concentrate on my work. I'd realized that the printed books that had crescents at the top of the pages all came from the same source, and I would shortly find who was using this paper in their printing press.

41

"I reckoned you'd bring a few galiots," Burak Reis said, "but where did you find these galleys?"

Burak Reis and Kemal Reis were standing on the deck of the Blue Lion.

"Sultan Bayezid knows there's not much time left to help the Jews and Muslims in Spain—we might not have another chance after this, so he ordered these galleys built, the largest that can sail the seas."

Burak Reis looked in amazement at the two galleys following behind the Blue Lion and Crescent of Victory. He leaned on the gunwale.

"So much timber, heaps of sails—one of these could make ten galleys, old man."

"You're right. Tons of trees were taken from the lush forests in Ilgaz, Kastamonu and along the Black Sea to the Gallipoli Shipyard. They brought so much hemp from Tashköprü for the rigging that I thought it was only for the ropes." Kemal Reis pointed to the ship Burak was looking at. "The sultan named that one the Göke—*to the sky*. He said that since everything in the world is created in pairs, so should these, and he called the other one the *Göke II*."

"Maybe he believes such huge ships could even sail to the sky," a voice from behind them said.

The two men turned around to the dark, short man standing behind them. Burak Reis could see from the man's heavily calloused hands that he'd been a ship caulker for many years.

Kemal Reis went up to the man and put his hand on his shoulder. "Here, the ships' architect's come. Burak Reis, meet Master Yani."

Master Yani bowed his head, which Burak Reis reciprocated with his hand on his chest in the greeting particular to pirates.

Master Yani took a look at the Göke and began to tally off its specifications.

"She's one hundred eighty feet long and eighty-two feet wide. Her stern is fifty-two feet tall. She has thirty rows of benches with seven men on each oar. She has nineteen double gun ports on the deck above the oars and each one has a pair of canons. Port, starboard, stern and bow all together have forty-four."

He then pointed up at the masts. "She has four masts along with the bowsprit—a foremast, mainmast, mizzenmast and jiggermast—and each one has a top with thirty archers a piece. The main mast with the square sail is one hundred eighty feet tall. She can easily carry two thousand people."

The eyes of two great captains of the Mediterranean looked over the Göke—the tips of its masts, some painted blood red and others navy blue, and its flags, rippling in the wind and bathed with sunlight, looked like golden brocaded satin. The brown, wooden boards of the ship seemed to shine like gold with the sparkling sea beneath and the blue sky above.

After Master Yani had finished, Kemal Reis turned back to Burak Reis, who was still marveling at the ship. "Master Yani here lived in Venice for a long time and knows how they make ships there and all the tricks—he learned it all in and out. Then he came to Constantinople and started working for Sultan Bayezid at the Gallipoli Shipyard. They say you could make it from one end of the Marmara Sea to the other just on two boards if Master Yani fitted them together."

"Why'd you come to Constantinople from Venice, Master Yani?
"Burak Reis asked. "It's the main center of this business after all."

"It's true. Venetians born and die on the water. The captains
are betrothed to their ships and married to the sea." He pursed his
lips and went on. "But Italian crews are sneaky. There's no blunder
they won't make for business, and nothing that they wouldn't sell
for higher gains. They want the keels to be gold and the sails made
of silk—they want you to deliver their ships no less than perfect,
but won't pay the debt until they make double the profit with the
ship. I didn't chase after the captains or beg on my knees in front of
the admirals for the money I had a right to—it wasn't worth it." He
looked at Kemal Reis with a confident smile on his face. "But is the
Ottoman sultan like that? Whatever's your right, he gives it that
day. He doesn't endlessly bargain and doesn't condescend the small
laborers and shipyard workers about what's their right. If you do
your job well, you'll be granted a purse of gold."

Burak Reis had picked up on Master Yani's accent.

"Are you Armenian, Master Yani?"

"My father's Armenian, my mother's Greek and I was born in
Constantinople. But when Eastern Rome fell, they were terrified
and we all fled to Venice. The more my father heard how well Sultan Mehmed treated the non-Muslims who stayed behind, though,
the more upset with himself he'd get from time to time. He wanted
to go back after a few years, but he was old and stayed in Venice.
If you ask me of what people I am, captain, I'm Ottoman. I work
for Sultan Bayezid and I live in his service. If word comes one day
that one of my ships won't sail anymore, I'll throw myself into the
salty waters of this Mediterranean. If God gives me a long life, I'll
keep on building ships for the Ottomans. The Muslims are hard-
working here—it's tough to find honest, hard workers in Venice.
Everybody's scrambling around for easy money. I had a very honest
Venetian master who was the head of the yard, and after he died I
had nothing in Venice to keep me there."

"God bless you, Master Yani," Kemal Reis said. "By the way, you filled the topside paints at the depot I told you about, right?"

"Don't you ever worry, Captain—we'll have the broadsides all painted in two hours on your order. I've taken up enough of your time, though. With your permission, I have to go to the Göke and check her ballast to make sure she can sail."

The ship's chief cook, Hard-Nose Ibrahim, came up to Kemal Reis while Master Yani was leaving. "The grilled bream's ready, Captain. Want me to bring it here?"

"Thanks, Ibrahim, don't trouble yourself. Burak Reis and I'll eat on deck with the crew." He turned back to Burak Reis. "It's a way to get to know the men on the Blue Lion. What do you say, Burak?"

"I smelled the grill, too. I was wondering if they were also going to offer it to me," Burak Reis said half joking. "It'd be my pleasure to join you all."

The first-class officers were seated around a low, circular table at the stern of Kemal Reis' galley—some on their knees and some cross-legged, although most in the common position with one knee up against their chest and one leg tucked beneath them. Kemal Reis and Burak Reis were seated together along with First Mate Piri, Yardman Jevher, Overseer Jihan, Helmsman Musa, Watchman Isa, Doctor Ilyas, Orion Orhan, Mahmud the Kurd and Fingerless Shakir enjoying the sea bream Hard-Nose Ibrahim had so carefully prepared.

"I've heard these fish are both male and female at the same time, Doctor Ilyas. There any truth to that?" Fingerless Shakir said.

The man was missing three fingers on his left hand.

Doctor Ilyas finished the bite in his mouth and looked angrily over at Shakir. "What, Shakir? You think I'm a veterinarian? What would I know about a bream being male or female?!"

Everyone at the table burst out laughing.

"What're you getting mad at, Doctor? Man or animal, they're both alive after all, aren't they?"

Doctor Ilyas muttered to himself, "God Almighty," and then spoke up again. "And with this head of yours you've only lost three fingers. You should be thankful your head's still where it's supposed to be."

Kemal Reis went on introducing the men to Burak Reis.

"Fingerless Shakir got captured five years ago when we were fighting against the Italians and was imprisoned on a crusader fleet. Our fleet was going to leave the Gallipoli Shipyard in two groups. We were going to meet up with Shakir off the coast of Lemnos and go to take on the Italians in Mytilene on Lesbos. The crusaders attacked Shakir's only ship five to one and slaughtered nearly everybody on board. Then they tortured him to give up our location, but he spit in their faces while he took the beating. Finally, an Italian knight drew a knife and splayed out his hand on a chest, and after every question he didn't get an answer to he cut off one of his fingers."

"I don't miss the other ones, Captain, but I grieve most for my little finger," Shakir said. "The bastard's knife was so sharp he hacked off my fingers like he was using a clever. Then I thanked my lucky stars he didn't chop off my limbs instead, otherwise I'd be missing both my arms and a leg."

"You're a real man, Shakir. You nearly lost a whole hand's worth of fingers and your still grateful. Well done," Overseer Jihan said, laughing.

"Then what happened?" Burak Reis asked.

"The bastard had come to my pointer finger, Captain, when a noise like a clap of thunder made everyone jump. I looked behind me through a wide window that'd opened and there outside was Kemal Reis' galley with its cannons still smoking."

"We knew something had gone wrong when Shakir wasn't at the meeting place on time," Kemal Reis said. "We went hard alee to the southwest and broke through the smoke and caught up with the crusaders before long."

Shakir picked up a piece of bread with fish on it with his good hand and squeezed a lemon over it with the two fingers he still had on his left hand.

"Thank God there's nothing I can't do with these two fingers. But it's like I said—I had a silver ring on that little finger that was passed down from my father. It went with the finger. I still grieve for it."

He shook his head and bit into the fish in his right hand.

Yardman Jevher spoke up. "You're right, Shakir. They call them hermaphrodites."

Everyone at the table looked over at him like he was crazy.

"I'm talking about the bream. Shakir knows. They're born both male and female. The Greeks call them hermaphrodites. He's Hermes and Aphrodite's son in Greek mythology. The water nymph Salamacis thought the boy was such a looker that she asked the gods that they never part, so they put their two bodies into one, both male and female. Breams are born male and turn into females."

"There's really no book this yardman hasn't read, Burak," Kemal Reis said.

"A ship's sails and the pages of a book bring a smart man wherever he pleases, Captain," Yardman Jevher said to Burak Reis. "The pages of a book start out white and blank like sails—it's man's smarts that give them meaning."

"I don't get this male or female thing, boys." Mahmud the Kurd said. "My compliments, Hard-Nose—this bream is so good I'd give an arm for it."

"Be careful there," Hard-Nose Ibrahim said. " If you lose an arm, you'll both be missing something and who'll fire the cannons?"

Piri stood up while everyone was laughing. "With your permission, I have some calculations I need to finish."

"See, this is what my nephew's like," Kemal Reis said. "He scarfs down his food and then runs back off to his maps. He does separate calculations in the day and night, then writes and writes in his log."

"It should be by maps during the day and the stars at night," Burak Reis said.

"Quite so, Burak. I've never gone astray after all these years thanks to him and this crew. God bless them all."

The men bowed their heads to their captain and repeated, "God bless you, too, captain."

"There's no way we can repay our debt to you," one said.

"Alright, Mr. Hard-Nose, sir. Pass out the fish and bread to the galley slaves. They must've smelled it and must be dying for it—they've got a right to eat, too," Kemal Reis said.

"Yes sir, Captain," Ibrahim said. He got up with his assistants and headed off for the galley slaves. The crews and galley slaves on Ottoman ships were always afforded the same meals. The oarsmen on European ships, however, were treated more like slaves, subsisting on only dry bread and water. The slaves on those ships were forced to be there whereas those on Ottoman ships were nearly there voluntarily.

The Blue Lion and Crescent of Victory were sailing abreast in the lead, followed by the Göke and Göke II and the galiots, the sun at their bows and with a favorable tailwind, speeding full-sail ahead. A dozen dolphins had joined the fleet, swimming alongside the ships as if in a race and playing off the bows, accompanying Kemal and Burak Reis' ships on the way. The fleet resembled a flock of birds from a distance, ready to take to the sky.

It crossed neither Kemal Reis nor Burak Reis' mind at that moment that in less than a week's time they would lose over half their ships and more than half their crews would be killed.

42

It was night.

An owl hooted off in the distance. A man was waiting in the darkness, hidden in a corner of the walls outside. He reached for his waist when he noticed the door of the tavern opening and knew the moment he'd been waiting for had come.

A jug of wine fell in front of the tavern and shattered to pieces.

Muayyedzade Abdurrahman was part of the group at the tavern with Prince Bayezid—the young governor of Amasya—and, having once again drunk too much wine, Abdurrahman was swerving around as he walked. He picked up the jug of wine in a stupor on his way out of the tavern but forgot he was holding it and let it crash to the ground outside. The prince had given up on his promise to Hamdullah, abandoning his lessons and dallying around with his mates in a tavern.

Half a dozen soldiers—the prince's palace guards—were following behind the group and keeping watch, but their eyes were heavy with sleep at the late hour. The guards wanted nothing more than to return to the villa as soon as possible, go to their quarters and turn in, but instead they were looking at each other annoyed as the prince and his friends slowly stumbled ahead.

"It's this tavern that's my bad fortune
—But there is not one equal to wine."

Hizirpashadaze Mahmud kept reciting couplets from some poet or another, stumbling around and yelling.

"It's not, *there's no equal to wine*," Hamzabeyzade Mustafa slurred. He was famous among his friends for his strong memory, even when, and despite, being very drunk. "It's, *there's nothing like wine*. Damn it Mahmud—you'd sell us anything if we didn't know better. The poem's full of mistakes."

"It's not that I don't know it, Mustafa, sir. It just sounds better my way."

They both stopped when they were talking and blinked slowly, then kept staggering off as if they'd forgotten what they were talking about.

If this had been a different group and not the prince and his friends, the city's judge would have given them a fitting punishment and made them think twice about disturbing the neighborhood the next day. Prince Bayezid didn't listen to reason anyway.

He stopped his friends and looked up at the sky.

"I once loved a graceful girl whose body was like the stars in that swan *Cygnus* "You're a prince, they said. Know your place, they said. One marries in one's station, they said."

His curiosity piqued, Abdurrahman asked, "Oh, my dear sir. If I were a prince, what I said would go—you said the word and you still couldn't give it to the little bird just one night?"

"My dignified father said one night of pleasure isn't preferable to a man's honor."

They all shouted out when they heard him refer to his father, "Long live the sultan!" half serious but also mocking—the soldiers, too, were obliged to join in.

"Look," Bayezid said, pointing to the constellation. "My swan's there." He put a hand on Abdurrahman's shoulder and pointed out the stars to the rest. They all looked up at where he was pointing. The soldiers also looked up at the sky.

The man biding his time in the darkness snatched at his opportunity.

He jumped behind the prince before the soldiers knew what was happening. He wrapped his left arm around Bayezid's head and held a dagger to his throat with his other hand.

"If anyone moves, I'll kill him!" he said, the certainty in his voice was unmistakable.

Everyone froze in place. One of the soldiers was slowly and gently moving his hand to his sword, but the assassin pressed the dagger softly into Bayezid's throat. He started bleeding from his neck.

"Don't mess with me!" he snapped. The soldier reaching for his sword took the warning and hung his hand back by his side.

No one could make out his features behind his hood to see what or whom he looked like.

The assassin dragged the prince back on his heels about fifteen or twenty steps from the group and backed up against a wall. He whispered in his hear so only the prince could hear.

"So, son of the khan, the great Sultan Mehmed the Conqueror—Bayezid son of Mehmed Forever Victorious. So is this how you prepare to become sultan?"

Bayezid swallowed the lump of fear in his throat. His heart was pounding and beads of sweat were pouring from his forehead.

"So that life you speak of, that holy war, that fight—is it in the corners of the tavern, then? Your life's over now as fast as you can blink. What do you have to say to the other side?"

Bayezid struggled to speak, "Who are you?"

"It's not important who I am. Know this, though. Let's say, I'm Khidr, or you can call me Azrael, you could say I'm the thief who doesn't plunder. Anybody could get you into the palm of their hand with you like this. It's not me that matters, but actually who you are. Who are you? What are you? Ask yourself that."

After he finished, he kicked Bayezid forward to the ground, turned the corner and disappeared into the darkness. The prince was on his knees with one hand on the ground and the other on his throat, trying to get over the shock. The soldiers quickly turned the corner and ran off into the darkness in pursuit, but there was no one to be found.

Bayezid's friends went running to his side and leaned over him, asking him if he was all right.

He waved all of them off. Abdurrahman and Mahmud looked at each other astounded and then back down at the prince on his knees.

The prince was staring at the ground and growing paler.

Nothing remained the same after this night.

Bayezid would realize only decades later after he had become sultan that this moment had been a turning point for him. It was going to change him forever.

43

A horse carriage came to a stop in front of David's workshop in the dark of night. De Silva's carriage would come to the workshop in the town of Montalban every Sunday night and then continue on to Toledo with a new load.

As always, David and Samuel quickly and carefully loaded cases onto the back of the cart from both sides. David knocked on the door of the carriage once to let the driver know he could go—but the cart didn't move. He rapped on the door a couple more times. The carriage still didn't move, and as Samuel walked toward the horses in front, David opened the door and Esther stuck her head out. She was the last person David had expected to see there.

"What're you doing here?" It was all he could say through his shock.

Esther's face was hard. "I didn't come willingly. My father sent me."

Samuel walked back to the carriage. "Come inside. We're being very careful, anybody could see at any time," he said, looking around.

David and Esther went into the workshop and sat facing each other beside the worktable.

Esther was angry. "I don't know what your carrying in these carts, but it seems to me you've put my father in a great deal of danger."

David didn't know what to say to this accusation and he hung his head.

"My father can't trust anyone anymore. He's quite different now after the *Alhambra Decree*, he doesn't say a word. Anyway, you're the only people he sees other that Isaac Abarbanel from the royal advisors."

Esther de Silva started looking around the shop at all the gold and silver jewelry and all the odds and ends lying around.

"That's why he sent me. Abarbanel's gone to the king and queen to talk with all that's in his power to do and get their decision. The king and queen will apparently propose the payment of a very large ransom. Señor Abarbanel is coming to my father tomorrow with the news." She looked back up at David. "My father's also asking for you to come. He says it's very important."

"Why didn't he send someone else with the news or tell the driver to tell me?"

"Like I said. He doesn't trust anyone anymore. He wanted me to tell you in person."

Esther saw a glinting piece of silver as she wandered around the workshop. She leaned over and picked up the metal bar, about as think as a little finger, and noticed a letter *aleph* on its end. She turned back to David. "What's this?"

David reckoned it was pointless to hide anything from her, even his most precious secret, since her father had sent his own daughter with a message. But he figured the less Esther knew the better, and had believed he'd kept her out of this dangerous work he'd been doing.

Esther walked back over to David. "What's this?"

"The first letter of your name."

"I see that, but what's it for?"

David stayed silent for a while, looking at Esther. Then he took a large key out of his pocket and put it in the recessed lock in the door in the back. He turned the key twice and the bolts slide open.

He cracked opened the door and called Esther over to his side, then showed her the workshop that was at least five times the size of the front shop. "This comes in handy," he said.

Esther was taken aback and brought her empty hand up to her mouth in amazement—there were thousands of pages and hundreds of books rising in front of her.

"Why didn't you tell me earlier?" Esther said, walking out of the back room. Her face had softened and was showing compassion, as if her earlier anger had melted away.

David came back into the front room and locked the door behind him.

"The fewer people know, the better—both for those who know and those who don't. It was for your own safety.

"So, does my mother know?"

David nodded. A look of light disappointment crossed over Esther's face. "Your father didn't want you involved with this."

"You still should've told me. But there's something more important." She took David's hand and looked up at him. His heart started racing. "I owe you an apology—a big one. Will you be able to forgive me?"

"There's nothing to forgive," David said, putting his hand to Esther's cheek.

"So, what'll happen now? You know, after the *Edict of Expulsion?*" Esther asked.

"I don't know. For now, we're keeping on working like nothing's happened. But it's best for you all—"

He didn't finish before Esther interrupted him, knowing what he was going to say. "Don't you say it. I was born Jewish and I'll die Jewish."

"I just mean for show, on the outside."

Samuel came up to the door from outside. "It would be good if you set off without attracting any attention in front of the door.

"He's right, you should be going, Esther."

"My father will be waiting for you on Friday," Esther said as she climbed into the coach. David closed the door behind her and the driver gave the horses a whip as they speedily set off on their way.

Esther looked at the shining, metal letter *aleph* in her hand.

44

Piri's eyes flashed as he looked up to the night sky and saw *Vega*—
he cracked a slight, confident smile. He was looking at one of the
brightest stars of summer, and at such moments he felt satisfaction,
serenity in his heart and an uplifting of his soul. He jotted down the
star's coordinates in his notebook and turned to speak to Orhan,
who had been watching him attentively.

"The Bedouins call it *Waqi* and in Latin it's *Vega*. The Arabs
for years found their way through the desert by the stars and they
likened this one to a diving eagle. The Europeans learned and got
the names for hundreds of stars from the Arabs, just as *an-Nasr
al-Waqi*—the Falling Eagle—became *Vega*. It's my uncle Kemal's favorite star." He turned his head back to the sky. "If you look closely
you can even see with the naked eye that it's different from the
other stars and has a bluish shine."

Orhan peered up at the star. "Oh yeah, it's really faint but it does
have a bluish tint to it, doesn't it."

He looked back over at Piri, who was holding his fingers up to
the sky. Piri was opening and closing his fingers, squinting with
one eye and looking with the other and then switching and making shapes with his hand as if he were casting shadow puppets. He
mumbled something after making each shape with his hand and
continued scribbling down notes in his book. Orhan could just

barely make out the numbers he was muttering. He liked looking up at the stars and taking them in, not Piri's calculations.

"What's that Orion Orhan?" Overseer Jihan yelled out, drawing out the name of the constellation of Orion. "S0 you're busy with the stars again with Piri and have forgotten to sleep. You'll definitely be seeing stars if I see you sleepy on deck tomorrow morning."

Ever since his first days working on the ship, Orhan was smitten with how Piri—the ship's first mate—read the stars as if they were a book, and would be at his side whenever he could, listening to the stories Piri explained as if they were sacred. Piri had told him about the constellation of Orion his first days on the ship, and he was so taken by it that nearly all winter, whether at sea or on dry land, he looked up at what he considered the season's, or even the year's, most splendid constellation. The ship's crew had long taken to calling him Orion Orhan.

"He's right," Piri said and smiled—he always smiled whenever he heard Orhan's nickname. It wasn't a bad one after all. "I still have quite a while to work. It'd be good for you if you go rest."

Orhan didn't pull his gaze away from the sky. "Alright, but I don't see an eagle or anything. I can't tell where the falling eagle is."

Piri started to go over the sky as if it were an oil painting. "So, there's *Draco*. Look, that there is what they call *Delphinus*. Oh, and this one is *Ursa Major*." Orhan always hoped he would see the patterns, the zoo in the heavens, every time he looked, but he was always disappointed—he could never make out a dragon, dolphin or bear.

"How many times do I have to tell you, Orhan? You give the shapes to the stars when you look up at the sky just like looking at clouds and seeing what they look like. The Greeks, Persians and Arabs have done the same thing for centuries, grouping what seem like meaningless clusters of stars into constellations and making them a lot easier to remember."

Orhan looked for the falling eagle of *Vega* again, taking in the nearby stars and trying to imagine the bird. There was no eagle, though, no matter how hard he tried. Months before he was able to make out the bear of *Ursa Major*, the snake of *Serpens* and even the hunter *Hercules*, but he couldn't see an eagle or any other animal in the constellation he was looking at now.

"Are you sure that both the Greeks and the Arabs called these stars an eagle?"

Piri stopped his calculations. "You're smarter than I expected, Orhan. Of course not—the Greeks call the constellation *Lyra*.

"That square-type musical instrument with strings?"

Piri nodded.

Orhan looked back up.

"All right, now I see it." He smiled. "I'd say the Arabs used their imagination a little too much to come up with an eagle. It's much more a lyre than an eagle."

Orhan looked back up at the constellation with pride as if he'd made an amazing discovery—*Vega*, *Waqi*, the *Falling Eagle*, *Lyra*. He could make sense of a little more of the night sky every time he looked after this, creating various stories in his mind about them and the stars illuminating the darkness bit by bit.

"Now I'll be able to go to sleep to the sound—no, the shining of *Lyra*," he said and headed off.

Kemal Reis came up to Piri and greeted his nephew as Orhan left.

"The kid's something, that Orhan," Piri said with a smile. "I should be afraid he'll take my job from me one day."

"It's obvious he's keen on it. But he's more interested in the fables and legends." Kemal Reis looked at the figures, triangles and cosine and tangent calculations on the sheets in front of Piri. "I've worked with a lot of first mates and mappers in my life, nephew. There's very few I've seen do calculations like you at such a young age. You produce a map of the sky from a single star and the latitudes and longitudes all at night."

"You're exaggerating, Uncle. I'm only standing on the shoulders of giants. I only use the findings of Ptolemy, al-Sufi and our master Ulugh Beg."

"There's no need to be modest, nephew. The whole of the Mediterranean knows of your talents already at your young age. I don't doubt it one day your name will be among those giants—man will know the earth and the sky better from your drawings."

Piri kept looking up at the sky and back at his book, making calculations as if he wasn't listening to his uncle at all. He didn't like this kind of praise—he never knew what to say.

"What do you say, Piri Pasha? How many days do we have until Sicily?"

"Three days, seven hours," Piri said without a pause.

"How can you be so sure?"

He looked over at his uncle, not understanding the question. "Are you really asking or are you testing me?"

The captain's voice was quite serious. "I'm really asking."

Although not very convinced, Piri started to quickly rattle off the explanation. He pointed at the moon. "The position of the moon gives the time of night, and I take the relative position of *Vega* and *Polaris* as proportional to the time of night. Then I find the longitude from our angle to *Polaris*. Then I compare the coordinates in Ulugh Beg's *Zinj-i Sultani* and the *Alfonsine Tables*. That gives exactly seventy-nine hours, forty-two minutes, which is roughly three days, seven hours. And of course, if we go at our average speed from over this past week—"

Kemal Reis looked proudly on his nephew.

"But uncle, don't make me explain what you already know, let me look to my work."

"What do you think the weather will be like?" Kemal Reis asked, turning to look off at the horizon.

"You're confusing me with the palace astrologer, Uncle," Piri said. "But according to the records, the water should be calm on the way to Sicily. Look how bright the sky is. I'll produce a map of the whole Milky Way if I have enough time."

Piri set aside his book again, composed himself and lowered his head. "It's not the weather you need to worry about, uncle, it's the Maltese knights."

Kemal Reis nodded dismally. It was without doubt that the Maltese knights would be one of the most dangerous groups to run across on this journey. The knights had taken up position on a magnificent piece of land between North Africa and Sicily, making it impossible to reach the northwest Mediterranean and Spain without running across them. The knights attacked everything on the sea save for Catholic ships and weren't content without capturing booty and prisoners. The captain was seriously concerned, but nonetheless turned to his nephew with a smile.

"You're confusing me with the janissary conscripts at the palace. *My* calculations tell me that the Maltese knights won't deter Kemal Reis."

45

Prince Bayezid had arrived at the mosque that bears his name before the morning call to prayer had sounded. His great, great grandfather Mehmed I had built the Bayezid Pasha Mosque a half-century earlier in the northeast of Amasya next to the Yeshilirmak River when he was the governor of the city. His special interest in the mosque was not because it bore his name, though. He would leave the palace when he was troubled and go the mosque as a commoner so as not to be recognized—the architecture, its location and the serenity he found within himself while he was there always fascinated him. Although it still wasn't all of this that affected him—there was something mystical about it that he couldn't name or put into words that drew him here.

He had come early in the morning this day before dawn. He had stopped before crossing a bridge that went over a small creek that ran off from the river.

Three days and three nights had passed since the attempt on his life. He had shut himself up in his room at the villa since that day and had nearly never left unless he had to. Apart from the one or two hours he would sleep, he would lay at night with his eyes wide open thinking about the past, the future and life.

And now, three days later, he was facing this mosque. He stepped onto the bridge and walked toward the mosque's courtyard full of flowers.

The mosque had one central dome surrounded by five smaller domes and had a colonnade leading to its entrance running east and west. A pair of arches supported each one of the successive rows of small domes. The mosque's extraordinary entrance was the first thing that captured Bayezid's admiration. The eastern and western gates to the entrance were done in the Andalusian style, surrounded by red and white marble arches. Above the arches supported on columns were red, geometric patters and the eaves were carved from stone into dazzling lacework. Nearly all of the walls were adorned with Andalusian style Arabesque patterns and geometric *Kufic* script. Bayezid felt as if he'd long ago lost his way amid the labyrinthine *Kufic* lettering of the arcade, but now reckoned he was approaching the exit.

A twelve-pointed star winked down at him from the ceiling under each small dome he passed beneath. He got goose bumps when he first set foot on the stone and felt a shiver in his soul.

He stopped in front of the door of the domed entrance adorned with muqarnas. There was a masterfully carved inscription about the mosque's architect and benefactor on the top of the wooden door just below a cupola carved into the wall. The walnut door had a fine elegance, carved with Quranic verses, stars and assorted geometric ornaments, inviting the faithful to enter.

The prince removed his shoes and set his right foot forth into the mosque. The fragrance, solemnity and calm inside penetrated deep into this spirit. He softly stepped on the green carpet and walked under the main arch rising above two marble columns and below the central dome and headed straight to the mihrab. The oil lamp hanging down from the ceiling was half-lit but was still enough to illuminate the interior. All the lamps hadn't yet been lit since the imam and muezzin still hadn't arrived, so the light was dim and somber.

The muqarnas of the mihrab were octagonal and dodecagonal with star-shaped figures. Bayezid kneeled at the far side of the minbar, far from its center. He bowed his head and breathed in deeply while he bent forward twice. He examined his life. The emptiness in him was slowly beginning to fill up.

He was ready. He was finding responses to the questions and hesitations he had. The discomfort that had been haunting him slowly began to disappear.

He lifted his head and read the large inscription of a verse written in polished *Thuluth* script.

And whoever does a wrong or wrongs himself but then seeks the forgiveness of God will find God forgiving and merciful.

He quickly remembered that it was the 110th verse of the *an-Nisah* surah. His father had praised him when he was a young child in Constantinople for becoming a hafiz—memorizing the Quran. This, however, was the first time in his life he thought this verse was meaningful. He read the verse again and again—it was as if it was the first time he had. He felt that the Yeshilirmak River just on the other side of the wall with the carved verse was washing him of all his sins. He prayed to *ar-Rahman* and *ar-Raheem*—the vastness of God's mercy and His mercy for His creation.

He closed his eyes and listened to the sound of the river.

Then he heard a noise behind his right shoulder. No one was ever at the mosque this early. He focused his attention and listened—he was sure he heard sobbing from beneath one of the domes on the western side.

He stood up on his left foot, turned around and headed to where the sound had come from. He hadn't been mistaken—there was a young man the same age as him, kneeling on the ground and sobbing below the windows at the back below the northwestern domes. The young man was also trying to quiet himself as if he was embarrassed of what he was doing, his head buried deep into his knees. He was working through the ninety-nine beads of his *tespih* in the palm of his hand with his thumb and forefinger.

As he approached the young man, Bayezid noticed he was repeating something amid his weeping—a name.

He waited by the young man, not knowing what to do.

He could hear now the name the young man was repeating—Elif. The man continued deliriously, his sobs burned and cut through the prince.

Bayezid was so quite that the young man on the ground hadn't noticed that someone was at his side. The man startled when the prince put his hand on his shoulder. He looked up at the prince with bloodshot eyes.

"Forgive me, brother," the prince said, still not able to find the words. "I wasn't expecting anybody else to be here."

"I'm the one who should apologize, Prince," the young man said, composing himself. I wasn't aware of how much noise I was making." He tried to stand up but Bayezid stopped him and knelt down beside him.

"How do you know who I am?" He was surprised—the man couldn't have seen his face clearly in the dim light. It was clear this tormented young man had a strong memory.

"Sir, I saw you with my father once in Constantinople at Topkapi Palace a year or two ago." He looked ahead, still kneeling and forcing his tears back.

Thoughts raced through Bayezid's head—this would mean this man was from a distinguished family, maybe the son of a vizier. What was he doing in Amasya, who was Elif, why was he here, alone, in such sorrow?

He wanted to ask the man so many questions, but it was apparent he didn't want to be disturbed. If it had been anyone else, they would've their hands on his feet incessantly supplicating themselves. It seemed more so, however, that this man was waiting for the prince to get up and leave him be.

"So, who are you?" Bayezid was finally able to ask, gently. If he could get an answer to this, he could get the rest later.

The young man didn't answer, rocking slightly back and forth, trying to soothe his pain. Bayezid only had more questions—what kind of pain is this, what kind of suffering, why was he here at this mosque and at this hour?

Bayezid was just about to lose hope and leave when he heard the man speak.

"Davud. My name is Davud son of Mahmud son of Muhammad."

The prince was going to listen to the man's story, invite him to the villa in Amasya and befriend him. He would become the empire's best spy in the years to come—it would be the cure for his sadness.

Now, however, it was Bayezid in need of a remedy, and he knew very well whom he needed to find.

The prince headed straight for Hamdullah the Calligrapher as soon as he left the mosque.

46

"There's no hope," Señor Abarbanel said, shaking his head.

Abraham de Silva was at the window of his grand house in Toledo's Jewish quarter and looking out at the Tagus River. It seemed to Abarbanel that the river, flowing swiftly to the south, was also carrying away the Jews from Spain.

De Silva was sitting on a carved wooden chair with dark blue cushions—an heirloom from his grandfather—listening to the painful news his old friend had come with. The shelves covering the wall behind where de Silva was sitting had blue on white Iznik pottery displayed on them. They'd all been brought from Asia Minor, from the land of the Grand Turk. Toledo's Jewish merchants had carefully selected this set—which de Silva used while entertaining guests—like so many of the other valuable goods from the east. A red Persian rug from Mamluk lands covered the floor and a Genoese glass vase stood on the large table in the middle of the room. All of the furniture in the room, like all the rest in the house, was covered in Venetian lacquer.

De Silva was slumped in his chair, devastated by what Abarbanel was saying, having waited out like the rest of the Jews with a last hope for him to bring good news.

"The queen is acting like she's completely lost her mind," Abarbanel continued. "She's even swept aside an offer of thirty thousand gold ducats. Torquemada has Isabella in the palm of his hand and plays her as he pleases."

De Silva's mouth was twisted as if he wasn't surprised by what he was hearing. "When you look at the material side, she wouldn't accept anything we offer, no matter how much, even though it's for her own benefit. If we were to convert, all of our assets would be under the shadow of the Inquisition." There was no accounting for the extent of how many houses or tax and land had been seized from Jewish converts to Catholicism in recent years. "But then if we don't agree to be baptized, we'll have to leave the country and all our property and possessions will be left to the kingdom or the Christians with royal favor. The thirty thousand pieces of gold we would give, and give dozens of times over, would be under their control in any case."

"There still must be a way," Abarbanel said. He couldn't fathom pulling up and leaving the land where he lived, where he was born and raised, the land of his ancestors that had seen the greatest Jewish golden age—no matter how hard he grappled with it, he couldn't accept it. The Abarbanel family was most likely the most rooted in all of Iberia. According to some, his family could even be traced back to King David. They had been prominent for centuries in Iberia—in Castile and Leon, in Seville, Cordoba and Toledo.

De Silva looked at his old friend, silent. There was nothing passing through his mind that Abarbanel hadn't also thought of. He finally spoke. "It's a disgrace for me to even think of such a thing. It'd be a disaster for all Jews if the Abarbanels were baptized."

"The de Silvas and Abarbanels must remain Jewish, Abraham."

De Silva was in thought, his eyes on the Iznik pottery on the shelf.

"I've lost you, old friend. What're you thinking?" Abarbanel asked.

"Sometimes I think—there're rumors that the Grand Turk is sending ships here. The chief rabbi in Constantinople is calling all Jews to the city—he must be thinking of our situation here."

"Hamon and Nassi hope to escape to Portugal, but I'm afraid that if this edict works in Spain, then all the kingdoms will take it up. That's why I think escaping isn't the solution. There must still be something that can be done." He knew as well as de Silva that what he was saying was nonsensical.

Esther and David kept talking in the kitchen while de Silva sadly showed out his guest. Esther was drying the dishes her mother was washing. At least three servants had worked in their house until the previous year, but now they had to do all the work themselves as the Inquisition had forbidden Jews to have servants. The Inquisition first decided that Christians couldn't be employed in Jewish homes, and when Jewish servants were brought in to replace the out-of-work Christians, Jews were banned from hiring any servants, and those who did would be punished.

Esther's mother Hannah de Silva left the kitchen to bring the dishes to the other room.

"Please, Esther," David implored from where he was sitting off to the side. "If you persuade your family, then you could be baptized just for show at the least."

"I'm not convinced—how am I supposed to convince them?" Esther snapped, still drying the dishes.

David looked out the kitchen window and tried to see who was coming and going on the street. He was anxious and restless. He thought for a moment that he'd seen Yehuda on the far side of the street, but wasn't quite sure.

"Look at yourself," Esther said. "You can't even stand up out of your fear. You're scared to death that the Inquisition will find you with Jews and know that you're still Jewish. Is this the life you want for us, too?"

"So what'll happen when the month's up? What're you all going to do?"

"I don't know. My father says we'll survive this hardship somehow. He says that Jews have overcome many troubles in the last hundred years and that every king has issued similar decrees but that none of them are ever implemented properly. He thinks that's how it'll be here, too, after the drunkenness of victory over the fall of Granada dies down. If the decree stays, then we'll need to wear patches that show we're Jewish."

As Spain had gradually passed into Christian hands, some kings had required Jews to wear a yellow star or circle sewn onto the breasts of their clothing. The rule was sometimes applied and sometimes forgotten altogether according to the whims and characteristics of the kings.

"Thousands of people are already beginning to flock to the harbors on the southern coast. You think these people are running away for nothing?" David said. He thought about what the Turk who had visited the previous day in Montalban had said. "They've even started to baptize people by force in Seville. It's all very serious this time, Esther."

"Please. Enough already, really." Esther's nerves were well worn out as she dried the dishes, so much so that she dropped the plate in her hands when a knock came at the door.

"Open the door! In the name of Jesus Christ, open this door at once!"

A large beam started pounding on the door as the shards of the plate spread over the floor. Esther, David and de Silva were all terrified and showing it.

The Inquisition guards broke the lock with a battering ram and flung open the door before anyone inside could get there. The guards stepped to the side and revealed Cardinal Cisneros. He looked straight at Esther who stood with her mouth agape in the kitchen.

Half a dozen Inquisition guards and knights poured in after Cisneros—knights of Santa Hermandad were among them. Cisneros' personal knight stood out from the rest due to his elite armor and cloak. He went straight over to de Silva as if he'd been ordered to do so. The guards and knights had surrounded everyone in the house, with nearly two soldiers for every one of them. The cardinal walked around the large room and approached de Silva with a challenging air.

"I said I would settle with you later."

De Silva had no chance to rise from his seat and was still sitting, now with swords drawn on him.

Cisneros slapped him across the face with the back of his hand when de Silva opened his mouth, before he had a chance to say anything. The thick, bejeweled ring on Cisneros' finger split open the old man's lip and blood dribbled into his white beard.

"Quiet you cur! Your lies don't trick me. I know what cases move in this house and I know you're hiding someone."

Cisneros ordered his men to search all the floors of the house and then walked over to Esther in the kitchen. She was standing stiff in the middle of the kitchen as if she'd just seen a ghost. Cisneros ogled her red lips, round breasts and thin waist. He put his face close to hers and started running his fingers over her face and lips. Esther slapped his face hard enough to leave behind a handprint. Cisneros flew into a rage and grabbed her by the throat "Heretic—I'll show you!" he bellowed.

Yehuda came up from behind. "This wasn't our agreement. You were going to let the girl and her father go."

Cisneros turned around. "You imbecile. Who do you think you're dealing with? Do you have the power to bargain with God?"

A sword was drawn to his neck before Yehuda had a chance to respond.

Cisneros turned back to Esther. He was going to give the impudent girl a lesson right there. As he had done with so many witches before, holy water would burn the belly of the Devil. Cisneros believed his own seed was sacred. This was a mercy he would show to cleanse heretical women.

He lightly pushed closed the door behind him, grabbed Esther by the throat and spun her around. He bent her over the table and lifted her skirt, groping at her undergarments.

David had hidden in the pantry, but couldn't stand it any longer—he burst out through the door and vengefully grabbed the man by the throat with both hands. He pushed the cardinal back onto the counter full of plates and bowls, tightening his grip on his throat as much as he could. Cisneros' face was starting to turn purple—but with the sound of breaking plates and pots crashing to the floor, it didn't take long for two guards to rush in and pull David off the cardinal.

"You're all going to die!" cried Cisneros. He was bent forward holding his throat and coughing to one side. "No, no. I won't kill you—I'll burn you slowly. You'll be begging me to kill you!"

Everything was over for the de Silva family and David. Becoming Catholic wouldn't even save them now.

47

Davud approached the guard waiting at the door and punched him hard in the neck right wear it was left open between his helmet and his armor. A blow to the nerves just below the ear and above the carotid artery interrupts the blood flow to the brain and makes a person lose their equilibrium. This spot is as small at the point of a needle and needs to be struck perfectly to be effective, but Davud knew the spot well from his years of experience. The man's eyes went black as he teetered on his feet and dropped his sword. The monk caught hold of him before he hit the ground.

Before the guards knew who it was who had just suddenly entered the house, he elbowed one and took his sword, sent the man next to him crashing against the wall with a kick and thrust his sword into the belly of another, sending him tumbling to the ground. The people in the house, the guards and Cisneros most of all stood for a second staring bewildered at this warrior monk. Nobody knew who he was other than David.

The soldiers rushed Davud as soon as they shook off their initial shock. The first to come slashed across at his head, but missed as Davud ducked and stabbed him in the waist. He parried off a blow from the left from another and pushed the man back, crossing back with his sword and slashing the man's throat, then turning around at the last moment and sinking his sword into a knight's face before he had a chance to attack. The man fell back into a glass cabinet and sent all the pottery crashing to the floor.

The knight who'd been standing next to Abraham de Silva could tell that this man was a master swordsman from his first movements, striking back and forth like a viper with a speed he could barely make out. With his men falling to the ground amid shrieks and screams, the knight took his ax from his waist with his left hand and his sword in his right and came at the monk.

Davud reckoned this man was no novice as the knight took his guard and his first ax strike tore through the left sleeve of his cassock. If he hadn't darted to the side when he did, his arm would be lying on the ground. Davud's first blow struck the knight in the shoulder, but had no affect as two layers of armor covered all the knight's joints and vulnerable areas. Taking the opportunity before Davud could take his guard again, the knight swung his ax overhand down toward Davud's head. The monk threw himself to the floor to evade the blow and the ax plunged into the dining table and split it in two. Davud knew his sword wouldn't be any match for the knight's armor. He swung his sword once again at his foe, but the knight fended it off and broke it in half with his ax.

David, Esther and the rest of the de Silva family thinking that this was a miracle was short-lived—even Yehuda looked worried. Cisneros grinned and waited for the knight to make the final blow.

With full confidence now that the monk's weapon was broken, the knight quickly struck with his sword at Davud's head. Davud saw and took his chance—he bent low and shot toward the knight, stabbing what was left of his broken sword into the man's armor over his heart.

David was quite aware that a broken, steel edge was sharper than even the world's finest blade—it was just the nature of steel.

Cisneros fled the house, not looking back once.

As the knight fell to the floor in spurts of blood, Davud looked over at David from where he stood amid the dozen of guards he'd cut down and asked, panting for breath, "So, you still set on not going?"

48

"Where're we going, Hamdullah, sir?" Prince Bayezid asked again.

The two had been walking through the streets of Amasya in the dim early hours for half an hour after the morning prayer.

"You'll understand when you see. It's not much farther."

Bayezid wasn't even certain if he'd come to this part of the city before. He had no idea. He had no other choice but to follow the calligrapher, though, come what may. The prince had come up to the calligrapher the day before while he was writing and, standing straight, said, "I'm ready. Teach me how to write. Teach me how to wash my soul with pen and ink."

Hamdullah had lifted his head. "I have one condition."

The prince had never been bound by any conditions his entire life, or had always run from them—he'd been the one giving orders. But he nodded in assent.

What the sheikh then said cut him like a knife.

"The one sitting across from me is not a prince, but a pupil, an apprentice. Like every apprentice, you will not talk back to your master and you will not make me say something twice."

Bayezid was relieved when he heard this, having expected something tougher.

"I'm under your command."

"Good, then," Hamdullah said as he turned back to his writing. "Go today and come back tomorrow."

Now tagging along behind Hamdullah after the morning prayer, Bayezid thought maybe it wasn't such a good idea to have accepted the man's condition. He hadn't the slightest idea where they were going and, climbing up a hill, the prince was thoroughly confused. He was amazed by the man who was at the very least fifteen years his senior never stopping to take a break while climbing the steep slope that rose in front of them—more a wrestler than a calligrapher.

Hamdullah stopped as if they'd arrived at where they were going.

"In order to be brought back from the dead, one must die first."

"But I am alive!" Bayezid said.

Hamdullah smirked. 'You've been the deadest of the dead."

He went to the right and opened a door made of three timbers in the middle of a fence that surrounded a large enclosure.

Bayezid was surprised when he saw what was behind the fence—hundreds of tombstones rising up from the rolling hill in front of him.

Hamdullah brought him over to one of them. The prince thought maybe he was going to pray for some deceased relative.

"This is our first lesson," said Hamdullah. "One who doesn't understand death can't understand life. There are no favorable winds to a captain who doesn't know where he's heading. As of tomorrow, you'll come to this cemetery every day after morning prayers, you will go to forty stones and commit the names to memory and you'll recite the Quran's *al-Fatiha* to those forty people."

Still not over his initial shock, Bayezid was frozen after hearing this.

"But—" he said before Hamdullah went on.

"Don't interrupt me again. Follow behind me and keep listening."

Having no other option, the prince shut his mouth and went behind Hamdullah. The calligrapher meandered between the gravestones.

"What you say is writing is memory, dear Prince. Writing is many things, in fact, but we'll call it memory at first— then destiny, then providence, then resurrection. Now, you think there are a thousand six hundred dead in this cemetery. If you don't think, you need to. Forty deceased per day in forty days would be how many? One thousand six hundred dead. Let me tell you the answer now. Here it is. You'll ask later how I know. There're at least five hundred stones here. That's wrong. There are a thousand nine hundred tombstones here, dear Prince. I'm not even counting the six hundred ninety-eight whose inscriptions can't be read any longer, or the ones that have crumbled, or the ones that are now under other stones."

It was like Hamdullah was reading from a book, listing off all the figures, but he was speaking fluidly with no pauses.

"Writing is a reflection of memory on paper. If your memory is no good, is it because of what you wrote? A calligrapher's memory is like nothing else. If you twist a letter, so too will you be twisted. It doesn't stop at that—you twist the sentence, the universe. Oh my dear, you make a letter like that, what will come from it? And if you say you'll start fooling around again in life—have you begun to see that mistake correctly, that there's no benefit from that letter or from that life? You're a prince, son of the sultan and in line for the throne. You're memory should be better than everyone's and your letters should pursue a greater truth than everybody else's."

The prince stayed silent but realized as he listened that he was taking everything in more keenly and with more trust. It also wasn't that he waivered in finding himself with good fortune to rediscover his life in a center of death.

It seemed like Hamdullah could tell what he was thinking.

"One who does not know death cannot know life, dear Prince. The fate of both man and society is in this dirt. He who doesn't know the dead won't understand the living."

Hamdullah and Bayezid wound their way carefully between the gravestones.

"Look," Hamdullah said, stopping in front of a stone about three feet tall. "Look at this *elif*." Hamdullah pointed at the tremendous *elif* that covered nearly the entire inscription on the stone. "This might be the most beautiful thing that can be carved in stone—a flawless *elif* in *Thuluth* script. It's the unity of existence—Allah, Ahmed, all the children of Adam—it's the sultan of the letters. I don't think there's another letter that explains so much, or maybe everything. It's clear that the man lying here was a master of his trade. The style of the turban on top of the stone also shows this."

Hamdullah opened his hands to the sky as he read the inscription on the stone, the Fatiha for the soul. Bayezid followed.

Hamdullah took two more steps and stopped in front of another stone and read the inscription on it.

"*Relinquishing and leaving this ephemeral world, no fame and station were left to this gentle body ruined by the will of the universe, and falling into hopeless illness, there was no remedy*—Pity. God rest her soul. It's clear this girl died from sickness at a very young age."

"How do you know it's a girl?"

"The gravestone's triangular and there's no man's headpiece." Hamdullah continued as if Bayezid had asked another question. "One who doesn't know the identity of the dead is incapable of knowing the living."

The two recited one Fatiha and moved along on their way.

"The best place to understand what has happened in life on earth is a cemetery. These inscriptions explain what has happened in life quite seriously."

Hamdullah put his hand up to a stone and wiped away the accumulated dust and dirt from between the letters.

"Look closely at this one, for example. *I never found any comfort in this life. I grew old and grey and that's how I passed away. Let those who are wise learn this lesson from me.*"

Then he read the next stone. "*I passed at the age of forty-three, leaving at home without having my fill of my princess, my daughter, my husband and my friends.* One never gets enough of the world. Don't expect to be satisfied. If you always stay hungry, maybe then you'll have your fill of the world inasmuch as man is condemned to hunger as long as he breathes."

The two wandered around the cemetery, stopping in front of gravestones and reading their inscriptions, trying to get to know and imagine the lives of those buried beneath them before reciting the Fatiha for each and moving on to the next.

Hamdullah pointed out a stone with a letter *kef* at the top that was nearly as high as his chin.

"This is a solder's grave. Since *kef* has the meaning of a company, they put it before the number of the janissary battalions. The anchor next to the number shows that this man was a sailor. Think— who knows what vast seas this man sailed or which sunlit horizon he chased. Maybe the day came when he thought he was the sole ruler of the seas. But now he lies under this stone you see here. God is so gracious that He is a giant garden of paradise from the islands where the soul is conquered."

"So, what's the meaning of this *lam-elif?*" the prince asked, pointing at the carving on the headpiece of the stone next to him—a beautifully carved *lam-elif* on the front of the turban.

"They call that the *lam-elif* turban, Prince. It's *'ilaha 'illa'llah— there is no god but God.* Some people tie it to their turbans like that while they're alive. They reckon they wear a shroud on their heads so they think about death every day, every moment, and don't forget about the fleetingness of life. When unwound it's a shroud and when wrapped it's a turban. Have you ever carried death on your head, dear Prince? Have you walked with death? God make this wise man's place in heaven."

Prince Bayezid would understand coming here over the course of forty days what life is and what its purpose should be, seeing the death in every life he memorized and finding the secrets in the inscriptions. The prince first committed the inscriptions on the stones to his mind and then his heart, and gained new meaning for life and what is with death and life together. The tombstones would speak to him and he would understand the Creator much better.

God was *Alive, the Forgiving, the Compassionate, the Merciful* and *the Restorer. The world was evil, unfaithful, not a place of pleasure, a place with no order, a warning. The dead want the Fatiha, they want intercession, they plead for their offences to be forgiven and for mercy. Man was not satisfied with his youth, couldn't see the loyalty of the world and no one interred was comfortable. Rosebuds wither and never-sinking ships cast their anchors to the seafloor.* Here, Bayezid saw turbans of grand viziers, the conical hats of the Mevlevi order, the ceremonial turbans of viziers, the hats of other orders, swords, flags, fish, birds, ships, anchors and beautiful women's headdresses. A few times he saw stones in the shape of a veil and wept—the graves of women who died right before they married. He would get to know pashas, aghas, gentlemen, master teachers, viziers, governors, gardeners and madrasah instructors—all of them now lying beneath a stone and covered with dirt, all of them dead.

"Take a look at this cabbage," Hamdullah said, smiling next to a gravestone with cabbage carved at its top and base.

Bayezid had seen this before but had no idea of its meaning, if there was one.

"These are our master javelin infantry from Amasya. We call them the cabbage men since the cabbage here is famous."

Hamdullah had turned off to another stone while Bayezid was reading the inscription and the prince heard him take a deep sigh. He looked behind him and saw Hamdullah in front of a stone with a pen and inkpot carved at the top of the inscription—obviously the grave of a master calligrapher. Bayezid started to quietly recite the *Fatiha.*

Hamdullah dug out a rock from the base of a cypress next to the grave, and to Bayezid's astonishment pulled out two reed pens.

"Reeds that have been buried write well—they're strong. See, Prince? Even a pen finds itself after being buried. This is really where life starts."

The prince would understood the same thing over and over again with every inscription and line of *Thuluth* script he memorized, every image etched into his mind—not only an understanding, but a feeling in his spirit with his mind and heart engaged with the same truth. Then, while his memory strengthened and reinforced his practice, Hamdullah's true target would slowly but strongly be realized without Bayezid even noticing, with the prince's heart and spirit pulling away the curtain of the hereafter. Prince Bayezid would come to know the sanctity of writing and the might of letters in this cemetery. The truth that had been carved in hundreds of inscription around him was also carved letter by letter in his heart. Bayezid would be reborn in this cemetery and his addictions and false pleasures of not so long ago would be replaced by real love and truth—the truth that is written on every tombstone—*Huve 'l-baki—God alone is eternal.*

49

Davud ran up to David from behind and flattened himself to the ground as soon as he saw the two-dozen knights of Santa Herman-dad three hundred yards off. David was terrified when he saw them on the slope of the mountain and was petrified in place. Davud grabbed his leg and pulled him to his side. David and Davud were coming to get the printing press from Montalban in the wake of the fight in the Jewish quarter of Toledo after the ruckus had calmed down.

They realized something had gone wrong when they saw two rising plumes of smoke near the town. They had split off from the main route and were approaching from the back of the house and workshop. David had jumped off his mule and come running when he realized the smoke was coming from his land and was now watching from a hillside the terrible scene that was unfolding in front of him.

Black smoke and flames played in his eyes and he could barely speak. "This is barbarity!"

The Inquisition guards and knights of Santa Hermandad under Cardinal Cisneros' charge had already set the house ablaze and were now setting flame to the piles of books and bundles of paper they had taken from the workshop. The guards came out with armloads of books and tossed the gleaming white pages into the flames.

His eyes were bloodshot and David wanted to run and take revenge on a knight at the very least—he would risk also burning in the same glowing flames. He was getting ready to run when he felt Davud slam down on his shoulders with the force of a lion and he couldn't move.

"It won't help anything."

"Let me go. Please." David was crying. "Please, let me go. I'm going!"

There was no chance of Davud releasing his grip.

"Think of Esther."

David calmed slightly hearing Esther's name and put his head back down.

Four Inquisition guards were laboring to carry the printing press out of the door of the destroyed workshop. Even with each one holding one side of the wooden contraption it was still much more difficult than they'd expected.

When the printing press was finally outside, one of the knights took his ax from his waist and plunged it into one of its middle boards. The plank didn't split, but the ax left a gaping crack in the middle. The knight hacked at it again and sent the press splintering in two. Then another knight and a guard came holding hatchets. They took their places on two sides of the printing press and hacked the boards to pieces— the flames of the nearby fire growing ever taller as they threw in the splintered boards.

The last few guards came out of the workshop with the inkpads, printing plate and composition sticks and threw them on the fire.

Davud saw that Cardinal Cisneros had kept and was holding some of the pages as examples. The cardinal was holding the pages up to the sun like he was looking for a marker in the empty spaces. A smile spread across his face as if he'd found what he was looking for. Davud could guess what it was.

"How could they have found out about this place?" Davud asked.

David was distraught and shaking his head. "I don't know."

Then he saw a boy sitting in Cisneros' carriage, his hands bound and face covered with blood.

"I know that boy." The words fell from David's mouth. He pounded his fist on his forehead. "He's Abdullah—Abdullah of Xativa's apprentice."

It was clear the boy had been made to talk. David thought of what could have happened to Abdullah.

The last Inquisition guard to leave the workshop was holding a printing plate full of type and emptied into the fire.

A letter fell in front of Cisneros and he bent down to throw it into the fire. The nearby flames had heated it up and it burned his fingers as he flung it into the blaze. When he pulled his hand away, he saw that the metal letter had burned into his skin. The *aleph* started to blacken in the fire and then melt away, disappearing like the hundreds of Arabic and Hebrew letters in the fire.

50

Davud raised his head from the letter he was holding and looked at the gigantic castle in front of him. He was thinking this wouldn't be easy—Alcazar Castle on the highest point above Toledo. After the destruction of the printing press in Montalban, David and Davud went off to rescue Abdullah and learned when they went to his shop in Toledo that Inquisition guards had hauled the poor man off and were holding him in Alcazar Castle.

"Are you sure you want to come?" Davud asked David. "We might not be able to get out of this."

"I owe Abdullah this. I brought this on him."

He raised his head as he spoke and looked over the Alcazar's towering height. The magnificent castle, with six floors and dungeons underground, completely surrounded a central, rectangular courtyard. High towers rose above each of its four corners, and from where Davud and David stood, it looked to be protected by knights in the towers and under the watch of all the soldiers in Toledo. Davud knew there wasn't much left of what the Muslims who built the Alcazar—perhaps the largest structure in all of the Kingdom of Castile.

"So you say this letter will help?" David asked.

"It has to. We don't have any other chance. Anyone can see that even an army couldn't capture this castle. There're ordinary guards on the first floor, royal guards on the second floor, Inquisition guards on the third and Knights of Santiago on the fourth and upper floors. Only Alfonso knows which prisoner is in which dungeon.

"Who's Alfonso?"

"Alfonso is the Alcazar's chief commander. There's something they say about the people who live here—that their one pleasure is using a sword and also—"

"And what?"

"And chess."

"How do you know so much about the Alcazar? I've lived nearly my whole life in Toledo, but I don't know any of these things about this place."

Davud smiled. "If you spent five months in its dungeons you would've learned, too."

Davud had already come up to the castle's main gates before David could even ask him when and how this all happened. He fell in behind Davud.

Alcazar Chief Commander Alfonso was sitting in a room on the sixth floor in between the northeast and northwest towers, stroking his pointy beard and looking at the game board where he was seated. The lines at the edge of the eyes of the commander, who was in his forties, weren't from age, but rather from the many hours of thinking he had done while playing this game, as he was doing now. He was wearing a black cape lined in red with a dueling sword on each side of his belt, one with a hilt of gold and the other silver, and long-toed, goatskin shoes. The armored knights around were pacing, clearly bored from watching the game.

The prisoner across from Alfonso was shackled around the wrists with thick irons—his hand shaking, he moved one of his last three pawns forward. The dirt under the man's fingernails might have drawn attention, but this shame was the last thing the man in a ragged, burlap tunic was worried about. Three guards stood at the ready beside him even though he could barely muster the strength to pick up the marble pieces.

Alfonso countered the prisoner's move and sighed. "I really thought it would be this time. I reckoned I'd found a worthy opponent. Don't expect anything."

With the movement of the pawn before, he slid his bishop through the open space across the black squares.

"Check and mate."

The guards abruptly grabbed the prisoner's arms and hauled him up to throw him back in the dungeon.

"But sir, give me another chance, I beg you!" he cried as they dragged him out.

Alfonso stood up and walked over to a big window and sighed again from boredom while looking out at the courtyard below the tower.

A guard came in and greeted him while he was standing there.

"Sir, there's a monk. He's brought a letter from Seville."

He handed the letter to Alfonso. Over the last half hour it had been examined once on each of the six floors.

The commander read the letter carefully. "Show him in."

In between six knights, the monk and David bowed their heads in greeting to Alfonso standing at the table.

Alfonso looked over the two men carefully—the monk's brown cloak and rope around his waist and the simple jacket and breeches on the man next to him. He looked over the monk again.

"How long has the Suprema been working with Franciscan monks?"

"Nearly all of the Dominican priests are engaged in Granada," Davud said coolly. "You would appreciate that they have much work to do. The Holy Church utilizes all types of labor."

This answer didn't seem to convince Alfonso much. He pointed over at David. "So, who's this man?"

"He's a guide for me on my travels. We need to take a prisoner safely to Seville."

Alfonso walked around to the front of the table and approached the monk and his aide quite closely. He clasped his hands behind his back and shoved out his chest, looking carefully at them. He motioned over to David with his head.

"He doesn't look like a soldier at all. And what's more, he has a Santa Hermandad sword but not the armor.

David thought about what Davud had told him—that no matter what, he mustn't get nervous or excited.

"The Jews prepare themselves and hide when they see us. Some of us decided to travel in daily clothing after the *Alhambra Decree*."

Alfonso looked David in the eyes. The slightest sense of faltering in his eyes or halting in his speech could have been enough for the commander to have the two tossed into the dungeon.

Alfonso turned his back and walked back to his table, unrolling the letter again and scrutinizing it for a second time. He ran his thumb over the raised seal of the Suprema at the bottom. Davud had prepared the false letter and its text himself using his mastery of handwriting techniques.

"This prisoner was just brought here. Why is Seville so interested in this Abdullah?"

"The authority of the Suprema is taken from the king and queen themselves, you must appreciate," Davud said. "We, however, only perform the task we're given. It falls on neither you nor me to question." There was a light, threating tone to his voice. Davud knew that Alfonso wouldn't want to run counter to and anger the Suprema. It was also widespread practice for the Suprema to bring the most important prisoners from around the country as they pleased to the center in Seville where they were questioned and their punishments meted out.

"Impossible," Alfonso said.

This was the last response Davud had been expecting. David was breaking out in a cold sweat and gulped.

"There's something about this that doesn't still well with me. I won't allow you to take this prisoner."

If Alfonso had learned one thing in his near lifetime of service at the Alcazar—other than playing chess—it was that he had to trust his instincts.

"I hope you know this is in contradiction of the laws of the Suprema," Davud said. "My superiors in Seville won't be pleased with your response."

Alfonso looked up. "Go then and complain. Now go before I lock you two up as well."

Davud caught sight of the chessboard in the middle of the room. Two of the guards came over to them and opened the door.

"Alright," Davud said. "Let's come to an agreement." He pointed at the chessboard. "Let's play a game."

Alfonso waived off the guards and Davud continued his proposal.

"If I win, you'll heed the Suprema's order and the prisoner will be ours."

This bold offer piqued Commander Alfonso's interest.

"So what if I win?"

Davud looked over at the sword at David's waist. "The Santa Hermandad sword is yours—and we'll be your prisoners."

David looked over at Davud, astonished. He couldn't believe what was coming out of this madman's mouth.

Alfonso smiled with glee. Maybe he would finally find a worthy match.

"It's a deal!"

"How did you know he'd keep his word," David asked as he, Davud and Abdullah hurried toward the house where Esther and the others were hiding.

Abdullah kept on rubbing his wrists that had just a short time ago been freed from their shackles. He had been hopelessly waiting to die, and being saved from the Alcazar by a monk was the last thing he'd have imagined.

"Alfonso is grim, hard and cruel," Davud said, "and a host of many other things, but he's fair. He would never want such a stigma."

"It's unbelievable," David said. He'd been confused about it for the past day. He had trouble figuring out what he believed anymore. "And what if you lost?"

Davud had been hard pressed for more than an hour during the game and it wasn't until the final moment that it was clear who would come out on top. Alfonso didn't understand where his opponent's final move came from and Davud checkmated him with a knight, but he was more than happy to play against somebody who could best him after so many years.

"In that case, we'd be in the dungeon making our own chess pieces."

Next in line was the papermaker, Zayd ibn Uthman. They had to find Zayd before the Inquisition did, otherwise it would be too late for anything.

BOOK FOUR
Dream and Reality

Mundus Imaginalis

According to what was written, there were not many people at the funeral of the great ibd Rushd in Cordoba—the commentator, Averroes. Doctor Maximus was thirty-three years old then and watched the noteworthy scene in silence—they'd slung the books the philosopher wrote from one side of a mule to balance his coffin on the other side.

Death and books, pages bearing a corpse, a body carried by the books written by a great mind, dried ink balancing clotted blood, yellowed pages opposite a pallid body.

It's said Doctor Maximus turned to the people next to him and said, Here is the imam and his works. How much would I like to know whether his hopes came to be or not.

I leraned this story about who the Arabs call ibn Arabi and Shaykh al-Akbar—the Greatest Master—who they call Doctor Maximus in Latin, long after my first encounter with him in the texts. It's strange that like this story, the first text from ibn Arabi's hand was also about death, or more correctly, a metaphor for death.

We continued our routine book hunting in Seville, or Ishbiliya as the Arabs call it. We collected books in Arabic, Hebrew and Latin that deviated from our Lord Jesus Christ and spread slander. Then we sorted through them in one of the monasteries in the city and burned the ones that needed to be destroyed. While I was sorting the books, a ten to fifteen page treatise fell out from the pages of a Latin Bible as I leafed through it.

I started to read the Hebrew text that I knew right away was the work of a printing press, that Devil's plaything. It was from the same press, too. This booklet, bearing the title The Message of Moses, described things about the prophet of the Jews that I'd never heard before, putting in order the essence of the wisdom of Moses. I devoured the whole thing as if a guide from beyond this world was sharing secret knowledge with me and inducing insight. After I'd read it over many times, I realized I had missed many aspects when I read it the first time. Then I read it again and again. Even after months, what was said in the tractate continued to resonate in my mind.

The baby Moses was dead in the symbolic coffin in which he was left in the water. The wooden case he was placed in represented a coffin. The body inside was his corpse. The water the coffin was placed in symbolizes being, life and the world of creation. Thereby the corpse rejoins spirit, matter converges with meaning, the external with the internal, and earth with water. It was this water that gave Moses such profound enlightenment. One must also search for the profundity in his name. In the Coptic language, mou means water and she means wood—that is, his name gives what is found in Moses, or Moshe as the Jews call him—and this wisdom, or more accurately, the trace of Absolute Mastery he shaped, continued throughout his life. It was Moses who tapped water from the soil with a piece of wood, who turned his staff into a living creature and who split an enormous sea and commanded the waters. He is host to much secret knowledge of nature, of water and earth. Only those who reach this secret distinction can understand the mystery of seeing God as water's contrast to fire.

God directs creation with creation—so it directs itself by means of Him. Just as the existence of a child is dependent on the existence of a father and is bound to the causes responsible and definite reality, so is the world of existence directed by the world of creation. This is the Providence of the Lord God.

At this point, many questions about ibn Rushd's thinking were poking at my mind again. Ibn Arabi seems to respond to ibn Rushd, who he'd visited as a child, from a different point of view—about whether many

metaphysical matters such as whether God's way of reason and logic can
be found as the cause for the existence of the cosmos and whether rational
thought can provide answers to divine topics.

After coming across these two interesting men in Cordoba, I found in
my hands and read Shaykh al-Akbar's masterpiece in thirty-seven volumes, al-Futuhat al-Makkiyya—The Mecca Illuminations—written in his
own hand. I read Mashahid al-Asrar—Contemplation of the Holy Mys-
teries—and Mishkat al-Anwar, or Divine Sayings, a collection of hadith
qudsi of the Muhammadan's prophet, all with the same enthusiasm. I was
also astonished to see that there was no doubt that for his Divine Comedy,
Dante had drawn from the works of ibn Arabi and his Sufi counterparts
such as al-Ma'arri, on the metaphysical power in these books, their universal vision and hidden meaning in the material.

Ibn Rushd, who was a qadi in Cordoba at the time, had wanted to
see the young ibn Arabi, who had begun to have interesting dreams and
visions of things since his childhood that even the master scholars couldn't
notice, and to grasp the secrets of the world and divine order. When the
two met, ibn Rushd stood up and embraced ibn Arabi in a show of love
and respect. Then he straight off asked, Yes?—and the young ibn Arabi
responded, Yes. Ibn Rushd was pleased and his eyes sparkled, believing
that he understood ibn Arabi. But as soon as ibn Arabi saw that the great
philosopher was pleased by the wrong thing and misunderstood him, he
said, No. Averroes was annoyed with this, his color changed and he asked
more openly, How did you find divine enlightenment with exploration—is
it the same thing that we learned of the way of reason that our minds give
us? Ibn Arabi then said, Yes, no. Between yes and no is where the spirit
flies from matter and the mind from the body. With this, ibn Rushd was
thunderstruck, his face went pale and he began to shake.

I read every single of ibn Arabi's books I found so I could understand
this answer of yes and no. Between these two propositions of positive and
negative, I tried to discern in the thousands of pages I read secretly at the
monastery how the spirit breaks away from the material and in what
meaning the mind is released from the body. What I had to overcome,
however, was not the mind, but the heart. Continuing from the treatise

on Moses that I first came across, I persisted in learning about the other prophets from what I could find. I seized books in my searches of the libraries of Cordoba, Seville and Toledo.

A treatise just as short and dense on the divine wisdom of the miracles of Jesus Christ pushed me much harder to understand what is said about Christianity and other religions.

Jesus had come into this world when God assumed human form through Gabriel before Mary and blew from his spirit into the pure and immaculate virgin. Jesus Christ is the only being in history to have descended to earth in this way. The power to create from nothing is God's alone and it's the part of His spirit in Jesus that gave our Savior the ability to rise from the dead, make the blind see, heal the sick and make a living bird out of clay.

What's striking is that ibn Arabi says that some of those who have attained this secret knowledge can themselves perform these miracles of the prophets. It brings to mind Bayazid Bastami, a Muslim saint who once accidentally stepped on and killed an ant but brought it back to life with his breath. He says that Bayazid Bastami knows very well whose breath he blew and that he is a successor to Jesus.

Ultimately, man was not created in the image of God, but is it not the spirit of God that breathes into the perfect human?

This question, however, is not one of man, but of the entire cosmos— from the grains of sand of the Sahara to the planets in the heavens, whatever is of the world and in the heavens, grasping that God appeared as a form elicits emotions in people and its explanation brings difficult sensations. Just as ibn Rushd said to look from all sides, embracing the mind and thoroughly and closely observing with the power of reason, ibn Arabi was now saying to keep the heart, courage and the whole spirit, to leave oneself to come to the self, to look at being and all of creation.

I found a treatise on Muhammad hidden between the pages of a Hebrew Torah on one of those strange days when I couldn't tell whether I was more confused or if my spirit was more at peace.

It said Almighty God is man's original and elementary source and this is why man knows his own self and his Creator. The prophet of Is-

lam said, I was made to love women, perfume and prayer. I struggled to understand this at first glance, but it's nothing other than a different way of expressing the preceding statement. God blew His spirit into Adam and created him in His image. Everything in nature is given to his order and he was created above everything else. Adam is God on earth. To be superior to other creatures, however, is to hold everything in one's own quality. Therefore, the words Adam, creation, and God are a composite. Likewise, in the same way woman is created in the form of a person as female, woman longs for man as man longs for woman. This situation is in fact a being's longing for its own being and the self's self yearning. Woman takes interest in man, man for God, and then both woman and man take interest in God and long for Him. Thus begins the relationship between man and woman, and God and humanity. When man joins with woman and woman joins with man with pleasure and sensual desire, they see Truth in another body. Many people unknowingly isolate spirit from the material, though, and put a physical body in the place of real love. It isn't with the substance of the being, but with a resemblance of love.

The profundity found in perfume is the secret in social ethics. Good men will be together with good women and good women will be with good men. A rotten corpse smells of filth and the material that feels no spirit cannot pass. A dung beetle doesn't search for roses after all. And here the good servants of God also strive to find benefaction and perfume. Finally, the best way to do this is through worship, which is the wisdom at the end of the promise.

A formerly Muhammadan Christian priest was displeased when I mentioned this work of ibn Arabi to him. He told me he was a heretic and that many Muhammadan rulers had forbidden his books. He told me he'd once read the work The Interpreters of Desires and explained that he tried to rid himself of the bedeviling book.

I wasn't surprised in the least, as the God of ibn Arabi can be misunderstood by many people with shallow minds and cloaked hearts—those whose eyes and souls are veiled by what is material. It's no wonder why some Muhammadans might call him a heretic.

Ibn Arabi said he saw Muhammad in a dream, who then ordered him to write this treatise on the prophet in his twenty-seven volume compilation of the wisdom of the prophets, Fusus al-Hikam—The Bezels of Wisdom. But ibn Arabi lifting the curtain to reveal this fantasy world, this mundus imaginales, to show the main secret of existence would remain futile for those whose hearts and eyes are closed shut. What's in front of our eyes, however, isn't a curtain, but a series of walls fitted with steel doors. As with Adam's superiority over the angels, Abraham's divine action in service to God, King Solomon's power, King David's wisdom as a blacksmith with command over fire, the nobility of Jesus and Muhammad's love for God, the light of all the prophets' provenance, esoteric interpretation and that which sustains mankind can be found in the Essence of Wisdom.

According to ibn Arabi, Reality can only be gleaned in dreams and visions in this imaginary world. The world is made of a fantasy and there is no real Existence. Man himself was made as a likeness. As such, what is called the world of man's existence is actually a dream within a dream.

This doesn't mean, however, that what we call Truth is trivial, devoid of essence, void or unstable. And so what we call Truth is not Truth in itself, but a symbolic representation, and man can perceive genuine Truth through this symbol. Just as if we interpret what is seen in dreams and attempt to divine their substance, so must the cosmos be interpreted in this way and the meaning behind matter be understood so as to interpret its hidden essence. As the holder of such perception, man must view the world as a dream to be able to access the level of what ibn Arabi calls the perfect human—and to which he says everyone who strives can attain. If one is to dream, one must sleep. All the senses are inactive in sleep—eyes don't see, ears don't hear and hands feel not—but what's seen is real. In the same way, it's necessary to go beyond the senses to be able to see the world as a likeness and interpret its hidden essence—for the body to die, so to say. With the death of the body, the curtain concealing the mystery opens and man perceives genuine Truth. It's this that's the level Sufi masters speak of as annihilation. The action of annihilation, or al-fana, in mushahada— the unity of vision of God—discusses this concept deeply.

When man wakes from such sleep, he no longer sees the world as before and the shackles of mind and reason are cast off. So then what does it look like and how does it feel? Here, Doctor Maximus labors to explain in his writing the extraordinary experiences he lived throughout his life. Therefore, according to ibn Arabi, the world is a likeness made up from a dream and nothing more than an illusion as expressed in the holy books. Its existence continues under the command of the Divine Power that constantly creates and destroys it.

The wisdom in the reply ibn Arabi gave ibn Rushd centuries ago is also hidden here—in yes and no there's a secret that's perceived as Absolute Reality that goes back to all things between existence and nonexistence amid the likenesses.

Sheikh al-Akbar's Truth, therefore, goes much beyond religions, rituals, traditions and sects, and instead occupies a much more sacred space. The enlightenment he attempts to impart in his writing is so vast and profound, however, that one lifetime might not be enough to fully understand it.

Whichever of ibn Arabi's books I cracked open, I felt I was standing at the shore of a boundless ocean, helpless to even set foot in the water. This ocean was so vast that its waters and mercy embraced all of existence. The scholars he mentions are no different from him, especially those he speaks of in Ruh al-Quds—The Holy Spirit in the Counseling of the Soul. He speaks with fondness of many holy women who were ascetics and saints. These saintly women, some of them sheikhs and some disciples, can be likened to our Holy Catholic saints. Of these, he gives particular mention to Fatima bint ibn al-Muthanna, a woman more than ninety years old who lived in a hovel for one or two years, recalling that she said of him, I am your spiritual mother and the Divine Light of your earthly mother, explaining the honor with which he held her.

It shouldn't be surprising that she dedicated herself to God the Truth having seen three of the great prophets in a dream when she was a young child.

According to ibn Arabi, what we call God is not superior or sublime, or a Being separate from everything. Quite the contrary, God is Existence itself. Existence is a likeness of Him, and the image is man's bringing to existence that Being, and because of this, it's ridiculous to ask what is God. God is the heartbeat, breathing—God is the yes and the no. He who reaches the paradox of this secret is the perfect human.

At the end of his meeting with the young ibn Arabi, ibn Rushd said, One with your worldly eyes enters seclusion with ignorance and emerges wise—I would be thankful to see this achievable existence without studying or debating and without resorting to research or the laws of reason.

I understand that these two scholars are separated into two fine distinctions—the Commentator and the Sheikh, the Philosopher and the Complete, the Mind and the Heart. Ibn Arabi saw behind the curtain whereas ibn Rushd continued to think. Explorers continue on the way from where dialecticians stop. The horizon of the heart exceeds the borders of the mind.

All of us are asleep and will wake only in death.

52

Davud and the group following him stopped just outside Toledo, in a forest on the banks of the Tagus River. He was thankful they could finally head straight for the Malaga port. Abdullah and Zayd bin Uthman had also joined the group of Jews. Together with the de Silvas, they were a group of seven.

No one was making a sound. David was the first to break the silence.

"Where are we going?"

David still wasn't certain whether it was such a good to follow this Turk who they had latched themselves to— and now they were headed in the opposite direction to what he'd planned in his head.

No one answered, so David raised his voice. "I asked you where we're going!"

The group stopped and Davud turned back to David. "How many more times do I have to explain it? We're continuing to the south. We'll reach the port of Malaga after passing Ciudad Real and Granada. Ottoman sailors will be waiting there for us. This is the only way out of this hell."

"If we keep heading south like this we'll have to stay far from all the main roads and use the byways," David said, "but if we follow the line from Cordoba to Seville, we'll reach Cadiz and can go by boat to Malaga."

Samuel, Esther, Abdullah, Abraham de Silva and the others all looked around at each other. No one was in any state to think or object.

Only Samuel spoke up. "My brother's right."

Davud was fierce. "Every Inquisition guard, Knight of Santa Hermandad and crusader returning to Granada there will be on our trail if we go on that main route and they'll have us before we even get to Cordoba."

The group was with Davud this time, but David didn't let up. "But we might lose our way and not reach the Malaga port if we cross through these mountains and forests. Wild animals, bandits and the Almohads won't make it easy to pass. We'd at least have a chance if we took the route straight from Cordoba to Seville."

Davud was growing angrier. "I would prefer wild animals to bandits, Inquisition guards and knights. And all of the places where people live are clear on the map I have, so we'll be able to stop in the villages we pass through and get provisions. All of the big cities like Cordoba and Seville are full of Catholic celebrations now. You can be sure that all of the Jewish groups trying to reach the port from there are already regretting it."

Jews and Muslims were coming in droves to the port from everywhere in the kingdom in a river rushing to the sea.

"I'd prefer to die with my fellow Jews than to follow a Turk," David said.

Davud had reached his breaking point. "Fine then, go die! Those who think this way is safer can follow me!" He turned around and continued steadfast through the scrub.

"Davud's right," Abraham de Silva said to David. "We have no chance on the main road. It would be found out sooner or later that without the *limpieza de sangre*, we're fugitives."

The Inquisition had produced the certificate of pure blood given to only those born of a Christian mother and father in such a way that it could not be faked and it was impossible for Jews or Muslims to obtain this document. The Inquisition guards and royal knights could demand to see it from whomever they wanted and whenever they pleased, and those who couldn't produce it were promptly arrested.

"Still, the safest way is what the Turk says."

Esther walked up to David. "Come on, David. We've seen nothing bad from this man so far. Let's go as far as Ciudad Real and then think about it."

David saw that everyone was with Davud.

"Fine, we'll so what you say," David said, finding no other way out.

Abdullah ran off from Zayd bin Uthman and caught up with Davud. "You won't make us walk through half of Spain, will you?" he asked, half joking.

"No, we won't walk, sometimes we'll run." He laughed and looked at Abdullah, whose face had fallen. "It would also help if you worked off some of that belly fat."

Abdullah rubbed his belly.

"We'll try to find a horse or mule from one of the first settlements we run across," Davud said after a while.

Abdullah took a deep breath. "How long do you think it will be until we get to the port?"

"I don't know how many days it'll be, but we'll miss the Ottoman ships if we don't get there in five days. It would also be the end of us. We're already two days late now due to his stubbornness. If he'd listened to me when we first met we'd be close to Granada by now. We have to move quickly."

"And what if the Ottoman ships aren't at the port when we get there?"

Davud looked over at Abdullah—he didn't even want to think of what the answer would be. "They'll be there. They have to be there."

53

Lookout Isa was holding onto the mainmast at the highest point of the Blue Lion, squinting and trying make out the galley approaching through the fog. The fog was so thick that he felt there was a wall between him and Orion Orhan standing bellow at the bow. It was like a gigantic barrier rising from the sea. Orhan had never seen such thick fog in his life.

"Be quiet!" Kemal Reis whispered to his men.

Yardman Jevher signaled to Overseer Jihan, who then passed the signal on to the other yardmen and, getting the order, the soldiers repeated it to the men on deck. The sounds of the rigging, clamor of feet, rustling of the sails, churning of the galley slaves' oars and the pirates shouting to each other all fell silent.

Kemal Reis leaned his hands on the gunwale next to the bowsprit and listened in silence to the surroundings. Yardman Jevher could tell something was off by the seriousness on the captain's face. Kemal Reis knew that this unfavorable fog and surrounding silence wasn't a good sign.

The galley entered the fog, first its ramming spur, then the bowsprit and lion figurehead, then the mainmast, mizzenmast and jigger. The fog hung so thick that no one could see from stern to bow. Kemal Reis' galley, the galiot and the Göke under his command slipped into the fog behind the Blue Lion.

The captain raised an eyebrow and tuned his ears, trying to make sense of the sounds emerging from the silence. There was no wind and barely even the sound of a wave here in the middle of the Mediterranean. He heard the wood creak and footsteps on deck but couldn't tell if they were coming from his own ship or some enemy vessel.

He then turned Piri, who was standing on his left. "Are you sure we're sailing off of Malta now, nephew?" he whispered.

His answer came quickly and just as quiet. "We're passing exactly three miles to the south, Uncle."

Orion Orhan turned to Overseer Jihan with a quizzical and worried look on his face. "Is it true the Maltese Knights have nearly a hundred ships patrolling all the way to a mile off the African coast and that no one's made it past this part of the Mediterranean? I've heard they swamp every passing ship, take it for booty and enslave the people."

"I don't know how many miles out they patrol, but I do know that the Catholic knights here make this place hell."

Orhan was confused. "Catholic knights? There're both Catholic knights and the Knights of Malta there?"

"They're the same, you idiot," Jihan said, smacking him over the back of the head. "On Malta, they call the Maltese knights the Catholic knights."

"They're also called the Order of Saint John and the Knights Hospitaller," Yardman Jevher added.

"This man who reads has a different way," Jihan said.

Orhan scratched his head and opened his eyes wide as if he'd just had a great revelation.

"Shut up," Kemal Reis snapped, still trying to make sense of the sounds coming from within the fog.

It was just in time—the captain heard what he needed to.

He heard whispering in Italian about ten arms' lengths off from the Blue Lion.

They had sailed directly into the middle of the Knights of Malta.

The captain felt like a minnow preparing to sail his fleet into the mouth of a whale.

Yardman Jevher gave a signal to the Overseer Jihan, who gave it to Mahmud the Kurd, and shortly the entire crew had taken their battle positions. Fenders were quickly placed on the bulwark to prevent damage from cannonballs, and Orion Orhan and others spread sand over the deck to soak up blood so the pirates who climbed back to deck from the sea wouldn't slip. Mahmud and his men prepared the dozen cannons on both sides of the ship and the gunner took their posts beside each one, ready to fire. The men formed a line to carry cannonballs up from the powder room and Fingerless Shakir and Hard-Nose Ibrahim and his team strung wet sailcloth and blankets across the entrances and door to the powder store to keep out any sparks and cannon attacks. Doctor Ilyas set up his station for the wounded in the safest place on board, quickly lining up everything he would need on hand—cotton, dressings, bottles of alcohol for cleaning and his knives. Helmsman Musa had one hand on the wheel and the other on the cutlass at his waist, his head up and waiting for the order from the captain.

"What do you say, Shakir? We've finally found a worthy ene-my," he said with a crooked smile. "You think the things they say about them are true?"

"Are you asking about what they say that a blade can't get through their armor, their swords are as long as a man is tall and two hand spans wide, and that they make prisoners sit on stakes at the bow for days half alive and half dead until they pledge fealty to the captain?"

Shakir looked over at Musa, his tone full of spite and winking. "Uh, they're all fairytales."

He knew as well as Musa that most of the stories of the Maltese Knights' ruthlessness were true.

Kemal Reis recited the *Throne Verse* of the *al-Baqarah* surah un-der his breath in Arabic, as he did before every battle.

"—He knows what is before them and what will be after them, and they encompass not a thing of His knowledge except for what He wills. His throne extends over the heavens and earth, and their preservation tires Him not. And He is the Most High, the Most Great."

He heard a bell ring out from the silence about twenty yards off as soon as he finished the verse. Then three more followed, one fifteen yards off from the other side, then another off the bow and another off starboard. He could feel his fleet surrounded by half a dozen Maltese galleys, and the bells were their signal to attack.

"For the love of God, how many ships are there?!" Orion Orhan said, not believing his ears and standing dumbfounded in the middle of the deck with a bucket of sand in his hand.

After the bells, a terrific blow came to the Blue Lion's stern. A cannonball nearly blew the quarterdeck to pieces. No one could tell from which direction the shot had come. Two of the gunners there were sent flying and bloody into the air. A splintered board lodged into another's throat and he writhed as he died on deck.

A second and third shot followed, driving up columns of water off the port and starboard sides of the Blue Lion.

Kemal Reis was at the stern chose messengers from amid the rowdiest soldiers at the ready to order the other ships to veer forty-five degrees port and for the oarsmen to row full speed. It was vital the ships weren't abreast, but following being each other one buy one.

A messenger scrambled to the top of the jiggermast and, clinging to it with one hand and cupping the other to his mouth, shouted out three times, "Forty-five degrees port! Churn the oars! All together!"

Each ship's messenger repeated the order from the jiggermast, ensuring it passed on to the entire fleet. The other two galleys, two galiots and the Göke pulling up behind all quickly crossed into position behind each other. The crews could barely see the ships in front of them, but the captains of each ship kept their bows closely following the ship they were trailing.

Kemal Reis was planning how to get out of this trap they found themselves without ramming his own ships while passing through the fog and with fire coming from all sides. The angle the ships were running would confuse the knights, both opening up room in front to target their ships and making it easier to penetrate to the front of them.

The captain gave the order to Mahmud to open fire as soon as Helmsman Musa brought the ship into the position he was waiting for. Mahmud gave the order and a dozen cannons fired in unison from port and starboard. Neither Mahmud nor Kemal Reis, however, could see if they hit anything. For every cannon they fired, twice as many came whirring at them, sending up foaming white columns of water on all sides. Water came pouring down on the deck and drenching the sailors and soldiers.

The captain knew they'd elicit such a reaction and so had stationed an extra man for every gunner with a blanket so they could hold it up stretched over the cannons to try and block the water from soaking the touch-holes and gunpowder.

"We'd be more comfortable if we could see what we're up against," Overseer Jihan said. "I can't even tell who these men are, let alone see them."

Then a cannonball came crashing into the mainmast and split it in two. The flying pieces cut down four men close to the mast—one was crushed under a falling timber, his entrails bursting out of his belly.

Piri felt a breeze on his face amid the cries and shouts and turned to his uncle. "Get ready to come face to face with the enemy, captain."

A wind blew up from the northwest and strengthened quickly, completely clearing out the fog in three minutes and revealing the scene.

Kemal Reis and his soldiers looked around in amazement as the fog lifted.

The Ottoman fleet was right in the middle of a crusader squadron facing a throng of the Knights of Malta. They were surrounded by dozens of enemy ships—galleys of Hospitallers from Provence and Auverge in France; Messina, Rome and Pisa in Italy, including Ludovico di Varthema; Clerkenwell in England; Amposta in Spain, and many others deployed on Malta.

Their red flags with a white cross fluttered from the tops of their mainmasts above the flags from their own lands. The emblems of the independent commanderies of the order were also on most of the ships.

He couldn't account for them all in only a few seconds, but the flag he saw a hundred yards away on the galley of the famous French Prior of the Langue of Auvergne, Philippe de Villiers de L'Isle-Adam, worried Kemal Reis. On the other side off port waved the flag of the Genoese Piero del Ponte. It was clear these two famous commanders were in control of the right and left flanks of the large Maltese fleet.

The Knights of Malta outnumbered the Ottomans nearly eight to one.

If Kemal Reis didn't come up with a solution immediately, both he and his crew would find themselves at the bottom of the Mediterranean in the blink of an eye.

The Blue Lion at the head of the Ottoman fleet had taken so much cannon fire from the surrounding Maltese forces that it had started to burst into violent flames. Del Ponte smiled as the flames rose higher into the sky. He'd heard countless times of the Ottoman sailor Kemal Reis' renowned Blue Lion and he now thought that it was going up in a ball of flames.

The ship's gunpowder stores ignited, sending of a terrific explosion and billowing plumes of smoke into the sky. The knights burst out cheering at the scene. They were so numerous that from afar they looked like a metal field of wheat on the sea, waving their weapons overhead. They were all ecstatic because Kemal Reis, the renowned Ottoman sailor whose name they'd heard or whose wrath they'd encountered before, could've possibly gone up with the explosion on his ship—and the Ottomans never abandoned ship.

The knights, though, realized something was amiss. The French commander Philippe could've sworn he saw a small rowboat off the Blue Lion's stern just before the explosion. The small boat was rowing swiftly to the galley behind the Blue Lion. The knights soon lost their smiles.

There was something strange going on.

54

The Knights of Malta looked like hundreds of insects scurrying from under a rock with the break in the fog. All the knights on board every ship had their eyes on Kemal Reis' Blue Lion in the center of their fleet. The knights' armor began to shine as the sun broke through, glinting white light into the eyes of the soldiers on the Ottoman fleet.

"They've sent quite the welcoming committee, old man," Fingerless Shakir said. "These bastard's need to be given what's coming—they are well prepared, though."

It only took Kemal Reis a few seconds to go through his options. He might've thought about turning and running since he was an experienced commander who would never intentionally send his men to their deaths in unnecessary shows of valor. If they were to reach Spain, however, it they needed to overcome this barricade, and so turning back was not an option—moreover, his men wouldn't accept it. He could've thought about continuing straight ahead, but the wind was blowing against them and it would be impossible to shake off and escape the Maltese fleet. It would be a long and strenuous death to fight against these men, but there was no other option.

He was convinced that continuing with the plan he'd devised when he first saw the fogbank ten miles off was still the best. This way they could catch the knights off guard.

He had also ordered the main crew remaining on the Blue Lion to attack when the ship exploded.

It all started when Kemal Reis saw the fog bank off of Malta. The captain knew the knight on this part of the island attacked those who sailed past and had always heard that they were superior in number. He first called for Burak Reis and told him to follow him ten miles back to the real Blue Lion, having been painted black and anchored off a small island. They had painted their weakest galley blue in its stead. He had gotten five barrels of paint while at the Gallipoli Shipyard and ordered Master Yani to load them on the Göke.

Since Kemal Reis' Blue Lion was renowned throughout the entire Mediterranean, the Knights of Malta had concentrated and spent all their effort on sinking the great Ottoman captain's ship—so his estimates had proven correct. The knights immediately headed for the fog to wait in ambush when they heard from their scout that the Blue Lion and its fleet were approaching.

In the meantime, the black ship trailing behind—the real Blue Lion—would stun the Maltese fleet and attack when they least expected after the knights had spent most of their energy on destroying the dummy Blue Lion in the lead and exhausted themselves.

The only problem had been who would captain the dummy Blue Lion since using this ship would mean willing going to one's death. It would be impossible to escape at the last moment.

Pierro Navarro had taken on this duty with pleasure in order to show Burak Reis the faithfulness and gratitude he'd promised for the Ottoman sailor who spared his life when he'd been captured weeks before in the waters off Rhodes. Although the pirates had suspicions and were concerned about whether Navarro would do something against his own men, Kemal Reis was a good judge of character and had believed the old knight and given him command of the old galley together with his own men. The only thing the man had to do to keep his word was drag the dummy Blue Lion into the fog. The Knights of Malta would have thrown him in a cage the moment they captured the blue galley.

Navarro had been good on his word—he'd leapt with two of his men into a small rowboat right before the ship exploded and was able to get to the following galley.

This is what the French commander Philippe had seen.

Now it was the Ottomans' turn to attack.

The Prior of the Hospitaller's Langue of Auvergne, the Frenchman Philippe de Villiers de L'Isle-Adam, was ogling a woman standing opposite him.

"*S'il vous plaît vous asseoir mademoiselle?*"—*Would you please sit, mademoiselle?*

The famous sea captain was sitting on a chair in his cabin with his legs crossed. He asked the woman to take a seat, but she stayed silent, her head hanging forward and angry. Philippe couldn't get this spoiled princess—the daughter of Lord William from the royal family—to listen to him no matter what he did. He sighed as he stared at the girl's white breasts while she stood firmly planted on her feet.

"I can't conceive of what right you have to hold me on these wild seas!" Mademoiselle Veronica spat in her own language.

Philippe sighed in vexation. The young woman was as beautiful as he'd ever seen his entire life—she was beautiful, but she was also a rare flower who'd never allow one to smell of her perfume.

"My father's orders to you were quite clear. You were to take me from Italy and bring me to the chateau in Paris."

"You're correct Mademoiselle Veronica—but right now my men tell me the fleet of a famous Turk has fallen into our net. We'll take care of that rightly and then continue on our way. My men have likely now caught this Turk as a slave and are busy bringing him to my ship.

Philippe got up and poured a large glass of wine from the jug on the table. He set it back down, walked to the young woman and extended the glass to her.

She stood still, angrily looking at the glass of wine. "I order you to deliver me to France at once! Your battles don't concern me!"

Philippe put the glass of wine back on the table. He was slightly taller than the young woman and so could look down on her. He lustfully gazed at her breasts in her low-necked, red satin dress, moving the taper to her waist and taking in every detail on his way down. He twirled the beautiful woman's auburn hair in his fingers and slowly fondled her silky tresses.

"Maybe while my men were seeing to the Turks, I thought we could get up to a little something."

He brought his face close to hers before she had a chance to say anything, wanting to kiss her with his entire body. Veronica recoiled and slapped him across the face.

"Now that is audacious! You are a knight who's sworn yourself to the Church and taken a vow of celibacy. Are you not embarrassed?"

His mouth stank of drink. He flew into a rage, grabbing the young woman by the hair, pulling her head back with one hand and grasping her throat with the other.

"Look here, mademoiselle!" His mouth was nearly touching her cheek. "I'll take you to France, but on this ship, my word goes and you must obey my orders. If you don't do this nicely, I'll do it by force."

Veronica felt she would die with Philippe's hand tightly gripping her throat, and with her head forced back that her hair would be pulled from its roots. She knew not to trust the knights, but she didn't think the French commander would be this uncouth.

Philippe slid his hand down for the woman's throat to her breasts, and with a quick and violent tug, ripped the front of her dress down the center, her breast bursting out, exposed. He greedily fondled them and then laid her on the table and got to lifting her skirts. The knight slapped her across the face so hard as she struggled to cover herself that she slumped half conscious to the table.

Satisfied that the woman wouldn't put up any more of a fight, he slid her skirts up her legs while unbuckling his belt and opening his trousers.

Then his assistant flung open the door and burst into the room. "Sir! Sir!"

"You idiot, didn't I tell you not to bother me in no uncertain terms?!" Philippe roared.

The assistant was frantic. "You did, that's what you said. But Sir—" he didn't know what to say and was growing paler.

"Say it, you fool. What is it?"

"Sir, the Turks, the Turks—" he gulped but couldn't speak.

"Say it already, you idiot! What's happened to the Turks?"

"The Turks, Sir. They, uh, we—we've fallen into a trap!"

55

Kemal Reis gave the signal and they started to open fire as they chanted the *mehter* hymn.

Then Mahmud the Kurd banged cannonballs against the deck to the shocked looks of the knights. The French commander and the hundreds of knights under his charge had been certain the Blue Lion had sunk and the Ottoman captains would surrender their fleet. But now the third ship—black, but blue at the waterline as it sailed over the waves—was heading for the front of the fleet, firing cannons as if it had been waiting for this moment. Each one of the cannonballs the galley was firing was striking the Maltese ship and tearing open massive holes. Mahmud was loading the cannons with as much gunpowder as they'd take.

Philippe's face was red with rage. *"Nous sommes trompés! Nous sommes trompés!"—We've been tricked! We've been tricked!*

Kemal Reis had already turned the tide against the French and Genoese captains' ships and the three others around them in a hail of cannon fire without affording them the opportunity to respond.

Kemal Reis called for galley slave Overseer Jihan and ordered for portside to back down and starboard to row full force.

He then went to Helmsman Musa. "Pull the wheel hard starboard as soon as we run abreast the galley."

"Yes sir, old man," Musa nodded, understanding what the captain was trying to do.

With the captain's orders, Yardman Jevher furled the jib and jigger sails and ordered his men to keep the yards bare.

The Blue Lion maneuvered swiftly on Kemal Reis' orders to the shocked looks of the French and Genoese captains, pulling up opposite one of the command ships and using the galley it had just disabled as a screen. It was now raining cannon fire and arrows down on three separate ships.

The captains of the other galleys and galiots kept pace with Kemal Reis and took their own lead, pulling away from the line and exchanging fire with the nearby Maltese ships. The Göke was taking shelter at the very back of the fleet, as Kemal Reis would need it against the Spanish galleons off Andalusia. Sultan Bayezid had specifically commissioned these ships so that they could carry the most people possible.

The knights had pulled themselves back together from their surprise by the time Kemal Reis had taken his new position, and they let loose with another vigorous attack—all of them now trying to attack his ship.

Kemal Reis flew from stern to bow of the Blue Lion, running from the gunners to the yardmen, giving seamless orders one after another everywhere on the ship. The battle plan in his head was like sunlight through a prism, multi-faceted with one each stage folding into one other. He gave orders quickly and ensured the entire crew was working in unison.

"Load these three cannons with naphtha, oil-soaked cloth and rags!" Mahmud ordered, setting to work with his men.

The captain called for his archers and ordered them to target not the people, but the sails on the enemy galleys and to have fire at the ready by their side.

A cannonball then came hurling from an enemy galley and pulverized the jiggermast like a piece straw. Doctor Ilyas pulled four men who'd been below the mast and were hit by the flying splinters off to the side to a sheltered area and began to dress their wounds.

Once Mahmud had the cannons loaded and ready with naphtha and rags, the captain gave the order to fire. He fired the cannons, covering the opposite galley's sails and yards with the mixture.

The captain then ordered for the archers to let loose their flaming arrows at the same target. The arrows hit the naphtha-covered sails, setting them alight and sending the galley into a ball of flame. The fire spread so quickly that the men with the water pumps on the enemy galley didn't know where to aim.

"Oars, full speed!" Kemal Reis bellowed as the enemy soldiers began to abandon their cannons and throw themselves into the sea to save their lives. The Blue Lion was swiftly nearing the flaming galley and every fifth man on deck grabbed an iron grappling hook and extended them over the bow so they could keep the ship at a distance so their own wouldn't catch fire. The men on the Blue Lion pushed the flaming ship into the closest enemy galley.

"Oars back down!" yelled Kemal Reis, and his galley pulled away.

The fire was quick to spread and now two Maltese ships were engulfed in flames.

The Maltese galleys had come so close to each other and left so little room for movement that they had no way to stop the blaze from spreading.

"Superiority in numbers isn't always the best, nephew," Kemal Reis said to Piri.

The knights were seething and out for vengeance, bearing down on the Blue Lion and trying to bombard its port, starboard, bow and stern. Some even tried to broadside Kemal Reis' galley to set ramps out and board. The Blue Lion, however, was able to drive off each ship like a lion fighting back a pack of jackals. They caught some of the attackers by the neck, tore open others' bellies and beset on others with their teeth. The enemy galleys were drawing away from the Blue Lion, some of them with their sterns destroyed, some with bows smashed to pieces and others with their hulls pockmarked from cannon fire while others found themselves under a barrage of arrows.

But then something happened that could change the fate of the battle—a galley to Kemal Reis' right and a galiot to his left burst into flames at the same moment. Knowing that he wouldn't be able to pull alongside the Blue Lion without first overcoming these two ships, the French commander Philippe had sent galleys in groups of three to constantly bombard them. And it had finally paid off.

One of the last cannonballs from the enemy ships crashed through the deck of the galiot and ignited the powder stores below. Kemal Reis and his crew were nearly deafened by the blast, and when they looked over, saw that the galiot had been blown to pieces.

"Well, that's no damn good at all," Fingerless Shakir said. "No good at all."

Philippe Villiers de L'Isle-Adam then yelled out as loud as he could, "*En avant! En avant! La mort aux les Turcs!*"— *Forward! Forward! Death to the Turks!*

Hard-Nose Ibrahim heard the captain's screams like everyone else on deck, as the French commander had left the safe position he'd held since the beginning of the battle and brought his ship close enough to fire on the Blue Lion and the two other ships.

"Looks like the captain's upset the French," Ibrahim said.

Fingerless Shakir grinned. "The bastard's angry at the captain and he'll take it out on us all. We'll see about that."

Philippe brought his ship broadside to the Blue Lion and opened every gun port facing the ship to reveal twenty cannons.

Kemal Reis also had all his cannons ready to fire.

"*Le feu!*"—*Fire!*

With the order from both captains, the two galleys each let loose a terrifying salvo of cannon fire crossing between the two ships. The two captains also knew that the capture of one ship or

312 1492: THE GATES OF HEAVEN

the other would change the fate of the battle. Some shots fell short of both ships and sent up towers of white foam while others came crashing into their bulwarks and prows. There were wounded on both ships and both were heavily damaged.

One of Mahmud's gunners had overloaded one of the cannons with gunpowder and it went flying when Mahmud ignited it. A young gunner nearby was pulverized, his guts, head and limbs raining back down to deck. Mahmud felt a pain on his right side and looked, but the arm he'd used to light the touchhole wasn't there anymore. His arm was lying on the deck, his hand still clutching the touch rod.

"Doctor Ilyas! My arm's gone, come and at least save my body, man!"

The doctor wrapped a dressing tightly around the remaining part of Mahmud's arm so he wouldn't lose any more blood while Mahmud kept talking.

"God is great—I'll fire cannons with my left arm."

Doctor Ilyas poured alcohol on the wound to disinfect it, burning and sizzling, making Mahmud's eyes water and go bloodshot.

"God is great—I'll fire the cannons with my left arm!" he screamed louder, trying to abate the pain.

Doctor Ilyas was finished up dressing the wound.

"Damn you boy, you've burned us this time!" Mahmud yelled—the gunner he was admonishing was already scattered in pieces across the deck. "So be it! One's not enough—let a thousand arms be sacrificed for the House of Osman!"

One of his gunners had jumped into Mahmud's place and the cannon fire continued unabated—the two ships like fire-belching dragons. Kemal Reis had enough artillery left in the stores to hold off the French commander for a while longer, but two Maltese ships had come to where his own two had sunk and started to fire barrages at his bow and stern. Three ships at once was much more difficult to deal with than one and the French commander was inundating the Blue Lion with unbelievably fast salvos of cannon fire.

Kemal Reis ordered Overseer Jihan to have the rowers on port-side push the ship starboard.

The Blue Lion came broadside to the French ship and Kemal Reis roared out the order. "Quick, to the ramparts!"

His men went running to lay down gangplanks to the French commander's ship. Orion Orhan and Lookout Isa reached out their long grappling hooks and pulled the enemy ship closer along with thirty others— the Blue Lion looking like a centipede as the grappling hooks waved off the side.

The archers skewered all of L'Isle de Adam's men who emerged over the ramparts. The French knights were accustomed to wandering around deck no matter how close an enemy ship was or how vicious the battle due to the security their armor afforded them, as it was so thick and protective that ordinary archers couldn't penetrate it. The Ottoman archers, however, targeted the joints in the armor and shot with such force that their arrows even pierced the armor and struck the knight through the chest, heart and guts.

The two ships were nearly about to collide when Kemal Reis saw the Genoese commander Piero del Ponte's galley approaching from the stern. He also had an inkling that the Göke was running out of ammunition.

There wasn't much time left. They'd still be prey for the Genoese commander even if they boarded L'Ilse de Adam's ship.

Kemal Reis grabbed one of the boarding ramps from the deck and threw it against the French ship with a cry. "*Ya Bismillah!*"—*In the name of God!*

There was now a bridge between the two ships. He drew his scimitar, which had remained at his side since the beginning of the battle, jumped onto the gangplank and threw himself onto the French ship followed closely behind by Yardman Jevher and Overseer Jihan. Jevher was wielding two scimitars and Jihan a mace and a sword. The Ottoman sailors had no armor to speak of while their enemies were covered from head to toe with steel.

Kemal Reis' blade flashed on the gangplank and a head fell to the deck. He swung again and a hand went spinning. A limb flew into the sky or fell to the deck with each strike of his scimitar, glinting in the sunlight like a sliver of a moon in the night. Jevher harvested the enemies' legs with his swords while Jihan caved in the knights' helmets with his mace.

The Ottoman soldiers then threw up a dozen more gangplanks and descended on the French ship like a horde of locusts. The angry shouting on both ships had now reached a fevered pitch—both the Ottomans and the Maltese knights attacking each other with seething malice. All the same, the skilled knights repelled the Ottoman sailors' attacks. The knights pushed the pirates back onto the gangplanks as if they were running into a stone wall and kept them from stepping foot back on the French ship.

Fingerless Shakir, Hard-Nose Ibrahim and Helmsman Musa took the lead and sent the knights amassing in front of them falling lifeless to the deck and tumbling to the sea. The knights' greatest protection became their greatest enemy as they fell into the sea, where many of them sank under the weight of their armor. The Ottoman sailors, however, were barefoot and bare-chested, and when they fell into the sea, they climbed back up its hull and attacked the knights from where they never would've expected.

Two Ottoman sailors threw themselves at a master French knight, who made short work of them, slicing them both in half with his thick, five-foot sword. Holding his sword with both hands, every one of his attacks and counters were evidence that he'd spent his life fighting either on the battlefield or a crusader ship. His helmet was cylindrical with a flat top and a thin opening in the shape of a cross to see through above breathing holes. As if his great height and bulk weren't enough, his elaborate, sturdy armor made him look like a frightening war machine more than a man.

He cut down three more Ottoman soldiers, severing their arms and legs with swift and powerful strokes amid their screams as they collapsed to the deck. He wasn't able to parry the strike from the next pirate to come at him, though. It was clear this man was different from the others. Fingerless Shakir looked at the dozen of his mates who the knight had chopped to bits before his eyes and swung his sword vengefully at the man's throat.

"Come on you bastard meat bag—come at me if all that bores you!"

Kemal Reis was under the mainmast with Yardman Jihan to his right and Overseer Jevher to his left, all three of them slashing and swinging their swords and taking down as many knights as came at them.

Philippe Villiers de L'Isle-Adam confronted Kemal Reis—the French commander clad in a black burgonet helmet with gold purling, cuirass armor with an embossed cross over his chest and a white cloak with the red cross of the Knights of Malta. The fighters around the two commanders scattered to the sides of the ship. The knight thrust his long sword down on Kemal Reis, who nimbly parried the blow at the last moment and the sword cleaved into the mast Kemal was standing against. Kemal Reis was going to finish Philippe off while his sword was stuck in the mast, but the French commander's men descended on him. Philippe pulled his sword from the mast and turned back to Kemal.

Kemal Reis had one eye on the fight while the other stayed on the ever-nearing Genoese commander's ship.

Fingerless Shakir lunged at a knight, but he blocked the strike and countered, swinging his sword across Shakir's belly. He'd cut many opponents in two with this strike in the past. But Shakir leapt back as the knight's sword whistled through the air and rushed him with all his strength before he could steady himself. The knight evaded to the side but couldn't fend off the blow from Shakir's scimitar slicing up to his left arm. Shakir severed the man's arms so swiftly that it lay twitching on the deck, the hand still clutching the sword as the knight fell in a pool of blood.

316 1492: THE GATES OF HEAVEN

Kemal Reis brushed aside a strike at his head from L'Isle de Adam and came down on him as he righted himself, plunging his scimitar into the crown of the Frenchman's gold-adorned helmet and coming out at his neck. Philippe's helmet went tumbling to the deck and rolled around as if it were empty. It rolled to the other side of the deck and spun at the feet of the commander's knights who stood still in astonishment at the death of their captain.

Kemal Reis and his soldiers were about to take over the ship, but the Genoese commander had pulled alongside the Blue Lion and was readying the cannons to fire at its broadside.

He, Shakir, Jihan and Jevher all watched the Genoese galley as it prepared to fire—the battle was about to turn again. The cannon fire they heard didn't come at the Blue Lion, though, and instead came raining down on the Genoese galley and the other nearby enemy ships.

Burak Reis had come with his Crescent of Victory in the nick of time. Kemal Reis breathed a deep sigh of relief when he saw the flag of the master pirate.

The Knights of Malta now only outnumbered the Ottomans three to one. The Maltese knights still had the upper hand in numbers and ships, but this was only something that would please Burak Reis' men.

"You're alive, Little Ahmed!" Rattler cackled from the Crescent of Victory. "These Maltese bastard's got us three to one. Let's deal with the Genoese and then start counting the booty!"

The pirates whooped and shouted at the set upon the knights.

Kemal noticed Ludovico di Varthema's ship fleeing far from the battle under a favorable wind. Di Varthema, however, would come head to head with Kemal Reis again, more powerful and when the Ottoman captain least expected.

56

Fingerless Shakir was hesitant as he approached Kemal Reis. He wanted to tell the captain something, but seemed unable to speak. They were still on Philippe's galley—the battle had ended and they were counting up the booty and prisoners on the ship.

"What are you chewing on, man? Speak up!"

"Captain," Shakir stuttered, "there's a woman down bellow raising hell. None of us can get close to her and we don't know what to do."

"My God, that's your trouble?" he said and followed Shakir below deck.

"Don't get near me! Stay away—don't touch me! I'll kill anyone who comes close!" Mademoiselle Veronica howled in blood-curdling screams. She was yelling in French and no one could understand her—all were wary of approaching this woman wildly waving around a knife.

Kemal Reis was charmed as soon as he saw the woman. He'd never before run across such a show of beauty and courage. He watched the woman without saying a word—it seemed everyone around her had suddenly disappeared and only the Frenchwoman across from him remained. He looked over every detail of the woman's nose, lips, eyes and figure.

Kemal Reis spoke to the woman in French after a long while. "No one has any intention of touching you, madam. Unlike your soldiers, we don't touch the women and children. You're free and we'll leave you at the port of your choosing."

She was surprised to see an Ottoman in the flesh speaking such fluent French, but she quickly pulled herself together.

"I've heard much about the barbarity of you Turks! They say you put every man to the sword on the ships you capture, rape the women and throw the children and elderly overboard. You plunder the houses where you go, burn them down and leave nothing behind. I'd rather kill myself than be taken by a barbarian Turk!"

Mademoiselle Veronica had never seen an Ottoman before in her life and was reciting what she'd heard in church since her childhood.

Kemal Reis smiled. "Yes, yes. We Turks also make shirts from human skin and drink blood with our meals. He took a couple steps toward the young woman. "Come now, madam. Stop this ridiculousness and give me that knife before you hurt yourself. I promise you, no one will lay a hand on you. I'll give you my own cabin. You'll be comfortable and alone there—I won't even enter."

Veronica couldn't deny the trustworthiness in his eyes or the kind look on his face. She would've preferred to be thrown straight into his arms, but she had heard such terrible tales of the Turks that she was overtaken with fear. She didn't know what to do.

Kemal Reis took advantage of her indecision, snatched the knife from her and handed it over to his men. He picked up a long coat and put it over her shoulders, covering her breasts and her torn dress.

"Now then, relax. My men will take you to my cabin and you can rest there. We'll deliver you to the French at the first port along our way."

Mademoiselle Veronica was speechless. She hadn't expected such courtesy from a Turk, the type of which she hadn't even seen from French aristocrats.

Piri was, as always, with his notebook. He was going back and forth from looking at the stars to the pages.

From the Notes of Piri Reis— The Compass

The compass is always in pursuit of the truth.

It always points to the same direction no matter where one is in the world. In Constantinople, the Black Sea, the Mediterranean and now off the coast of North Africa, the tiny needle of the compass always points in that direction. Neither time nor place can fool it. Whether in the dark of night or glory of day, on the water or dry land, in the desert or at sea, on mountain peaks or in the depths of valleys, this needle, a little elif, never deviates.

I get ashamed of myself the more I look at this little needle. I sometimes sit for hours on the deck of the Blue Lion while I look at this wondrous device in my hand. Such consistency, such command and its oblivion to time and place makes me jealous. Whatever conditions and circumstances a man finds himself in, it's a great blessing that he can always pursue the same truth—never deviating from the truth. To walk with the same trust in the same direction without regard for location or position, without being taken by passing whims and without being fooled by the deceptive matter of nature, whether amid boulders or on a feather pillow, in a hovel or a gold and ruby-encrusted palace—to be the elif of a compass.

All other directions can easily be reckoned once the compass finds its way. One can distinguish north from south and east from west. Man can distinguish right from wrong when he isn't separated from the truth. It's quite difficult, however, for a man to determine they way to go on a journey in foggy weather with a cloudy horizon. So, how does the compass do it? The needle knows itself, its substance, and that is what it searches for. A magnet never forgets that it's of the north and that it's from there that it comes. No matter how hazy the sky or how short the visibility, the compass' elif feels the north—it knows it and is one with it. If man knows where he is, his substance and his existence, then he can easily see where he's going. The spirit knows and the heart perceives what the eyes can't see and the ears can't hear. If the spirit and heart forget where they've come from, then the body is lost, loses its bearings and wavers. The man dependent on that body is lost, whereas he who trusts in spirit lives in heaven on earth.

That's why a man who needs to find his way must first know himself. To know one's course is to know one's self, and knowing one's self starts with understanding the world and creation. A sailor is completely alone in the middle of the sea and the view is the same no matter which direction he looks—uniformity in three hundred sixty degrees. Dry land is beyond sight, the waters don't speak and everything stays silent. It makes a man feel solitude and loneliness, nothingness and futility, and absence and existence more deeply than he ever has. A man understands in the middle of the sea that it has no drops, but that without drops there would be no sea. Man understands more than ever before that there is a piece of land in the middle of these waters. Every patch of earth is a part of the world and a piece of the world is part of creation.

Is the man who understands this any different from the compass? To be the compass' elif, that's the entire point.

58

The young man whispered, staring at the brown eyes facing him.

"Elif. I love you, Elif."

His grandmother always called her almond eyes—*When will you bring her to us? When will you introduce us to almond eyes?*

Elif blushed and smiled, although she was embarrassed and trying not to show her delight.

"Love is no empty word, Davud," she said looking straight at him. "Ask my father for my hand."

Elif then took three cups from the larder's wooden shelves and placed them on an embossed silver tray.

Davud had started to secretly go in the darkness of night to Elif's family's house a few neighborhoods over several weeks ago. He would first jump over the wall into the garden of the three-story house, then climb the grates over the windows, over the curved coving, up to the crossbeams on the second story and the wall behind the larder. Then he'd push open the unlatched shutters and throw himself onto the sacks of food. The room had everything one could imagine—dried apricots, figs, sacks of flower, salt and sugar, jars upon jars of sweet-smelling rose jam, assorted pickles and layer upon layer of stacked, dried fruit pulp.

"I'll ask as soon as my father comes back from Italy, Elif."

"I told my mother, as well, and I've turned everybody around on it."

"He didn't bring you this time?"

Davud's father was still angry that he'd gone missing for three full years on his last trip.

"It's very secret. Even the grand vizier doesn't know where he went or why, but I hope he'll come back quickly this time."

He tore off a piece of dried beet pulp next to the sack he was sitting on and tossed it into his mouth, chewing heartily while he rummaged through the sacks to see what else there was.

"How many times have I told you to keep your hands out of there?" Elif said, giving Davud's hand a quick slap as he reached for the food.

"Please? What about just a little?"

"You think they won't notice that someone's been rifling through the food sacks?"

"What? Aren't there any rats?"

Elif smiled. "Well, there's you."

Davud looked away embarrassed. Then Silver, one of the two cats in the house, came poking around, rubbed against his leg and looked up at him, trying to figure out who this stranger in the house was.

"Look, I'd say Silver's smelled you out as a big rat."

She couldn't stop herself from laughing and covered her mouth to try to stifle the sound.

Davud picked up the cat and put it on his lap. Silver seemed happy with this lap and didn't make any protests, licking Davud's fingers sticky from the dried fruit paste. His short-sleeved, deep blue caftan, which went down slightly below his waist, was getting covered with cat hair. Davud liked cats but had never gotten used to this side effect—he always had to takes minutes to clean himself off. Silver had jumped back to his feet and was sniffing at his brown, gazelle hide boots with great interest.

Elif had been running through his daydreams for days now. He watched her swaying body in the room as she gracefully ladled ayran from a bowl with her delicate hands, not spilling a drop on the tray as he poured it into cups. He looked her up and down. She was wearing a white dress with pistachio green lining, a golden yellow belt around her waist and light pink, satin shalvar he could see coming down to her ankles. The collar of her white shirt poked up from the neck of her dress and a silk scarf with embroidered flowers in its corners and lacework covered half her hair.

Davud couldn't stand it anymore. "Oh, please would you give me a little kiss?"

His heart was thumping. He'd been thinking for days about how to put it into words and had run all sorts of lines through his head, but the more excited he got he found himself more unsure and timid. He eventually wrote a poem, but forgot it in the moment and the few words he said were as difficult for him as reciting an entire book.

Elif stopped what she was doing and turned around. "What did you say?"

Davud felt a lump sink in his throat. "No—nothing," he stammered. "I asked if you'd please give me a cup of ayran. I got a craving."

His face was red—he didn't know if she'd heard what he had first said or not. Elif looked at him slyly and turned back to the cups. "All right. Come in if you'd like and have a chat."

A voice came from inside the house. "Come now, Elif, where'd you go off to?"

Elif's parents and her grandmother were sitting on a couch under the trellis and talking.

She was flustered. "Ugh. You're going to get us both in trouble. Come one, quick, go back wherever you came from. I'm not going to leave these shutters unlatched again and I'm going to tell my father to get new locks for everything."

Footsteps started coming up the stairs to the top floor.

"Oh no! Come one, please, go already, quick!"

Davud stood up and ran over to the window, sending Silver flopping down to the floor from his lap. She seemed angry when she got surprised, and just when she was getting comfortable.

"I'm going, I'm going," Davud said. "But on one condition."

The footsteps were on the third floor now and getting closer to the larder.

"What condition? You're going to make me crazy. Come on, go!"

She didn't raise her voice but was glaring at Davud.

"You know what it is," he said.

Elif looked at his eyes—sometimes blue, sometimes green—when he was half out of the window. She thought he wouldn't actually leave if she didn't do what he asked.

She was holding the tray of ayran when her mother opened the door to the larder. The cat was in the middle of the room licking its mussed fur.

"God darn it, what a shame," her mother said.

Elif looked at her mother in shock. Her heart was in her throat.

"I'm going to chase these two cats out of the house. Look at the fruit paste—who knows what animal's been rummaging through here."

Elif took a deep sigh of relief.

Davud might have been clinging to the wall outside, but he was flying high from the kiss he just got on the cheek.

59

Be... be... be...

And then another. And then another.

The raw silk Prince Bayezid had placed in the inkpot quickly drew up the black ink. He watched delightedly for a couple seconds as the white silk absorbed the highest quality lampblack ink mixture. It seemed something spiritual was hidden in how the ink spread. He'd collected the soot for the black ink from the oil lamps in the city's mosques just as Hamdullah had told him. He went from mosque to mosque, asking the imams' permission to take the soot, and then add it to gum arabic, measuring everything as if he were weighing gold.

One-fifth soot and four parts gum arabic. The ink will be more like a sticky glaze if there's too much gum arabic and it'll harden on the pen tip and dent in the paper. If there's too much soot, though, it'll spread too quickly and all the letters' details will be lost—they'll shoot over the paper and aggravate you if your hand touches them.

Be—

Prince Bayezid was writing the letter Sheikh Hamdullah had put in front of him to practice perhaps a hundred times today.

Touch the pen to the paper with confidence, and after pulling down a little, go left as if drawing the hull of a boat, then curl back up. Make the left side of the be sharp like a bull's horn. And don't forget to put a diamond—its eye—below the body.

The prince wrote out the letter with his master's instructions running through his mind while words with the letter *be* passed before his eyes. *Be* was the first letter of his name, after all.

Bayezid, be'—which means *power*, or *the second*, according to the alphabet—so, *Sultan Bayezid II. Bedii* for beauty, *ba's* for resurrection, *bab* for gate, *bahr* for sea, *baht* for luck, *bais* for the Resurrector, *baki* for eternal, *bari* for perfect, *batin* for hidden, *behisht* for heaven, *baniadem* for the creator of man, *beyyede* to make white, and *beytullah* for the Kaaba. And then *berr* for truth and *bedi* for unmatched.

After months of writing *elif, be* and the other letters of the Ottoman-Arabic alphabet, he started lessons writing words, and of the hundreds he wrote, two stood out and hung in gold frames in the boundlessness of his mind—ibn al-Bawwab and the *Basmala*.

Bayezid was fascinated that just this morning he'd learned how the letters come together to form the *Basmala*, which he'd seen hundreds of times in his life.

"Do you know what the khat of Basmala is?" Hamdullah had asked him.

Make the be higher up, elongate the letter sin, don't break the mim, write Allah well, keep the Rahman long and make sure the Rahim is impeccable.

Bismillah ar-Rahman ar-Rahim—a door of ink in nineteen letters.

Be patient at first, then you'll gain mercy and blessings of abundance. Look well to the letter sin and the blessings that come after the letter mim. Look well to the sin and then the blessings that come after the mim. Everything is dry and lame with Allah—bare and mute. A servant learns of Allah with mim, that is, Muhammad, and the rest is blessings. The life that you say is the world is an illusion—nothing more than a long, thin line. The hereafter is reality—don't believe in the blessings of the world, but the blessings of the hereafter. The letter sin is as thin as the as-sirat— the straight path—but then abundance and blessings await when you pass to the other side.

Don't boast that you're a prince and don't regret that you're a doorkeeper. One's rank is in piety, not on the throne.

Bayezid was finally listening respectfully to Sheikh Hamdullah.

He wasn't impatient as he was before, he didn't succumb to his anger and Hamdullah didn't have to repeat himself. He greatly enjoyed listening to Hamdullah tell the story of the letters of the Basmala, which he'd seen his entire life over doors, on fountains, at the beginning of books, in mosques, villas and palaces and many other places. Hamdullah smiled as he told the story of ibn al-Bawwab.

Think about it, Prince—ibn al-Bawwab means son of the doorkeeper. This man lived in the eleventh century at the time of the Buyids and Abbasids and was the son of a palace doorkeeper. The aristocrats treated him with contempt his entire life and humiliated him on many occasions. Ibn al-Bawwab never paid heed to the fanfare of the palace or the sycophants and pretentious tricksters around the caliph. He devoted his life to Islamic letters, wrote thousands of Qurans, filled tens of thousands of pages and became one of the three greatest figures of all time of the six styles of calligraphy. He saw the endless light of God in a dream one night and listened to all the details of how to write the Basmala that you now see before you. That is the story of the Basmala with the long letter sin that adorns nearly every Islamic building. We don't know what has happened to the souls of those Abbasid aristocrats, but what ibn al-Bawwab—this son of a doorkeeper—gave to the Basmala five centuries ago adorns the place of honor of countless palaces, villas, mosques and fountains. This enchanting talisman is written above every door and at the opening of every book. It's the gift from the calligrapher ibn al-Bawwab.

The more he thought about it, Bayezid likened the form of ibn al-Bawwab's letter *be* to a crescent moon with its horns pointing upward. This comparison had more meaning for him since ibn al-Bawwab's full name also included ibn Hilal—son of the crescent. He wondered how these two parts of this calligrapher's name could be in such contrast to each other—one a doorkeeper, condemned to the ground and attached to the earth, and the other the crescent, the most beautiful object in the heavens and perhaps the most beautiful thing in existence. *Hilal*—one *he*, two *lam* and one *elif*— just like *Allah*—one *he*, two *lam* and one *elif*. It was ibn Hilal who most beautifully wrote the name of God. The fortune of man is full of so many secrets for those who know how to read it, he thought.

Bayezid thought about his own name. Caliph Yazid I had perpetrated one of the largest massacres in the history of Islam. He had killed Hasan and Husain—the grandsons of the prophet, who had caressed their hair. Yazid is a symbol of fire and wickedness. The prince thought this name explained his past from which he was now slowly starting to break away. And his name wasn't Yezid—it was *Ba*yezid. He thought maybe the initial *ba* could be a negation—*biedeb* means ill-mannered, *bidin* means unreligious, *bigünah* without sin and *bimekân* placeless. The name *Bayezid* includes *Yezid*, but he thought maybe it was possible it had overcome it. *Ba* had a connection to the meaning for after—*ba'de* means after, *ba'delmilad* means after the milad, *ba'dema* means herein after—so, *Bayezid* could mean *after Yezid* and have a separate meaning from it. Everything in the world is in direct opposition and understood with contrasts—white cannot be understood without black, water without fire or darkness without light. He thought maybe these two opposing natures of *Ba* and *Yezid* could be summed up in their spirits. After all, man can be more degenerate than the Devil if he pleases, and likewise could attain the loftiness of the angels. Was this not the greatest reward given to man? It isn't freedom, but what is it? Which religion has bestowed such a right to man? Christianity proclaims original sin and Judaism asserts all Israelites are the chosen people.

In Islam, though, all things are in the hands of the servants of God. Being a sinner or a saint is a choice for mankind—to be Yezid or Bayezid.

The prince turned the sheet so he could continue to use its empty corners and wrote the letter *be* in its initial, medial and end forms. The word *muswada* in Arabic means a draft or notes and comes from the word *sawada*, or blackness. The white of the paper is *bayad*, or whiteness, from *bid*, to whiten or make impeccable. Bayezid thought of the connection between his name and the clean whiteness he filled in the empty spaces. Hamdullah had told him that as a man's heart becomes pure as he fills a sheet of paper.

The ink flowing on the paper is actually a waterfall from your heart, Prince. The groaning you hear is not from the pen as you write, but from your own soul. The paper laughs as the pen weeps—but remember, one cannot practice without love.

Be... be... be...

And then another. And then another.

While writing out these letters, due to his ability, Bayezid would sometimes moan like the *nun* in between the two *elifs* of the word *ana* and other times when writing out the letter *kaf,* he felt he was at its zenith.

Two main parts comprise every letter. A letter has a quintessence and supplementary features. Its essence is the letter's substance—it's the smallest feature that distinguishes it from the other letters. The head of the letter ha that resembles a rising cobra, the ruby of a dot below the letter be, the head of the letter mim slopping forward, the foot of the letter re twisting like a dagger—these are their essences, and the rest of their forms are their supplementary features. Without essence, the supplementary features are nothing. You will first find their essences and then the rest will come. Is man not also like this, Prince? What benefaction comes from the body whose essence isn't processed. Every letter is like a person. Not just their essences—they have heads, torsos, shoulders and feet. A calligrapher who understands these letters understands man, and a calligrapher who serves these letters serves man. The secret of life is hidden in letters. Memory is a composition of letters. History owes its existence to letters.

The Arab poets of old said give them three letters and they would beget creation. From the letters kaf, te and be there're the words kitab, mekteb, katib, kuttab and mektub—book, school, scribe, scribes and letter. From elif, be and de there are abd, ibadet and mabud—slave, worship and divinity. The letters elif, lam and mim give us alim, ilim, alem and ulema—scholar, science, universe and theologian, while ha, fe and zad make hafiza, mahfaza, hafiz and hifz—memory, keepsake box, one who's memorized the Quran and to conserve. Kaf, lam and mim also give us kalem, kelime and kelam—pen, word and speech.

And where do these three letters come from? What is Arabic if not a divine language, Prince?

Just thinking about these letters is enough to explain to man the sacred language and existence that it has created.

60

Davud came to an abrupt stop when he came to the Monastery of San Jeronimo in the middle of a large plain. He was out of breath. He'd taken off running when he saw smoke rising from a half mile away, pulling far ahead of David, Esther and the others who were following behind—he wanted to see what had happened to the monastery as soon as possible. It was the monastery on the road to Malaga where he had lived for months.

The monastery was the most important of the Franciscans, and under Father Paulo, they had hosted him for months and provided him with a hidden safe haven. The flames that had engulfed the building were now dying down. What remained of the place where he'd spent countless sleepless nights, his room where he'd had nightmares, the roof of the kitchen where he ate, where he had secretly recited verses of the Quran as he knelt in front of a statue of Christ in the small church, the horse stables and everywhere else was reduced to half-burned timbers and the acrid smell of black smoke.

David came up behind Davud and couldn't tell if the tears in his eyes were from the smoke or sadness. He didn't ask.

"Was this a mosque or a synagogue?" he asked as he looked at the rising smoke.

He was thinking about whether those who were killed or abducted were Muslim or Jewish.

Davud's eyes were filled with tears and bloodshot. He smiled wryly. "Neither. This was a Catholic monastery."

David struggled to understand. "But how could this happen? Are the Catholics burning their own monasteries now?"

Davud turned back to the smoking ruins and approached what had been the church. "The only thing I know is that the men who did this have no religion."

Davud had been a monk at the monastery, and the same question he had when he first saw the smoke rising from the building kept running through his head—was Father Paulo safe? He walked through the blackened timbers as he tried to find some trace of Father Paulo.

"Was this—" David started to ask, forcing himself to go on. "Was this the monastery where you hid?"

He could reckon what the answer was from the look on Davud's face.

Davud was lost in the ashes—he pulled out a figure of Christ on the cross hidden behind a piece of wood on the ground and placed it on a blackened but still standing piece of marble in the center of the church.

He then heard a muffled sound coming from behind him. He made his way through the ruins, following the sound, and heard that it was coming from underneath wooden planks by the wall in the kitchen. He tapped on the planks with his foot to try to figure out which had something under them and which didn't. He realized from the sound they made that there was a secret chamber under where he was now standing. He saw an arm covered in ash where the wall met the floor and heaved open the trapdoor with all his might. There was an old monk with bloodshot eyes and tattered robes coughing and trying to pull himself up.

"This man's about to die from the smoke." Davud said. "He must've been hiding here when they were attacked."

He and David each grabbed one of the old man's wrists and slowly pulled him up, trying to get him to breath more comfortably again after a while in the open air. The monk, however, had inhaled a lot of smoke for hours on end and couldn't stop coughing, although he still tried to speak. Davud leaned over the man lying on his back and tried to hear what he was saying.

"The Dominican—the Dominican knights," he coughed.

Davud was trying to make out what he was saying in between coughing fits.

"The Dominican knights attacked. They were—they were looking for Father—for Father Paulo. They took away—they took everybody—everybody who wanted to protect him."

"Where did they take them?" Davud asked. "Where's Father Paulo?"

The man couldn't stop coughing anymore and had started wheezing heavily.

David looked anxiously from the old man to Davud and back. Esther and the others had also come and were watching the tragic scene unfold, feeling powerless and sorry that they had nothing with them to help.

"Cor—" the old man said, but couldn't finish the word.

David and Davud looked at each other to see if the other had understood. The man tried desperately one more time.

"The Great Cor—" he couldn't finish.

His eyes and mouth closed.

The monk was dead.

David and Davud were knelt down at his head, looking at each other in silence.

"This is savagery," David said. "I couldn't understand where he was talking about. If I could've, maybe we'd have had a chance."

Davud stood up and looked to the southwest, his fists clenched and knuckles turning white. "I did. I know where they have Father Paulo."

David was surprised. "Where?"

Davud set his eyes on the horizon. "The Great Mosque of Cordoba."

"You mean the Great Cathedral of Cordoba?"

"It might be a cathedral for you, but it's still a mosque for me."

David could tell from the look on Davud's face that their journey had just been extended. Davud would certainly go no further without first going to Cordoba and learning what had happened to Father Paulo. That meant the route would change, and with out the *limpieza de sangre*—the certificate of pure Christian blood, there was no way they could go beyond Cordoba.

61

"Have you lost your mind?" David said. "What? You think you'll be able to just freely walk into the Cathedral of Cordoba and leave with him?"

He'd been trying to convince David for the past half hour that it wouldn't work. Davud, however, hadn't moved from the ground where he was sharpening his sword, as if he hadn't been listening to anything David was saying.

"My brother's right." Samuel said. "The dungeons in the cathedral are one of the best protected places in the land—maybe only second to the Suprema's dungeons in Seville."

"And they'll also grab us as soon as we get to Cordoba and throw us to the Inquisition," Esther said.

"Who said we would go together?" Davud said, breaking his silence.

He stood up and started turning his sword from side to side. The fire at the monastery hadn't at all affected the small arsenal he had buried there while he was a resident. Lying in front of him were two double-handled swords, knives and daggers of various sizes, more than a hundred arrows, three Ottoman bows and quivers, leather belts, hilts and scabbards to easily carry them all.

"But what'll we do when you're not here?" Abdullah asked, his voice tinged with worry, as Davud meticulously placed the weapons under his cloak.

"You'll stay on the road to the Malaga port."

Esther was angry. "You know we'll be easy prey for bandits, the Almohad fanatics and thieves while you're away, don't you?"

"And don't forget that all of southern Spain has been crawling with crusader knights since the fall of Granada," Samuel said. "And now these mongrels are out on the hunt for Muslims and Jews."

None of it changed Davud's demeanor. He spoke as if he'd thought of all this before and that he'd everything planned out. "You'll keep on going due southeast. I'll explain in detail what direction you'll follow and what you'll need to do. By tomorrow you'll join other Jewish caravans—you'll be more secure when you're in a large group. I'll try to meet back up with you in three days in Rio.

"Of course. If you're still alive," Esther scoffed.

"In that case, let me go with you. David said. "You'll need someone."

"Not a chance. The more men in the group the safer you'll all be, otherwise the bandits will more readily set their eyes on you.

"Father Paulo might also already be dead," Abdullah said calmly. "You're throwing both yourself and us in a lot of danger for nothing."

Davud seemed like he had also thought of this earlier. "I very well could be. Either way, I need to find out what's happened to him."

"Why is this priest so important to you?" David asked.

Davud paused. He looked straight at David and gave an answer to the question everyone in the group standing in front of him had.

"He saved my life. I'm indebted to him." He gave a final warning before he left the group. "Don't anyone follow me, for anything, and if you can't find me in Rio in three days, don't look back and continue on the way."

Then he opened a map and explained at long length what they were to do.

62

Davud was making his way under the velvety lavender light of the full moon. He had taken a mule so as not to draw attention to himself, and in his full cassock and cowl, he looked more like a specter on its back. He looked at the Mosque of Cordoba rising like an oasis in the desert as he came under the silence of night to the far end of the Roman bridge over the Guadalquivir River. It was like a dagger to the heart every time he saw it—he wasn't easily able to dispel the burning in his chest and he couldn't stop tears from welling in his eyes.

Maybe the Arabs had built this gigantic mosque with brown, yellow and golden walls and roofs in the rainy and fertile land of Andalusia dominated by flowers and orange trees to evoke the majestic sand dunes of the Sahara so they would feel at home. The columns rising from the forest row after row to rectangular roofs were like the mystical desert mountains of the Arabian Peninsula. It was without a doubt that the Great Mosque of Cordoba was the most beautifully designed house of worship in the world—until the Catholics took it in a bloody battle two centuries earlier and converted it into a cathedral.

Davud looked at the northwestern wall, added on like a makeshift patch, and the bell tower where once there'd been a minaret. He knew the Inquisition held its captives here in the cells they'd added and the dungeons they'd built in the inner courtyard. It was also clear from the amount of Inquisition guards and knights of the Order of Santiago stationed there. He thought Father Paulo should here, and turned his mule to the tower.

He'd try the same method he used to free Abdullah from the Alcazar Castle in Toledo. If by chance the aide went along, he'd be out with Father Paulo within ten minutes.

"What's the matter, Brother? What're you doing here at this hour?" one of the guards at the gate asked Davud.

"May the grace of our Lord Jesus Christ be upon you. I've come from Seville. I've been charged with bringing the prisoner whose name is on this paper to the Suprema.

"You couldn't wait until morning, Brother?"

The guard had a menacing look on his face and his voice had gotten increasingly harsh. Davud had begun to sense that something could go wrong from the first moment, but he kept his composure.

"We are servants to orders, and I must be back in Seville by tomorrow morning. The timing of it is out of my hands."

The guard stared at Davud's face and looked up and down at the monk's cassock. He wanted to find out what all the slight bulges around the monk's waist and on his back were, and Davud was trying to reckon whether the guard had noticed the weapons under his clothing or not.

"Let's see the papers," another guard said.

Davud quickly reached into the leather bag slung over his shoulder and handed over the sealed letter. The guard examined the document and handed it to the one who had been wary of Davud since the beginning—and who still was. The man looked over the letter with a suspicious eye still trained on the monk.

"Alright," he finally said, his expression unchanging. "Enter."

Davud dismounted his mule, walked in between the guards and through the open gate. He had a feeling the guard he was leaving behind wouldn't sit easy.

Davud entered the dungeon accompanied by two soldiers. He was relieved when he saw Father Paulo, slumped at the wall but still alive. But when the man lifted his head in his miserable state with scrapes and bruises on his nose and brow and dirt on his beard and looked up at Davud, the monk knew it was too early for relief. It was clear he'd been soundly beaten. The priest was baffled seeing this monk Daniel there and at a loss as for what to do. Davud shot him a look to make sure he kept quiet.

"You wait outside," he said to the guards as he entered the cell.

The guards looked at the monk as if they hadn't been expecting such an order.

"I need to check the prisoner's state and bear witness to the confession of his sins before the return journey. This is the only way to save his soul if he ends up dying on the way."

The guard with the keys was too tired to argue. He stepped aside to wait outside the door.

"Father," Davud whispered as soon as he was inside, "who did this to you?"

He pulled the old man up by his arms and sat him upright.

"The knights of Santa Hermandad," Father Paulo said softly. "They got the order from Torquemada. They claim we hid Jews and Muslims at the monastery. Apparently there's a spy among us."

Davud felt responsible for what had happened to Father Paulo, and the priest seemed to understand.

"Don't be upset, my son. If not today, Torquemada would've found another excuse for it tomorrow. Spain has long turned into a hell for true believers."

He fell into a coughing fit before he could go on. "I'm at peace since I'm not in their ranks."

Davud tried to encourage him. "I'm going to take you from here, Father."

The priest smiled. "I'm already about to be saved from here, my boy. You've come needlessly."

"We need to get out of here, Father."

The priest nodded twice. "I'm very tired, Daniel. I'm in no state to walk or even move."

"You can do it, Father. You only have to walk a hundred yards, then I'll put you on a horse and take you away from here."

Father Paulo knew quite well that Davud wouldn't give up. "Alright. I'll try, but I don't very well think I can," he said, moving forward.

"I need to put these on your wrists for show," Davud said, and clasped the iron shackles he was carrying on the old man's hands.

Davud saw the guard who had interrogated him at the gate with half a dozen men waiting when he came back to the head of the corridor with the prisoner.

"We'll take you here," the guard said with a sly smile.

This didn't make Davud happy.

"The head guard of the Cathedral of Cordoba wishes to see you. He has a message to send with you to Seville."

Davud knew this was not so much a request as an order, and so he nodded, not knowing what game these men were up to. He and Father Paulo started to walk into the cathedral with two guards to the front and back of each of them.

It was midnight, but the inside of the cathedral was as light as day. There were hundreds of majestic chandeliers suspended from the ceiling, the largest with a thousand oil lamps—all the triumph of Muslim engineers—beaming their light at those passing below. The burning in Davud's chest grew as he passed the granite, marble and porphyry columns in the shapes of date trees and palms in the section of Abd al-Rahman I. He had absolutely no desire to go into and wander through the masjid of what had been the greatest and most beautiful mosque in the world, looking at its walls now as a cathedral. He'd never been able to accept that that this greatest form of Islamic beauty had become Catholic. Possibly its greatest feature, unmatched the world over, was its rows of columns opposite each other, increasing as if in infinite reflection, and the semi-circular arches rising above them. The twisting capitals of the columns looked more like the palms of Medina than actual stone.

The grand sanctuary's domes ornamented with golden mosaics where Muslims were no longer allowed to enter seemed to greet Davud like an old friend. He felt as though he was rubbing shoulders with the likes of ibn Rushd, ibn Tufail, ibn Arabi, ibn Hazm and al-Qurtubi as he walked past the columns and under the horseshoe arches, which centuries later were the inspiration for the architecture of Gothic cathedrals. The arches of red and yellow stone in the square of Abd al-Rahman II rose over the thousands of transcendental columns in an image of night and day, earth and air, desert and sea, and servant and faith. It was as if all of creation—the world and the heavens, woman and man, substance and meaning, and the sun and moon—had been preserved here in the old Mosque of Cordoba. The Iberian Muslims of the tenth century had succeeded in transforming eternity and faith into a house of worship here.

The rulers of Andalusia had built each of its sections, and walking through it was like experiencing the history of Muslim Iberia. Each ruler tried to show the splendor of his own time in the areas they had created, seamlessly fitting with the mosque's character. Davud averted his eyes from the left when he came to the arches of Abd al-Rahman III, as this was where walls had been erected in the center of the old mosque with depictions of the story of the Church. Where once there had been the most beautiful mihrab ornamented with flowers and rows of emerald green, golden yellow and ocean blue stone along with *Kufic* script covering the walls was now home to a cathedral. Walls now wove between the columns, the interior set in rows, and there was a marble altar—the Mosque of Cordoba had become the Cathedral of Cordoba.

"This way," the guard in front of Davud said.

Davud snapped back to reality from his melancholy dream and saw another group of knights waiting for him at the end of the corridor. Torquemada's brutish personal guard Lucas was there in the middle of the men, his strange pig-nosed helmet down over his head. Two more fully armored knights stood to his right and left, all of them surrounded by the cathedral's other guards. The man who drew Davud's attention most, though, was the priest standing in front of them in the back in the white vestments of the Dominicans.

Davud could tell they were in the section of al-Hakam from the Byzantine-style mosaics on the walls. The gold mosaics that the Byzantine masters al-Hakam had brought from Constantinople had spent years making still shined as if they had just been finished.

"A monk or whoever you are, you better tell us without making any trouble," Lucas said with one hand on his waist and the other on the handle of his dagger next to his sword. "Otherwise, we know how to make you talk."

Davud suppressed his surprise. "What are you trying to say? How can you talk to a clergyman from the Suprema in such a manner?"

Then the Dominican priest spoke. "Brother, either I'm blind or you're a phantasm. I've been within the Suprema for thirty-six years, and in that time I've neither run into you nor been witness to such an assignment. Does it not boggle the mind for a monk to come alone in the middle of the night to take away such an important offender?"

Davud felt a knot forming in his throat.

"I commend your daring, though," the knight said, and laughed. "Whoever you are, you're head must be full of quite the fantasies."

The smile suddenly disappeared from Lucas' face and he motioned the guards to seize the monk.

Two guards stepped forward, grabbed Davud by the arms and set to shackle his hands. Only then did Davud lift up his outstretched arms with a speed too fast to see, grabbed the two guards by the ears and smashed their heads together. Their skulls crashing into each other sounded like a jug shattering to the floor.

David then drew his sword from beneath his cloak with the same agility and pulled Father Paulo behind him. He dispatched a knight of Santa Hermandad and two cathedral guards who had attacked first before he rushed into the forest of columns in the section of al-Mansur. He would've been able to move much faster if it hadn't been for the aged priest and he could've easily evaded his pursuers, but the old man was struggling and could only run so fast. The granite columns, however, provided good cover from the arrows flying at them from behind. Davud knew the only way out was through the southwest gate and he was doing his best to get there. He came upon two guards on patrol, sliced one across the throat and sent his elbow into the face of the other, sending both to the floor as he and the priest sped on their way. He felt something whir past to his left as he took the priest on his back so he could move faster. When he turned to look, he saw an arrow hit the column in front of him and fall to the floor. It seemed the columns of the old Mosque of Cordoba were on his side, fending off all the arrows bearing down on him and Father Paulo like a fellow warrior.

But they found themself vulnerable when they turned into area that had been turned into a chapel. There were much fewer columns here than in other areas to allow room for the large open space of the Villaviciosa Chapel. Davud's arms and legs were burning as he passed through the chapel as if the stonecutters who had shaped these marble columns centuries ago were instead working on him. They came opposite the main altarpiece flanked by statues of Saint Peter and Saint Paul. Father Paulo exhaled heavily. He stopped moving and seemed to be stuck to the floor. Davud pulled at his arm, but when he turned to look he saw the old man was about to collapse. He caught the priest by the back and slowly lowered him to the floor—his hand came across the cold handle of a dagger sticking out of the old man.

Lucas had been looking for a clear shot through the columns since they first entered the open space of the chapel and, seeing his chance, flung his dagger from afar straight into Father Paulo's back. Davud couldn't do anything other than look into the priest's

bloodshot eyes. The moonlight streaming through the commanding dome overhead fell on the two men in magical geometric patterns beside a partition screen.

"Divine justice," Father Paulo said.

Davud didn't understand what he was talking about. The guards
were quickly drawing nearer and the old man knew he didn't have
much time left.

"We thrust this chapel into your beautiful mosque like a dagger
and we turned it into a church. It's fitting for me to have a dagger in
my back and die here at the main altarpiece in front of Saint Paul."

Davud looked wide-eyed at Father Paulo. He was astonished
that the old man referred to him as a Muslim.

"Go," Father Paulo said with his final breaths. "Save yourself. Go
to Malaga and find the book hunter Brother Santiago. He'll help
you."

Davud closed the old man's lifeless eyes and laid him to the
ground before he stood up full of vengeance and cut down the
guards bearing down on him. He looked back for a moment and
caught the eye of Lucas at the end of the corridor—but he had no
time now. He flung himself back in among the columns, mowing
down whoever he ran across with his sword, firsts, elbows and
kicks as he kept on his way. A sword swung at him and glanced off
a column, but he couldn't stop it from slicing his arm.

Davud was thinking about what Father Paulo had said as he
found a horse in a courtyard and galloped away, leaving the old
priest behind in the Cathedral of Cordoba quickly disappearing behind him.

*We thrust this chapel into your beautiful mosque like a dagger and we
turned it into a church. It's fitting for me to have a dagger in my back and
die here at the main altarpiece in front of Saint Paul.*

The wound on his left arm was quite deep and his cloak was
soaked with blood, but he didn't feel it.

He wondered who this monk—Brother Santiago—could be.

Sefer Yad ha—Ḥazakha

It wasn't long after throwing the works of heretical ancient Greek phi-
losophy on the cinders that ibn Rushd's works also met the flames. We'd
proceeded in our important duty in the name of Christ and in service to
the Holy Church and had saved the hearts and minds of good Christians
from a very many of these poisonous and wicked books.

At least that's what I thought. How wrong I was.

This time I came across these so-called fools, who take the intertwining
roads of mind and reason as superior to the Holy Bible and God's supreme
teachings, in a place and in a way I never would've expected. I'd been
resting in a room at one of the Dominican monasteries in Zaragoza with
a fellow servant of God who'd been asigned to me as an assistant. It was
night, but I couldn't sleep. It wasn't something easy to bear like the smell
of a monk's feet after traveling thousands of miles. Lying on my bed, my
eyes were fixed on an odd crack in the ceiling that somehow held my gaze.
The shapes the crack took in my head were sometimes a snake, sometimes
a mountain range and sometimes ocean waves. What kept me awake,
however, was something different—ibn Rushd and Aristotle continued to
gnaw at my mind like hungry wolves. It was as if I was no longer in con-
trol of my thoughts.

I left the room and decided to pray in the small monastery's church,
which had once been a synagogue. The sky was completely clear, there
were millions of stars in the blue-black of the night and the silvery light

of the full moon illuminated everything clear as day. I lifted my head and looked up at the moon for a while. I thought it unnecessary for me to understand what kind of entity the moon is in order to believe in God.

I felt relief in my heart when I entered the humble church and made the sign of the cross with the holy water. I walked past the pews and knelt down at the altar, my head bowed in front of the statue of Christ on the cross. I beseeched Him. I wanted him to gird my faith and show me the right way. I suppose I was waiting for a miracle.

I don't know how long I stayed there, but there was no lighting bolt or any movement from Christ on the crucifix. I didn't even hear a whisper. I rose to my feet, and even though I was a little more at ease, my despair came back as I headed for the door. I heard a scratching to my left just before I was about to step out through the church's possibly centuries-old wooden door. I didn't take notice of it at first, but turned toward it when the scratching turned into little taps and I saw a very fat mouse scampering along with a black cat in quick pursuit. The mouse wasn't what frightened me, but the black cat. I was outraged with this devil in a house of God.

I was going to have that cat's life.

I snatched a candleholder as I rushed after the two scurrying creatures and readied it both to light my way and to bring down on the cat. I followed them down a stone staircase through a narrow opening I'd never noticed before. There were the sarcophagi of three saints in the subterranean chamber. The ceiling was low and I had to stoop down to keep going. I lost sight of the mouse, but I could still easily see the cat's shadow. They both suddenly disappeared when I came to the far wall. I ran the candle along the bottom of the wall but couldn't find anything. Everywhere was stone. A while later I noticed a dark opening at the edge of one of the sarcophagi. I brought the candle to it and saw that there was a space below the tomb. I put down the candleholder and pushed the sarcophagus with what strength I had. I knew it was nearly impossible to move these masses of stone, but I just needed to budge it a couple of feet—and I was able to shift it just enough to squeeze through.

I luckily could still reach up and grab my candle from where my feet met the ground. I moved the candle around and saw cobwebs covering everything. It was obvious no one had been here for a long while. There was nothing there other than mouse droppings, some bugs and small bits of rubbish that must've fallen through the hole above. More importantly, though, there was no cat and no mouse.

All at once I felt foolish for coming down here and I wanted to pull myself out as soon as possible and get back to my room in the monastery. But then the candle flickered and I saw a wooden door illuminated on the far wall. I broke off the lock on the door that had moldered and rotted from dampness, and I remember overflowing with excitement as I ripped out the lock and swung open the door.

Inside was a room of about fifty square feet with shelves completely covering its walls—all filled with books. The cat was sitting in the middle of the room, its ears pricked and looking up at me. I looked over at the shelves to my right and saw the fat mouse again, now greedily gnawing on the corner of a book. I could tell that it and all its friends had been at it for a long time when I saw that all the books' spines were full of holes. The cat took off and flew out between my legs as soon as I took another step into the room.

I put the candle in the middle of the room and set to going through the books.

Every book I picked up was in Arabic. The mouse kept on gnawing at its book without a care. At first I'd always thought these Arabic books were the holy book of the Muhammadans due to my instincts as a monk. I never paid attention to what was written inside them. Perhaps it was because I was in a church that I was searching for a Bible or at least something written in Latin as I quickly went through the books. But there were none. Every book I took from every shelf on every wall was in Arabic. I tried to get an idea of the subject of the books for once and held them under the candlelight, for once paying attention to the words on the pages. Then I got more confused—nearly all of the texts were Jewish teachings from the Torah and the Talmud or about Moses or other similar things.

There were Jewish teachings written in Arabic in a Christian church—a Talmud in Arabic in a church.

I had originally left that night to find peace, and I'd now ended up thoroughly confused.

This is how I came to know Maimonides. I was confronted with the corpus of the famous Jewish thinker Moshe ben Maimon, or Musa bin Maymun, as the Muhammadans call him.

In my investigation in the following days I found that the church had been hastily converted from a synagogue years ago, and it was clear the underground library had escaped their attention and had been completely forgotten with the stone floor built on top of it. This library of ben Maimon had been hidden away for dozens of years, if not centuries.

But I wondered why these works by Maimonides were written in the language of the Muhammadans. I needed to do much more research on this Jewish scholar and learn much more about his life and works to understand this. I learned in the following days from the pages of the books in the room I entered that night in a twist of fate that this philosopher was born in the Andalusian city of Cordoba under Muhammadan rule. He was subjected to such ill treatment, like so many other Jews, at the hands of the rulers of the fanatical Muhammadan Almohad Caliphate, who forced him from his homeland that, seizing on the ancient Greek philosophies he read and learned from in Arabic from the old scholars of Baghdad—ibn Sina, al-Farabi and many other Muhammadan philosophers—he asserted there is no discrepancy between reason and religion, philosophy and faith, or intelligence and belief. He had done in Judaism what the Muhammadans like ibn Rushd who introduced these concepts and made this place flourish with them had done for Islam. I learned that he was the author of the greatest work of hakakhah, his fourteen-volume Mishneh Torah: Sefer Yad ha-Hazakha—Repetition of the Torah: Book of the Strong Hand—that he fled the Muhammadan Almohads in Andalusia in his youth and that some Jews claimed he was a heretic in his old age— some even claimed he was a secret Muhammadan.

To understand Maimonides is to understand Judaism, or to understand Judaism is to understand Maimonides.

The holy book of these heretics, the Torah, is the first five books of the Old Testament—Genesis, Exodus, Leviticus, Numbers and Deuteron-

omy—the Written Law that God sent down to Moses on Mount Sinai. Judaism, however, doesn't stop there. This is only one side of the coin. On the other side is the Oral Law that God inscribed in Moses' mind and isn't found in the Torah.

I wondered how this information was handed down from generation to generation. There is the science of the Talmud, which means instruction in Hebrew and for which every Jewish scholar for centuries has devoted themselves to better understand and explain this Oral Law. This reminds me of the corpus of sayings of the Muhammadan prophet called the Hadith that they have in addition to their Quran.

For both Jews and Muhammadans, why the Laws of God were not completely written down on the parchment of scrolls or pages of books, and that from there they continue with oral rituals, is to stress that religion shouldn't be trapped by its letters and that its members should rather hold it in their hearts, minds and on their tongues.

The Talmud covers all the dietary laws of the Jews, the details of keeping kosher, how one should marry, how prayers and worship are to be performed, how to determine the time of holy days such as the Sabbath, how to dress, what to overcome and much practical knowledge about how Jews should conduct their daily lives in both public and private from beginning to end. Maimonides' book explains for pages on end the reasons why pigs are not kosher and why circumcision is obligatory. It's no surprise then why the Mishneh Torah has fourteen volumes.

I read much of this book in revulsion. There was no doubt, however, that this type of book on the form of Jewish practices would aid the Inquisition priests in revealing the hidden marranos they were charged with finding.

What mainly confused me was Maimonides' Dalalat al-Ha'irin, or Guide for the Perplexed. I remember that I cracked it open on my first night in that room and began reading with interest under the flickering light of my candle as soon as I saw the title. I had left my room that night to clear my head, trying to escape from ibn Rushd, but then I started confronting names like Aristotle and Plato. As if he were in agreement with ibn Rushd, Maimonides explained there's no conflict between reason and religion and that reason is a great virtue and talent bestowed on man in order to find and reinforce faith. It isn't there to suppress understanding of God, and rather must be used at its full potential.

God created man in His own image. Does this mean God has hands and feet? If so, then all animals, all living creatures, also have these joints, organs and senses. If the body is in the image of God, then impossibly, so is a donkey or goat His likeness.

According to Maimonides, however, it's precisely because of these reasons that man's likeness to God cannot be his form. It must've been something like this that made man different from all the animals and rendered him unique in the world. It's this difference—man's mind and ability to think—that Maimonides speaks of. This means that what is said as God having created man in His own image is actually just the one similarity that man and God have—the faculty for reason, the power to think. So perhaps the mind is the greatest of curses, placed as an obstacle before belief or to ignore needling questions as if one has no power to reason so as to suppress this ability. This is why in many of his works, similar to ibn Rushd, Maimonides says that God can be found through the way of reason and that the laws of nature do not constitute an opposition to belief and faith. On the contrary, he says that man attains stronger and more powerful faith the more he thinks and reflects.

Of course, since every person's power to think, upbringing and scientific knowledge are different, individuals will have different perceptions and understandings of God, which is why anecdotes are so often used in religious texts. Some interpret these anecdotes literally and have faith in God as such while others take each as an allegory and find faith through their meanings. As Maimonides says, it isn't written in the Tanakh that God has hands, that God created Adam with His hands or that God has a body like that of man.

Everything is fine up to here, but this is where the trouble begins. Who decides which stories in the sacred books are literal truth and which are symbolic? For example, will man truly be resurrected with all his bones, flesh, organs and senses and continue living, or as Maimonides claims, is it the sacred wisdom of the spirit that God has breathed into man that

sustains the eternity of creation? Did God truly inscribe the Ten Com-
mandments in stone Himself, or is it an allegory for something else? As
the body is composed of parts but God is one, wouldn't these parts harm
His unity? Even though there were inklings of the answers to these ques-
tions in the Guide for the Perplexed, I was certain it would serve to only
further confuse me.

Maimonides does something surprisingly different, however. The fi-
nal conclusions he gives for these investigations, the cruel laws of reason
and the power of thought are thought provoking. In the end, he says while
man has set out to better understand God, so long as it's done through the
use of thought and reason, man is in fact unable to understand God, as
man's mind is wholly inadequate for the task.

He says it is this that is the best way to understand God.

There's something in Maimonides' silence after so many queries that
is powerful. In man's weakness and the awareness of this incapacity to be
able to understand the Creator, ultimately, is surrender to the helplessness.

Maimonides explains in the Mishneh Torah the concept of tzedakah—
doing right and giving charity, what the books of the Muhammadans
call sadaqah—the particulars of observations while helping others and the
eight levels of giving charity. At the bottom is giving money to help some-
one in need without interest and at the top is to feel sorry for, but not pity,
the one in need while providing help. A still higher type of tzedakah is to
help those in need voluntarily and on one's own accord. Like ibn Rushd,
Maimonides clearly explains these concepts and others in religion and
seems to want to show that there's no conflict between inferences from
reason and the teachings of religion.

Another of the concepts of this Jewish philosopher who wrote in Arabic
that I labored to understand was his use of negative philosophy. No matter
how man uses his mind and the laws of reason, and even though his faith
is strengthened while trying to understand creation and the Power behind
it all, language is insufficient to describe his enlightenment, as language
is a tool of man that's inadequate to completely describe the divine. As
such, it's more useful to describe what God is not with negative statements.
For example, we cannot explain God as a being that resembles man or

creation, as these are lesser than Him. We can say, however, that God was not born and does not stand. We cannot say that God is one like the unity of man, but can say that God has no multiplicity. As a result, it is a more trustworthy practice to describe what God is not than to describe what God is. I perceived a similarity with these negative statements particularly when I read Maimonides' concept that God was not born and does not stand in the al-Ikhlas prayer of the Muhammadans and in their shahada—'ilaha 'illa'llah, there is not Got but God.

I would need many more days, weeks and even years to understand Maimonides. Although about a week after I had discovered the hidden library beneath the monastery's church, all the books were collected and burned in front of it due to incitement from other meddlesome monks. An old rabbi and a few Arabs in the city even watched delightedly as the pages curled in the flamesand turned to ash. There seemed to be no doubt that Maimonides was a heretic. The black cat that wandered around the church would look at me when I was there as if to ask if I was happy with what I'd done, or at least that's how I remembered it months later. Only our Lord Jesus Christ knows what else that mouse went on to nibble.

This Jewish philosopher not only wrote on halakha, he was also a learned physician, and what was running through my mind that night were the lines in his book of anatomy that explained the need to sleep. He says lying on the right side is healthy practice for the body's anatomy. I've also read similar commentary from the Muhammadans' prophet in a book. The important thing to me was that if I was going to try to sleep at the monastery that night, reclining on my right side and without turning to the ceiling, neither would I see the crack there nor would my mind be racing and my sleep would come.

Maybe if I'd done it earlier then I wouldn't have been able to go out and discover Maimonides.

His books possibly would've continued to stay there hidden away for another hundred years. Maybe this would have been the best for me.

64

Davud reunited with the group of Jews and Muslims around Rio after his unsuccessful attempt to rescue Father Paulo at the Cathedral of Cordoba. He'd so far been able to keep Lucas and his men off his trail. The half-dozen *limpieza de sangre* certificates of pure Catholic blood he'd swiped from the guards' quarters while escaping from the cathedral had made things easier. They had been able to pass quite easily through the control points the Catholics had set up thanks to these documents.

This is how Davud and his companions proceeded on the three-day road to Montilla.

De Silva suddenly stopped as if he'd seen a ghost cross their path. He stood still, his lips mouthing something. "Oh my God."

"What it is, father? Esther asked.

De Silva lifted his hand and pointed at the village they were approaching. The group looked at the village he was pointing to about three hundred yards to the northeast and saw rising smoke.

Everyone gulped.

"This's the end of us," Yehuda said. "We've walked to our deaths on our own feet. I knew a Muslim couldn't be trusted."

"Don't make any trouble now," Abdullah said, his voice ominous. "Maybe there's a festival in the village or maybe it's from a burning pan. I mean, why not? Maybe there's soup on the stove."

He didn't actually believe anything he said, but he didn't even want to think about what was going through the others' minds.

"We're done for," Samuel said.

David looked over at Davud as if he was interested in what he was thinking with a look on his face asking what his next genius plan would be. The others were fixed on the smoke.

"Abdullah's right," Davud said, turning back around to the group.

Yehuda laughed as if here were joking.

"What? So they're cooking food in the middle of the village?"

"No, but this isn't an *auto da fé*. The Inquisition wouldn't burn a man in a village, they prefer much larger cities since the audience is bigger and it's more effectual."

"So what's all this smoke, then? Esther said.

"We'll go and see."

"Are you crazy, man?" Yehuda snapped. "We should change our route while we still can if you ask me."

"We need to know what's happened here," Davud said. "If there're really Inquisition guards in the area, then they'll soon find our trail."

The group shot worried glances at each other.

Davud gave the reins a shake and kept going on his horse without waiting for the others to decide anything. The smoke grew larger and rose higher into the sky as they neared.

"I beg you, I beg you. Have mercy. I didn't do anything!"

A woman of about twenty-five or thirty was weeping and screaming with her hands tied behind her around a stake. The brush and thickets around her were slowly starting to burn. Nearly everybody there was holding a pitchfork, shovel, pickax or thick piece of wood. The woman looked to have taken quite a beating before being tied to the stake—her clothes were torn to shreds and her face was covered with scratches and cuts. A group of men set fire to the brush while another threw whatever they got their hands on at the woman and slung insults.

"Quiet you damn woman!"

"Die, you dirty witch!"

"You'll find your worth in fire, you whore!"

Davud and the others watched the dreadful scene unfold from afar behind a stand of trees, more at ease but also sorry for the woman.

"It's not the Inquisition, thankfully," Yehuda said. "Come on, what're we waiting for? Let's keep going."

Esther looked at her mother. David and Samuel looked at each other, not knowing what they were to do. None of them wanted to pass by as if nothing were happening, but they all also knew quite well there was nothing they could do.

"You all keep going as we planned. I'll catch up," Davud said as he took his sword from his horse and strapped it to his waist.

"You're thinking about running in and saving that woman in that big crowd all by yourself, aren't you," David asked.

"I can't keep going as if nothing's happening. They're going to burn the woman alive!"

"Very good, but what can you do by yourself?" Abdullah said. "Be a little more reasonable, Davud. At least don't put our lives at risk,"

"That's why you all need to keep going. I'm not putting you in any danger."

He started walking toward the crowd without giving anyone else the opportunity to speak up.

"Alright, then, so that's that. We keep going without the Turk," Yehuda said, turning and walking away from the village. "What else were you expecting?"

The others were unsure but followed after him.

One man in the front was doing the most agitating and getting ready to throw his torch into the brush at the woman's feet.

"I wouldn't do that if I were you," Davud said as he made his way through the crowd.

The man stopped suddenly and turned around with the rest of the crowd, trying to figure out whom this stranger was. The people impulsively thought they knew who this monk was—some of them greeted him and made the sign of the cross.

"Welcome to our village, Brother," said the man with the pitch-fork and torch—his air much more threatening than hospitable.

"What's this woman's crime?" Davud asked.

A woman in the crowd yelled out. "She sold our baby's soul to the Devil."

"Yes, yes," another said. "And the baby died."

"They're lying!" the woman on the stake cried. "I've done nothing!"

"On what basis do you declare this woman a witch?" Davud asked.

"She's the village midwife and the last two babies born have died."

"That's right," another man said. "And I saw her yesterday with a black cat on her lap."

The woman they had accused of being a witch was trying to cry out through her weeping. "I've been with you all for five years! I've attended to dozens of births—nothing happened at any of them!"

Davud could tell from the first charge that he was surrounded by ignorant villagers.

The woman looked at the man who had been inflaming the crowd. "This man tried to use me and take advantage of me. He started this slander when I rejected him."

She was trying to save herself, but the villagers had long ago made up their minds and were growing restless to give the woman her punishment now.

"Well now," Davud said, stepping in between the woman and the crowd. "I'll take this woman and bring her to the Inquisition where the necessary judgments will be made before she is given her punishment."

The villagers were not pleased with this and began to murmur. Davud knew he had to act as fast as he could. He went forward to take the woman from the stake, but the agitator stepped in front of him.

"We judged her, Brother. There's no need for an inquest. We're going to burn this woman here, today!"

He looked at Davud menacingly as the crowd began supporting him.

"You know the laws," Davud said. "There must be an inquiry so the Church can save this woman's eternal soul. You cannot make this judgment on your own imperative like this."

"Look, Brother," the man said, this time nearly growling. "We love the clergy, but you're sticking your nose into our business. What order are you from anyway? I've never seen a monk carrying a sword before."

Davud hadn't expected this much resistance and responded with the same severity. "I don't have to answer to you. I'm untying this woman now and delivering her to the Church."

He took another step forward, but the man beside him thrust his pitchfork in his way. Davud quickly sidestepped and snatched it from the man's hand, spun it around and in a blink had the tines at the man's throat. The man winced with the tips of his own pitchfork now pointed at him. The villagers had also frozen.

"Listen to me well. If you move against me once more, I'll bring down the forces of the Inquisition on this entire village and we'll burn all of you at the stake! The woman is coming with me."

He untied the woman before the villagers could get over their shock. He took the woman and was putting her on his horse when the agitator walked up behind him with more men.

"You're mistaken if you think you can leave here this easy, Brother."

They rushed Davud, some with axes, others pickaxes and a few with breadknives and cleavers. He told the woman to get on the horse immediately and drew his sword.

A man with a pickax swung it down at Davud as soon as he could. Davud stepped to the side and the pickax plunged into the ground. He gave the man a swift kick and sent him down with broken ribs. Then a man with an ax swung it with all his might. Davud ducked under and stabbed the man through the foot with his sword and pulled it back out. The villager dropped his ax and fell down screaming in pain. Two more men both threw themselves at Davud at the same time. He rammed the hilt of his sword into the belly of one wielding a breadknife and sent the other who was flashing a cleaver flying with his free hand. The man who had first argued with Davud had his pitchfork back and was watching from a distance. He was going to jump and plunge his pitchfork's three rusty tines into this monk the first chance he got.

Davud knew that fighting the inexperienced could sometimes be much more difficult than taking on skilled knights and soldiers. The moves a knight made could be predicted from their specific training, but it was a mystery from where and how these wild villagers would attack. He'd so far tried not to kill any of them, but he saw now he could just as easily fall to a pitchfork, cleaver or breadknife. They left him no choice. Even though they weren't dead, the first three men would already be crippled for the rest of their lives.

One man came at him with a breadknife outstretched. Davud flashed his sword and sliced completely through the man's arm, swing his blade back up and driving it through the man's belly before his arm had fallen to the ground. He sprung up at the man who had stopped him with a pitchfork and with one blow sliced through both his arms.

The men were all on the ground wailing in pools of blood and the villagers were stepping back. Davud's face was smeared with the men's blood.

"I told you," Davud said, his voice low. "This woman is coming with me!"

The villagers stared at him with their mouths agape.

Without losing more time, Davud mounted his horse and sped off with the woman.

65

Alonso Clavijo had stopped and was looking around the stern of Columbus' flagship, the Santa Maria. He had a giant hand ax strapped to his belt that extended over his belly.

"Go on," Juan de Moguer said. "The Genoese bastard's at the bow with the maps."

Clavijo nodded. One of the man's eyes was covered with a leather eye patch tied around his head. He'd lost an eye in his pirating days and had a deep scar across his face to match.

The Spanish sailor climbed over the gunwale at the stern, down the boards of the ship and slipped into the water. He took a deep breath and disappeared below the surface.

De Moguer was rummaging around, trying to make sure the captain didn't leave the bow. Clavijo and de Morguer weren't alone in their scheme, either. Thirty-two of the thirty-three men on board had agreed to carry out this mutiny. They didn't even consider Columbus to be the captain of the ship—instead calling him the Genoese—and believed he was bringing them all to their deaths with all his absurd ideas.

It had been three weeks since Columbus and the Pinzon brothers had set sail with three ships, and talk of mutiny and disorder had begun on each of them. Isabella and Ferdinand had offered amnesty to any convict who signed on for Columbus' voyage to the other side of the ocean. The crew was made up of many Muslims and Jews who'd fallen victim to the Inquisition, along with Clavijo, de Moguer and a few other criminals. Their tune had changed, however, when they found themselves in the hands of this maniacal Genoese sailor and his questionable ships—all of them well worn, two second-hand and one third-hand. The only thing this rowdy, quarreling group of seamen could agree on was to head off this voyage and turn back while it was still just beginning

Clavijo and de Moguer had realized they were left with no other option when their words failed to convince Columbus, so they had set to work.

Clavijo was in the water at the stern of the Santa Maria. He took the ax from his waist and started hacking away at the carrack's rudder. It cracked after a couple strikes. He kept hacking at the timbers until the ship's rudder was in pieces. His face was red from holding his breath and expending so much effort and veins were popping out of his forehead. His work was done and he climbed back up to the deck.

Columbus saw that the ship's direction was changing from the position of the sun and quickly ran to the helmsman on the quarterdeck.

"What happened? Why're we heading southwest?" he barked.

"I don't know, Captain. The rudder's not doing anything," the helmsman said hopelessly, as if he didn't know what had happened.

Columbus pushed the man aside and took the wheel, turning it to the right and left. The helmsman was right—the wheel wasn't doing anything and wasn't any more useful than a cudgel. Columbus didn't know how such a thing could've happened. They wouldn't be able to continue their voyage if the ship couldn't be steered. The Santa Maria was also the biggest of the three and the flagship, no matter if the crew didn't consider him the captain.

"How long has it been like this?"

"Maybe half an hour, Captain."

"Why didn't you tell me, you fool?"

"You said not to disturb you no matter what, Captain, didn't you?"

The crew on deck started laughing. Columbus could tell something had turned.

"You idiot, of course you would come and tell me about something like this!"

The helmsman then turned to speak to the crew gathering around. "Tell him. What happened to the rudder?"

"Maybe a fish ate it, Captain," Clavijo smirked.

De Moguer and the others laughed.

"No need to get wise. Tell me now. What'd you do to the rudder?"

Clavijo and the others began to walk toward the captain.

"And what'll you do if we don't say, Captain? Oh, sorry—Admiral."

They all snickered again.

"You'll pay for this! I'll show you," Columbus said as he pointed off port to the Pinta, captained by Martin Alonso Pinzon.

"Did I agree with you that these men would mutiny against me?" Columbus shouted.

Martin Alonso Pinzon had rowed over to the Santa Maria and met Columbus who'd been raging at him as soon as he set foot on deck.

He began to think while Columbus was still railing at him about his unmaneuverable ship and the men's insubordination. The crew was still laughing and aping him.

Pinzon wasn't exactly against the men, though, as he wasn't so fond of Columbus himself. But he had given a promise, and wouldn't go back on his entire life no matter what were to happen.

He listened in silence to Columbus and then walked over above the rudder. He stripped his shirt and removed his sword before checking over himself, his face indignant, and jumped into the water.

Clavijo and de Moguer looked at each other. The crew had stopped laughing when Pinzon jumped into the water.

He reemerged from the water after a while, picked up his sword from where he'd left it and went to the wheel.

"Speak up. Which of you destroyed the rudder?!" he shouted, his face creased with fury.

"What? It's destroyed?" Columbus was exasperated. "In the name of Christ. The rudder's destroyed? Why? How?"

"Stop screaming like a woman, Admiral," Pinzon snapped.

Columbus fell silent in shock at what was happening and began looking at what was going on around him.

Pinzon took two steps forward, looked down at the men and repeated his question.

"I'm not going to ask again. Who destroyed the rudder?!"

One of the crew found some courage. "Why do you listen to this Genoese, Captain?"

Another spoke up, encouraged by the first. "Yeah, this bastard's taking us all to our deaths. It's time you put an end to this bullshit already."

The others piped up with everyone yelling something.

"Look at the ships, Captain. The biggest isn't even sixty feet from stern to bow. This ship's no good for fishing let alone conquering the ocean."

"All these ships need repairs, Captain."

"You couldn't even fish on a lake with them."

"This isn't the sea, Captain. Who knows where we'll end up if we keep heading west at this speed."

It was no surprise to Pinzon that this is what the men thought. He listened to them all patiently, but his anger didn't leave his face.

Clavijo grabbed his ax and stepped forward when he sensed that Pinzon was siding with Columbus. "It's time to end this bullshit!"

He swung his ax at Pinzon's head.

The experienced mariner dodged the ax blow and with blinding speed drew his sword and swung down on Clavijo.

"I said I wasn't going to ask you all again," Pinzon said calmly as Clavijo writhed and screamed in pain.

"The man who bashed the rudder's flat on the deck, Captain," de Moguer managed to say through his fear.

Pinzon called for the doctor and gave orders to a few men. "Go on, get this man's arm wrapped up."

Columbus was silent. Like the others, he'd been watching what had unfolded in utter disbelief.

Pinzon sheathed his sword. "Now you all listen to me well. I don't trust this Genoese," he said, pointing at Columbus, "but I gave this man my word and I have no intentions of going back on it. And as for your worries, I've returned every ship I've ever set sail on back to port so far. I'm on this voyage because I believe it can be done. We've got more maps and more tools than anybody before us. You're right. The ships are old and the crews are small, but it's worth it to try our chances."

Another crewman tried his courage despite Pinson's determination. "This voyage isn't for me, Captain."

"What're you talking about? You were going to be burned alive the next day when we found you. And now you start this in the middle of the ocean?"

The sailor hung his head in dismay.

Even though Pinzon didn't like bringing up these men's previous transgressions, he knew that if he wouldn't be able to head off the mutiny on this voyage, or on any other, if he didn't take a hard line now. The slightest clemency he showed the crew would be taken for weakness and they would find themselves in the middle of the ocean up against an army of mutineers ninety men strong.

"Above all, great rewards will be waiting for us when we get to the other side of the ocean." He looked over at Columbus. "Won't there, Admiral?"

Columbus was best at knowing how to give men hope with talk of money.

He thought for a bit. "That's right. There's gold in China—and silks, spices and all types of valuable stones we don't even know about in India—diamonds, rubies, sapphires. It's all waiting for us in these lands."

Pinzon walked over to the bow while Columbus was still talking. Niño was there peering out at the horizon.

"What do you say, Niño? Do you think there's any truth in what Columbus says?"

Niño looked over at Pinzon and smiled. "It's certain some will be very rich if this voyage is successful, but I've got doubts we'll be them."

It seemed that Niño and Pinzon weren't only looking out at the horizon over the open ocean, but out beyond time.

Columbus was thinking about the crises that had arisen again and again before they'd set sail. He'd gone from palace to palace and from kingdom to kingdom but hadn't been able to convince either the Portuguese king or the Ottoman sultan. He would've been a toy in one's hand and found himself opposite distrustful looks from the other. He was grateful as he remembered those earlier days that he could go on with his voyage, even among the hardships.

66

"So, what you're saying is you'll cross the ocean. You'll go and go and go, and then India will pop up in front of you. Right?" Portuguese King João said to the mariner standing in front of him in the main hall of the São Jorge Castle. He was having trouble stifling his laughter while sitting on his throne, raised five steps above the floor, and listening to this man. He took a glass from the tray his servant was holding and took another sip, bringing it to his mouth with his fingers covered with gem-encrusted gold rings. The crown sitting atop his purple, velvet cap was the same color as his yellow stockings.

There was also the kingdom's geography and astronomy commission at the day's meeting in addition to the king's usual attendants, dukes, lords and knights.

Christopher Columbus' hands were out in front of him as he tried to explain the same thing dozens of times. He had no doubt the king was a fool.

"Yes, Your Majesty," he said. "Since the world is a sphere, I'll get to Asia if I set sail from Portugal and keep going west. My only need at your expense is three ships, a crew for each and a three-month stipend.

One of the king's loyal clergymen, the cardinal of Ceuta, couldn't hold himself back any longer. He spoke angrily, waving his nearly concealed hands from inside the ample sleeves of his black cassock.

"This man is a heretic, Your Majesty. It's written in the Bible that the world is flat—and it's a fact all our geographers know."

King João knew the common conception well enough, but he'd received the man as a type of jester, and he was enjoying himself.

He looked over at the head of the geographers and astronomers.

The kingdom's most distinguished—the provost of the University of Lisbon—spoke up. "We agree with the cardinal, You Majesty. If one keeps going west, as Senhor Columbus says, one would reach the end of the world and, God forbid, fall into the void. And even if one weren't to fall, having sailed to the other side of a tall mountain, there's no way a ship could return to Portugal on any wind."

Columbus could tell it would be very difficult to convince these fools that the world was a sphere, but had come prepared.

"This isn't only my idea, Your Majesty." He turned to the provost, pulled out one of the maps he'd brought and continued. "It can even be seen on the map by Pierre d'Ailly, the famous cartographer. Look how close Iberia and Asia are to each other. There's an ocean in between that can be crossed in only a few weeks."

He pulled out more maps while the provost begrudgingly looked at the map.

"The renowned Florentine mathematician Toscanelli also says that this ocean is one thousand nautical miles wide and is easily crossable."

"We also know of Toscanelli, of course," the provost said. He had no intention of letting this simple sailor humiliate him in front of the king. "Just as we also know that some of his calculations are wrong."

Columbus then turned to the cardinal of Ceuta. "Is it not written in the Bible that Jerusalem is the center of the world?"

He pulled out a Bible and started to read from a page he had marked the night before. "Ezekiel, chapter five, verse five. *Thus saith the Lord God—This is Jerusalem, and I have set it in the midst of the nations and countries that are round about her.* It's written in the Bible."

The cardinal was quick to refute. "We don't deny that Jerusalem is the center of the world—far from it. What we say is the world isn't a sphere. Saint Augustine covers this in detail in his writings. Both his books and also Bible verses explain at length that it's impossible to pass from one side of the world to the other."

Columbus thumbed through his Bible, stopping at another verse. "So then, what's more, the land or the water? It says very clearly in Second Ezra, chapter five, verse two that water covers only one-seventh of the world and dry land makes up the rest." He put away his notes and went on to the changing looks of the cardinal and the king. "We can cross the ocean much easier than we'd thought and take hold of the treasures of the East while bypassing the Turk's hold over trade on the Mediterranean and Black Seas."

Columbus knew the king chaffed at the Ottomans' conquest of the last holdout of the Byzantines and their newfound dominance of trade on the Mediterranean.

King João put his wine glass back on the tray that his servant was still holding when he heard Columbus mention treasure. He was pleased that this scrubby yet crafty man had finally said something to interest him right when he was growing tired of the whole affair.

"What kinds of treasures?"

"Those like the ones Marco Polo and Sir John Mandeville wrote about on their travels to the East, You Majesty. They say the treasures of the East are boundless." He went on eagerly, passionately explaining to draw in the king. "There're so many gems and precious stones in the East that they make ships and dishes from them. The palaces of the empires there are made of diamonds and ivory, their windows are crystal, their dining tables from gold and emeralds, and the stairs in the cities are made of marble and polished coral. The columns in the palaces glimmer with gold and the emperors' beds sparkle with sapphires, Your Majesty."

King João's eyes shimmered as he listened as if he could see the treasure before him.

Columbus didn't stop. "The balls of gold on the towers in the cities shine so brightly that they light up the night sky. The throne of the Sheba, Ophir's island of gold and the treasures of King Solomon the Bible speaks of will be ours, Your Highness. The trade we do now is nothing compared to this—the Silk Road will go back to being a deserted and desolate route. It would be a great blow to the Turk's dominance on the Mediterranean, too. Even the gold cornices and marble bridges of the island of *Cipangu* will be ours."

"So," the king said, reclining in his throne, "what will you get from all of this?"

"I ask for one-tenth of the treasure we find and for the rank of Admiral of the Ocean Sea and for lord to be bestowed on me, as well as for my debts to the crown and others to be forgiven."

He was drowning in debt and needed to find the impossible sum of six hundred fifty gold ducats by the end of the month.

The cardinal of Ceuta didn't miss the opportunity. "I think we understand this man's principle misery," he said, chuckling. "He's looking for a benefactor to close his accounts."

The king grew tired again when the tales of treasure suddenly came to a stop. "Very well, but there's one thing I don't understand. If the world is a sphere, as you say, are the people below us walking upside down?" He started laughing as soon as he said it, accompanied by the rest of his attendants in the hall. "Don't they fall off?"

Columbus didn't know how to answer and hung his head.

He turned back to the cardinal and tried his chances one more time. "Is it not our mission to spread the message of Jesus Christ to the entire world and teach God's compassion to the Muhammadans in the Turk's dominion and the Asians?"

The cardinal had no intention of entering this game. "We are very much engaged with supporting the holy war against the Muhammadans in Granada and along the African coast. Our sea captains have already started to completely dominate the African coast. And outside of this, treasure from unnecessary places would lead to trouble."

The king sent Columbus on his way. "Such madness is only for the Turk!"

Columbus got an idea in that moment he'd never thought of before.

Maybe the king was right, but maybe he could try his luck in Constantinople.

67

Columbus felt out of place among the others in the Audience Hall of Topkapi Palace with his snug breeches, pointed shoes, the frilly cuffs and collar of his white shirt and his short jacket. Everyone else was wearing flowing, fur-lined caftans, and each had a different grandiosity from head to toe. The merchant Rodrigo by his side had succeeded in receiving an audience after months of writing letters, and now, despite his warnings, Columbus wasn't prepared for the timidity he felt in the moment. The sun shining through the window on the sultan sitting on a throne inlaid with mother of pearl gave him an ethereal quality—it made the affair seem holier and made Columbus grow even more excited. The sultan was perhaps a few years older than him—in his forties.

The calming and pleasant gurgle of a fountain just outside the door sounded through the Audience Hall along with birdsongs from the trees in the palace's large courtyard.

"You provide me with ships and I'll find you a new route," Columbus repeated in Genoese.

Rodrigo had a deep command of both Ottoman and Italian dialects and nearly simultaneously translated for the sultan and local officials.

Sultan Bayezid was sitting upright and looking Columbus up and down from under his brow. His green, velvet caftan was covered with crescent and tulip designs and his shirt buttons extended down to his white belt from where its ample fabric fell around his legs. Bayezid's wide shoulders and white turban with green quilting made him appear well built. He had one hand on his knee with his elbow sticking out and the other resting on the throne.

Next to the throne was the vizier with whom Rodrigo had arranged the audience. Next in line were two other viziers, then sea captains who'd been called for this meeting and the sultan's personal guards in the back along with other palace officials. Maps, an astrolabe, a quadrant and other tools of the sea were spread out on a table in the space between the sultan and his guests.

Bayezid was wavering as to whether he should believe what this man was saying or not—he didn't really strike much confidence. The sultan looked at Kemal Reis, who was standing at the ready next to the viziers. He and the cartographers had held an hour-long meeting with Columbus beforehand.

"What do you think Kemal Reis? What's this man saying?"

The captain's face was steely, his left hand on the hilt of his scimitar and his right on its pommel. He was wearing a sea blue caftan lined in white.

"If you ask me, Sultan," he said looking over at Columbus, "all these calculations are wrong."

Rodrigo quietly translated for Columbus.

"For starters, the circumference of the earth is calculated wrong."

The sultan looked back to Columbus. "How much do you calculate the degree of longitude to be at the equator?"

Columbus was glad that he'd finally found someone who didn't accuse him of being in work with the Devil or crack jokes like the Portuguese king about falling into the void at the end of the ocean. But he'd found it difficult to understand the calculations of the sailor he had met that morning. Kemal Reis had been mentioning calculations and sea routes that he'd never heard of before.

"Forty miles at the equator," Columbus answered.

Bayezid smiled as if he was not expecting this reply. He already knew that the distance between to lines of longitude at the equator was sixty-nine miles.

"You see, this man's half confused. I don't understand how he can be a sailor," Kemal Reis sniffed.

Columbus spoke over Rodrigo as he translated. "There may be some approximations in the calculations, but what's important is that I'm the one willing to try."

"These approximations you speak of are unacceptable errors. This's no undertaking to just try one's hand at. Is it so easy to put the lives of hundreds of crewmen in danger and waste dozens of ships?" Kemal Reis shot back. He looked to the sultan. "The calculations Eratosthenes and Ptolemy made centuries ago even had a fifteen percent margin of error, but this man's are at least thirty."

"So then, on what strength does he speak so confidently?" Bayezid asked.

"Sultan, God save us, there's no limit to ignorance. He doesn't know of the writings of the Andalusian captains since he obviously doesn't know Arabic. All of the charts and maps he has are either in Spanish or Latin."

Bayezid looked to his vizier who'd arranged the audience with an expression as if to ask why he'd brought such men to him. The vizier was already quite embarrassed, but there was nothing he could do about it other than sweat.

The sultan still didn't want to underestimate this man or send him away, so he proceeded with the meeting.

"So, why do you think we're in need of such a voyage? Trade on the Mediterranean is already under our near complete control. Why would we even need a different route?"

"If you don't do it, then the Portuguese will. The alternative route I find will compete with the Silk Road from India. If I keep heading west, then I'll reach India from the Atlantic. If you fund the expenses for his voyage it will strengthen your sovereignty and the taxes you levy on the routes will be guaranteed. I'll be the first to find this route."

Kemal Reis had grown testy. "God Almighty, he's lying. The Portuguese king already rejected him, which means he's trying his luck with us now."

"So I've heard. Was it about this business of reaching India?" Bayezid said.

"He's full of it, Sultan. The Muslims in Africa and Andalusia have been sailing the Atlantic for centuries."

Kemal Reis requested permission and stepped forward. He picked up some of the maps and brought them to the sultan, pointing at the land and continuing his explanation.

"Take a close look at these dark areas, Sultan. We have dozens of sources like al-Idrisi's maps, the drawings al-Ma'mun made, ibn Aswad's travel diaries and ibn Farrukh's maps. All sailors have heard there's a large continent in the middle of the ocean. But since this man's unaware of this and has miscalculated the distance by a third, he thinks the Atlantic Ocean leads straight to India, even though there's another large continent there. We also know that the Umayyads in North Africa have trade agreements with most of them. In other words, Sultan, there's no danger of finding an alternative to the Silk Road."

He stepped back to his place.

Columbus was baffled as he listened to this bizarre sailor, and his astonishment grew hearing these vague tales the Ottomans had heard from the Moors about earlier voyages. He took note of the names Kemal Reis had mentioned and tried to memorize them, wishing that he could pack up his books and maps and leave.

Kemal Reis pointed at Columbus and had one last word. "This man will neither be the first nor the last to cross these waters."

Columbus tried desperately to defend himself. "I don't understand what you're talking about, but I'll be able to reach India in two months' time if I have good ships and enough men."

Kemal Reis had now lost his temper. "Don't you understand, man? You're talking about sailing around the world. You would need a full year for that, even with the best ships of the day. Even if you don't count the landmass, there is no ship that can sail for a year without docking at a port."

"Just think, Sultan," Columbus said doggedly. "If we're success-ful, then the land that no king has claim to will be yours. You'll be the greatest sovereign on the face of the earth."

"The greatness of a king is not measured by the breadth of his land, but judged by his justice and competence in that land. An emperor who rules his small territory justly is greater than a high-handed king who rules the world," Bayezid said calmly.

Columbus was taken aback by what he was running up against with this response. Any European king would be watering at the mouth faced with such a possibility. He opened his mouth to say one more thing, but Sultan Bayezid motioned for him to be quiet.

"So, it's understood," he said, turning to his vizier and waving Columbus away. "This poor fellow has strived this much and come here. Prepare a bag of gifts for him, some *lokum* and the like, and send him on his way." He rose to leave. "We don't have the treasure to spend on such absurdities. We have power and work to do," he said, turning around at the door with a cross look at his vizier.

Columbus decided that day that as soon as he returned to Spain, he'd have to somehow find the maps he heard Kemal Reis speak of.

68

"Come on, tell me," Beatriz said, her back against a tree as she gently slid closer to Davud while he looked up at the stars.

The others were a little ways off eating around a fire.

"What's your story?"

Davud and the group had been continuing on to Malaga. One night had passed since he had saved her from being burned as a witch, and since then she hadn't been able to take her eyes off him for a moment.

Davud all of a sudden felt he'd been caught unprepared. He would've left if he'd seen Beatriz scooting closer to him. She'd picked up on his quiet temperament, though, and so got close to him silently and then set to talking.

David could feel the heat from her arm on his. He was lost for what to do.

"What're you trying to say?"

"I mean, why're you here? Why're you helping us?"

Beatriz stopped with her mouth open as if she were holding herself back from saying something, then she hung her head.

"And who's the woman yourself lost in thought with all the time?"

Beatriz was always curious, and she was finally able to ask the question that had been on her mind. A man or woman's fantasies could have such a deep effect to make one feel as if they were sleep-walking. Beatriz had made up her mind to learn who this man was no matter what Davud did to evade her. She'd taken a liking to him. The wayward man's wide shoulders, large biceps and well-muscled chest, chiseled and strong hands, long neck and sensuality coupled with his quietness had taken her over. If she weren't ashamed to do it, she'd find no end to caressing his face and kissing his handsome brow and well-cut neck. To feel his lips on hers would've been enough.

Davud sighed deeply.

It'd been ages since he'd sat this close to and talked with a woman. He could tell Beatriz had taken to him—and worse, he found himself attracted to her, too. Her hair the color of a fiery, setting sun with curls like the waves on a rough sea, the freckles on her cheeks, her eyes each a deep blue sea, her full lips and her plump breasts peeking above the neckline of her dress that she always left open excited him. His heart beat faster whenever he was near her and reminded him of emotions he hadn't felt for a long while.

"Do you see the stars of *Pegasus* over that hill?" he said, pointing to the sky.

The constellations were twinkling between the branches above where they were sitting. Beatriz smiled, knowing he was again evading the question, and looked at him awhile instead of the sky in an attempt to draw his attention. Hopeless, she resigned herself to listening to what this tight-lipped man had to say.

"What *Pegasus?*" she asked, looking up at the night sky. "I don't see anything other than stars."

She knew the twelve constellations of the zodiac and the famous ones like *Hercules* and *Ursa Major*, but she'd never looked for *Pegasus*.

"Look at those four stars," he said, easily giving in and pointing to the same point in the sky. "Do you see?"

She scanned over the sky looking at the stars and then nodded. Davud looked at her to make sure she was looking at the stars.

"Now draw a line between the stars going out to the right and left of that square to this square and imagine a winged horse."

Beatriz had a confused look on her face at first. She tilted her head to one side and then the other, trying to imagine this flying creature in the sky. The constellations of the zodiac—even Leo, Aries and Cancer—were obvious, but it didn't seem possible to make a winged horse out of these stars. It was worth a try, though, for Davud's sake.

He waited patiently and got a little closer. "Look, those are its head, those are its legs and those are its wings."

Her face brightened after a while and she started to smile. "Ah, I see it now."

"My father showed me this constellation when I was small. I'd watch it rise in the sky from the window every summer night before going to bed. Then I imagined it would come down to earth and take me away between the other stars to different lands and kingdoms. I dreamed that *Pegasus* would take me to fairytale houses I'd never heard of among people I'd never seen like the flying carpet in *One Thousand and One Nights* that my mother used to read to me before bed."

Beatriz turned and looked at him, listening interestedly.

"It seems my wish was granted even though the flying horse never came to get me. My childhood and youth were spent with my father who sometimes worked as a diplomat and sometimes a spy, moving from one European kingdom to another—in Buda and Pest, Rome, Naples and Paris. It seems like we made our home everywhere in the world like nomads and we only stayed a few years in each before we moved on. I was happy that I could always see the same stars whenever I looked up as I went from land to land and kingdom to kingdom like a migrating bird. *Pegasus* rises on summer nights and *Orion* in winter—it reminds me how small a land the world is. I look at the stars and think no matter what land I'm in, I'm on the earth, and no matter what culture I'm in, I walk around on a small sphere and feel safe. The stars saved me from my sense of being lost and reminded me that I'm of the earth. *Pegasus* is in Constantinople and Rome." He looked back up at the sky. "I didn't know then that I'd share the same fate as my father because of my familiarity with the languages and cultures of these lands and spend two-thirds of my life as a spy outside Constantinople." He paused. "Then something happened. Something I'd never reckoned and never wanted."

He was quiet for a moment and licked his lips. "Years later—" he said, skipping this part of his life that he didn't want to tell like a novice storyteller who quickly passes through some episodes to get to the end. "Years later I dreamed many times that this winged horse would come get me in Spain and fly me back to Constantinople, where I was born. As a child I had wanted it to take me to different lands, but as an adult I begged it to take me home."

He looked at Beatriz and smiled. "And now we are. Maybe not on a winged horse, but one way or the other we're going to Constantinople, and I promise you that after what you've experienced here, it'll seem like heaven."

Beatriz looked at him tenderly, appreciating that he opened up about himself even this much, but she wondered about the secret he was hiding.

"What happened, Davud? What happened in Constantinople? What's this thing in your life that's made you so angry?"

Davud pursed his lips as if to say her entreaty wouldn't work. "We all have secrets, Beatriz. It's these secrets that define us. The secrets that only we and maybe those closest to us know." It was clear Davud didn't want to talk about this any more. "And what about you? What're you going to do when we get to Constantinople?"

Beatriz thought for a bit as if the question hadn't ever crossed her mind. "I'll find a rich Turk and marry him," she said, half joking.

Davud smiled.

Beatriz looked back up at the stars as if to cheer Davud up again and dispel the heavy air. "I don't know about a flying horse, but you look much more like that *Hercules*," she said, and pointed at the well-known constellation in the August night sky. "Your arms, your strength, your vigor—they look like him much more. If *Hercules* were a sign of the zodiac, that's what you'd be."

Davud blushed and didn't know what to say.

"Being a Leo wouldn't be so bad for you, either."

Davud eyes widened. "How'd you know I'm a Leo?"

Beatriz let out a sneaky giggle. "How soon you've forgotten that I'm a witch."

With this, she got up and walked over to the others, not wanting to bother him any longer.

Davud looked back up at the stars.

The Arabs call him *The Kneeler*, the Greeks *Heracles* and the Romans *Hercules*, but the stars are all the same, as is the character. The huge hero, kneeling on his right leg with his club raised and ready to strike, has the easiest stars to see in the summertime night sky. Davud thought about the Herculean myths. The Greek poet Aratus had said of the constellation that *no one knows how to read the sign clearly, nor over what task he is bent.* Another bard of ancient Greece claimed that the hero had fought in a battle and had been wounded, and so was kneeling. But the greatest myth accepted in every culture was that *Draco* the dragon directly below *Hercules* had crushed the head of *Serpens* the snake as his eternal sentry. Davud slid his eyes over to the stars of *Serpens*, what the Arabs call *al-Hayyah*.

He'd forgotten that Hercules wears a lion skin according to legend.

69

Piri did his ablutions and then went back topside, tucking his shirt back in. He'd been preparing for his prayers as the sun set. The crewmen were going about their usual work. Those who were hungry were eating, the yardmen were manning the sails, the boatswain's mate was watching the hourglass, one of the crew was measure the sea depth with a rope and Helmsman Musa was leaning on the tiller and letting out a sigh.

On deck, Piri stopped and turned his head to the sky. He froze in place. Seeing the newly risen full moon stopped him in his tracks. He was transfixed for a while, but then pulled himself together and ran over to port. He quickly pulled up a glass and wood device—some kind of ancient temperature gauge—that was hanging from the gunwale into the sea. He hadn't even had enough time to fully button his shirt.

He hastily snatched up and read the device. He couldn't believe his eyes and looked at the numbers again and again. Something must've gone wrong. Then he pulled up the second one and looked at it. It was the same. He tossed the device to the deck, cracking the glass, the liquid inside leaking out and running in between the cracks between the wood planks.

He went running and yelling to the quarterdeck. "Uncle, Uncle!"

Kemal Reis was sitting cross-legged and looking over maps spread out over the deck. "Whoa there, nephew, don't be so rattled. What is it?"

Piri turned and pointed at the moon. "Don't you see the full moon, Uncle? Look at it," Piri panted.

Kemal Reis stood up, took a couple steps forward and looked up at the sky. The full moon was red.

The captain was surprised.

"What's this? Or is it—?"

"Yes, Uncle. It's the *One-Eye!*"

"Come on, though, can you be so sure?"

"I took readings of the sea temperature. I checked over and over—the water's too hot."

"What're you saying? Are you sure?"

Piri looked worried and nodded slowly.

Kemal Reis looked back up to the full moon. He needed to move fast. Once a year or every few years a cyclone would form on the Mediterranean—the *One-Eye*—in the middle point between Europe and North Africa, and one was about to strike right where Kemal Reis and Burak Reis' fleet was sailing. A red moon and unusually warm water were the clearest signs of the coming of this terrifying storm.

Burak Reis looked worriedly at the red moon and then at Mute Yusuf, who was just as worried as the captain. Both of them were deadly silent.

"Ahmed, would you call this the One-Eye?" Rattler said, jabbing the merchant in the side.

Big Ahmed's mouth hung open as he stared at the moon.

Yasin didn't understand why everyone had suddenly stopped and looked up at the full moon. "What's going on, Yunus? For God's sake, what the hell's all this rumbling about? Who's One-Eye?"

Helmsman Yunus' voice was serious. "Don't you see the moon, boy? We're about to be caught up in these sea's wickedest storm."

"Why aren't we steering straight for the coast, then?"

"Why not? Because we're in the middle of the Mediterranean right now. The closest land is at least three hundred miles away. Which direction would we go? The storm'll bear down right on top of us."

Rattler's dog sensed the anxiousness in the air and started barking nonstop.

"Rattler, mate, my nerves are already frazzled without your damn mutt making that racket," Big Ahmed said. "Shut it up already."

Rattler picked up the little dog and cradling it in his arms as he took it down to one of the storerooms below deck to be safe. He didn't do it because of Big Ahmed's nerves, though—he was more worried about the little thing falling into the sea in the storm.

"Yardmen, reef in the sails," Burak Reis called out.

Mute Yusuf and his men set to tying up all the masts' sails. Yusuf's riggers climbed up and swung like spiders from the top of one mast to another and tied the sails to the yards as fast as they could.

"Wear ship!" Burak Reis yelled out to Helmsman Yunus. The wind left the sails with the turning of the galley.

This would make the job of the yardmen climbing up the masts with grappling hooks and out on the ends of the booms much easier.

In the meantime, dark, black clouds had hidden the full moon and the sky was wrapped in a leaden grey. The blue sea was calm and looked more like a sheet of steel.

As they drew closer and he saw the spiral in the sky, Yasin finally understood who, or what, the One-Eye was. The clouds were swirling dark as pitch as if it were Judgment Day. The weather made all the pirates' hearts knot up and sink in their chests. Beads of sweat started building up on all the their foreheads. The wind swept over the deck in ferocious gusts, licking the crew's faces like a whip.

The ropes began to whistle, turning into a howl and then a scream.

Having had the yardmen tie up the sails, Mute Yusuf had opened space for the wind. The pirate flag on the main topgallant was being whipped in the wind so relentlessly that it looked as if it had gone stiff. The ropes and pulleys squeaked and chattered like they were trying to tell the crew something. What had been gentle waters slowly picked up, carrying the Crescent of Victory and sending it undulating over the waves.

The pirates were running around trying to collect everything that could go overboard—water buckets, knives, weapons, stools— bundled them together with tethers and shoved them up against the bulwark.

Burak Reis glanced over at Kemal Reis' Blue Lion sixty yards away as he was completing preparations on his own ship and then back to gigantic galleys and the others following behind.

Rattler was shooting off at the mouth, as always. "For the life of me, Captain, I don't much know old man Kemal, but I'm not sure those two hulking galleys'll make it through this storm in one piece."

"Come on Rattler, say something worthwhile for once, mate," Big Ahmed said.

"What's the use of hiding what God knows from His servants, Little Ahmed? Look at these damn waves already."

"Isn't it better that they're big?" Yasin asked. "Do we really have to worry about it?"

Rattler laughed. "Oh, you young'un, skill's not with the ship, it's with the captain."

"Here it comes, boys. Here it comes!" Gunner Topal yelled, pointing at the approaching darkness.

The sky looked like a hole had opened up to unleash the hounds of hell on the earth. I lightning bolt whipped the sea as everyone stood staring at the sky, followed by such crashing thunder that the heavens seemed they would split in two. Another lightning bolt struck soon after, its force sending the Crescent of Victory hurtling forward.

Burak Reis called out to Watchman Mikhail. "You pulled in the oars, didn't you?"

"We did, Captain. All the portholes are closed."

Burak Reis looked up at the masts—all of their sails had been tied up. The ship had no oars out or sails up to drive it, but the galley was picking up so much speed it seemed the oarsman were churning away and the sails were full.

"It's damn frightening this plowing wind is enough to drive the ship just hitting the masts," Blind Ali said.

Boatswain Mahmud pointed down at the sea. "Don't take the sea lightly. Look at these swells."

Kemal Reis couldn't reckon anything from the direction of the waves. The Blue Lion was dwarfed by the towering waves rising around it, rocking in the trough like a cradle.

Mademoiselle Veronica was on the deck screaming.

"This woman's getting on my nerves—she's worse than the storm," said the captain.

The current was running in every direction, sometimes sending waves crashing into each other and erupting with white foam.

"Hold tight!" the captain shouted as he saw an incoming wave—a mountain of water bearing down on them.

Everyone looked for something to hold on to—the gunwale, ropes, the masts. The storm grew larger as they neared it. The bow of the Blue Lion shot so steeply into the air it seemed the ship would keel over, bucking from side to side like a wild stallion. The galley rose up high on the water as if it had run onto the back of a sea creature. Another wave passed and the ship went speeding down from the crest. Water was pouring over both sides of the ship as it cleaved through the sea, sending foam off its broadsides as if it had fallen from the sky. Nothing was stable and the ship started to list to port.

"Fill the starboard ballasts!" Kemal Reis ordered.

A group of crewmen went to the storerooms below and tried to move barrels, sandbags and sacks of wheat to starboard while the ship listed. They ran into each other as waves hit the ship and had trouble carrying their loads to the other side of the rocking ship, losing their balance, falling down and tumbling back and forth from storeroom to storeroom. A hundred pound barrel fell on its side and, with the steep incline from the waves, quickly rolled onto one of the crewmen. The others rolled the barrel off him, but he'd been crushed under its weight. They brought him to a safer part of the ship and called for Doctor Ilyas.

The Blue Lion slowly righted itself as they filled the starboard ballast, but it didn't last long, as the ship had to contend with the pouring rain driving down on the deck and the indiscriminant waves.

The crewmen manning the pumps were working nonstop to clear the deck.

Overseer Jihan came running. "Captain, Captain! The slaves are going mad and revolting because the ship's taking on water. They're screaming that they don't want to drown chained to their seats."

"Unshackle all their legs," the captain said. "Give each of them a bucket so they can bail out the water.

"What'll happen if they revolt, Captain?"

"I wouldn't send dozens of men to a watery grave. They're right. If they rise against us while we're sparing their lives, then that's their choice. Do as I say."

Jihan went back below deck and removed the chains from around the slaves' ankles. Not expecting this, they all took a bucket and started bailing out the water for dear life. Both the rain and the waves were constantly spilling over the deck.

The jiggermast top yard snapped off and flew away as the ship listed from side to side. The top of the foremast also cracked as the storm shook the ship like a pile of sticks.

"Help!" someone yelled out from on top of the mast.

When they looked up they saw Lookout Isa stranded on the yard of the shattered mast and holding on to two ropes that passed over the yard and through the pulleys. It was only a matter of time before the mast split down the center, sending the ropes streaming through the pulleys and the yard, and Isa into the angry sea. He was stuck—he could disrupt the balance or make the mast split faster if he moved. He was clinging to the yard for dear life as it spun around in half circles back and forth. The crew looked on helplessly.

The mast let out another loud crack and Mademoiselle Veronica started screaming again. The crack was spreading.

Kemal Reis threw off his sword and belt and stripped his rain-sodden shirt and tossed it into the sea. He scrambled up the foremast like a wildcat. He climbed up to where Isa was stranded—hand over hand on the ropes with his feet making their way up the mast as he blinked the rain out of his eyes.

"Reach out your hand!"

The rain was coming down in sheets and the captain had to spit water from his mouth as he was yelling to the boy.

Isa reached out his shaking hand, but there was still an arm's length between them. The captain realized there was no way to reach him from where he was, so he grabbed a rope and swung himself toward the boy with his other arm straining and outstretched, but still a hand's breadth remained between them. The ship then listed starboard, bringing the mast nearly parallel to the sea, and he had to twist and turn to stay balanced. The ship then listed back to port in an instant.

The captain looked around from where he was atop the ship, but couldn't see any of the rest of the fleet. They were all seeing to themselves.

He noticed something else, though—half a dozen cannons on deck were straining at their tethers. He yelled down to the crew. "Open the gun ports and cut the cannons' ropes. Tear them off if you need to. Let them roll into the sea!"

Mademoiselle Veronica was watching Kemal Reis in wonder and suspense.

Yardman Jevher and Overseer Jihan saw the danger and set straight to work when they saw the cannons kicking around like angry bulls. If the cannons—some of them half a ton—were to break free, they could roll to the other side of the ship and smash through the bulwark and take out anybody in their way. Jihan, Jevher and other crewmen grabbed axes and ran to the cannons to hack through their tethers so they would roll into the water when the ship tilted starboard and port.

The ship listed starboard again while the crewmen worked to untether the cannons, and Kemal Reis used it to make a powerful lunge for Isa. He caught him by the wrist and pulled, throwing him to the deck as the ship righted itself. Isa fell to the middle of the deck and, unhurt, ran to find a safe place to hold on to.

The burden put on the mast when Kemal Reis took hold of Isa was too much and the timber snapped. He tumbled with the top of the mast toward the fierce waves, but reached out for the gunwale and caught himself with half his body hanging over into the sea. He pulled himself over and ran straight for Helmsman Musa, who was about to completely lose control of the ship.

Jevher and Jihan had released all the cannons on the starboard side into the water and the men on portside had cut loose and sent off three of them. One of the men lost his balance and sliced a tether, sending a cannon careening into the others. They all sped across the deck as the galley listed to the other side. The three cannons then came rumbling back with the pitch of the ship, one of them crashing through the bulwark into the sea, leaving behind a three-foot-wide hole.

"Run, run. Save yourselves!" the crewman yelled.

Another of the cannons came rolling back to starboard with the motion of the ship, directly onto the deckhand who'd set it loose, crushing him like a walnut between its mass and the bulwark. The third cannon flew over the deck and over Hard-Nose Ibrahim's foot as he bailed out water before it smashed through the bulwark into the sea.

"I'm done for!" Ibrahim cried.

Water was now pouring onto the deck through the two large holes on either side. The Blue Lion was inundated.

Another loose cannon was now rolling around and smashing through anything in its path. The deck looked like a battlefield. It had rolled over a man's head, leaving him unrecognizable with blood spurting out of his ear.

Blind Ali was at the bow of the Crescent of Victory looking at the deep cut in the palm of his hand. He tore a piece from his shirt and quickly wrapped the wound. He'd been holding a rope to keep his balance, but the power of the storm ripped it from his hand, cutting like a knife as it flew through his grip. He used all his strength to keep his balance, but the master archer was thinking about whether he'd be able to shoot again with this hand.

Mute Yusuf, Rattler and Big Ahmed were near him on the forecastle deck, and when they looked to the quarterdeck of the pitching ship they saw Burak Reis flying through the air. Like Kemal Reis, Burak Reis had also taken on the helm and was wrestling with it as if he were trying to subdue a wild animal. The stern had risen so high with the waves passing under it that the bow looked like it was going to drive into the water, the stern towering a hundred sixty feet above.

The dark, towering waves kept rising to both sides and the rain was vicious and relentless.

"For the love of God, mate—you coming from below or above!" Rattler shouted at the storm.

It seemed as though the sea had been set on end and was crashing over the pirates' from head to foot.

"Mate, if the ship's not already sunk, then would you say we're wallowing in purgatory, Little Ahmed?" Rattler yelled out.

"Don't give me that crap, Rattler!" Ahmed yelled back through the water streaming over his face and into his mouth. "If it were that, we'd be winding up straight in hell and not some purgatory or other. And if it were that, there'd be fire roasting us all, so I've heard, instead of this damn wall of water!"

The pirates kept on with each other and were keeping up their moral even when looking death in the face.

Then the thing they needed least happened—a deadly cracking sound came from the keel. The Crescent of Victory was about to split in two.

70

Elif... lam... mim...

Prince Bayezid entered the room that had been prepared as his writing room in his villa in Amasya, and rolled up his sleeves. He wouldn't write without first doing his ablutions, as Sheikh Hamdullah had told him, explaining that the water would clean his body and the ink would clean his heart.

Bayezid had sat down to write so much recently that he was at no loss for letters looking back at him—*elif, lam, mim*—all repeated over and over. But he'd finished the lessons on letters and words and had now started on sentences.

The prince selected a piece of paper the color of sugar from the cabinet and laid it on the table inlaid with *rub' al-hizb* designs. There were stacks of paper on the top shelf in different whites and yellows. Damascus and wood pulp *hashebi* paper was good for scribbling but low quality, Hatay and *Adilshahi* paper was good for daily exercises, and slightly higher quality Indian paper was more suitable for writing sentences. But today Bayezid was a bit more confident and chose the highest quality Samarkand paper, the yellowy pink of a newborn baby.

You should know the nature of the paper well—is it soft enough, can it withstand erasing when you make a mistake, does ink take to it? You should understand all of this.

He took some chalk from the lower shelf and used it to remove the oil from the paper.

Removing the oil from the paper is just like repentance. First you must remove its flaws so that the surface you work on is beautiful and sturdy.

He started going through the reeds on the middle shelf after he had prepared the paper.

The reed should be neither hard nor soft. A hard pen won't bend enough and a soft one will have you make unnecessary mistakes.

He found the reed he was looking for—one with a dark chestnut color—and went to his writing table where he took an ivory-handled sharpener and carefully sharpened the nib. As the reed took more the shape of a pen, he placed it on the sharpening area of the table to work on it more. He held the knife at a forty-five degree angle to the nib and pressed the steel down with his left thumb in a curve to sculpt it in the style of Yaqut al-Musta'simi. One of the three greatest figures of calligraphy, al-Musta'simi had begun cutting the nib with a curve two centuries before, which had given the letters an esthetic quality never seen before.

Lastly, he held the pen in his left hand and drew the knife up from the nib less than half an inch to make the slit.

Don't assume that it is easy to split the nib. If you press quickly and without planning, the binder in the ink will damage the edges and wreak havoc on you. You'll have to split the nib again if you can't do it correctly at first. Then you'll have to do it over and over until there's not enough of the pen left to hold. Don't do anything thoughtlessly. This art is not for waste—it is work of putting together balanced movements. How can you expect well-balanced writing if you yourself aren't?

Now that the paper and pen were ready, it was time for the ink. The prince selected one of the inkpots from the cabinets, opened it and started to stir the contents with a quill. The writing would come out grey if the water and ink weren't well mixed and it wouldn't allow the calligrapher to use his talents. He added a piece of rough silk and a few drops of grape juice to the ink that had been made from soot, as Hamdullah had instructed him. As he dropped in the grape juice, he remembered the bacchanalias he and his friends used to have in this room with countless glasses of wine. The corner of his mouth turned up in a smile. There were dancers sensuously moving their lithe bodies in the middle of the room, his friends clinking their glasses over in a corner, everyone in reverie. Those days had passed and now simply made Bayezid smile.

After mixing the ink, he checked to make sure it was the right consistency and thought about what he would write.

The correct adjustments for the ink must be determined according to the features of the writing.

Bayezid had now prepared his three materials—paper, pen and ink.

The tools do the work and the hand does the boasting. By the time I became a calligrapher, I'd spent so much gold on these materials and benefitted from many artisans. You will not make waste—there is no waste in searching for and finding good materials and spending money and effort for its sake. Extravagance is needless, but investing in these tools is indispensible. Should we tear paper when we have scissors? What point is there in doing nothing when there's a good place to cut a pen in the hand?

The prince sat in the position that ibn al-Bawwab had described centuries before in his qasida, *Rhyming in R*, as hundreds of calligraphers from dozens of communities had and, of course, as Hamdullah had taught him. His left leg was tucked beneath him and his right knee was against his chest, he brought the writing platform to his knee and set the trimmed paper on it. He moved his right hand back and forth to loosen it up and be more fluid while he prepared the fur pad for his writing hand.

One must remove pride and ego from one's heart before one begins to write, trust in God and write with devotion as if He were the word. You must rid your mind of negative thoughts and trust yourself. Don't curse if your writing is not beautiful when you start—this work is hard, but it gets easier with practice. Isn't it the same for all work? Every difficulty is followed by facility.

Prince Bayezid's lips moved almost imperceptibly, saying *bismillah* as dipped his pen into the ink and placed a dot in the upper right corner of the sheet of paper. Hamdullah had taught him to put this diamond-shaped dot on the page, as this way, he could test the color of the ink and the nib of the pen before starting. He wrote out the *Rabbi Yassir* prayer just to the left of the diamond—*O my Lord, make things easier for me, do not make things difficult for me.* These words were like a charm for the thousands of calligraphers who had come and gone. No matter how heavy his heart, it would lift whenever Bayezid wrote the letter *re.*

Then he wrote the first letter of the sentence a line below. He held his breath as he wrote, only exhaling when he paused.

Hamdullah had once explained this with a smile on his face.

They say that the lives of us calligraphers are long. A calligrapher holds his breath as much as he writes. That's life, isn't it, the culmination of breath?

The letters you write must be fluid like a breath—they should look like breathing. You don't actually breath, but through this the letters begin to breath. Letters written with a trembling hand while breathing are dead from the start, but if you kill yourself, then the letters will live for eternity. Do you understand now why calligraphers can never talk about themselves? The writing shows you, even the breaths you take. You wouldn't know, though, but you'll have true life by crushing the self thanks to that writing. Writing is full of such secrets, and as you do it competently, so is it faithful.

He tilted his head from side to side after he finished the first word and before he moved on to the second, thinking about whether his writing was beautiful or not.

What is beauty? According to Plato, all of what we call the fine arts are a shadow of earthly ephemeralities. If man attempts to imitate nature, he can actually go no further than making the shadow of a shadow. That's why true art is that which shows the eternal, hidden beauty behind these ephemeralities. According to Aristotle, beauty is the imparting of art with the breath of life.

Calligraphy, however, dear Prince, is the uniting of esthetics and mathematics, geometry and art, and substance and meaning.

He dipped his pen into the ink again before starting the second word. He held the pad with his left hand, and the pen started to groan again as he touched it to the paper and drew it along.

There's purity in beautiful calligraphy like in nature. Dirty consciences and broken spirits cannot touch this purity. Beautiful calligraphy requires a beautiful character. Being a man of letters is not for just anyone, Bayezid my boy. For the first months of my apprenticeship, my teacher wouldn't start until after I'd written Right Life or God a hundred times every day. Your willpower is reflected in the writing. You learn about a person who's shabby and wretched, whose shirt is dirty and a mess, and like that so is calligraphy a mirror to your soul.

A story that Hamdullah had told him sometime before was running through his mind.

There was once a great caliph who held writing in great esteem. One of his viziers wrote a letter to air his complaints and gave it to him. The caliph read the letter but didn't give it any credence. He told the vizier his writing was ugly and that if he had had good intentions, that grace would've been reflected in the letter. He told the vizier he would be ready to listen when the letter comes beautifully written.

The writings of a man of letters are not only tied to himself—they're connected to the people, religion and land whence they come. People will look at your writing and pass judgment on your civilization. The letters you write will be a sign of the character of your empire. Know that the lines you write will reveal your intelligence, will and esthetics, and not only yours, but those of your forbearers.

Don't forget, dear Prince, that when you're writing, you're walking on the straight path of a sharpened knife-edge as thin as a hair.

Hamdullah knew that as a calligrapher holding a pen becomes inflexible, so too does his writing.

It must be as though you're not in this world when you're writing, just as the ascetic cares not for anything. They say that our sage Yaqut al-Musta'simi was so engrossed in his writing that even while the Mon-

gols were sacking and burning his city, he went up a minaret and continued writing. He'd already continued to write new books on whatever he
could find, writing on discarded shirts and towels whatever lines came to
his mind as the barbarians were burning books.

Bayezid finished the line he was working on and looked at the
letters. He also paid attention to how the writing progressed.

*Novices, and even worse, those who know little try to place the letters
in the lines they draw beforehand. This's what unrefined, half-baked and
flat minds do. This is the way of those who see life as black and white,
horizontal and vertical, and are beyond their depth with more than two
options. The issue, though, is not whether or not there are guiding lines
for the letters, but their placement. This what they call the throne of
letters. One who hasn't studied under a good master wouldn't understand
this. No matter how beautiful your letters are, if the letters don't sit on
their thrones, then you're unable to go beyond mathematics, which means
you're unable to see beyond the material.*

The prince was eager to show Hamdullah the sentence he wrote.
He wondered if the letters were on their thrones or not along with
dozens of other details.

*When you finish writing, it's like a flower breaking through the soil
on the page. It should elicit a feeling as if the writing had been hidden
within the paper for centuries and you just now drew it out.*

*That's the thing, Bayezid, sir. If you keep writing patiently, eagerly
and persistently, your writing will change according to that. This is your
summer for august writing, dear Prince.*

*The pen is powerful—more so than the sword and the tongue, and the
war hammer and spear.*

*In that case, give thanks to God and abide by his approval when you
attain your wants and desires. Don't write a line or move the pen an inch
for the benefit of the world—instead encourage yourself to write and do
the beautiful and good things that will ensure you remember the goodness
in the world.*

*For tomorrow when people are presented with their books of deeds at
the Day of Judgment, everyone will receive their judgment.*

The prince looked out the window toward the sun and got lost in thought. The drying ink on the paper in the sunlight looked like little rivers and the letters of the fourth and fifth verses of the *al-'Alaq* surah sparkled—*He who taught by the pen, taught man that which he knew not.*

71

Davud looked at his wife as she slept peacefully under their supple, yellow Kastamonu sheet. He thought these were his wife's most beautiful, innocent and sweetest moments when he would wake up at night and watch as she slept. Elif's mother had sent for hand-woven sheets from Kastamonu whose edges she then worked with silver and gold silk over the course of twenty years, filling up a chest for the dowry for her only daughter.

Even a few years after marrying, Elif was still pulling out a tablecloth, towels, bath mitts, woolen socks and many other things Davud had never seen and had no idea existed. He'd joke that if they were left without anything, they'd still be able to furnish a house just with what came out of this chest.

She had taken out this sheet that night.

"The magic chest opens again," Davud had said and laughed. "Every house needs a chest like this."

He saw his wife as just as elegant, beautiful and precious as the supple, yellow sheet they were lying under. It was the picture of innocence for him as he looked at her while she breathed slowly and deeply within the folds of this sheet. His wife had a particular specialization for sleep—Davud would watch her do what she needed to every night, repeating her routine every evening as if she were going through the fine steps of a ritual. He watched her as she fluffed the pillows like a bird preparing its nest, as she curled up beneath the quilt and laid her head down, warming up the covers, and then as she slept, unconsciously moving her right leg back and forth, and sometimes curled up tightly like a baby.

On warm summer nights like this one, she would throw off the sheet or quilt and take it between her legs.

He looked at her body beneath her fine-spun and nearly transparent nightgown, her hair spread across the pillow, her crimson lips and rosy cheeks. He took in her black eyelashes, each the curl of a little crescent, her elegant neck—long and thin like a swan's—her full breasts, thin waist and smooth, curving hips.

Davud most loved to get close to her in her most innocent moments when she was sleeping the deepest. He gently moved to her and put his hand on her hip. He put his face to her neck and inhaled deeply as if he were in a flower garden, and kissed her where her neck met her shoulder.

She smiled, her eyes still closed.

Taking it as a sign, he started to move his hand up her body.

"Davud," she said, drawing out his name quietly but annoyed, "you're waking me up."

Davud liked this even more—he enjoyed nothing more than nettling his wife.

He took a chance at it again, gently sliding up her nightgown and caressing her hips.

"Davud, I'm tired."

She was much more clear this time and he didn't persist. He gave her one last kiss and withdrew to his pillow.

He turned onto his back and stared at the ceiling with a hand beneath his head. He wasn't sleepy at all and kept his eyes on the ceiling and the wooden slats forming hundreds of overlapping six-pointed stars. This ornament was found in the houses of Constantinople's wealthy residents. The craftsmanship was laborious, as each of the hundreds of slats had to be placed on the ceiling individually. He stared at the center of the eighteen-pointed star in the middle of the ceiling. The more he gazed at it, the concentric stars appeared to move and rotate. He would often do this when he couldn't sleep—sometimes it would lull him to sleep and other times it would bring thoughts to his mind and keep him awake.

He was lucky tonight, though. He felt a stirring next to him. He looked over and saw Elif looking at him, her eyes mischievous.

"You woke me up," she huffed, although with a smile.

Having already lost hope for the night, Davud didn't want to pass up this opportunity and leaned in to her lips and kissed her hungrily.

The two embraced and entangled each other amid the folds of the supple, yellow sheet. The stars on the ceiling started to spin faster.

Davud was leaning back on a hillside and watching the stars through far away, teary eyes, his hands folded behind his head. He wasn't so much looking at the night sky, but rather at the past.

"I'm not bothering you, am I?" David said as he sat down beside him—although he moved to get back up and leave after seeing Davud's red eyes.

"It's nothing," Davud said. "I couldn't sleep."

David laid down beside him and Davud turned his head to wipe his eyes.

"The sky's clear tonight," David said.

"It's the middle of summer," Davud said, just to say something.

"You like looking at the sky. You're always looking up at the heavens whenever I see you alone at night."

"It puts me at ease. The stillness, silence and calm of the stars in the sky gives me peace while people on earth hack away at each other and chase endlessly after other creatures. It reminds me of how empty and meaningless the things we pursue are."

"Of the books I printed, one of the most sought after in Italy was the *Alfonsine Tables*. We sent a dozen each month to the University of Padua. It makes a lot of sense why scholars have tried so much to understand the sky when you look up at that enchanting spectacle."

Davud smiled when he heard David mention the renowned astronomical text with calculations of the stars and planets named for King Alfonso X of Castile, who had lived in the thirteenth century.

"What a shame there aren't any Catholic kings like Alfonso left in Spain. I often wonder what Ferdinand and Isabella would think of Alfonso the Wise as fellow Catholics but so different in actions."

"My grandfather had explained it to me when I was a child. My great, great grandfather Yehuda ben Moshe ha-Kohen was one of Alfonso's translators and had told him of it. I still remember those days—" David said.

Davud cut him off. "Moshe ha-Kohen is your great, great grandfather?"

David nodded humbly. "He translated al-Tusi, al-Sufi, al-Farghani, al-Khwarizmi and a whole bunch of other Muslim scholars' books. I was getting ready to print all their work."

Davud couldn't believe what he was hearing and looked back up to the sky. "No wonder you have such influential friends in Constantinople and are in such demand."

He couldn't believe he was next to the man whose ancestor had translated nearly the most Arabic and Hebrew works in Spain into Latin after Gerard of Cremona. These renowned translators of the thirteenth century had over a century transferred all the scientific knowledge acquired by Islamic civilization to Western Europe through their renderings of these books. And now, this great, great grandson of one of them had made it his mission to distribute them to the rest of Europe with his printing press.

"They said Alfonso was really liberal and clever. He also laughed at the sight of the kingdom's greatest astronomers, most Muslims, bringing together the most valuable astronomical manuscripts in Toledo along with Ptolemy's peculiar accounts and said that if God had consulted him when He created everything, he would have given Him a couple hints to make the system simpler."

Davud couldn't help but smile. "How could it be God's fault? It's Ptolemy who's at fault—or more correctly, the ancient Greeks and those who don't question Ptolemy and take his work as sacred. What else would you expect from a geocentric view of the heavens? All the calculations are easier with the sun at the center."

"I'd gotten my hands on a Muslim scholar's manuscript that mentioned similar things. There're others who have related theories, too, but those views aren't so much in demand yet."

"There's an astronomer in Samarkand called Ulugh Beg. I heard of what they were doing in his observatory from Ali Qushji, one of his students who's now at the Constantinople observatory. Scholars from the previous century like al-Tusi, al-Battani, al-Farghani and ibn Yunus all mention the heliocentric heavens." Davud smiled again. "I'm really curious about what the Inquisition will do when they hear these theories that subvert their whole discourse on the Bible."

"I don't know what the Inquisition will do, but you can be sure I won't be there when these ideas spread among Catholics," David said

They both looked at the night sky. The *Summer Triangle—Vega, Altar* and *Deneb*—were twinkling brilliantly.

"The more you look at the stars, you understand why the ancients worshipped them and saw the moon and sun as gods," David said. "If faith isn't strong then people beseech the stars. Maybe looking at the stars and making a wish is a relic from those times. What do you think?"

"I don't understand those people. I think Abraham's the best answer to that. When he noticed that the sun set at night, that the moon isn't present in the day and that the stars couldn't be seen in the light of day, it wasn't for nothing that he said his God must be everywhere, in the light and the darkness. Someone who uses their mind can easily see there's a higher power behind these things, despite all their beauty. Nothing else is necessary."

"Abraham's father sold God." David said. "More than pagans, his business was to make and sell idols. You know the story—Abraham's father left his shop to him one day and told him to mind the stock. He came back at the end of the day and saw all the idols smashed. Only the largest one made from wood was in one piece.

He asked Abraham what he'd done to the idols, and Abraham said he'd done nothing, that the greatest one, God, had killed the others. His father got angry and said it was only wood so how could it kill the others. Abraham then told his father that he admits it then, that God cannot be of stone or wood."

Davud knew the story. He'd once enjoyed listening to it from a Jewish man.

He almost said that he wished Jews would—but stopped himself. He wanted to say the Israelites had been just as foolish as the pagans and remind David that even after Moses had performed the miracle of parting the sea to save the Jews from Pharaoh, they wanted Moses to make an idol for them. He could've listed all the verses in the Quran about how despite all of Moses' advice, the first work the Israelites set to was to fashion a golden calf as an idol to worship. But just thinking about these people who were now being burned alive for their beliefs made him keep his mouth shut.

"I know what you're thinking," David said.

Davud looked at him without saying anything.

"So why are you saving us, then? David asked.

"True, I don't share your beliefs, and it's true that I hate your beliefs. The true religion of God is Islam. That's my belief." He was quiet for a while. "But this doesn't entitle me to kill, torture or destroy you. There's no coercion in religion. That's what my religion orders of me. I'd try to convince you, but I wouldn't force you. Your religion is for you all and mine is for me. We don't look at religion while we save people butchers oppress."

He stood up, not wanting to continue with the conversation, and returned to Abraham's fight against idols. He recited the forty-sixth verse of the *Maryam* surah in Arabic.

"Have you no desire for my gods, O Abraham, his father said."

How nice, Davud thought, that they could at least meet in their love of Abraham, and that it was enough to bring people together on common ground.

72

The Blue Lion and the rest of the fleet had passed Sicily and were slowly making their way through the waters off Sardinia. Burak Reis had saved his ship from the cyclone by emptying it of everything it had on board. They had repaired the ship and made it sturdy again—replacing the caulking and the shattered parts of the deck—at the first island they had run across. The Blue Lion had escaped the storm with minor damage but the cannons on Kemal Reis' ship had crippled half a dozen crewmen and torn holes through the broadside that let the sea rush in, but it still sailed. The other ships were not so lucky, though. A galley and galiot from each of the two groups had sunk. Fortunately, both the Göke and Göke II were still seaworthy.

After the storm, it was as if Kemal Reis and Burak Reis had found themselves on another planet as the black clouds dispersed and the sun began to shine. The water was still and as smooth as a mirror. The ship was rocking gently while everyone on board—soldiers, galley slaves and crewmen—had fallen asleep. Piri and Orion Orhan, though, were keeping the watch in the crow's nest. The night sky ran into the dark blue sea, the stars reflected on its still surface, giving the Blue Lion the look that it was sailing through a fantasy. There was no distinction between the stars on the horizon and their reflections, and they shined from every direction.

Piri couldn't miss this opportunity. He'd noticed that the sky would be clear from the early hours of the evening and had sat in the ships most stable part in the middle of the deck with all types of star maps laid out around him. His trunk was full of books, rulers, quadrants, astrolabes, maps and charts, and now he had al-Sufi's star map and Ulugh Beg and Ali Qushji's drawings in front of him.

His greatest motivation for joining his uncle's campaigns was to see how the stars looked from different areas and different degrees of longitude and latitude. The horizon was as wide as the sea, and the entire sky turned into a laboratory for the young astronomer. He kept alert while everyone else was sound asleep, looking on the heavens with admiration as he started to read the stars again.

Orion Orhan knelt down next to Piri and watched him work. He had just begun. Piri lifted his arm up to the sky with his thumb and little finger extended and looked up squinting through one eye. He slowly moved his arm, mumbling calculations. He dropped his arm as if he'd found what he was looking for, picked up his note-book and very carefully plotted the measurements with a ruler.

"Hey Piri, you've never taught me about these finger measure-ments," Orhan said.

He knew that Piri was always busy and he didn't want to bother him, but he also couldn't help from asking what he was measuring when Piri was looking up at the sky. His curiosity was eating away at him.

Piri smiled. "That's the easy part, Orhan. What's difficult is rep-resenting the stars on paper and comparing them with the stars hundreds of years ago." He put aside his ruler and notebook. "Here, look." He put up a fist and extended his little finger. "The little fin-ger is one degree in the sky. So, the highest point of the heavens is ninety degrees from the horizon and from one horizon to the op-posite one over the sky is one hundred eighty degrees, and the little finger is one of these. The tip of the little finger is also enough to cover up the moon or the sun since they never appear larger than one degree. The tricky part is to stretch out your arm well. The degrees will be off if you don't hold it out perfectly straight."

"Can everyone to do this? I mean, some people's hands are small and some are big. What do I know—you know, children's hands are small and adults' hands are big. Like that."

"That's true, but remember that no matter how short or long one's arm is, they all have the same ratios. The important thing is the ratio of the eye to the length of the arm, and for everybody it's nearly the same. And then when someone is accustomed to the proportion of their little finger to the sky, converting it into calculations is easy."

Orhan made a fist like Piri and stuck his little finger out to the sky with his arm straight. He put his finger over the moon and blocked it out.

"Now here it's important to find how many of your fingers are equivalent to how many degrees." He extended his index, middle and ring fingers. "Look, these three fingers are five degrees in the sky, so five times what the little finger makes. You see those two stars shining there? Put these three fingers in between them. You see? These three fingers fill up the space between those two stars— al-Dubb and al-Maraqq—since the space between them is five degrees. Al-Dubb means the bear in Arabic, like the constellation Ursa Major, and al-Maraqq means the loins. They likened it to the bear's loins since it's lower."

Orhan put three fingers between al-Dubb and al-Maraqq as Piri described—he smiled with glee when they actually filled the space.

"Now make a fist and put it next to al-Dubb. What do you see?"

Orhan did what Piri said and saw another star shining on the other side of his fist. "There's another star."

"That's Alioth. It's also been called Aliore and al-Hawar, or the white of the eye."

Piri then stuck out his thumb and little finger and stretched his arm out.

"You'll see another star to the left when you line up your right finger with *al-Dubb*. That's *al-Qaid*—the furthest out in *Ursa Major*, the leader star. There's about twenty-five degrees between these two fingers, so it's twenty-five degrees between those two stars."

This discovery gave Orhan the same joy a conqueror feels when taking new territory.

"So that's how you can find the positions of the stars in the sky, their movements and the constellations even without any instruments. For example, if you follow the line up from *al-Dubb* and *al-Maraqq*, then you see the *North Star*—the brightest in the sky. There's about twenty-eight degrees between *al-Dubb* and *Polaris*."

Orhan imagined lines running from star to star as Piri was explaining, and he came to the two Piri had mentioned, which then became clearer than the hundreds of others, drawing his eye to the *North Star* winking back at him.

"When you follow the tail of *Ursa Major*, you'll find *Ursa Minor*. Look—the group with a square and a tail. The upper two stars on the left are called *al-Farqadain*. The one shining just below it is *Kochab*. It comes from the Arabic *al-Kawkab*, which means star. But the thing I love about these stars is that I liken them to Kemal Reis and Burak Reis because they call these stars the *Guardians of the Pole*. They constantly revolve around *Polaris*, and *Polaris* is always fixed. It's the one that shows you they way. It's as if it's the duty of these stars to protect and watch over *Polaris*."

Orhan enjoyed the story.

"All the stars move. It's only *Polaris* that's fixed. All the others revolve around it."

"How's that? Isn't it a star, or is it something else? Why doesn't it revolve?

"It actually does. Or, really, none of the stars revolve. It's the earth that turns. It's like when we look at the sun from the earth and it looks like it's moving. That's what the stars do, too."

"So this *Polaris*—what's it's secret? How does it always stay in the same place? If the world is turning, how does it always point in the same direction?"

"There are two important points here. The first is its position and the second has to do with its distance. The *North Star* is aligned with the Earth's axis, so no matter how much the world turns, it always stays on that line. But even so, the star changes position throughout the year. It concerns the annual movement of the stars, like how we can't see your so-admired Orion right now. You see different constellations every season, just like how the zodiac changes every month. But the *North Star* is always in the same spot. The star is so far away from us that even with the earth revolving around the sun, it looks to be stable and fixed. The star's distance also makes it look fixed like how a far off horizon seems to stay at the same distance no matter how fast the galley is going,"

Piri and Orhan both had their heads at forty-five degrees, gazing up at the *North Star*.

"You know what the interesting thing is though?" Piri said. "These stars that look so stationary actually move, too. They move at speeds more than hundreds of times faster than any object on the Earth. The *North Star* also makes this movement. You see that star shining between *Ursa Major* and *Ursa Minor?*"

Orhan looked up and nodded.

"The Arabs call that one *Thuban*, which means snake. Did you know that it was the pole star four thousand years ago in the time of ancient Egypt?"

Orhon looked on in astonishment.

"And those stars I told you about, the *Guardians of the Pole*—*al-Fargadain* and *Kochab*—centuries ago those were the pole stars. People looked up at them and got their bearings."

Piri sighed and looked back up at the *North Star*.

"A day will come when *Polaris* will pass on its turn and another star will come to the center. People will discover the world on routes with a different star. Absolutely nothing lasts forever. Only God is eternal."

Orhan's neck hurt from craning it at the sky and he hung it down.

"How do you know this much? Like about the *North Star*? If the movement of these stars can only be seen over centuries and millennia, then howcan anyone alive now know it?"

Piri picked up his notebook. "This is how. You're right. A star moves an inch and a half over four thousand years. This isn't something you can measure with your fingers like I showed you. It's only a practical way for us to describe the heavens—a blessing from God. The real science requires making records and using instruments." He pointed at his rulers and astrolabes. "It requires the accumulation of the knowledge of all civilizations. We wouldn't be able to read the heavens now if it weren't for the star maps from Egypt, if we couldn't read the observations of Hipparchus and Ptolemy from ancient Greece, if we didn't know the calculation of the stars by the Persian al-Sufi, if it weren't for the work that astronomers like the Timurids Ulugh Beg and Ali Qushji did in their observatories, and if we never saw the *Alfonsine Tables* created by the Muslim, Jewish and Christian scholars in Spain. And not just the heavens—the whole of the cosmos would have no language and creation would be left stuttering. Science isn't the holding of any one religion or people, Orhan. It belongs to all man."

"So these thousands of years of notes are checked over and over, get added to each other and keep a record of what's in the sky. Is that it?"

"Precisely."

"So that's how we learn about the previous pole stars and the movements of the other stars."

"Those who come after us will learn from us, as well. A European could read it, or an Arab, or someone from some other place. But there's no doubt that he who can read the heavens will rule the world. Science and power have always gone together throughout the ages."

They both sat and watched the sky for a while in silence. It was so clear that they could make out all the details large and small of the millions of stars of the *Milky Way*.

One star seemed to signal to them, quickly arcing overhead and fading away.

"Did you see that?" Orhan said.

Piri smiled. "Uh-huh."

He'd seen countless shooting stars while making observations, but it was the first for Orhan. His heart was thumping with excitement and he was fascinated.

"Those whose eyes are open while everyone else sleeps are always rewarded, Orhan. If you give yourself to science, it'll offer many more things to you."

The Blue Lion continued on its way like a mystical ship sailing on a sea of stars.

BOOK FIVE
Calligraphy of the Stars

73

"Si *enim secundum carnem vixeritis moriemini si autem Spiritu facta carnis mortificatis vivetis.*"

Verses from *Romans* echoed throughout one of the underground chambers of the Suprema in Seville, as happened every night, each verse accompanied by the crack of a whip.

For if ye live after the flesh, ye shall die, but if ye through the Spirit do mortify the deeds of the body, ye shall live.

The only thing lighting the chamber was a fireplace in the corner of the moldy, damp room. The smoke from the flickering flames rose through the flue in the wall and up the chimney. On the other side of the room was a man wearing a pointed hood kneeling on the ground, his dark shadow playing on the walls as the fire quivered, making him look like a wraith.

There was a shadow cast on the wall of a man's arm holding a whip as he lashed his back. The whips twelve tails cut deep into his flesh and opened painful wounds. The heat from the fire was making him sweat, and it poured down his body searing his wounds all the more.

His shadow covered the entire wall like a hulking monster. Even if not for that, Lucas was already a brute, tall and broad, who stood a head and shoulders over an average tall man.

"*Qui autem sunt Christi carnem crucifixerunt cum vitiis et concupiscentiis.*"

The whip cracked again.

His hood came down over his face with only holes for his eyes and mouth. Other than that he was completely nude. His back was bloody, and each lashing added freshly torn flesh to the old scars already there, reopening some that had partly healed. His hand holding the whip had scars from where nails had been driven through.

And they who belong to Christ have crucified the flesh with the passions and lusts.

Torquemada had met Lucas when he had been stealing from the monastery when he was young. As he listened to the boy's story, he was convinced that Lucas was a prize sent by God to punish the people.

As he was now, Lucas' past was just as wicked.

A child born to a girl raped by her father, his mind was underdeveloped from the incest, but his body grew uncommonly large. His wide and sloping forehead, uneven eyes and brow, large ears, and massive bones, hands and feet had disgusted people since his childhood, and upon seeing his face they took him for some sort of creature. He set fire to his house one night in a fit of rage, killing both his father and sister-mother. Torquemada had adopted him after the boy had been sleeping on the streets for days,.

"*Vae tibi Corazain vae tibi Bethsaida quia si in Tyro et Sidone factae fuissent virtutes quae in vobis factae sunt olim in cilicio et cinere sedentes paeniterent.*"

The whip cracked again, this time sending blood spattering.

Woe unto thee, Chorazin, woe unto thee, Bethsaida, for if the mighty works had been done in Tyre and Sidon, which have been done in you, they would have long ago repented, sitting in sackcloth and ashes.

Lucas lashed his back with more vigor every time he recited this verse.

Torquemada had given meaning to his meaningless life, having explained that while man was born in sin, one's salvation is within himself. Torquemada had taught this verse to Lucas when he was a boy and had named him after it—*Luke*, chapter ten, verse thirteen. He'd told the boy that man is sinful, but can find freedom through living in pain like Christ and had given him a wide brimmed hat of the Dominicans to fend of the looks of disgust. He'd then had the knights of Santa Hermandad raise him, ensuring a helmet always hid his face. Lucas quickly found success in his new life and felt as though he'd found his place in the world. He was able to cut down even the most expert knights with the swords he wielded, and though his body shouted to him as the handiwork of a sinner, he'd found a new mission with what Torquemada had taught him.

Lucas believed body and soul that men are sinners. He found a village girl on the street the previous evening and had taken her to the woods. Now he was punishing himself for his indulgence. Each lash from the whip was purifying his soul over and again.

"*Ecce dedi vobis potestatem calcandi supra serpentes et scorpiones et supra omnem virtutem inimici et nihil vobis nocebit.*"

Torquemada had made this obedient man the head of the special guard corps made up of the knights of Santa Hermandad. As time passed and Lucas grew up in Torquemada's hands, he had made him see all sorts of unlawfulness. Lucas knew that Torquemada's enemies were his enemies, and never went outside without word from the grand inquisitor. Torquemada overlooked Lucas' heresies, and Lucas repeatedly forgave himself as he purged his sins in this room, lashing himself a hundred times every evening.

Behold, I give unto you power to tread on serpents and scorpions, and over all the power of the enemy, and nothing shall by any means hurt you.

The whip cracked the hundredth time.

Torquemada appeared behind him. Lucas rose to his feet. He turned around and took two steps toward the Grand Inquisitor before falling to his knees.

Torquemada slowly lifted the hood covering Lucas' face from his head. His face was nearly level with Torquemada's despite him being on his knees. He took Lucas' head in his hands and kissed his forehead.

"Father," Lucas said quietly.

"I have a new duty for you."

Lucas lifted his head, his face full of rage and submission, ready to hear what it was.

Torquemada told Lucas to kill the Ottoman spy and his group who had been causing trouble throughout the kingdom in the last two weeks. As his right-hand man, Lucas, a master knight, had already taken action.

74

It was early in the evening and the stars had just started to show themselves. Juan de Moguer, one of the three-dozen men aboard the Santa Maria, looked at the old compass he was holding and shook his head. Clavijo didn't know how Martin Alonso Pinzon would respond to his and his mates' recent mutiny, but alarm had already been raised.

"What is it, Juan? It looks like you're chomping on something again," one of the yardmen said.

"What is it? Don't you see the compass? It's not lined up with the North Star anymore. It's at least five degrees off."

The yardman was alarmed. "Oh my God, you're not lying are you?"

Another sailor heard him as he approached. "Are there demons in the middle of this dark ocean?"

The man's shouting caught the attention of two deckhands swabbing the quarterdeck. Murmuring and confusion spread throughout the whole ship like rings in the water from a dropped stone.

"Our compass is worthless!"

"We're done for! How'll we find our way without a compass?"

"This is the Devil's work. We'll never get out of these waters and get back!"

"We're being punished for taunting the Lord!"

Columbus was in his cabin also looking at the stars through the window and then at the compass. He angrily clapped his hand over it. Something was definitely going wrong.

He went out on deck and ordered two crewmen to prepare a rowboat, without paying any heed to the other crewmen and their mutterings. He was going to go to Martin Alonso Pinzon's ship the Pinta.

"Captain, the compass isn't working anymore," de Morguer said.

Columbus forced a smile. "You must've put it by your nails again. Check it again after it gets demagnetized."

The men looked over at de Morguer. Unable to respond to the crew, Colombus hopped into the rowboat and started rowing toward the ship behind his own. He had to tell Pinzon of the situation immediately so he'd know what was going on.

When he got to Pinzon's ship, he found a young deckhand at the bow pouring water over the captain's hands and feet. He emptied the tankard into Pinzon's hands, who then scrubbed at his arms and ears. Colombus had much earlier noticed that this man was quite fond of water, but this was the first time he'd seen him using it like the Moors did.

Pinzon sent the boy away as soon as soon as he saw Columbus and the two headed for the captain's cabin.

Pinzon and Columbus were standing over the compass in the spacious captain's quarters of the Pinta. There were quadrants, pens, various rulers and other instruments for calculating latitude and longitude lying on the maps spread out on the table in front of them. Niño was at the other end of the table bent over a map and drawing lines from point to point with a ruler.

"I've been a sailor for forty years and I've never seen anything like this before," Columbus said, exasperated over what was happening.

"Where was it when you saw the compass didn't align with the North Star?"

Pinzon had his hand on his chin, scratching his beard as he slowly paced back and forth. He stared at the floor, trying to figure out what had happened.

"Or is there really anything to this talk of the Devil? Are we being played with?" Columbus said.

"Come on Admiral, don't talk that rubbish. There're enough men sick in the head already, let's not have you be one of them," Pinzon said.

"So what'll we say to the men? The compass will be well off in a few days."

Pinzon stopped pacing and looked over at Columbus. "What did you say, Admiral?"

"The compass was all amiss a few days ago."

"Are you saying you noticed this earlier and that the compass deviates from north more each day?"

"Yes, I've seen it for a week. North has been changing one degree nearly every day as we go," Columbus said reluctantly.

Columbus had expected Pinzon to be angry that he'd hidden this from him, but quite the opposite, he looked over at Niño finishing up his plotting on the map and smiled.

"But this can't be true," he said, shaking his head. "It's as if we've discovered a mystery."

"What can't be true?" Columbus shot back. "What're you talking about?"

Pinzon composed himself after the shock of what he'd just heard and began to explain.

"Do we not know that the Earth is a sphere? If we ignore the teachings of the Church and compare our own experience with the calculations of the Arab scholars, then it's obvious Earth is round."

"I wouldn't have set out on this voyage if I didn't believe that. What're you trying to say?"

"True, but the thing we haven't calculated is the position of north. Since the Earth is spherical, north must also change a degree or so over great distances."

"But I've never seen such a thing before."

"Of course you haven't, Admiral, because so far, you've never made such a far journey. The compass' unusual behavior is because of this. And as you say, it didn't happen overnight. There's a gradual deviation. If it had been sudden, then I'd say there was something off, but the increasing deviation from north just shows how far we've come."

This is also what Niño's calculations showed.

"Of course. Why didn't I think of it before," Columbus lamented and hung his head. "Well, if our compass doesn't do any good, how'll we plot our way with any certainty?"

"What day do the stars show?" Admiral, Pinzon said.

"I can also compare the deviation in the compass and the distance we've covered with these charts I've kept and determine the deviation of north to be included in the calculations," Niño added.

A pounding came at the door. "Captain, there's unrest on the Santa Maria. The crew's on edge."

Pinzon turned to Columbus. "You better go and tell the men what's going on so they don't keep on with these tales of the Devil, Admiral. My brothers and I will explain the situation with the compasses on the Pinta and Niña."

Columbus' hopes had lifted again as he rowed back to his ship. Perhaps they would reach Asia within a few days now and he would have limitless land and thousands of servants at his behest. This would be his most profitable expedition without doubt.

75

Neither David nor Esther were prepared for the sight when they came upon a Jewish quarter along the way to Malaga. David had always heard people deem proper the torture of Jews and all types of denigration of them and Muslims in the kingdom under Catholic rule. Most of them had witnessed it first hand. David couldn't discern anything humane in the scene he was about to encounter, there was no humanity in the very least, and he couldn't even reduce it to barbarism.

The Jewish quarter had been nearly totally emptied and the sense of dereliction spread to every corner of the city. Some of the remaining families were trying to sell the possessions they couldn't take with them before they left.

David saw two men haggling in a doorway as he passed a house. A mule stood tied to the fence in the yard just in front of the door. One man was Jewish, as his *kippah* and yellow ribbon on his arm gave away, and pleading with another man.

"But señor, I've given my whole life for this house. Everything in it is worth ten thousand gold ducats alone. The house is fifty thousand ducats at the least, and I'm only asking a thousand from you. I beg of you señor. This is only one-sixth of the house's worth. What's your offer?"

The man grew tired of the Jewish man's pleading and cut him off, wrinkling his nose and squinting his eyes, not wanting to haggle any further. "Take it or leave it, man. You've been holding out."

The man again turned and looked at the mule in despair. He was giving all his property—the furniture, house and a half-acre field—to this Christian, his closest neighbor, for a mule.

A group of thieves, both men and women, ran from another house down the road. They'd taken everything they could carry and were heading back home. A woman was clutching plates to her chest that rattled as she ran clumsily along, some of them falling and shattering on the ground. After her was a man struggling to carry off a polished mahogany table, its four legs sticking out in front of him. The small child following after them was holding a carved wooden horse and caressing its head as if it were a treasure.

Davud and the group made their way toward the synagogue at the edge of the neighborhood through a street strewn with useless housewares. Davud sensed they were being followed—it was the third time he'd seen the same man standing in a corner.

The street in front of them was littered with all sorts of things—chairs that had broken as people rummaged through the houses, broken porcelain, Persian rugs that had been dropped in the mud, and men's, women's and baby clothing scattered around—all the things that would normally be brought but were to much for those fleeing to carry. What they saw most often along the street were gold and silver candelabras. Looters had taken them from the houses without any notice since they were gold and silver, but they'd come to their senses once on the street and cast them to the ground, realizing they were menorahs. Having a Jewish object such as this in one's house was an invitation for the Inquisition to find it and burn the whole family alive as secret Jews.

David thought about the similar scenes unfolding in countless other Spanish cities, towns, villages and neighborhoods. He picked up a muddied piece of paper that had stuck to his foot and looked at the Hebrew text. It wasn't just a thousand-year Jewish legacy that was being lost, but all its history, as well.

Esther gasped just as everyone thought that it couldn't get any worse. "Oh my God!"

She was looking at the synagogue, ten steps away. The others looked and were stunned by what they saw.

Its windows were smashed, the roof tiles had all been pillaged, its wooden door had been carried off and its once pristine white walls were now smeared with mud. Even worse, there were animal sounds coming from inside. David went running in.

Pigs were running around inside. The *mechitza* curtain used to separate the men and women in the temple had been used to cover the straw along the wall. The central wall decorated by Arab crafts-men and the *tevah* platform from where the Torah was read that had once been there had been hacked to pieces with axes and carted off as firewood. Behind where the Torah scrolls were kept along the eastern wall facing Jerusalem was also filled with pig filth.

There was a mass of hogs grunting and eating their excrement amid the acrid smell of their manure.

Abraham de Silva dropped to his knees distraught in the middle of the temple and began to weep.

"They've made it a barn. A pigsty!" Hannah de Silva said as she went to her husband to console him.

Davud looked at the ornamentations on the walls that hadn't been ransacked and sighed. He could tell they hailed from the time of Caliph al-Hakam II, who ruled Andalusia in the tenth century. The tragic fate of the synagogue burned his heart. He wanted to pray that he wouldn't encounter a similar sight with the mosques in Granada, but he couldn't force to evoke the name of God amid swine and ran outside to the fresh air where he mumbled a prayer under his breath.

He had an inkling, though, that the fate of the mosques wouldn't be so different.

All of a sudden Samuel yelled, "Thief—he's stolen the documents!"

Davud and David went running to him just in time to see a man speeding off with a leather satchel and disappearing from view.

Davud could tell from the man's clothes that he was the one who'd been following them since they'd come to town. He had the man's face etched in his mind.

"Can't you even mind a bag!" David yelled at his brother.

"I dropped everything when I saw the synagogue. How was I to know?"

"Damn it!" David, Abdullah and Yehuda all said together.

Everything had again become much more dangerous.

"There's no point to arguing now," Davud said. "Abdullah and I will go after the man and you all stay and wait here. We need to get those papers back no matter what."

76

Prince Bayezid held his breath as he wrote a *mim* at the end of the sixth line on the paper on his knee. He had one eye on his writing and the other on the verse his master had placed in front of him for him to practice.

Sheikh Hamdullah was going through the books in the room, waiting for the prince to finish so he could check his apprentice's work. The room had filled up with books that the prince had sent for over the past few months from Constantinople. One of the walls in the writing room was completely covered with shelves with books stacked up like pyramids on each of them.

Bayezid stopped writing to take a breath and saw Hamdullah standing on his toes trying to reach a manuscript on the top shelf. Hamdullah was tall, but the prince had the shelves installed up to the ceiling so he could cram in as many books as possible.

Bayezid softly set his pen and paper aside and pulled a stool over to Hamdullah so he could reach. The manuscript was so high up, though, that he couldn't even reach it from the stool. The prince had noticed the day before that the stool wasn't tall enough and told the sheikh that he'd brought in a flat stone to put under it.

"God bless you," Hamdullah said. He was about to step onto the stool when he saw a carving on the stone. He stepped back and stooped down to look at the stone. "Where did you find this stone?"

"I just saw it. It must be from the old times, from the ruins of some Byzantine monastery nearby. There's Greek on it."

Hamdullah snapped back at him. "Oh, Prince, what've you done? Did you see whose writing we're standing on?"

"It's fine Sheikh. It's Greek, not Arabic."

Hamdullah frowned. He liked this response even less.

"What kind of thing is that to say, Prince? People may be Muslim or Christian, but are not both their writings religious? Is the prayer said in one not said in the other? Whether it's Greek or Latin, is the scripture still not sacred? God would send me tumbling straight to the depths of hell for stepping on this writing even if I had no sins."

Bayezid didn't know what to say. He knew well enough that Arabic writing was sacred. If he were to see a piece of paper with a verse in Arabic written on it, he'd immediately pick it up and put it somewhere high up. He'd never thought about it for any other language, though. He realized and regretted what he'd done as soon as the sheikh explained it. He was right, one could pray to God in any language.

"Take this stone and put it on the top shelf. Let it be a lesson for you. One who doesn't honor writing should give up calligraphy and can't be a mature person."

The prince did as he was told and sat back done and resumed his writing in silence out of embarrassment.

Sheikh Hamdullah went and sat in the opposite corner. "Now, write and listen to me.

"You might be sultan one day, and then you'll have two or even more jobs to do at the same time. You should get used to it now. Pay full attention to the work in front of you, but also give me your ear—your eyes and hand on the writing and your ears on me—so be it if the smell of the ink gets to you."

77

"There's something I don't get," Boatswain Mahmud said from where he was lying.

Blind Ali was lying above him in the crew's quarters on the Crescent of Victory. They were all in their small beds, squeezed in as if they were coffins. Everyone had lay down now that it was night and the captain was in his own cabin. The pirates were chatting as they did every night before falling to sleep.

"Why are we saving Jews? I mean, is this much danger worth it? If it were up to me with this fleet, I'd say lets go and take North Africa."

"Look at what you're saying, you prick. Is it being Muslim or Jewish that makes anyone a person? It's righteous to help the persecuted," Rattler said with Qitmir on his lap.

"That's all fine, Rattler, but would the infidels ever help a Muslim? Haven't you seen the crusader knights? They hack our people to bits where they see them. The Jews, you say—there's no prophet the bastards haven't cut down. And they've changed their holy books to suit themselves."

"Honestly really, I don't understand them," Overseer Mikhail said. "They see themselves as chosen above all other people. Can there even be such a thing? Why are they superior to everyyone else?"

"Come on, mates. What is it the bastards' religion has you all strung up?" Rattler said. "He who wants to sees himself where he likes. It's none of your business so long as they don't try to kill you or stop your religion. If the Lord had wanted the whole world to be Muslim then He would've made it so. And we're not even only going to save Jews. The Catholics are burning Muslims alive, too. There're loads of our fellow Muslims there who want to escape."

Helmsman Yunus nodded as Rattler spoke. "This crackpot's right," Yunus said. "If we demand everyone has to be Muslim, then what difference would there be between us and the Catholics slaughtering Jews and Muslims? Weren't we sent on this campaign since the Spanish are trying to make the whole world Catholic? People shouldn't think their truth is the only truth. Of course you should believe from the heart and live that belief, but you shouldn't breach someone else's truth."

"Well said, Yunus," Mahmud said. "Well said, but now let's say I, thank God, am Muslim, and you're an infidel. While I'll go to heaven and work to earn God's mercy, how can I conscionably be comfortable that you, a friend of forty years, God forbid, will wind up in hell? All the good I want for myself I want for you, too. So shouldn't I tell you, my good friend, to become Muslim because my religion is good in this and that way? Shouldn't I try to convert you?"

"Stop there and look," Yunus said. "You can explain and share your religion with others. No one said you couldn't explain it. Most of all, too, if it's like you're banging a man over the head with a hammer, constantly saying your religion is great like this and that, and, God forbid, that you'll make him Muslim, then you're making an enemy of Muslims out of him."

"I think it's best when people never get into this business," Big Ahmed said. "People's own religion is the best and they should try to live in the best way. Any way, if a man strives for God's mercy and acts like a true believer, then the people who see him try to be like him. Which of us is so sure we're the correct Muslims. There, I said it. I wonder—are we so sure we have the true faith of Islam?"

"Little Ahmed, you bugger," Rattler said. "You talk like a man since you've become a pirate. Look at this twist of fate—I never thought in a thousand years that I'd think the same as you on anything."

They all laughed.

"Look at Pier," the Rattler continued. "The man left behind his fancy knighthood and recited the *shahada.* The bastard got so sick of all the knights' shit that he prays more than us now. Well, I'll stop dead in hell and die again from resentment if he goes to heaven with his uncircumcised cock."

Pierro Navarro looked up from his bunk when he heard his name. He could pick out his name no matter how bastardized the pronunciation from the piles of words he didn't know yet, as he'd only recently started to pick up the pirates' Turkish.

Rattler saw Navarro poke his head up. "*Serenissima,* Pier, *Serenissima!*" he chuckled, waving his hand to tell him to go back to sleep.

Navarro had long ago accepted Rattler's ways. He smiled and put his head back down.

"There you go, Rattler. The bastard won't learn Turkish if you keep on with the Italian like that," Big Ahmed said.

The pirates all burst out laughing again, this time Qitmir joined in yipping along with them.

"I really don't know honestly," Mahmud said, "but they say the Spanish galleons have piles of gold. I swear to God, boys, I won't return without that gold. I mean all right, let's save the Jews, but let's make some profit, too. Am I right?"

"Better we have the darling gold than the Spanish. The bastards have ravaged the whole of the African coast—they enslave the people and take their gold. I wonder if it's possible to get on those ships and swipe a few sacks of it," Mahmud said.

"Don't get your hopes up," Rattler said. "Those ships are more like floating islands. It's like they make them more for living in than for sailing. If our galley's were to lay alongside them they wouldn't feel anything more for us than a bull does for a fly."

"Cram it," Big Ahmed said. "Would our galleys be nothing to those infidels" galleons? A galley can go and turn anywhere like a horse, and if someone like Burak Reis is commanding it then it really whirls. And what about a galleon? Without wind it just sits there like a two hundred pound sheep.

Overseer Mikhail picked up where Big Ahmed left off. "That's right. A galley's like a spry warrior. A galleon looks big, but it's just a lumbering fat ass."

"Fine," Rattler said. "Why don't you tell these stories again after you stick your fool head through each of the gun ports and meet fifty cannons."

Mute Yusuf had so far been silent, but jumped up from his bunk on the far side. He shot them all an angry look for keeping him awake. His scarred face looked even more frightening in the dark of night as he stormed out topside.

"Ah, we made him mad," Rattler sighed.

"No, he's just sad again," Mikhail said. "He gets memories from childhood as soon as he lays his head down. They've stayed with him since he was young and they'll be there in the future. His head got clouded once, and it's not easy to clear it back up."

"He's got every right," Yunus said. "He's seen and gone through more than any of us other than Burak Reis. Just thinking about what he's suffered makes me lose sleep."

"Is it true he was really handsome and happy before he got that scar?" Yasin asked.

"Oh, my boy," Rattler said. "We were strolling along the Algerian coast with him once and the girls were falling over themselves with the sight of him—they were dripping for him, if only you knew."

"So where's he going now?" Yasin asked.

Rattler's voice lost its constant joking tone. "He's going to look for a star. Every pirate has his star, son. You feel at home and find some peace when you look up at it at night. We're all objects revolving around a star."

Yasin was confused.

Having stayed silent so far, Blind Ali got up and walked out behind the others. "Here's another star for you!"

Mute Yusuf went up to the deck and found Burak Reis leaning against the gunwale, his elbow on his knee and his chin on his fist, thinking in the night darkness.

"What gives, Captain? Can't you sleep, either?"

The captain was deep in thought, looking off in the dark toward the horizon. He looked like he saw something there that Yusuf couldn't. He noticed after a while that Yusuf was standing beside him and turned to his right-hand man.

"What do the men say? They're most likely questioning why we set off on this campaign, aren't they?"

Yusuf smiled. The captain always knew what was on his crewmen's minds, and knew it before anybody else.

"You see that bluish star, Yusuf? The one above *Alioth*?"

"It's *Mizar*," Yusuf said, nodding.

"I once heard it's not actually a single star. I read that it's made up of seven very close stars that all shine together and only look like one to us. And the distance between the two closest stars is five times larger than the sun and all its planets and all the space in between. Now think—seven stars. So that's seven suns. If each one has planets and each planet has a moon, the single light we see is actually dozens of objects, the smallest the size of our moon. Each one is a separate world. Leave that aside, though. Each one is a cluster of separate worlds. So what is it when you think of *Mizar*—this star that's actually seven suns? You know?"

Yusuf smiled, as he so rarely did. "I don't know about you, Captain, but all these stars are keeping me up. I'm hanging onto a sun by a nail."

The captain smiled back. "Everyone on this ship seems like a sun to me sometimes, each one as far from each other as all the ones in the Milky Way. It looks monolithic from afar, but each has his own dreams, individual past and his own stories."

Blind Ali walked up behind them, also not able to sleep. "So what's the thing that brings us together, Captain?"

Mute Yusuf and Burak Reis turned around when they heard him.

Burak Reis looked back out at the horizon. "The destination. Our destination is us—our goal and our word unites us. We'll fulfill our promise by the grace of God. Our belief unites us."

Mizar looked as if it were shining brighter than usual—that its seven stars had united as a beacon.

Taurus the bull was now rising over the horizon of a different land.

78

A nearly half-ton bull was snorting angrily as the sun rose. The locals called it *el Monstruo Oscuro*—the *Dark Monster*. It had so far killed nine *toreros* in the ring.

The beast was already ill tempered despite it still being early morning, and the growing heat was driving it mad. The situation it was in also didn't help.

It butted another bull to its side with its sharp horns, trying to make space for itself. There were two-dozen bulls, each one more massive than the next and all fine specimens, standing in a cramped and narrow pen having stamped in their own filth for a night. The bulls were always kept in these uncomfortable conditions the night before a fight to ensure they'd be aggressive the next day.

Almost a mile away was the arena to where the bulls would run, careening through the narrow streets. The attendant in the plaza by the arena touched his punk to a fuse, sending firecrackers whirring into the air in a loud commotion and officially starting the hundred-year tradition of the festival of San Fermin.

The people of the town of La Campana and the surrounding villages had already started to fill the square. Men and women and the young and old had piled into the town's narrow streets and plaza to celebrate the saint's day. Those in there homes were on the balconies and roofs to watch the spectacle.

Although the Running of the Bulls for the Feast of San Fermin was held in the city of Pamplona in the old Kingdom of Navarre, it became a holiday for all of Spain with the fall of Granada. The end of eight centuries of Muslim rule was celebrated with festivals in every city and town.

Attendants were carefully placing the last of the wooden screens to block off all the entrances and exits from the winding streets the bulls would soon run through.

Davud and Abdullah were trying to follow a man among the crowd without losing sight of him. The two were both dressed as monks with cowls over their heads and could walk through the town without drawing attention. A few people were suspicious of two monks hurrying through the crowd, but everyone was much more interested in the festival than dealing with them.

They noticed the man at the fair when they least expected it. He was the thief who'd stolen their certificates of pure Christian blood. Davud knew their way out of Spain was in this man's hands, and he had catch him no matter the cost.

The man went on his way for a while suspecting nothing. He stopped by a monger along the road who had set up a stall and bought some pomegranate candies made from the fruit the first Muslims to come had brought to Iberia. Davud carefully watched the man from a hundred yards off—there was no doubt this man was the thief.

"Damn it!" he muttered from under his cowl.

He quickly bowed his head and covered his face with his hood.

"What happened?" Abdullah asked.

"I thought the guy saw me for a moment."

"There's no way he could recognize you from that far away."

Davud looked back up to see the man continuing on his way none the wiser, and he breathed a sigh of relief.

Davud and Abdullah picked up their pace when the man turned right down another street. There was no trace of him from the corner when they got there. There was also a huge crowd carrying an effigy of Santiago and singing hymns coming up the street directly toward them. The festival had indeed started, with dancers, drummers and other fanfare among the crowd whipping up a terrific racket.

Davud stood on his toes and craned his neck to try and spot the thief in the crowd. He saw him barreling through the mass of people behind the effigy, trying to make a quick escape.

"Damn it! He saw us and he's running away."

They dove in, trying to make their way through the quick-moving river of people. As in most Spanish towns and cities, the streets were narrow and winding. The dancing musicians, singers and women with babies held to their breasts filled the entire street as they streamed past. The entrance to a slightly wider road that led to the square had been closed off for the traditional running of the bulls, who were soon to be let loose.

Davud elbowed his way through the crowd flowing toward him, trying not to lose sight of the man, and Abdullah followed on his heels.

Two soldiers from the town guards standing off to the side realized something was wrong when they saw these two monks trying to cut their way through the crowd in the wrong direction and took off after them.

"*Paren, paren!*"

Davud and Abdullah were running after the man with the two guards and twenty or thirty people behind them trying to catch up. They were yelling for them to halt, opening up the way for themselves and drawing attention to the two monks.

A few meddlesome people in the parade heard the guards and tried to step in front of Davud to stop him. He elbowed one aside and shoved another out of the way, but the disturbance caught the attention of the people in front of them and they were now all trying to stop him. He punched, kneed and shoved his way through, doing everything he could to keep on the thief's tail.

The guards started closing in on them as the crowd tried to stop Davud and the thief was gaining ground on them.

"We're going to lose him!" Davud yelled.

Abdullah was panicking and constantly looking over his shoulder. "The guards are really close!"

"I'm going off onto that side road and I'll try to cut him off. You go off to the other side, hide behind the effigy, then turn around and mix in with the parade once they've passed."

Davud reckoned the guards would catch Adbullah as soon as he pulled away.

"But—"

Davud wasn't listening. "We've got no other options. Do what I told you. The guards won't recognize you when you're in with the crowd. I'm going after the thief."

Davud split off from the parade and cut down the first open side street to the next road over. One of the guards saw him and quickly followed after. Abdullah pulled his cowl over his face and mingled in with the parade behind the effigy of Santiago. The guards passed slowly by only three people behind him. He was safe for now.

Davud was running fast down the street, veering off when the way was blocked or wound the wrong way, having no other option. He finally found another route running alongside the parade and sped along his way.

The guard was blowing away at his whistle and now there were no less than half a dozen others chasing Davud.

He'd made good headway and turned off back toward the parade when he saw a side street from where he could head off the thief. The sound of two fireworks echoed through the town, their sparkling streams falling through the air—the bulls had been released and now the beasts were stampeding toward the arena about a mile away.

The thief felt safe and relaxed now that he couldn't see Davud any longer, but then he caught Davud's eye twenty yards away through a break in the crowd. Davud took off after him. The thief realized there was no way he could escape on these roads and looked around helplessly. There was only one thing he could do. He new it was mad, but with Davud bearing down on him he felt he couldn't wait any longer.

The thief leapt over a wooden screen to the left and jumped into the empty street where the bulls would come. Davud was at the barrier as soon as the man's feet touched the ground. They peered at each other through the slats and the thief ran off down the street with a victorious look. Davud knew what the man was doing was foolish, but this was his only chance to keep with him.

He climbed up and over the fence into the empty street.

"I can't believe I'm doing this," he thought, angry with himself as the thief ran with all he had through the empty street, fifty yards ahead.

Davud first felt a rumbling.

A thundering roar was getting closer. He looked over and thought of what else he could do other than dance with death. There were now a dozen enraged bulls stampeding toward him.

This was the first time Davud had noticed just how fast bulls can run and how sharp their horns could be. He recalled that a bull could run at least more than three times as fast a man, and reckoned maybe it'd be better not to know so much.

He knew any movement could provoke them and that the best thing to do when face to face with a bull was to stay still and calm. The thief would be long gone if he were to wait for the bulls to pass, though. He was already disappearing down the road.

"*Ya Bismillah,*" Davud yelled as he threw himself forward.

He ran after the thief as fast as his legs would carry him. He rounded a curve and found another obstacle waiting for him— about forty or fifty young men waiting with their backs turned to take off in front of the bulls in a show of bravery and to prove their courage. As per tradition, once the bulls got close, they'd speed off and then wait for the bulls to pass them after they caught up—if they were lucky.

Davud was running faster than he ever had before, but still the bulls were gaining on him. The thief had joined the group of young men ahead and began to speed along with them.

Davud was about to catch up with the group after a few minutes just as the bulls bore down on them. The three in the lead were rampaging and swinging their heads from side to side, tossing the men aside with their horns. Two men were flung into the air and lying bloodied in the street, one gored through the rear and other through the leg. Their horns could gouge through anything with the speed and weight they had behind them.

Davud was dashing to the right and the left as he ran, his head turned back to the bulls nearly on him. One of them had its eye set on him. Lowering its head, it picked up speed and lunged over him. The crowd behind the fences was cheering and yelling, which only wound the bulls up more and made them stampede more violently. People in the crowd had long, sharp sticks to prod the beasts that had slipped and fallen, enraging them even more. Others thrust spears at the beasts, most of them hitting their mark. The bulls were enraged, their backs streaming blood, and attacked anybody they could.

A bull was quickly gaining on Davud, but he threw himself off to the side and rolled into a corner right as it was breathing down his neck. The bull missed him and instead rammed its head into a wall, pulverizing the bricks and falling to the ground. A few other bulls followed its lead and also slipped and crashed to the street. The young men at the head of it all were still taking a beating, some tripping themselves up while others crashed into each other and fell to the ground together or were tossed into the air or crushed beneath the beasts' hooves.

Davud reckoned the best thing to do would be to curl up and cover his head where he'd come to a stop and wait for the bulls to pass, but he couldn't risk losing sight of the thief. He carefully got back to his feet—there was a group of bulls in front of him and another group quickly coming up from behind.

A third crack of fireworks echoed through the town, their sparks streaming down, signaling that the second group of bulls had been released. The nearing rumble was like an approaching earthquake and Davud could feel the ground beneath his feet shaking.

He took off running again, jumping over those who'd fallen and dashing in between the bulls that were still on their feet. He spotted the thief amid the lead group as he bounded through the chaos.

One of the guards who had been chasing Davud was standing by the fences to the side where the bulls were running and noticed that he was the monk who'd slipped them earlier. He blew his whistle and alerted the other guards who started following him along the side of the street.

Some of the bulls from the first group had caught up with the people in front. One of them gored a man through the face before trampling over him, leaving him pulverized and soaked in blood. Another bull coming from behind brought its hoof down on a man's head who was trying to stand back up and shattered his skull to pieces. The people watching the chaos from their balconies and roofs overlooking the disarray were all cheering and shouting.

Davud flew through the blood-strewn street, but saw two more groups of bulls gaining on him when he looked back. The thief had managed to evade even the slightest scratch from the passing bulls and was still on his feet and running, now about twenty paces in front of Davud. The bulls were at his heels and were lunging for him. He jumped up onto one of the fences as a bull came for him, pulling himself up and tucking in his legs as the bull passed below.

Davud found himself at the entrance to the arena when he let himself down from the fence after the bulls had all passed. He couldn't believe he'd covered over half a mile in only about four minutes. The crowd had funneled into the arena's narrow entrance after the bulls, the thief among them.

Davud wriggled through the doors just as they were closing and tumbled into the arena.

He was startled when he straightened himself up on the dusty ground of the La Campana Bullring. The *Monstruo Oscuro* was staring straight at him from about twenty-five yards away. The beast had set its sights on him before he could stand. He still had one knee on the ground. It was readying itself to spring forward and charge him any moment to crush him underfoot. Blood was streaming from the beast's back as it stamped its right hoof, waiting for Davud to make a move.

All the people in the stands held their breath as they watched this unusual scene unfold. The thief reckoned there was no way Davud could escape the bull and so joined the crowd, waiting to watch him die or, at the very least, be gored left and right.

The bull lowered its head and snorted as it stamped the ground.

Davud stood motionless as he looked at the hulking beast, trying to figure out what he could do. Running would be the most foolish thing. He knew that it wasn't red, as people thought, that provoked bulls, but movement. A scholar friend of his in Constantinople had once told him that bulls are colorblind anyway.

He looked around without moving his head to try to find something useful, scanning slowly and barely breathing. If he could find a rope or tether then he could wrap up the beast's horns and subdue it. He saw one lying two steps to his right and carefully reached out for it.

Even this, though, was enough to trigger the bull.

It bound forward as if it wanted to ravage Davud for all the bleeding lance wounds it had on its back. The effect this imposing charge has on a man is so great it's no wonder it was so often spoken of in the old myths—a symbol of the synergy on earth, portrayed as massive creatures bounding with their full force. It was one of the unique moments outside of man's influence.

Davud had to get the rope before his chances ran out. The bull lowered its head as it charged, its horns aimed straight for Davud's face, but he flattened himself to the ground and rolled to the side in a cloud of dust as he caught the beast's eye.

Having just missed him, the bull backed up and came charging again just as fiercely as Davud tried to stand back up. This time, Davud thrust out his hands and grabbed onto the bull's horns. He leaned in and pushed with the strength of his entire body. His face went red and all the veins on his forehead were popping as he tried to bend the bull's head back.

The bull couldn't resist anymore and Davud overpowered it—bending the tumbling to the ground and him on top of it, his knees so firmly set against it that it couldn't move. He swiped up the rope and in a flash bound three of its legs in the way he remembered from butchering a sacrifice.

He stood up, dazed by the strange scene and looked over the crowd for the thief. This wasn't what the thief had expected and he took off running again, although he was so spent that he was panting as he tried to escape. Davud followed him to the exit of the arena. He was just about to grab the man, but guards waiting for him at the door stepped in front of him.

"*Pare ahí!*"

Half a dozen soldiers had their swords extended at the monk as they ordered him to halt.

Davud could see the thief making a hasty escape behind the guards. There was no way he'd be able to take on these six armed guards with no weapon of his own. He stopped in his tracks with one eye still on the thief as he fled. One of the guards walked over and went behind Davud, kicking the back of his knee so hard and trying to break it that it buckled and he collapsed to the right. The guard sheathed his sword and pulled out a rope to tie up Davud's hands. This was the opportunity he'd been looking for and, with his hands clasped together, sent them smashing into the guard's face and breaking his nose. He drew the man's sword in a flash and rushed the remaining five guards. Their blood flew into the air with each strike.

He went limping away, leaving the six guards in a pile behind him. There was no way he'd be able to catch the thief with an injured leg, and he was already long gone from view. He had to though, no matter what, and he had no intention of giving up.

He saw some horses standing by a nearby fountain. He hopped on one and spurred it galloping off.

Davud caught up with the thief a few minutes later and jumped off onto him before the man knew what was happening, sending them both tumbling together into the field by the roadside.

Davud had him at last. He punched him with such ferocity that the thief's head fell unconscious to the ground.

From the Notes of Piri Reis—
The Map

Maps are a dream.

They're the depiction, perception and image of the world that is first reflected in the mind and then on paper. They're abstract images of man's worldly adventures and projections on paper of what he's seen. If the world is transitory, life short and there's no reality to life, then dreams are reality itself. So maps are a dream and more real than the world.

Drawing a map, for me, is diving into the world of dreams and tracking its reality. Reality isn't the truth—it's more precious and lasting than that—reality is eternal.

The eyes can't see the world. But is it only the world they don't see? They don't see the continents, kingdoms, cities, towns or even villages. They only see a small part of any of these. People take these small parts and assemble them in their heads like a puzzle and then imagine the whole. Then this mind's image is reflected on paper. And as such, maps are the likeness of this fantasy—the portrayal of man's mind and power of imagination with pen and paper.

Eyes constantly look over the world. We look at the sea, mountain peaks and over green plains, but it's the eyes of the heart and man's power to imagine that captures the true vista. What the eyes see is real, but they can't catch hold of naked reality. Reality is captured in dreams.

I've been thinking of the map I'm going to draw as I've taken notes aboard my Uncle Kemal's galley while we sail through places I've never been to before. I set my astrolabe to the stars, horizon, sun and moon, and my calculations of the distance we've traveled, the temperature of the air, the direction of the currents and the wind all build up and I imagine the world. My calculations mix with my imagination, my imagination mixes with daydreams of other lands, continents and seas, and then the map takes a more sure form in my head. The pieces come together, the small truths become reality and the whole comes forth.

I go through the maps in my chest when I'm not taking measurements and making calculations. I look over again and again and analyze Ptolemy's Geography, al-Ma'mun's atlas, al-Farghani and al-Khwarizmi's calculations for the Earth's diameter, the trigonometric calculations of al-Sabi' and al-Biruni's drawings of the lines of latitude and longitude. Ptolemy says land surrounds the oceans. Al-Idrisi asserts the opposite, that the world is mostly ocean that itself surrounds the land. The measurements I've made, the maps I've collected and my own calculations all show that al-Idrisi's undoubtedly correct.

We better comprehend the world the more we sail the seas and oceans. Some think seas and rivers separate people from one another. They don't separate people, though—they bring them together and make communication, trade and travel possible. The seas make it possible to get from one island to the next, to go between continents and to see other lands. The Lord created the heavens and the Earth, made rains fall from the sky and with them, myriad fruits for our benefit. Ships were made to conquer the seas and rivers. Yes, maybe deserts and mountains separate people, but not the seas.

From Odysseus of the ancient Greeks to Sinbad of the Arabs, haven't the main cultural heroes found their livelihoods on the seas? Was it not Noah's Ark that saved mankind and a giant fish that saved Jonah? I think the sea is a blessing—it's God's grace and a favor unto man. And thus we get to know each other and build civilizations.

Those who think maps only show places are mistaken. Maps tell of man—his future and his past. So many empires I've seen on maps no longer exist. The maps of hundreds of years ago show the Roman Empire as encompassing nearly all lands. There was a time when Alexander the

Great held that seat of honor. All the lands with cities that bear his name must've been greatly subdued when his map makers were depicting them— an empire spanning from the east of Europe through all of old Persia. I've seen such maps that can no longer even be read, written in lost languages that no one knows. There are some maps filled with tiny crosses over the entire world and others with large and small crescents in their place. These blend into each other on some maps and others were drawn with the world split in two as if a battle plan on the table of some commander.

East and west are only a part of the imagination of maps, because as far as maps depict certain places, they also speak of who drew them and for whom they were made. The maps from some periods have Jerusalem at the center, at other times Rome, and still others Mecca. The Mamluks are easterners on the maps of the Venetians but westerners as far as Chinese maps are concerned. Africa is a western land according to the Indians. The Turks coming from the Asian steppes must've come upon a sea and thought it was the largest in the world once seeing its immense waters. The sea was once called inhospitable, hence the Black Sea. The name of the Mediterranean comes from Latin for the sea in the middle of the earth. We know now though that neither the Mediterranean nor Europe and North Africa are the middle of the world. I remember once seeing a map that had come from the Chagatai Khanate at the other end of Asia. I poured over the map for maybe an hour, trying to figure out how it should be read. They had put Japan at the center, south was at the top and north at the bottom, and Europe and West Asia were placed off in a corner as if they were running off the page. Who can blame these men, though? East and west are relative. Once again, that's why maps are imagined—the reflection of a dream of he who made it and those looking upon it.

The viewpoint of man is therefore limited and an illusion. The east and the west both belong to God.

Maps take people from one place to another, although most the time they don't describe the destination, but the starting point.

There are the black dirt of dry land, deep blue seas, golden valleys and plains, and green meadows—red borders, ports, castles, temples, tents, palaces, churches, mosques and monuments—elephants, gazelles, tigers, camels, peacocks, pheasants and monkeys—ships, galleys, galiots, caravels and galleons—fish, dolphins, sea monsters and dragons—crescents, stars and crosses—flags, banners and swords—compass roses in red, blue, green, yellow, white and black—those who go naked, people in furs, sultans in turbans, kings with crowns, haloed faces, black faces and golden faces.

Maps are a dream world. It takes mathematics to draw them, but they feed our hearts.

Maps are our imagination.

80

The Guadalquivir River cut through the Sierra Morena in the south of Andalusia like a knife. The river through the rocky mountains was at times so deep and swiftly flowing that had cut miles of cliffs from the mountain sides, making it nearly impossible to traverse from one slope to the next.

Davud and the group had been walking along a cliff edge for hours and were relieved to come across an old rope and wood-slat bridge suspended over the chasm that looked like it might not have been used for the past ten years. Davud went up, grabbed the ropes and thought it over. It was about fifty yards from one side to the other, or sixty to seventy steps. He turned back to the group.

"There's no way we can all cross this bridge together. We'll go in turns—first the women, then the elders, then finally the men."

Everyone nodded in agreement.

Esther approached the bridge first and stepped on the remaining part of a broken plank. It immediately gave way under her as she hopped to another plank and gripped the ropes with both hands.

"Are you sure this bridge will hold us, even one by one?" David asked Davud.

"It'll be fine if we go slowly and hold onto the ropes, but wee need to avoid shaking it."

David had hugged Esther tightly before she went to the bridge stretching high above the chasm below. She'd also held on firmly around his waist.

"Don't worry," he said. "Hold onto the ropes tight and look before you put your weight anywhere."

"It'd be good if we got going without wasting any more time." Yehuda said. "It's starting to get dark."

Esther advanced over the planks slowly. She was trying not to look down at the drop below, but she also had to look where she was stepping and so couldn't look up. Another plank broke under her in the middle of the bridge and fell tumbling against the crags, into the gurgling Guadalquivir and out of sight. Her heart was pounding harder and harder as she kept going until she got to the other end.

David had been holding his breath nearly the entire time and finally heaved a sigh of relief.

It took an hour and a half for everyone except for David and Davud to cross. The stars had already begun to shine. The bridge had already taken quite a beating by the time it came for them to cross and there weren't many places left to step. The ropes had also worn thin and looked as though they could snap in some places.

David looked over at Davud. "Well, let's go. We don't have much time left."

David knew it would've been useless to hold out. He slowly and carefully began to cross as the others had.

Everyone on the other side held their breaths as David advanced.

"God damn it!" Abdullah yelled.

He was staring at the cliff on the other side as if he'd seen a monster. The others all turned to where Abdullah was looking and were equally terrified. Esther brought her hand to her mouth, her eyes opened wide.

"Davud, they're right behind you!" Samuel cried.

When he turned to look, Davud saw a priest and three knights of Santa Hermandad emerge from the trees. One of the mounted men fired his crossbow at the group standing on the opposite cliff edge. The arrow fell right at Esther's feet. Another shot at David as he was crossing, but missed.

"Quick, get away from there. Go into the trees!" Davud yelled across to them.

David was in the very middle of the bridge and looked helplessly over his shoulder back at Davud. He thought maybe he should go back and help.

"Keep yourself together!" Davud yelled. "You need the others. Keep going on the road we talked about. Don't you think about turning back now!"

Davud didn't finish speaking before another arrow kissed and sped passed David's shoulder.

"Quick, keep going, what are you waiting for!" Davud yelled at David.

David quickened his uncertain steps. The knights of Santa Hermandad had gotten quite close to Davud now. He drew his sword as David was taking his final steps off the bridge.

"No, don't!" Abdullah cried.

Davud swung his sword and severed the ropes suspending the bridge. David stepped onto the cliff edge with the others as the bridge swung down and hung against the cliff face.

Davud had ensured that the knight couldn't cross, but he was also trapped on the wrong side.

David, Abdullah and the rest watched with fear and worry from behind the trees to see what Davud would do.

Still mounted, two of the knights shot at Davud's shoulder and leg. The arrows came from such close range that they pierced deep through and stuck out the other side.

"We need him alive, don't kill him!" the priest shouted.

A third arrow struck Davud in his hand holding his sword. He dropped the blade as blood streamed down his fingers. One of the knights threw a line and roped Davud's neck. He pulled it tight and yanked him, ensuring he was held firm. David and everybody else's knees went out from under them. A knight walked up behind Davud and struck him hard across the back of the neck with the pommel of his sword and sent him unconscious to the ground.

The priest and the knights looked across the chasm and saw the group on the other side amid the trees.

"Come on, let's get out of here before they find a way to get to us!" Yehuda said.

The group fled into the trees under the watch of the knights.

Davud was lying still on the mountain at the feet of three knights and a priest. The arrows had pierced through his shoulder, leg and hand. His blood was flowing over the ground and seeping into the dirt.

81

"So, what? Are we just going to leave him behind after all he's done for us?" David said.

Abdullah, Samuel, Zayd and the de Silva family had taken refuge in an abandoned Jewish house to spend the night. They were going to set out early the next morning for Malaga, but David wasn't willing to leave Davud behind.

"But what could we even do?" Yehuda said. "They must've either killed him already or tortured so he can't even move. We should see to saving ourselves."

"Yehuda's right, my boy," de Silva said. "There's nothing we can do. How would we be able to find him anyway? We wouldn't be able to do anything even if we did find him."

David paced from one corner to the other of ransacked living room that had been emptied of all its furniture, his arms crossed, refusing to accept abandoning the man who'd saved his life. Esther and Beatriz were sitting against the wall with their knees pulled up to their chests in despair.

Abdullah lifted up his head from an old table at the other corner of the room.

"It was Dominican knights who caught him. The only church around here is at a small Dominican monastery on the southeastern slope of the mountains."

"How do you know?" David asked.

"It says here on this map." Abdullah pointed to a spot on a map spread out on the table.

David went over to his side and bent over the map. "How far away is it?"

"One, I don't know, maybe two miles, and on the other side of the river."

"Have you forgotten that the only way over the river isn't there anymore?" Samuel said.

"True, but the southeastern slope flattens out about a third of a mile from the church."

"You see this on the map?" Yehuda asked.

"The map's in Arabic," Abdullah said. "The colors on it show the measurements. The pale colors show where the mountains are lower. I've been buying and selling hundreds of these for years."

Beatriz got up and walked over to the table. "What're you saying, that we can cross the river and get to the monastery?"

"I think it's worth to try," David said. "But you—"

"But me what?" Beatriz shot back.

"It'd be better if the men handled it," Abdullah said.

Beatriz smiled. "And so what're you all going to do—get into the monastery and overcome three knights with the swords you don't have? A printer and a binder—you think you can be soldiers just because you're men?"

"It's better than sitting here helplessly," David said.

Everyone in the room knew Beatriz was right.

"I have a plan," she said.

The night sky was cloudy and there was neither the moon nor a star to light the Monastery of Santa Maria in the darkness. The guard at the door was half asleep on his stool, resting against his spear and waiting for his shift to end a couple hours later with the coming dawn. He saw the silhouette of something move in the darkness and first thought it was one of the many wild boars in the area. Later, though, he saw the figure of a woman with her breasts nearly completely out. He stood up when he saw the beautiful woman motion for him. He walked toward her, figuring she'd forcibly been brought to be a nun and had grown tired of it. After all, it wouldn't be the first time he'd had a nun.

He thought about how plump her breasts were as he got closer, her thick lips and the curves of her hips. He was delighted that some color had come to the night just as he was getting bored. The woman's chestnut hair shined even in the darkness. He thought maybe he was still sleeping and this was just a dream.

As the guard came up to Beatriz and reached his hand out for her breasts, he felt a violent crack over the head, his eyes went dark and he fell to the ground. David had come out from where he'd been hiding and swung a giant piece of wood over the man's head.

"Quick, quick. Get the keys off him and all the weapons he has," Beatriz said.

"What do you think I'm doing?" David whispered as he rummaged through the man's clothing. He stood up with the guard's keys, a sword, a knife and a crossbow. "Now it's time for the hard part."

They entered the monastery and found themselves at the head of a corridor lit by hundreds of candelabras on the walls, some burning away and some not, but enough to light the way.

"Which way should we go?" Beatriz asked. "I wonder where the dungeon is?"

Right then the shadows of two monks started to grow on the wall. David and Beatriz spun around. Down the corridor there was a narrow stairway leading down about thirty yards in front of them.

They reckoned they had found the right way from the strange smells wafting at them. The clatter and moaning got louder as they descended the stairs.

David was the first to reach the bottom—he couldn't see anything in front of him. Beatriz was following right behind. They waited for their eyes to adjust as they stood unmoving in the dark.

A voice called out right as David started to be able to make out the way through the middle of the dungeon.

"Stop right there!"

A guard was standing in front of them, his crossbow trained straight forward. David thought he'd just given himself over to the dungeon. Beatriz was staring at the tip of the arrow pointed at them.

82

A horse was carrying a young man and galloping through wheat fields as far as the eye could see. The sun was shining from between white clouds and making each head of wheat sparkle like little nuggets of gold. Constantinople was neither so hot nor so cold—one of those rare days with no humidity that comes maybe a few times a year. It was comfortable and relieving.

The fresh air blowing past Davud's face as he rode made him feel as though he was being caressed with a silk handkerchief. He spurred his snow-white horse on faster and faster as he felt Elif's smell embrace his face. The horse's mane played in the wind as it sped up, dancing in the crosswind along with Davud's tussled hair. Its gold harness sparkled in the sunshine like the wheat and its saddle blanket matched the attire of the warrior on top. Davud was wearing a white, linen shirt with an upright collar and well-spaced buttons. Over that he had a sleeveless caftan the same blue as his eyes and a crimson sash around his waist. His sword hung from his left side while his quiver and red shield with golden ornaments hung from either side of his horse. His armbands and leather chest plate made it seem as if he were returning from battle, his horse clad in a cloak with Chinese clouds emblazoned on it.

Davud didn't know from where he'd come. He only knew there was a long valley behind his house in the city and that he could see Elif waiting in the far distance with their baby in her arms.

The sun shined off Elif a blinding white from where she stood beneath a massive plane tree.

Davud shook the reins and spurred his horse on faster as he passed through the wheat field into the green valley. His heart beat faster the closer he got and as Elif grew bigger. He caught a glimpse of her face. She was smiling—a simple, shy smile. Davud would never forget her smile, her dimples or her fair lips.

Then suddenly her smile disappeared.

The horse stopped abruptly as if it had come to an invisible wall. It reared up with its front legs thrashing through the air. Unprepared, Davud slid off the back and his head struck a stone as he fell to the ground.

The sun and its brilliance faded and a terrific pounding started in his head.

Davud's head was throbbing. He wanted to move but he felt as if his entire body was being held down. He couldn't move his arms or legs and wasn't even able to open his eyes.

Then his head began to spin and his cheeks started to twitch involuntarily as he felt slaps on both sides of his face.

He felt a coldness wash over his face and he finally opened his eyes.

David, Abdullah and Beatriz were leaning over him.

"Come on, wake up, get up!"

If it weren't for the bucket of water they found in a corner and splashed over his face Davud wouldn't have been able to come to himself. The wounds on his shoulder and leg where the arrows had hit him had been left exposed.

David and the others, having just saved themselves, had found Davud curled up and unconscious in a corner of the dungeon filled with excrement, rat droppings, blood and dried vomit. As they'd agreed earlier, Abdullah had gone around to the back of the monastery and squeezed though a hole in a dilapidated wall. He had slowly come up behind the guard who'd stopped David and Beatriz and struck him over the head with a stone.

"We don't have any more time, there're people coming," Beatriz said as the sound of footsteps came closer down the stairs.

Davud had just opened his eyes and David and Abdullah were struggling to pull him up. Davud seemed to find his strength as he came to, but he still couldn't walk without being propped up from both sides. David and Abdullah had never noticed before how well muscled and hard his body was.

"My God, it's like he's carved from stone," Abdullah said.

It was nearly impossible to keep Davud upright, and the two had sweat pouring down their faces as they struggled with him. David clenched his teeth and tried to find the power to pull Davud along.

Davud began to come to more after a few more steps and started to be able to carry himself.

The two monks who were descending the stairs saw the guard lying on the ground and the door to the dungeon open and couldn't make heads or tails of how the prisoner they'd captured that evening could've escaped. Meanwhile, Davud, David and Beatriz were slipping through the hole in the wall Abdullah had found, replacing the loose stones behind them. They were able to get to the other side of the river in only half an hour. The biggest problem now, though, was whether Davud's wounds would prove deadly or not.

Finis Terræ

My heart ached when I heard there were banned Latin books from the printing press I had tracked down in Santiago de Compostela. My dearly departed mother was pregnant with me in this city while she was a nun at the convent there, but was treated as if she was a whore and was cast out of the Church.

She'd told me countless times before that she'd left me at the orphanage of a monastery in Toledo, that her only misdeed was that she'd helped a mysterious priest who'd come to the convent one night, stayed a month and then disappeared just as suddenly and inexplicably as he'd appeared. My mother had loved no one else in her life and had left me at the orphanage as she struggled for years with the pain and suffering of a fatal illness. Even in those days, though, she never spoke an ill word of my father—the priest I've never known. She always saw the convent in Santiago de Compastela as home, and so named me Santiago.

I suppose I was never able to go to Santiago de Compostela throughout my life so as not to bring back any clear memory of my mother's suffering. I'd never ventured to go to this city despite it being where the tomb of the Apostle Saint James is and the second most visited pilgrimage site after the Basilica of Saint Peter in Rome. French, Italian, English and Austrian pilgrims and those from more distant lands make the months-long journey, whereas for me it was only three days away.

I accepted this task right away in those days when my head was con-
fused and with a strangely tortured heart. It would've been unthinkable
for me to turn down such a mission the Holy Church thought me worthy
of, and I accepted the task thinking that going to the Cathedral of Santia-
go de Compostela, to which my namesake Saint James also lent his name,
would bring me peace. It was time I went.

On the far, northwestern edge of Spain, the Roman legions that came
here called it Finis Terræ—the End of the Earth. The peninsula, the last
land before the vast ocean, was indeed the end of the earth for anyone
making the months-long journey from the middle of Europe, Africa, Jeru-
salem or even Asia. Santiago de Composela must have felt like the farthest
place on earth to the pilgrims who travailed over muddy, rocky and crag-
gy roads in rain, snow and storms, sometimes starving and some afflicted
with plague and countless other hardships.

A Bible verse echoed in my mind—Sed accipietis virtutem superveni-
entis Spiritus Sancti in vos, et eritis mihi testes in Jerusalem, et in omni
Judæa, et Samaria, et usque ad ultimum terræ. These are the last words
the Lord Jesus Christ spoke to his twelve apostles before he ascended to
heaven shrouded by a cloud—But ye shall receive power, after that the
Holy Spirit is come upon you, and ye shall be witnesses unto me both in
Jerusalem, and in all Judaea, and in Samaria, and unto the uttermost part
of the earth. I wonder if it's possible that Saint James understood this as
a place rather than a time, and as such came to the end of the earth fif-
teen hundred years ago carrying the name of Jesus Christ to the Vandals,
Visigoths and other pagans to teach God's commandments and the mercy
and grace of the Lord so as to preach peace and compassion to a land full
of conflict, blood and plunder. Saint James was an ambassador for Christ.
Did Saint James do for Spain what Saint Peter did for Rome?

When Saint James first came to Spain, however, the pagans met him
with hatred and hostility and insulted him. They spat in his face and
threatened to skin him alive, accusing him of being a fraud and asking
why he couldn't show this God he so loved even once as they presented
their magnificent idols in stone, clay and gold. James was dismayed by

this storm of curses. No one believed a word he said and he couldn't convince even a single person of his holy message.

Then the Virgin Mary appeared to him as he was about to leave the country, two days from where I am now, outside Zaragoza. The Mother of God told him to not leave Spain so hastily and to have patience. James recovered his strength and courage after this and returned to tell the people of God and His compassion.

The tale doesn't end there, though. Centuries later, a hermit in the fields with his flock fell asleep under a tree. It had grown dark by the time he awoke and he noticed an unusual cluster of stars. He followed the light and below it found the lost tomb of Saint James. The local bishop at the time had a modest chapel built on the spot where the monastery in Santiago de Compostela now stands. How much I would've wanted Saint James' message of compassion and peace to have reigned over this land until the end of world. From the tenth century onward, however, this chapel became a symbol for the holy war carried out by the kings of Leon and Castile against the non-Christians.

Saint James, an ambassador of peace and compassion, became the icon for our five hundred-year war against the Muhammadans. What can be said to those knights who took lives in the name of Saint James? May God give man common sense.

Many books I've seen explain that the second part of the name Santiago de Compostela is derived from the Latin Campus Stellarum—the field of stars in which the tomb of Saint James was rediscovered. There's no doubt the kings and bishops chose this name to esteem their own glory. To me, though, it's incontestable Compostela comes from composita tella— burial ground. Do I really need tall tales to believe in Saint James, or a holy war to have faith in Jesus Christ?

I was in the throws of confused emotions on my way to Santiago de Compostela. It seemed I was going to the end of the world, returning to my own uncertainty, my birthplace and my origin.

I felt like a strange being stepping from darkness into the light, going from cold to hot and from one mountainside to another with every step of the journey. My beginning was in the place that was the end of the Earth for the Romans, Christians and Saint James, but maybe my real beginning would start after this end.

I came across a much larger crowd of people than I'd imagined would be there when I got to the city. Catholics had come to Santiago de Compostela from Rome, Paris, Vienna, Prague, Oxford, Canterbury and many places I'd never heard of before like Toul, Lyon and Reims—a motley group of myriad peoples, both young and old, men and women. This was the end of the holy road of pilgrimage for millions of people, but maybe this was also a milestone of spiritual life. The first holy chapters of many people's lives were beginning to be written here. These Catholics were a sublime and impressive sight and I got the same feeling I experienced while at Saint Peter's Basilica in Rome.

I needed to find a place to stay when I got to the city, but headed to the Santiago de Compostela Cathedral, bypassing the Hostal dos Reis Católicos that had been built to house the pilgrims. The place enchanted me as I entered from the western gate of the cathedral. I saw the statue of Christ as Redeemer and Judge, his hands and feet pierced through and his face somber, surrounded by depictions of His trials, angels and the tetramorph. Then I looked at the carvings of the old prophets and saw Daniel's enigmatic smile. All the statues were of a different color stone and they seemed to whisper to the people who gazed upon them for too long. But what held my view was the statue of Saint James, he whose name I've carried my entire life like the city and its cathedral. Alone on a central pillar, the saint's calm face was a mix of happiness and serenity. He was holding a sheet of paper that had Misit me Dominus written on it—The Lord has sent me. I read it again and again.

Misit me Dominus.

The interior was vaulted in a Romanesque style in the shape of a large cross—almost carved into a great mountain—the stones having been sculpted into columns and statues. I looked long on the reliefs of hell and Jesus saving the people. It was difficult to walk among the throngs of people but I managed to come to the place holding the holy relics of Saint James. I stared at the coffin behind the iron bars.

As I stood there, a very old pilgrim in front of me dropped a book. I bent down to help him and reached out to his arm to give it back. The book had opened as it fell and I knew right away from its pages both who wrote it and which book it was. I couldn't understand why this man had brought this book into the middle of a cathedral, let alone among those in reverence of Saint James. I nevertheless picked up the book, but the old man snatched it from my hands before I could give it to him. I was frightened when I looked at his face—his brow was furrowed and he was looking straight at me. His face was wrinkled, his eyes were lost between his white beard and hair, peering out, and his lips were curled in spite. I was afraid that if I opened my mouth this old man would've cut me down on the spot, grabbed me by the throat and taken my life in short shrift. His eyes burned with hate and chilled my insides. I was certain, though, that this was the first time I'd ever seen him.

I told him after a while that I had only wanted to lend my help. He shot back at me that the fire in my hands couldn't help his books. The sharpness and severity of his voice hit me like a slap to the face. I reminded him that he was speaking with an ambassador of the Holy Church, all the while trying not to show my fear. He then said that he should remind me of what God once said to one of his servants—I have not come here to find the fires of hell, but the springs of heaven.

With this, he disappeared into the crowd. It was as if his final words to me sealed my mouth and chained my feet. I couldn't response or follow after him.

I turned back to Saint James and prayed to him to deliver me from this crisis I found myself in. I then looked at the walls that my mother must've seen countless times, the stone floor she must've tread and the statues she'd run her fingers over. I prayed for my mother and appealed to God for her to protect and watch over me.

After visiting the cathedral, I forced myself to go to the Hostal dos Reis Católicos to get a bed.

Fatigue from the road and the spiritual exhaustion I experienced had worn me down. I decided to meet with the abbot and monks at the monastery the next day and laid myself down on the bed I was given. I fell asleep with hopes of seeing my mother in my dreams.

But neither was my mother in my dreams nor anything else to give me peace.

I had a nightmare all night and was soaked with sweat by morning. I was in an old, ruined library, although all of the books on the shelves were standing neatly and in order. It was a huge, three-story building with shelves on each floor, labyrinthine corridors and hundreds of books. There was a large owl keeping watch on a ruined column at the entrance to the library. I was throwing all the books from the shelves and scattering them on the floor with preterhuman strength as I tried to clear all the shelves. I was taking books from dozens of shelves on the third floor a throwing them into heaps in the corridor. There were pages covered with Arabic, Hebrew and Latin scattered everywhere.

I was out of breath and took a break, but when I looked up, all the books were back on the shelves and the corridor was completely empty.

I was enraged and attacked the shelves again as sweat poured from me. This time I threw the books further down the corridor. But after all this labor, the shelves weren't empty—they were fuller than before, with more books crammed onto them.

Then I flew into an even greater rage and threw the books completely out of the building and out into the square instead. I'd created a mountain of books outside after a few hours. I piled book upon book and page upon page. I found a torch and tossed it onto this pile of paper and ink. It burned with the ferocity of a forest fire and its flames were licking into the sky. Facing me on the other side of the inferno, however, was the looming visage of the old pilgrim I'd seen that day, smirking at me. He stood cackling and watching me from the other side of the burning mountain of books. The books had all turned to ash after a while and I turned to go back inside to look once more as the fire died down.

Alas, what I saw. The library was now endless and stretched as far as the eye could see as if two gigantic mirrors were reflecting the hundreds of shelves ad infinitum, the hundreds of books now millions.

Then I woke up screaming.

I ran outside as the sun was rising. That nightmare was a little messenger of the calamity awaiting me.

84

Davud felt a burning in his right shoulder and opened his eyes. Beatriz was over him, smearing a thick, dark green paste from a wooden bowl on his wounds. She was being soft and gentle, but the pain grew with each touch of her fingers.

"I know," she said, "it hurts a lot when I touch it and it'll burn for a bit. But be patient. You'll start to feel better very soon."

Davud was laid out on a mattress riddled with holes and with an old pillow under his head on the side of the living room of the abandoned Jewish house where the group had been hiding. David and Abdullah were watching curiously a little further away while the others were sitting or lying around the room. Yehuda was trying to bite the still edible parts of a rotten apple he'd found.

Davud looked at Beatriz as she knelt beside him again, the waves of her auburn hair hanging in front of her. He was trying to figure out what was in the bowl she was holding.

She had prepared it earlier and set it to the side and was now trying to make Davud drink.

"It's pomegranate juice. It'll give you strength and make your nausea go away."

He left himself to her hands without saying a word.

"What's she smearing on the poor man?" Abdullah asked. "I see now why they took her for a witch. Look, she went off into the woods, collected some weeds, came back saying it's medicine and now she's spreading it on him."

Yehuda snickered as he dealt with his apple.

Beatriz paid no mind as she took more of the mixture and smeared it on Davud's other shoulder.

"Don't pay attention to them," she told him. "It's willow leaves, pinesap, egg whites, labdanum, dried snails, copper and honey. It's good for open wounds."

Davud was nauseous and getting dizzy as he struggled to remember whether all the things she mentioned were useful. He'd read in al-Zahrawi's *Kitab al-Tasrif* that honey was an antiseptic, willow leaves can be used to suppress pain and that egg whites stop bleeding. All the same, he'd never heard of pinesap, copper or, worse, anything from snails as having any use. He figured it was most likely something ignorant people in far off villages made up from the teachings of Andalusia's scholars like ibn Sina and al-Zahrawi.

Be it so, he started to relax as she applied the mixture. He had no power to protest anyway. He continued to watch her without speaking.

Beatriz must've sensed what he was thinking. "Trust me. These're mixtures I've known for years. My grandmother taught them to me."

Adbullah and David looked at each other, both suspicious.

"Witchcraft must run in her family," Abdullah chuckled quietly.

"I'm amazed they didn't kill him," Samuel said.

"It's the Inquisition's normal way of doing things," David said. "Killing someone it the biggest favor they could do a person. They want to keep you alive as long as possible to make you suffer more."

"Yeah," Samuel said. "They probably waited for him to be conscious before they took out the arrows. They'd have started torturing him tomorrow."

Beatriz looked at his right leg not knowing how to stop the bleeding. It was spilling blood. The wound on his shoulder and hand were in better shape, but the one on his leg was getting worse.

Walking from the monastery to the house where they were hiding hadn't been any help, either.

""Wrap a rag above the wound," Davud said weakly.

Beatriz got a piece of cloth and twisted it, then wrapped it around his leg and tied a hard knot.

"You're making it hell for him. Come on and go a bit slower," Abdullah said.

"Don't stick your nose in what you don't know." Beatriz said. "It won't be any good unless it's tight."

A wine bottle on the table caught Davud's eye.

"Take that bottle and pour it over the wounds slowly."

His voice was barely loud enough to hear.

Abdullah took the bottle and gave it to Beatriz. She did as Davud said and dribbled the wine over his wounds. The true horror of his injuries became clear as the blood washed down his sides. The arrow that had hit his shoulder had shredded the muscle and the hole in his leg big enough for three fingers. Beatrice gasped when she saw them.

"Now go light a fire outside," Davud said, having to catch his breath. "Then heat up some metal in it like a knife or a fire iron."

"I'm not thinking about whether it'll happen but whether he'll be able to stand it," Samuel said.

He'd by chance read in some of the books he'd printed that burning a wound would close it up, although neither he nor the others had ever seen it done.

David came back inside after a while with a red-hot knife and handed it to Beatriz, who was waiting at Davud's side.

Davud asked for a stick to put between his teeth. He braced himself and then looked up at Beatriz to let her know he was ready.

She pressed the knife firmly onto the wound. The hot metal hissed as it touched the blood and water on his leg. Davud was biting down so hard on the stick that his teeth started to sink into it. She took the knife awaywhen she was sure the wound was well cauterized. The smell of burning blood filled the room.

Davud had fainted.

85

Columbus and his three ships had been sailing for nearly a month and there was still no sign of land. The food and water had been running low and the crew was restless. None of them had trusted Columbus from start and it had now come to a head. Not a day went by without the men getting into it with each other. All the three ships—the Nina, Pina and Santa Maria—were full of sick and wounded. Some of the wounded had lost control of ropes in storms and others when a mast broke in two in a squall, but most of them suffered from sword, knife and ax blows sustained in fights. There wouldn't have been anybody to handle the ships if not for Martin Alonso Pinzon and his brothers, as there were no yardmen or helmsmen left who weren't incapacitated in one way or another. Pinzon was grateful, though, that he hadn't been forced to come to blows with the unruly Portuguese mariners.

Pinzon, Niño and Columbus were meeting again in the captain's cabin on the Santa Maria, trying to figure out where they were on the maps and where they were going according to Niño's charts.

"I don't get it," Columbus said. "According to these books, we should've reached Asia long ago."

"I've explained it to you fifty times, Admiral," Niño said. "You're reading the nautical miles in those books wrong. When they say one nautical mile they mean one Arabic mile. You're using the Italian mile and doing the calculations based on what you're used to. But the Arabic mile is nearly two thousand yards and the Italian mile is just over sixteen hundred—there's a twenty percent difference. So do the calculations of the mistakes you made when we were talking about hundreds of miles."

"If you calculated the circumference of the world with these numbers, then yeah, you'd think you could sail around the world in a few weeks," Pinzon said.

Columbus had realized the miscalculations with the Arabic mile, but he still trusted the maps from Italian sailors.

"Toscanelli's map shows three thousand miles between Lisbon and Asia. It doesn't use Arabic miles."

"This man's going to make me go mad," Niño muttered. "You're right, Admiral, but most of Toscanelli's calculations are wrong. Like you, he confused Arabic and Italian miles and so his measurements are all off. He should be embarrassed—if he were right you'd be able to see the light from Asia in Spain. And again, all the maps he looked over are the ones we have in front of us now. The books we swiped from the Muslim libraries when Granada was burning were the ones men like Toscanelli and Martin Behaim used as their sources."

"You said it yourself, Niño. Al-Ma'mun and al-Masudi's books say the ocean can be crossed. They even say the Muhammadans did it in the ninth century."

Now it was Niño's turn to be silent. He knew this is what the books said.

"That's how it looks," he said after a while. "Their captains must've been more talented than ours."

With this, Columbus stormed out and slammed the door shut behind him. Pinzon and Niño looked at each other—neither of them knew where this would end up.

Columbus had just walked out when a loud commotion rose up on deck.

Pinzon ran out to see Columbus lying on deck surrounded by a dozen men, and worse still, one had a sword to his throat.

"Finish this son of a bitch—he's taking us to our deaths!" one yelled.

The sword was a hair's breadth from Columbus neck and trembling with the man's rage.

"Stay where you are, Captain," the crewman said.

Pinzon stopped in his tracks no less than ten feet from Columbus.

"Don't do anything stupid, boy!" Pinzon said. "Killing him won't bring us home."

"And if I don't kill him then we'll be lost in these waters. I'm settling it here!"

Columbus was short of breath. He was afraid to even swallow lest his throat nick the sword.

"We've come this far," Pinzon said. "We're basically at the end of the journey. Just be patient."

"I'll give you all the gold you want. All the locals you find are yours," Columbus pleaded.

Pinzon would've preferred if Columbus stayed silent.

"The gold and slaves you promised haven't come to pass now, have they, Admiral? Don't you see we're about to die? Some men are even drinking the ocean water out of thirst—it's that damn hopeless!"

Pinzon thought for a moment— it wasn't that he didn't want the crewman to rough up the admiral, but if Columbus died, he'd be forced to live as a fugitive on their return to Spain. He'd made the agreement with Isabella and Ferdinand in person. They'd take it as a personal insult if Columbus were murdered and the entire crew would most likely end up hanging at the ends of ropes. If they took their chances, they'd pay for their mutiny either with their heads or in the fire. Pinzon didn't know if they could sail from one end of the ocean to the other, but what he did know was that this ship would return to Spain and that's where he would live out his life. Columbus' death would take away this possibility altogether.

The crewmen were all yelling.

"Kill this Genoese son of a bitch!"

"If you don't do it, I will!"

Pinzon saw the crewman move his eyes to Columbus and reckoned it was only a matter of time before he slit his throat.

"Alright," Pinzon finally said. "We'll all turn around if we don't spot land in the next three days. I, Martin Alonzo Pinzon, give you all my word."

Pinzon's face had softened. Columbus looked at him wide eyed and would've protested, but remembered the sword at his throat.

The crewmen started murmuring to each other. Nobody seemed to know what to believe. They were trying to figure out if Pinzon had made the promise just to stop the man or if he truly meant it. Pinzon's own men who had sailed with him before knew that the captain would never lie about anything, large or small.

"Look, my boy. I'll cut your hands off myself if you kill him. But if you let him live, I give my word, if we see land in three days then that's that, but if we don't, then we turn around." He turned at looked at the rest of the men. "I make this promise to all of you. I'm at least as fed up as you are with the Admiral, but I'll give hell to anyone who touches him."

The man hesitated for a moment, then pulled back his sword and slid it back in its scabbard.

As soon as he stood up, Columbus pointed at the man a growled. "Kill this mutineer!"

Nobody moved.

Columbus looked at Pinzon. "I order that you kill this bastard!"

Pinzon stepped forward. "No. I've given my word. He'll live. We turn back if we don't spy land in three days."

Columbus walked up to him seething. "What're you talking about? You think I'll give up everything so easily?"

Pinzon was just as firm. "I just saved your life, Admiral. I wouldn't push my luck with men who want to kill you, if I were you."

86

Davud heard the rumbling of horse hooves from no more than three hundred yards away and pulled up on his reins. The group behind him also stopped. There was something peculiar about the trees and greenery. Davud spotted a mark left by a rope on a tree in front of him.

"We're being ambushed," he said.

At first he'd thought that people from the village they had made off with the horses from had found them, but this was something much different.

He'd recovered well after Beatriz had tended to his wounds and they had set off back on their way the very next day. The road was more perilous the closer they got to Malaga, and now they were on the verge of a disaster.

"Where'd you get that idea?" David asked. "There's no one around."

"Come on, let's keep going. What're we waiting for?" Abdullah called out from behind.

"Everybody stay where they are," Davud said, raising his voice.

David didn't have the chance to respond before a huge spear flew past his nose and plunged into a tree trunk.

Terrified, they all turned there heads to where the spear had come from and saw a man dressed in all black save for his exposed eyes. He had a *litham* veil around his head, face and shoulders that hung down his back.

"It's the Almohad!" Abdullah said.

Five warriors came from behind and beside the man in a black cloak. Davud looked to the other side and saw six more fully armed Almohads emerge.

The Almohad militants had come from the cities and kingdoms like Granada that the Catholic armies constantly attacked. They continued the fight against crusader armies with ambushes and raids. The groups were mostly Berber and didn't recognize the treaties the Muslim princes had made with the Catholic kings. They'd set up a highly organized hierarchy and operation and were attempting to spread their influence throughout Andalusia despite their sparse forces.

Another mounted group came out in front of Davud and the others as he saw the six other Almohads walk out from the trees. There was no doubt the man in the middle was their leader. Like the others, he was donning a black cloak with an indigo *litham* around his head and face. White cuffs emerged from beneath his cloak, a red sash was wrapped around his waist and the armor over his chest, shoulders and his codpiece were of thick leather and felt of the kind used in the Maghreb. The ornamented hilt of his sword fashioned from Damscus steel—the finest in the world—and ivory-handled dagger tucked into his sash set him apart from the rest.

Davud could see that the two-dozen warriors surrounding them had enough weapons to take on a small army. A man in a cloak to the right had an Arab scimitar at his side of the type master swordsmen wielded. On the other side, one of the mounted warriors had no blade other than his spear, speaking to his adeptness with the weapon. The rest had daggers strapped to their sleeveless arms and those with full quivers slung over their shoulders were the renowned archers from the Sahara.

David, Samuel, Abdullah and everyone else in the group had all heard at least a couple stories of how the Almohad took no mercy on the non-Muslims they captured and killed them with a thirst for blood. Except for Abdullah, though, this was the first time any of them had encountered the militants.

Davud greeted the man he took for the leader. "*As-salamu 'alay-kum.*"

The others kept silent out of fear as Davud stayed calm.

The leader in the indigo *litham* was startled when he heard this greeting. He tipped his head slightly back and looked at this man in monk's robes in the eye. The Almohad fighters had witnessed throughout many years of battles that countless priests and monks had given Islamic greetings to save themselves—some had even claimed to know how to pray. Nearly all of them, however, were found out while they were still doing ablutions, as any slight deviation from the norm made it clear they weren't Muslim.

"*Wa alaykumu s-salam wa rahmatullah,*" he said after a pause.

He kept looking over the group. He looked carefully at David, Esther, Beatriz and Abdullah before he turned back to Davud.

"I'm Ali bin Abdullah. Tell me now, who are you and where are you going?"

Davud took particular interest in the double-tipped *Zulfiqar* sword at the man's waist.

"My friends and I are heading for the Malaga port. There's a Turkish ship there we're trying to catch."

"Are you a Turk?"

Davud stayed silent and examined the Almohad, who himself had always had the innate ability to be able to easily read people's faces.

"Everyone's given up hope on the Turks," the Almohad said. "They say they're not coming."

"That's my problem," Davud said.

"And so who are these?" the Almohad said, pointing to the rest of the group.

"These are innocent people fleeing the Inquisition."

"Are they Muslim?"

"Only some."

"Which of you are Muslim," the Almohad said, looking at the group.

Adbullah and Zayd raised their hands, stunned.

Ali bin Abdullah seemed to know Abdullah from somewhere and spoke to him in Arabic. Abdullah got down from his horse, went to the Almohad leader and the two started speaking in different Arabic dialects.

Abdullah turned to Davud and told him he and the Almohad leader were from the same tribe and that the Muslims in the group would be allowed to live, but the others would be taken as prisoners.

The leader barked an order to his men before Abdullah had finished speaking. They pulled everyone from their horses except for Davud, Adbullah and Zayd, and set to tying their hands behind their backs.

"What are you doing?" Davud cried. "These people have done nothing wrong!"

"You and these two Arabs can go where you please, but the others are our prisoners," the leader said calmly.

David and Esther felt a chill of terror tremble through them.

"I can't allow this," Davud said. "These people haven't caused harm to anyone."

The Almohad leader hadn't expected such boldness. He prodded his horse forward and came up to Davud. He pulled the cloth from his face, revealing his jet-black beard, aquiline nose and swarthy countenance.

"Oh, they haven't hurt anyone, have they? Look here. I don't know how long you've been here, who you are or what you're doing here, but you must know the Jews have aided the Catholics with their war against Muslims with the money they've provided and have formed an army with their wealth against Granada to wipe Islam from the land."

Davud knew there was some truth to what he said—Ferdinand and Isabella survived and fed their armies for years off the fortunes of Jewish merchants and diplomats. This didn't make all non-Muslims guilty, though.

"Well then you should also know," Davud said, "that the Inquisition has targeted these poor people, confiscated all their belongings on the basis of no crime and would throw these innocent lives to the flames."

Ali bin Abdullah's mouth hung open, mocking what Davud said.

"It's no fault of mine they didn't know their time was coming. Divine providence really. They should've thought about that when they went against us Muslims."

"You can't possibly equate the hundreds of thousands of helpless Jews who don't even know the names of the king and queen and have lived with Muslims for centuries with the handful of palace folk whose religion has changed politics and trade."

Ali bin Abdullah voice was sharp. "You've taken too much interest in these Jews. You're nothing in their eyes. We're all nothing. You forget they believe they're the chosen people. If you were in their hands, though, they'd choke you with a spoon."

"Maybe so—and maybe you are right. Only God knows the future, though. It's not for me to question people's religion. All are free to believe what they will so long as they don't interfere in anyone else's life. They're the People of the Book described in our own scripture."

"The People of the Book?" Ali bin Abdullah laughed. "What of their book? They've doctored and changed their book just like the Christians have. They call themselves chosen and say all other religions are lesser. The hell with all of them and their books!"

"You're right, and I'm not defending their religion. There is no god but God. Muhammad, peace be upon him, is the messenger of God," Davud said before saying *bismillah* and reciting verses from the Quran.

"And believe in what I have sent down confirming that which is already with you, and be not the first to disbelieve it. And do not exchange My signs for a small price, and fear only Me.

"And if only they upheld the law of the Torah, the Gospel and what has been revealed to them from their Lord, they would have consumed provision from above and from beneath their feet. Among them are a moderate community, but many of them—evil is that which they do."

Ali bin Abdullah was listening carefully.

"But this is no reason for me to leave them to their deaths. They are oppressed," Davud said at the end.

"And those who disbelieved are allies of one another," the Almohad responded, citing another verse.

Davud responded to this verse from the *al-Anfal* surah with another.

"And who is better in religion than one who submits himself to God while being a doer of good and follows the religion of Abraham, inclining toward truth? For God took Abraham as a friend"

"These people don't believe in God," the Almohad said.

"You can't know that. There are unbelievers among those who worship God and unbelievers who find and worship God. God is All-Knowing."

The two continued to exchange verses.

The Almohad began. *"O, you who have believed, do not take the Jews and the Christians as allies."*

Davud knew the verses to respond to this. *"And if God willed, He could have made them of one religion. O mankind, indeed, We have created you from male and female and made you peoples and tribes that you may know one another. God is Almighty."*

"Be careful when you're saying you know them so you don't end up like them," the Almohad said.

"I do not worship what you worship," Davud started reciting. *"Nor are you worshippers of what I worship. Nor will I be a worshipper of what you worship. Nor will you be worshippers of what I worship. For you is your religion, and for me is my religion.*

"There shall be no compulsion in acceptance of the religion."

Ali bin Abdullah looked at Davud in silence. He could tell Davud had memorized the Quran and was a hafiz. He liked that, and a faint smile appeared behind his thick beard.

He barked an order in Arabic to his men as he had before. This time they untied everyone's hands and pulled David and the others off to the side.

"Alright", bin Abdullah said. "Be it as you say. But know this. If we ever cross paths again, it won't only be the Jews—I'll consider you an infidel as well."

The Almohad bin Abdullah called after them as Davud and the others set back off on their way. "If I were you I'd stay off the southeastern road. It's crawling with knights of Santa Hermandad."

He saluted Abdullah and then was lost from view in the woods.

He'd warned them and saved them from a great danger. That road, however, was the shortest to Malaga, and if they took another, they would miss the Turkish ships.

87

The Blue Lion was rocking gently in the quietness of night. There was no light other than a thin sliver of a moon in its first phase. Kemal Reis, his soldiers and crew were all sound asleep.

Two of the junior gunners—Grubby Tezjan and Fat Hamdi—were leaning against the wall of the captain's quarters, lost in the darkness.

"That whore's in there," Grubby Tezjan whispered. "It's time we got a taste of her already."

They'd had their eyes on Mademoiselle Veronica for a few days now and they knew she was inside. They'd been watching her and had waited for this night.

"Oh, I can't wait to get a handful of those gorgeous tits," Hamdi said, licking his lips.

Grubby Tezjan tried to open the door softly but it wouldn't budge. "The fucking bitch's locked the door!" he fumed.

He was sure this infidel, as he called her, was a hussy and was surprised to find the door locked.

"Step aside," Fat Hamdi said as he stepped up.

There was a reason for his nickname. He held onto the door handle and put his shoulder to the door, pulling the nails holding the lock in place out of the wood.

Tezjan looked around to see if anyone had come, and the door broke open with a short thud. They both stood there for a few seconds, making sure no one had heard before they slipped in after they were sure nobody was coming.

Hamdi entered first and opened his eyes wide when he saw Veronica asleep and alone on the captain's bed. She was sleeping deeply, sprawled out more than half naked in the comfort that she was alone. Tezjan joined Hamdi ogling her, moving their eyes up and down her body. They couldn't reckon how to approach her, like two jackals on the hunt against a dangerous prey. Tezjan was staring at her legs and hips and Hamdi at her young, firm breasts.

"This's our lucky day." Hamdi grinned as he headed for her legs.

With the instinctual agreement they made then and there, Tezjan went to her head to holding her down by the arms while Hamdi had his way with her.

Veronica opened her eyes to see two brutes standing over her and tried to scream after the initial shock. Grubby Tezjan had is large hand over her mouth so tightly, though, that she couldn't make a sound and was struggling to breath. She rammed her heel into Hamdi's nose as he came up her legs. When he saw the blood coming from his face, he grabbed her by the knickers and slapped her across the face. She went limp, as if lifeless.

"I'll fix you, you fucking bitch!" Hamdi snarled as he tore of her nightgown and got on top of her.

He was just about to get to what he'd most been waiting for when all of a sudden he was flung up to the ceiling of the cabin as if a whirlwind had blown through. He had no idea what had happened as he fell bewildered to the side of the bed just as fast as he flew off. He turned his head and saw Kemal Reis burry a fist into Grubby Tezjan's face.

The captain would know if even a needle fell on deck. He'd heard a noise when the cabin door broke open and came to see what it was.

Fat Hamdi got up to his feet and drew his knife on the captain.

"Look, Captain, we don't want any trouble. Leave and let us have a bit of fun. Is this worth it for some slutty infidel?"

Grubby Tezjan pulled out the razor he always kept in the back of his pants and steadied himself on the other side of the captain to strike. Grubby Tezjan had gotten his nickname from his usual filthy state and mind and his impetuousness this razor.

"Hamdi's right, Captain. We're under your command, but this is damn shameful what you're doing."

Catching the two unaware, Kemal Reis found himself in the middle of a fight, and both of them had blades. Veronica had come to and was holding her breath as she sobbed.

"You filthy bastards. You see the betrayal you've made slobbering over a guest entrusted on my ship?"

"What guest, Captain?" Grubby Tezjan said. "There's no man in France who hasn't fucked this bitch. You're defending this infidel whore over us?"

"Captain, if those French pricks got ahold of one of our women they wouldn't be as generous as you," Hamdi said.

"Oh good, there it is, as you say. Are we French? Do we also deem it proper to treat women as they do?"

Fat Hamdi knew he wouldn't be able to turn him as soon as he stopped speaking and lunged at him with his knife. The captain deftly grabbed his wrist and pulled him toward himself, head butting him in the face. Hamdi collapsed as if he'd been hit by a boulder. Grubby Tezjan was behind him waving his razor at the captain.

After a few swipes of the razor licking his cheeks, Kemal Reis snatched Tezjan's hand holding the razor and threw him into the wall.

He was stuck between the wall and the captain, and jumped for Kemal Reis with his razor flashing. The captain batted it away from his face and twisted it from Grubby Tezjan's hand. He sliced the man's cheeks from side to side, leaving his face seeping blood. Tez-

CALLIGRAPHY OF THE STARS **479**

jan had lost the power to resist. The captain twisted his hand back and threw him to the floor.

Having been there to save her every time and each time a hero, Mademoiselle Veronica was now more attached to the captain than before.

Piri, however, had been in his room with his notes during the ruckus.

From the Notes of Piri Reis — The Stars

One star is enough for those who want to believe.

Some people are fascinated by shooting stars, solar and lunar eclipses, and the rare celestial events that can only be seen every fifteen years or so. I fall back in love with all the stars every night. I don't think I'd get my fill of even one star even if I looked at it my entire life. What treasures lie for man when he turns his head to the sky. Those sleeping can't see the stars, though, and those who constantly observe the land are blind to the heavens.

Every star is a sun. Do they also have their own planets, their own worlds? I wonder if there's a Piri there as well.

I'm mistaken, though. Each star isn't one, but a thousand suns.

I wrestle with these questions that make my head spin every time I look to the night sky. I can't conceive of the size or dimensions of the heavens. And what is Tariq, the Morning Star—can you comprehend it? As I look at the countless stars in the heavens and try to calculate their sizes, I see that the Earth is no bigger in comparison to them than a grain of sand in the vast Sahara.

The Earth is nearly four times the size of the moon, Saturn ten times that of Earth and the sun eleven times the size of Saturn. Our gigantic sun—the source of life, light, warmth and energy—of course, is the sultan, the king, the padishah of its own galaxy. Our sun, however, is dwarfed when compared to other stars. Seirios to the ancient Greeks, Sirius to the Romans and al-Shira to the Arabs, the brightest in the night sky, shining blue, is twice the size of the sun according to al-Sufi's calculations. If my Uncle Kemal were a star, there's no doubt he'd be this one. What difference is there between the twinkling blue light of al-Shira and the Blue Lion? They eye of Taurus, what the Arabs call Aldebaran—the Follower—the red light winking at me below, is forty times the radius of al-Shira. And so what about the ruler of the night sky, Orion the Hunter? How should its parts be calculated? Rigel, the star of his foot, is one hundred times the size of Alderaban.

I've wondered by the Arabs called the star in what to me always looks to be Orion's shoulder, Yad al-Jauzah—the Hand of Orion. I've also seen in books that scribes working in Latin mistranscribed the Arabic as Betelgeuse. Whatever its name and position, this orangey-reddish star is the sun of winter's night sky. But it's a disservice to call this star a sun. We're accustomed to speaking of the sun in terms of size and grandeur, as the biggest and most sublime, but calling this star the Hand of Orion is not enough to describe it. Burak Reis would be this red star—like Yad al-Jauzah, his red Crescent of Victory is firm and bullish.

All these radii and sizes can be confusing when comparing dimensions, even when using the most practical method of praxis. Maybe one could explain it thusly, that if we liken the cosmos to a grand palace, we can think of the sun as a tiny fly on a high wall in one of the palace's many spacious rooms. The Earth isn't even a drop in the vast ocean of the cosmos, a speck of sand in a desert or a shred of a leaf in a forest. Every sun is a star, and every star is a snowflake.

Do those who reach this subtle distinction doubt the verity that those who are and will be created will exist for eternity in the hereafter after the body withers? After all, does this exponentially continuing wealth not make man tremble at the might of All-Knowing God and trust in that power while he looks at these millions of stars in the night sky?

I was stupefied earlier when I was confronted with volume as I looked at the stars. I see why the Bedouins refer to the stars as they do, how they find their way and how they make sense of their lives as they gaze up at this sparkling vista in the dark of night of their interminable desert. I'm now trusting in the same star aboard the Blue Lion on the Mediterranean that they do in the middle of the desert. Maybe a Bedouin was lost in the desert hundreds of years ago, hopeless and exhausted, but looked up and smiled at the sight of the North Star, and now I'm also determining our course by this same star. The enduring and staid immutability of the heavens leaves me spellbound despite the disorder, chaos and change on earth. Kings die, sultans are born, padishahs conquer lands, princes lose territory, they wage war, they die, others are born, some have disputes, some talk, they sleep, they work, they sail the seas, they conquer land, they siege castles, towers collapse and they build palaces. The time between the birth and death of empires is no longer than it takes a bird to alight on a branch and fly away again. The North Star, however, continues to show the way from the same place. Hunters have been watching the hunt in to sky for a thousand years.

Maybe a soldier centuries ago from Alexander the Great's army lost his way and looked up at the moon and thought of home just as I now look up from the middle of the sea and think about where we came from and where we're going.

During the years I was in Constantinople, Ali Kushji once told me that it takes Saturn thirty years to complete its orbit around the sun. That means that it makes a tour of the sun twice over the average man's lifetime. Man's life is exhausted when it's only been two years on Saturn. Two of Saturn's orbits is our entire lifetime. Most of us are born, get married, have children, become grandparents, age and die before Saturn has made only two revolutions around the sun.

All of this is what the planets do around our tiny sun. So what about the planets around Sirius, or those revolving around Betelgeuse? How can we account for those or understand them? There are planets that don't move a hair in four thousand years. This tranquility, dignity and constancy bring me peace. Everything on earth is kept watch over from the heavens. Then, what we reckon as a thousand years is one day for God.

Looking at the stars isn't only good for the spirit, it also guides man in a real sense. The North Star has been a dear friend to sailors for centuries. The Bedouins in the deserts and we on the seas take shelter by its light. Everlasting God is the torch that shows man the way, even in darkness. He has made stars as beacons for us to find our way in the darkness on land and at sea. When compasses break, maps burn and turn to ashes and any other of man's tools become useless, a star is all a man needs.

If I were a star, I would most like to be the North Star. I'd want to reassure and show people the way on the seas, through deserts and over mountains and plains, over the vast expanses on my maps, as the North Star does.

What is that beating star? Can we grasp it?

O, Piri, open your eyes while the world sleeps. You're here—let the Piris on other worlds sleep. The heavens are the prize of those who are awake.

BOOK SIX
The New World

89

The knights of Santa Hermandad under Lucas's charge weren't paying much attention when they found an old Jewish woman and her husband in the southern part of the forests outside Iznajar.

Hanna de Silva was boiling eggs in a pot next to and old hut in a dense stand of trees. Abraham de Silva had gone off to collect brushwood to keep his own fire going. The rest of the group was off trying to find medicine and supplies in the nearby abandoned houses while the elderly couple rested and prepared the food.

"It's that woman," Lucas growled to one of his men. "These are the de Silvas. The ones who ran away from Toledo with that Turk!"

Lucas and all the soldiers with him were armed and clad from head to toe in armor. Lucas was as frightening as always with his pointed helmet, his visor down hiding face, and chain mail over his neck and throat. The visor of his pig-face bascinet extended out like a hound's muzzle, with holes perforated around it and above was a single slit to see the outside world. As always, his chest plate had a large embossed cross.

Seeing him on the hill mounted on his horse, Hanna de Silva first thought it was a monster. This enormous and strange armored knight on horseback frightened her so that her arms hung down limp as she held the pot, spilling the water on the ground and cracking the eggs. Her hands started to tremble and tears ran down her face as if she knew what was going to happen to her.

A half human, half animal voice came from behind the visor. "Where are the others?"

Señora de Silva was heaving and sobbing. "I swear. I swear I don't know. They told us to wait here."

Lucas looked over at the two men next to him, who dismounted as if they understood some unspoken order. They walked over to the woman, took her by both arms and threw her to her knees.

"Leave me alone, I beg you! What're you going to do to me? Leave me be, I'm telling you the truth!"

She writhed against them and her grey *tichel* fell to her shoulders.

One of the knights found a log and brought it in front of her.

Hanna de Silva was trying to figure out what they had in store for her. She looked in the other direction to see if there was any way if she could save herself, but there was no way she could overpower these ruthless men. She prayed for her husband not to come and that at least his life be spared.

Two knights held her by the arms and placed her head face down on the log. Her knees gave out from under her and her chest and face collapsed onto the log. The two knights grabbed her arms again and yanked her forward. She had seen many times in the city square how criminals' heads were lopped off this way. She lowered her head, resigned to her fate.

Lucas had dismounted and grabbed a thick rope to tie her hands when she collapsed. He placed his boot on her head as the knights looked on in disgust as if she were a bug to squash.

Señora de Silva was willing to die, but she couldn't stand this man stepping on her head and dishonoring her.

She couldn't imagine worse degradation and pain. Then Abraham de Silva appeared from the woods carrying a bundle of wood opposite his wife and Lucas with his foot on her head. He threw down the pile save for a large branch and went running at Lucas.

"You Inquisition bastards!"

His face had gone red—eating Lucas' flesh raw wouldn't have sated his vengeance.

Three knights were enough to hold Abraham de Silva back. His blue-lined *tallit*, which he wore like a badge, fell from his shoulders in the fray along with his *kippah*.

"Careful. Don't kill him," Lucas said.

They pummeled his face and sides, sending him to the ground, then dragged him close to his wife. He was about to lose his mind forced to watch this scene unfold—his eyes had glazed over and he was as dead to feeling as a corpse. Señora de Silva looked at this man she had shared fifty years with as if to say that everything would be all right and they'd be happy again, as she had told him on his most difficult days. It was useless. She knew nothing would be as it had been and that neither of them would be able to recover after such barbarity.

Esther was the first to scream when she, Davud, David and the others returned to where they had left her parents. The others stood staring at the terrible sight in front of them, their faces pale and twisted.

Abraham de Silva was swinging from one end of a branch of a large tree and his wife Hanna from the other.

90

Prince Bayezid was sitting in front of Sheikh Hamdullah as his teacher checked over his script. As he did after every lesson, Hamdullah put his student's writing on his knee and marked the mistakes with red ink, and if necessary, wrote the correct version below the letters. Sometimes he would draw a square in the margins beside the letter and explain its orientation in the space.

"I had an odd dream last night," Bayezid said, clearly troubled.

Hamdullah put his pen down on the paper. "I hope nothing's wrong, Prince."

"I don't know if it's benevolence or malice, Master. But let me tell you and you can interpret it. I wonder what you'll have to say."

Hamdullah wiped off the tip of his pen and set it aside on a silver tray with the other writing instruments before turning back to the prince.

"I opened my eyes to a *vav* on a sheet of paper," Bayezid began. "The letter wasn't fixed on the sheet and was turning around itself with terrific vigor. It twisted like a whirlpool in the middle of the sea as it spun before me. I couldn't pull away my eyes from the influence of this motion no matter how I tried. The letter truly became a whirlpool, and it pulled me in as it grew wider. I was spinning around its edge, turning round toward the *vav* in the center. The current was so powerful that it could've not only swallowed me, but easily even a great Spanish galleon.

"I was waiting to drown as I was being dragged to the center and under water, but instead I opened my eyes with as much contentment I could muster. I was falling fast from the heavens to the earth. I hit the ground and looked back up at the sky where I saw a dome of a mosque, larger than any I'd ever seen. There was the same letter, a *vav*, in the center of this gigantic, central dome. There were more letters around it this time, though. The letters all came together at the center of the dome, along its edges and on the mosque's walls with a beauty I'd never before seen, forming various Quranic verses. They were moving as if underwater, but it didn't detract from their beauty—it rather gave the effect of them dancing. The hundreds or thousands of letters in the verses and hadiths—*alif, mim, lam*— were in black, red and gold, swimming across the walls of this huge mosque.

"I turned to the light streaming in through the door and looked outside. It was like nothing I'd ever seen. The light of a magnificent sun gave sharp shadows to everything around. These shadows astounded me—each one was a letter. The shadows of the trees along the road were cast on the ground as an *elif*, a *vav*, a *mim*, a *kaf*—forming another verse or hadith as they came together. The shadow of a minaret joined with those from the trees and towers and became a wondrous writing in *Jeli Thuluth* script where they fell. I went in among the trees and saw that the veins of every leaf were each a letter. There were millions of letters. Booksellers had opened stands in between the trees and people were competing with each other to buy the books that had all sorts of texts.

"I don't know how long a walked amid these letters, but I ultimately found myself looking upon a grand palace. The stones of its walls were carved with verses from the Quran. I entered through a door, its arch sitting atop two columns of cylindrical stones. Absolutely everything inside was decorated with letters—the marble columns, the porcelain plates on the shelves along the walls, hanging carpets, the patters in the stained glass and the tables.

"I found myself at an observatory after walking down a long corridor. I couldn't tell if it was connected to the palace or if I was in a different time and place from the rest of the dream. But when I looked through some kind of tube, I saw the constellations were Arabic letters. *Gemini* was a *sin*, the Summer Triangle a *nun*, Orion a splendid *sad*. Then—"

Prince Bayezid stopped. He looked out the window and heaved a deep sigh. He seemed to not want to go on, but he did reluctantly.

"Then I took my eye away from the tube and saw men in strange clothing and hats all around me. Their backs were turned to me as they fiddled with the instruments on the table as if they didn't know how to use them, turning them over and around. One held an astrolabe up to his ear as if he thought it would make a sound, and when it didn't, he banged it against the table as if it were a hammer. Another held up a board of the star positions and movements and tried to read it upside down, but he couldn't understand the figures, dates or lines on it. He gave up, threw it to the floor and stamped on it angrily. One of the others looked in wonder through the tube, but was distressed and said he couldn't see anything.

"One of the men I'd been watching from behind noticed me and turned around. I was petrified. He had no pupils—none of them did. They had eyes, but no pupils. I realized then why they couldn't understand what was written on the instruments—they couldn't see what it was, but they could somehow see everything else. They found what I was wearing just as odd as I regarded their clothing and they started walking toward me. I rushed out the door of the observatory and started bolting away.

"Everything was surrounded with the finest furniture, but when I got back to the palace that was decorated with the gorgeous letters, it had all turned to ruins. The magnificent marble columns had crumbled, the porcelain plates with Quranic verses were all broken and the walls covered with letters had been overtaken by moss. Some of the men who'd been chasing me had gotten to the palace.

One of them took an ax to a table decorated with writing and used the wood to build a fire off to the side. Another used shears to cut the rugs hanging on the walls into shreds. The men used all their power to destroy the writing as if they were under a spell. They went about their work dutifully, but then noticed me and took me for an enemy. Then they started closing in on me.

"I escaped through their grasping hands and ran outside into the woods. Alas, all of the leaves whose veins had been letters had turned to ash and the trees had become lifeless, black trunks. The sun had gone and in its place were dark, angry clouds. Even worse, the streets were full of people in strange clothing and with no pupils. They were all running about in what had been a haven of books and booksellers, trampling pages under their feet. There was a page with an *elif* on it under a man's foot that I wanted to pick up, but the man bit my outstretched arm like a ravenous dog and I ran back to the mosque.

"I couldn't get away. I wish the dream had stopped there and I hadn't gone back to the mosque where the Quranic verses and hadiths had been dancing.

"It was crawling with those unseeing men. The distressing thing, though, was that they all had hammers and were banging iron rings into the walls, stringing chains through them and tying up rabid dogs that were thrashing about. The dancing letters had become nothing more than lines, the verses had unraveled and fallen apart and couldn't be read any longer, and the hadiths were unrecognizable. I was transfixed by the terrible scene and had forgotten the pain in my arm. The ferocious dogs grew cross and started snarling when they saw me, as if I was a stranger in their house. The men who'd been chasing me were now piled up behind me. I walked around the mosque and there were unseeing men and snarling dogs all around me. I was in the very center of the mosque—the place where I'd fallen from the sky. I remembered and instinctively looked up to the ceiling. There was only one place left the men couldn't reach—the dome. The *vav* I'd seen at the beginning of my dream was still there, as prominent as ever. I don't know which verse or word it had been a part of since all of the rest of the verse had disappeared, but the *vav* was there. They all descended on me and were drawing closer and closer. I set my eyes on that letter and silently prayed to God.

"Then I woke up and found myself in front of the *vav* I'd been practicing. I'd been exhausted and apparently fell asleep right there facing the page."

Sheikh Hamdullah had listen intently as the prince recounted his dream. He was pensive and troubled. "A window was opened to you in your dream, Prince—a window into the future of the power of the Ottomans, that with God's permission will continue with you and after you. The world's most beautiful houses of God will be built in these lands and the zenith of science and faith will be reached in this empire. Calligraphy will be as precious as the stars and writing will be as much a part of everyday life as a plate of food. Man will be at the peak of civilization so long as he respects letters." He stopped for a moment and looked at the writing in front of him, then looked back up. "There will come a time, though, when our letters lose their meaning. People won't be able to read them or understand their value."

"But how could that be? Will people be burning books and libraries as the Mongols did in Baghdad?"

"Even worse. If you burn one library, ten will still be standing. If you tear one page, the others will be enough. It's not the kind of thing you saw—it's much more calamitous. People will be strangers to their own letters. The libraries and book will survive, but the people won't be able to read or understand them. There'll come a day when the beauty of a letter *vav* no longer enchants and an aged book is no more valued than the dust on its cover."

The prince was confused of how a world surrounded with letters wouldn't be able to read, how people wouldn't be able to understand their own words and how they would be blind to substance and meaning.

"When you have such a dream, Prince, do your ablutions right away and a two-rakat prayer. Ask All-Knowing God, Creator of letters, Teacher of writing and the pen, to not have us forget the meaning of letters and what they symbolize on earth, do not leave us blind to His verses on all in the heavens and on Earth and do not let us see but not read and read but not understand." He handed the sheet of paper back to student. "Now, however, learn how to write these letters properly so your prayers may be accepted."

91

Esther de Silva was staring out across the horizon as the rabbi was saying the prayers. The sun had just begun to color the sky behind the Villanueva mountains orange. The evening star shined timidly above the eastern horizon whose blue had grown darker and velvety. Its shyness could not stop it from showing its beauty in all its majesty to those below.

David and Esther were standing in front of the rabbi and holding hands. There was a square cloth above their heads large enough to pass under them. Davud, Beatriz, Abdullah and Zayd bin Uthman were standing around them, each holding a pole at each of the corners.

The rabbi recited the wedding prayer. "*Blessed are You, Lord, our God, sovereign of the universe, who created everything for His Glory.*"

Hannah de Silva had prepared a *chuppah* for her daughter's wedding while Esther was still a young girl, ornamenting the edges with silk lacework. This beautiful silk had been waiting for years in her dowry chest, but had been ripped to shreds by the countless, greedy thieves who had looted the de Silvas' home. They'd decided to use a cloth they'd found in one of the abandoned houses and fashioned poles out of fallen limbs from the forest for the *chuppah* to fulfill the custom for the Jewish wedding ceremony. Esther's mother had said that according to the Torah, it evokes Abraham and Sarah's hospitality to the visitors to their house and represents the union of a new couple beneath a roof and the need for them to be hospitable to others.

"*Blessed are You, Lord, our God, sovereign of the universe, Creator of man.*"

Esther had watched grand weddings in Catholic churches with great interest when she was a young girl and had wondered why Jewish weddings weren't held in such colorful buildings decorated with images. Her mother had once explained, asking her how a wedding under the sun and moon witnessed by the stars could take place between four walls. Even though the magic of this thought took her over for a moment, she soon continued with her enchantment with the flamboyant glamor at the Catholic churches.

"*Blessed are You, Lord, our God, sovereign of the universe, who created man in His image, in the image of His likeness He fashioned his form, and prepared for him from His own self an everlasting edifice. Blessed are You Lord, Creator of man.*"

Now, though, years later, Esther thought about how proud her mother would be to be there at a wedding ceremony under the stars, moon and setting sun among her bridesmen. She understood now that marriage is a door opening to the heavens and that it did not shut a woman out, but instead is a coalescence of her with the earth, nature and God.

Her eyes filled up as she stroked the *tichel* she was wearing that she had taken from her mother's body. It still smelled like her. She turned and looked at David, the man she would share the rest of her life with.

"*Grant abundant joy to these loving friends, as You bestowed gladness upon Your created being in the Garden of Eden of old. Blessed are You, Lord, who gladdens the groom and bride.*"

Abraham de Silva's white *tallit* with blue stripes was hanging from David's shoulders. It had gotten dirty when he'd been pulled along the ground as he fought against the knights of Santa Hermandad and one of the *tzitzit* on the edge had been torn. David had for years thought of this moment maybe a thousand times and imagined it in thousands of ways, but none of it had prepared him for the storm of emotions he was now feeling.

Letters appeared before his eyes, turning into words, words into sentences and sentences into lines as the rabbi who they'd found in a caravan escaping Andalusia and asked to preside over the wedding recited the prayer. Every letter of the prayer the rabbi said while performing the ceremony went through his head and touched his spirit like the clinking metal letters of a printing press set against a page as if his and Esther's future was being written on an invisible page of creation. The illusory pages emerging in front of his eyes were pure white like the moon illuminating the darkness in contrast to the situation they were in.

"Blessed are You, Lord, our God, sovereign of the universe, who created in the world joy and gladness, love and companionship, peace and friendship, bridegroom and bride—"

Both bride and groom were somber. They had become prepared for anything after what had happened to Hannah and Abraham de Silva, and at least wanted to guarantee they would spend eternity together in the hereafter.

"—Blessed are you Lord, who delights in bridegroom and bride together."

More stars emerged one after another as the sky grew a deep indigo. Davud was withdrawn as he held one of the poles of the *chuppah*, his face turned to the sky. His heart burned when he saw *Virgo* appear. The burning in his heart grew the longer this Turk in a foreign land looked up at the stars he knew so well.

92

Davud's eyes were awash with the Milky Way—what he knew in Turkish and Arabic as the Road of Straw—shining in the dark blue of the night sky. He was lying next to Elif on a slope with his hands behind his head, his eyes set in wonder on the sky and the millions of stars.

He thought about why this galaxy that stretched through the heavens like a caravan route was called as such. Maybe the Bedouins looked up at this dusty cloud running through the middle of millions of stars and likened it to a caravan route, calling it *Darb ut-Tabanah*, or the Road of Straw, as bits of straw would fall along the road from the bales on their horses and camels.

He thought this must be the reason.

He also thought about *Darb al-Libani*, which would have the meaning same as Milky Way like *Galaxias Kyklos*, or Milky Circle, in Greek, and weather it was a slip up in the language. Maybe the Muslim astronomers pouring over Ptolemy's star map and losing sleep over this dust cloud found it more appropriate to call it *tabanah* rather than *libani*—straw rather than milky.

"Why do you think the Greeks call it the Milky Circle?" he asked Elif.

She turned to him, her eyes the color of the soil of a glistening wet field. "My grandmother explained it to me when I was a child.

She used to kneel with me at the window in the evenings and tell me the old Greek tales."

With the stars sparkling on the woman he was in love with and listening to her velvety voice, Davud felt he was in heaven.

"In the myth," Elif said, "Heracles was sired by Zeus and born of a mortal woman. Zeus surreptitiously gave his infant son to suckle his divine wife Hera's milk as she slept to make him god-like, but Hera woke up and pushed the unknown baby away from her breast, making milk spill across the heavens. So they call it the Milky Circle."

Elif laughed after the two of them had stayed silent for a while as they looked at the stars. "If our Armenian neighbors were over when my grandmother was telling the tale, they'd grumble and say it was just something that the ancient Greeks concocted with all their gods and that everyone knows that its name comes from an Armenian myth. They said that eons ago there was a really cold winter and the sun god Vahagn stole straw from the Assyrian King Barsham. He fled across the heavens and dropped some of it along the way, which became the Milky Way, which they call the Straw Thief's Way. Once when her Armenian friend explained it this way she said that that yes, the old Greeks had many gods, but then how were those ancient Armenians with all their gods and their tale any different from the Greeks anyway. What's the big difference? Then they both just laughed and went on with their knitting."

Davud was listening to Elif, but he was caught on the Greek story. He wanted so much for this woman next to him to one day nurse their own children.

His eyes then fixed on *Virgo*. "There it is!" he said, pointing up. "That's who you are. You're her—the sky's pure beauty."

Ptolemy called the constellation *Virgo* and the Arabs call this figure of a woman *Malak Jamil*, or Beautiful Angel. Davud thought this constellation sparkled the most interestingly. There were thousands of different names and meanings for every constellation in the star maps he'd read. The Greeks, Arabs and Persians had even all given a different name to the gigantic collections of stars across the sky. In one culture one was a camel, in another a horse and still again a princess for others, or a bearded sultan.

Virgo though, was always depicted as a beautiful maiden holding a sheaf of wheat. Both Ptolemy and al-Sufi had it like this. The ancient Greeks, Christians and Muslims all saw love in it.

Elif blushed as she looked away from Davud and back up, connecting the stars and trying to imagine the figure he mentioned.

It's not for nothing that Muslims call it *al-Eadhra', the Virgin*, while the Christians liken it to Mary, the Blessed Virgin. Some Bedouins called one of its stars *al-Simak al-A'zal—the Unarmed of the Uplifted Ones*. In Egypt it was Isis, Ishtar for the Babylonians and the maiden goddess in India.

"Here's a Greek tale for you," said Davud with a smile. 'This Star Maiden once lived with man during the Golden Age. She roamed the land handing out ears of grain to the people. Man lived for hundreds of years, contented and happy, knowing nothing of corruption, war, hunger, illness or separation. There was harmony, peace, piety and potency. Then man forgot the gods, as they reckoned the perfect order was their doing and lost their piety. This maiden warned them to be ready for the gods' wrath, but man turned away from her. They found hunger, injustice, violent death and war, and the maiden who had distributed grain ran away to the mountain while wickedness and war took reign over the land and she ascended to the heavens. We're in those days now, looking up at this maiden while man has been at the mercy of his own war and sorrow for hundreds of years."

"Maybe one day she'll come back to earth. Who knows?"

They both smiled.

"She already has," Davud said.

She looked back over at Davud, surprised. She didn't understand what he was getting at.

"She's right next to me."

"Davud," she drew out his name, her voice betraying her timid excitement as the stars sparkled in her eyes.

He turned his head to her. He couldn't tell if he'd been carried away by the stargazing or if it was from the twinkling.

"We're getting married in a week, Davud. Then we'll live together until the end. Just think about it."

He took her hands and squeezed them. Elif looked from the stars to him. "Let there be a baby—a boy with your blue eyes."

"No no, a girl as sweet as you. Everything like her mother."

"You should know then the two of us will overpower you." Elif laughed.

Davud couldn't believe for a moment that they were going to get married.

"Alright you turtledoves," a voice said from behind them. "That's enough chit chat for now."

Elif's mother had been watching them from the window and had come down to where they were lying. There was an even bigger pile of business for the next day.

This was the last time they would see each other before the wedding, and the next time they'd look at the stars like this they would be husband and wife.

Davud looked at the stars for a while longer after Elif and her mother left.

He had no idea that only a year later his entire life would be turned upside down, that he would always be traveling far like on the caravan route of the Milky Way, or that his beloved daughter would tragically disappear like the maiden of the constellation in the tale. He was only thinking of marrying Elif, smiling with joy, a crescent moon on his face.

Virgo—the Star Maiden—twinkled in the midnight blue of the night sky.

93

Davud and the rest of the group were resting in the thick wood-lands around Antequera, one day away from Malaga. The orange of the sun was about to be lost to the evening. They were to set out on the road for the last time the next morning after spending a night here.

David had heard that there was an old library still remaining in the area from the time of the emirate and he'd been planning to go and find it while the rest were sleeping to get a few dozen man-uscripts. He'd told Davud of his plan a few times, and every time Davud said it would be a huge risk since the libraries were crawling with book hunters and it would only be a matter of time until the priests or monks caught him.

And so after the sun set and everyone was curled up beneath the trees, David slipped away without a word to go find the library some one or two hours away. Fleeing this land without these books for him would mean continuing life with no spirit. He needed these texts—they were important for the rest of his life.

As he set out, he hoped that at worst he'd be able to return to the others by midnight.

Esther was the first to notice he was gone in the morning and the others woke up to her screaming. Davud reckoned were he'd gone off to. He was fuming.

He cautioned everyone to stay at the camp and then warily set out to find the library.

He got back about three hours later holding a sack of books. His face was long and drawn.

He threw the sack into the middle of the group and a few manuscripts fell out. Everyone, Esther most of all, had their eyes on Davud for what I would say.

"He found the book, but he must've been captured on the way back."

"Where'd you find these?" Samuel asked.

Esther was heaving and sobbing.

"About an hour from here."

"We should go to the library and save him," Samuel said as he sprung to his feet.

"He's not at the library. It's way too late for that."

"How do you know?"

"Because I came from there. There were to knights of Santa Hermandad and a priest taking prisoners away as the sun was coming up."

"So where're they taking them?" Abdullah asked. "Could you at least find that out?"

Davud stayed quiet for a moment and heaved a deep sigh. "Yes."

He'd learned where David had been taken and had also met the monk Santiago, the one Father Paolo had mentioned. He'd already gotten all the information from him. What was certain, though, was there was no longer any way to save David.

"So, come on, say it. Where'd they take him?" Samuel said.

"Where's David?" Esther said between heaves.

What David said fell like burning cinders on the group. "Alcazaba."

"Damn it!" Abdullah said, stomping the ground.

David was now captive in Malaga's most heavily guarded castle in one of the last areas the Spanish kingdom had conquered.

They all knew it would be impossible to go there and get out alive.

The Library of al—Hakam

Nobody in our group believed it while I was an Inquisition clerk in the Antequera region when we heard that the library of al-Hakam was hidden with
its hundreds of books somewhere close to the Alcazaba, only one day from
Malaga. Like all the long-suffering servants of the Holy Church, I knew quite
well that the fabled library of this Muhammadan ruler, who lived a thousand
years after Christ, had been destroyed centuries ago. First the Almoravids,
then another dynasty from Morocco—the fanatical Almohad—then finally
our own Holy Church and the triumphant Catholic sovereigns had all left
nothing of al-Hakam's trove of thousands of books.

And so I and two other monks headed to the nearby madrasah that
had long ago fallen into ruin. A few Inquisition guards held sentry at the
door. The first order of business when a new library was found was to
protect it from theft by Jews and Muhammadans. It didn't seem, however,
that many people would come upon this out-of-the-way place other than
us. We frankly didn't expect to find any manuscripts in the crumbling
library, let alone books.

But we couldn't believe our eyes when we entered the stone building and
ascended the stairs that were still standing and sturdy despite their cracks. An
entire floor, nearly the size of a small field, was full of books. There weren't
only shelves upon shelves lining the walls, but also rows of shelves running the
length of the floor. There were so many shelves running parallel and crossing
through each other that I felt I was in a labyrinth.

I saw the mixed looks on the other two monks' faces. One looked like a jackal that had just come across a butcher full of meat. He had a devilish grin as he took account of all the books to burn while the other was disheartened at the prospect of the amount of work awaiting us. Standing between them, I was thinking about all the difficult work of how we would classify all these books, which ones would be found to be prohibited and which would be delivered to the church library. And we only had half day for all of it.

At first, we all decided to go through and eliminate all the Arabic and Hebrew books without touching the ones in Latin. We'd learned already that every book in Arabic wasn't the Quran and every one in Hebrew wasn't the Torah, but we also all knew Cardinal Cisneros' thinking and prudence on this subject, that nothing beneficial comes from Arabic or Hebrew. We would then go through the books in Latin afterward according to their contents.

We set to work in three different corners of the library like hungry bulls wandering through a field full of wheat. It was all going well at first and we thought we were making good time. We took books from the shelves, haphazardly leafed through the pages and tossed them to the ground once we saw that they weren't in Latin. The books would all be collected later for the Inquisition guards to burn. Sometimes there wasn't even need to open them up—they had extraordinarily beautiful binding and the title or author embossed on their covers and spines.

We sifted through hundred of books like this. We looked around after a couple hours had passed and tried to take account of how many books we'd cleared from the shelves. I thought we'd presumably gone through half the library, but when we looked under our feet and then back up at the shelves, we saw that we'd only touched a hundredth of the books. The shelves along the walls and in the middle of the room were still full. We started going through the books simply by their appearance, without even opening them, now aware what we were up against. We pulled books out and tossed them to the floor if there was no Latin or if there were any Arabic or Hebrew letters on their spines or covers. We were so arbitrary, it reminded me of months earlier when Inquisition guards decided if non-Christians were Muhammadan or Jewish based on how they looked and tossed them in the dungeons. Ibn Rushd and Maimonides were in a corner of my mind while a voice was crying out to me as if to suppress them, telling me to not stop and keep going.

We stepped back and looked around again after two more hours and saw that we'd now cleared a fifth of the books. We'd be rid of all the Arabic and Hebrew books in a few more hours if we picked up the pace.

We got back to work, now going faster than before as we went through the books two at a time with both hands. My arms were sore and aching after another three hours. I cleared off the last shelves in the area I was responsible for and then went over to my two companions and looked at what we'd accomplished. We'd done well. There was nothing left on the shelves other than books we were certain were in Latin. The labyrinthine corridors had become waves of piled up books and we were proud of ourselves when we saw open pages with Arabic and Hebrew lying on the floor.

There's no point to deceiving myself any longer, though.

I was distressed, not proud. I thought every book and every manuscript in Hebrew, Arabic or Latin I burned, would quench the fire inside me, that I would find relief and win the battle raging inside me. But I was only fooling myself. Every book I burned only fanned the flames of that battle.

Then something happened. It was night and our work somehow still hadn't finished even though we'd planned to return to Malaga in the early morning. I heard a noise come from the lower floors. I went downstairs and found out that the Inquisition guards had caught a Jew stealing books. He'd run away at first, but they caught him on the road and brought him back. Everything was quite ordinary up to this point. A monk came to me the next morning, though. He told me about Father Paolo, under whom I'd grown up many years ago. It was as if I returned to my childhood right there upon hearing the name of the priest, which hadn't come to my ears for decades, and I was ashamed of what I'd done. All of my inner troubles surfaced and I was ashamed of myself for having become a book hunter.

I trusted this man then and there—this monk—his looks and what he said, and agreed to help him.

I still don't know why I did.

95

Davud could tell his wife was washing when he heard the sound of water coming from behind the wooden closet painted with flowers in the bedroom. Even the sound of water spilling from a jug to the floor was enough to excite him, imagining her body, how the water flowed over her delicate curves, her wet hair falling to her shoulders and down her back and drops of water running down every intimate crevice.

Davud slowly opened the door to the washroom and found Elif sitting on a wooden stool with her back to him. She was sitting in front of the heating stove and lathering up her hair. A shining copper basin full of hot water was resting against the curved pipe coming out and up from the heating stove. The fire in the stove that heated both the water and the washroom was burning brightly, but it was the enchanting beauty he saw, not the fire, that was heating him up.

The hot water steaming off her wheaten skin and the smoke from the stove looked like fog lifting from the land as the sun rises. For Davud, though, the sight was more beautiful than any sunrise or the moon shining in the night sky.

He walked in, not even removing his clothes, approached his wife and dabbled his fingers in the copper basin. Her eyes closed, Elif reached out for the basin to rinse her head. She felt around but couldn't find it.

"Davud," she said, mostly but not all jokingly, "there's soap in my eyes. Come on, give me the basin!"

He smiled and slowly poured the water over her head. The soap rinsed from her auburn hair, over her shoulders and curved down her arms and over her breasts. The soap seemed to have the same idea he did, lingering on her breasts before it wound over and cascaded down.

Davud put down the basin and sat behind Elif. He embraced her. He didn't smell her fragrant skin, he drew it in deeply—her neck, her throat and shoulders—as if it were a life-giving spring.

She shuddered and turned her head around. Sparks popped from the stove the moment Davud's lips touched hers, full and flushed from the heat. Their hearts were both beating as if they were going to burst. More than kissing, their spirits were intertwining with each other. Davud felt as though he'd been lost in the desert for days and was finally able to drink at an oasis. It was as if Elif had been held prisoner for years in a tower and now her prince had come to save her, and she offered the keys to her body and spirit to him.

Elif stood up and turned around once Davud's head had been soaked from the water running off her body. He held her and put his head against her belly. He kissed her and breathed in deeply as if he were a traveler who had wandered the world for years and finally found its center. Elif held his head and stroked his hair. He put his ear to her body and listened to her heartbeat and the blood running through her veins—the sound of her whole being. He could listen to this heartbeat his entire life and would give up what was left for the sake of this woman.

They both couldn't tell if the sparks were from each other as they held each other or were from the crackling wood and cinders in the stove. Elif sat across from Davud and pulled his dripping shirt over his head, revealing his broad shoulders and chiseled chest. His arms were like ivory. She ran her fingers over his body, as hard as marble, and looked at him in wonder as he gazed at her as if she were the only woman on earth. Powerful and dangerous yet elegant and daring, this warrior was in love. She took his face in her hands and pulled him to her. She felt she was lost in the waters of a deep sea as she looked into his blue eyes, then as though she were flying through the sky. She couldn't close her eyes as she kissed him and stared into the blue. It numbed her whole body and took her strength like a snakebite. This body, according to Elif, was the definition of valor and virility.

Davud ran his hands over her as if he were tracing the lines and curves of a map, drawing his fingers across her like a sailor searching for hidden treasure.

The sweat from their bodies mixed with the water and slowly flowed down their skin like lava down a volcano. The sweat flying from Davud's body pelted the stove like the warriors who tore down the walls of Rome. Their hot breath rose from their mouths like steam from a geyser.

There were Adam and Eve finding their lost Eden.

They were unaware as they breathlessly climbed the tall mountain that they had planted a seed for a flower that would sprout on a spring day after three seasons.

Elif looked into Davud's eyes. "I love you, Davud."

Davud was transfixed by her gaze. "I love you, Elif. God, don't ever let us part."

Martin Alonso Pinzon rowed to the Santa Maria and went straight to the admiral's cabin to tell Columbus that he'd looked at the horizon there were some signs that they were nearing land. He rapped on the door and it cracked open.

Pinzon entered, thinking Columbus was inside.

Columbus' cabin was small but ostentatious. There was a pelt hanging on the wall of a leopard he'd caught in Africa while voyaging with the Portuguese, the head of a stag whose antlers were five times the size of the rest of it, zebra skins on the ground and African carved wooden masks the size of a man in the corners.

Pinzon saw a wicker basket full of elephant tusks. One of these would fetch an unimaginable sum from some aristocrat in Italy. He wondered how many chess pieces could be made from just one tusk. He walked through the room looking at all the strange objects, smiling with a slight look of contempt.

He realized that Columbus wasn't there and was about to leave when he turned around and bumped into the table in the middle of the cabin. A notebook fell to the floor. He leafed through its pages before he put it back on the table, thinking it must be the admiral's logbook.

He began to read a random page.

October 7, 1492

This voyage has made my hair go grey like never before. I see that my hair's grown whiter every time I look at my reflection in the water. Maybe I can find some sort of dye that the locals have discovered, some plant from the rich soils when I get to Asia, some remedy that the Spanish and Italians haven't found yet. I went through Pliny's Historia Naturalis by candlelight in the silence of last night. He says the semen of a donkey stops hair loss and greying. He explains at length how to harvest the semen from the animal's loins. Although I haven't made use of his previous suggestions so far and I've vowed not to listen to him anymore, I have no intention of aging prematurely now that fortune is smiling on me again. True, powdered Saint John's bread didn't help my hair even though I did everything as Pliny says.

But, I have nothing to lose and should find a remedy for this white hair no matter what.

I'm trying to reinvigorate my hopes by writing these notes in my logbook. I'm working to encourage myself with thoughts of the land I'll acquire, the gold, jewels and whatever other vast riches we don't know about yet that I'll find when we ultimately spot land and these ships get to India.

This voyage becomes even more impossible with every passing day. The crew's morale has been used up. Not one among them trusted me anyway. They've rather become my foes since we've not come across any piece of land despite only a few weeks having passed until now. I take note of our course in my logbook every evening.

We've gone one hundred thirty-eight nautical miles as of sunset today. This figure, which I've gotten by dead reckoning, redoubles every evening, but I fear telling the men of it. I take this measurement, decrease it by a third and then tell them of our course. By doing so, I ensure the crew thinks we've gone slow and so, also not too far, ensuring they don't know how far we are from Spain. The men would slaughter me straight away if they knew how far away from land we are now.

My many thanks to our Lord Jesus Christ, that Pinzon is a captain of his word and no one would go against it. The problem, though, is that it seems to me that Niño knows the actual course we've been on and how far it's been since he never leaves the maps, star charts or astrolabe. He must know that it'll bring nothing other than ruin. Nevertheless, I'm grateful I got him for the voyage in Granada. He's very tight-lipped. He doesn't speak unless he's asked. He answers questions and is constantly making calculations. He holds two astrolabes, one in each hand, the Arabic letters and numbers on his alidade are smaller than anything I've seen before, no bigger than an ant, and the brass plate it sits on has star maps according to the seasons, lines of latitude and longitude and other markings I don't understand.

He goes above under the sun, looks up at the sky through his shining, golden astrolabe and immediately knows where we are and at which latitude. Then he looks at me and gives me a knowing grin as if to tell me I'm still lying. There's no problem so long as he doesn't tell the crew what he knows. It would be unfortunate for the both of us if he did.

If only he had some other gadget to see land, then we'd be saved from thinking dark, far off clouds were dry land. Just like those lost in the desert think they see oases and water, so do lost sailors, the other way around, always think they spy land. Not a day goes by that some hopeless sailor on deck points out over the ocean yelling about land. And we always get excited and look where he's pointing, thinking maybe this time it's real, maybe this time we've reached Asia. Then we turn the bow in that direction and sail for hours and sometimes days. But at the end, since we haven't come across any land, we deviate from our course and lose time. It also wreaks havoc with the men's morale. I don't know if we can go on much longer like this.

A large fireball fell fifty miles from us yesterday. The men claim it was the Devil's fireball and that we've come to the end of the world. I, however, am certain it was a star falling to the earth. Niño and Pinzon laughed when I said this. When I asked why they were laughing, Niño said that even the smallest star is dozens of times larger than the earth and that there's no such think as a star falling to earth. Then when I asked what it was, he said it was either a meteor or lava from a nearby volcanic eruption. The men forgot about all the Devil nonsense when they heard this and we continued on our way. I'm confident, though, that chaos will erupt again soon and the crew will be hung up on turning back.

If these men knew what I know and saw what I've envisioned, they'd be able to endure this voyage for months instead of only weeks.

We'll be directly at the foot of Asia's treasures when we reach the Indian shores by continuing west, bypassing the Muhammadans' monopoly on Mediterranean trade and the Silk Road. Reaching these lands will the rediscovery of a lost paradise. There will be fruits we've never seen, foods we've never tasted, gold and precious stones as valuable as maravedis, and thousands of slaves under our charge.

We saw a white swallow in the afternoon. Pinzon said it was a blackbird and that it wouldn't be able to fly too far offshore. This means that we're quite close to land. The seaweed and rocks on the surface of the ocean are other signs.

I did well to get Luis de Torres in Toledo. The men we meet on the other side of the world will most likely speak Arabic or Hebrew. So far, these cultures have produced the quality and valuable developments we have. The astrolabe is from the Arabs, they discovered and named the stars, they've made the most detailed maps I've ever seen, the most exhaustive accounts of the globe and measurements of the distance of the sun and the moon. There's no language this converso doesn't know—Arabic, Hebrew, the Italian languages, Ottoman, Greek, Latin and many others I've never heard of. I'm certain that whatever language the people we'll meet speak, it'll be one he understands. The man pays no regard to how I treat him after the barbarity in Spain, and never makes me repeat myself. The only thing he wants from me is to not take him back to Spain. He's dead set on settling where we land no matter whom we meet there. I haven't said anything about it so far, but he's dead wrong if he thinks I'll release him from duty when we reach Asia. I plan to use him longer for my dealings with the Arabs and the Turks.

It makes no sense to me why Isabella and Ferdinand are discarding these skilled people. It makes no difference to me if they're Jewish or Muhammadans. I've actually begun to think the Pinzon brothers are Muhammadans since we set sail. Maybe the Inquisition had reason to throw Martin Alonso Pinzon in the dungeon. I saw him once washing his arms and ears when I came to the Pinta. There was a man holding a water pitcher opposite him and he mumbled something and washed his arms and feet like the Muhammadans do. He was startled when he saw me on deck, but then collected himself. I'm uncertain as to whether he was just washing his hands or cleaning himself as the Muhammadans do before prayer, but I suspect him. He knows Arabic very well, even though he tries not to let me know. He shows extreme diligence in fulfilling his word like most Muhammadans. What's more interesting is I've never heard him say the name of Jesus Christ. When he swears he says things like for the love of God or for God's sake. There's no pork on his ship, either. When I asked him about it, he said pork makes him ill and elided the question. He also doesn't drink wine, saying a wise captain stays sober. He dislikes talking of himself and changes the subject whenever I ask these types of questions. He says one doesn't have to be a Muhammadan to not drink alcohol and claims all religions ban wine.

I don't care at all about Pinzon's religion so far as he obeys me, but if he does something to set me back, the first thing I do when we get back to Spain will be to hand him back over to the Inquisition. So far I've treated him the same as Niño and the converso de Torres, and haven't said a word. I wouldn't do the slightest thing to imperil this voyage. Still, if something becomes of me or I lose my memory, as happens to so many lost at sea, this *logbook will reveal the truth. This voyage will do the greatest damage to the Muhammadan Turks when we find land. It will break their monopoly on trade over the Mediterranean and through the East and we'll rule over the land as God's faithful servants.*

After reading this, Pinzon rifled through the maps on the table and started to read the second logbook Columbus mentioned. It was like a letter he had prepared to send to the king and queen. The entries for the same days explained everything differently. It had no mention of Pinzon or Niño's contributions to the voyage and Columbus attributed everything to himself. Pinzon's surprise didn't last long, though, and he soon reckoned what the admiral was up to. For his own safety, Columbus was keeping one logbook only for himself and a second to show everybody else and trick the crew.

98

October 7, 1492

The voyage is continuing as planned with the support of the faithful servants of our Lord Jesus Christ, King Ferdinand and Queen Isabella. We've made it seventy-eight nautical miles as of sundown today. We've gone a little slow owing to unfavorable winds and currents. I have no doubt that we'll reach land very soon. My calculations, the information I obtained from the maps and my reckoning from the stars at night show me that we're on the correct course.

This voyage has already begun to prove fruitful. The ocean is a radiant, dazzling blue I've never seen on the Mediterranean. The weather is cool with little humidity. The waters, too, are as calm as the Guadalquivir most of the time. I can almost smell the earthly paradise we're nearing—only the song of the nightingale is missing. After ridding Spain of the Jews and Muhammadans, there's no doubt that we'll spread the goodness and justice of the civilization of Jesus Christ to the uncultured inhabitants of the continents we reach. The world will be freed of the heathen Muhammadans' yoke and justice will hold reign over the entire world thanks to us noble Catholics.

I came to believe that the time if the heretical Muhammadan is over and that we, the true servants of God, must hold everywhere in the world in high honor when I saw the flag of our great kingdom in the Alhambra, from where the Muhammadans had ruled for centuries, and when I witnessed the Arabs' great King Boabdil kiss the skirts of Queen Isabella.

Eastern Rome fell to the Turks after the unfortunate events of 1453, but before fifty years pass, we will reach the center of the world in Jerusalem from the west and make the Catholic flag wave once again in the holy land. The Turks punished the Orthodox Romans of Constantinople for deviating from the way of the pope and using their religion as an instrument of heresy. However, our Lord Jesus Christ will continue to reward us as we spread Catholicism and treat the Jews and Muhammadans as they deserve.

I, poor Christopher Columbus, Great Admiral of the Ocean, have been keeping supporting logs of the calculations I've made throughout the voyage, my observations, charts of latitude and longitude, and other charts so that our holy kingdom will be able to continue with or without me and all of humanity can benefit from the message of our Lord and Savior Jesus Christ. I write in the evenings, comments on my observations of the morning sun, wind and currents, and calculations of our course and time by the hourglass. Yes, maybe it's from lack of sleep—I'm surrendering my health, but it's of no importance to me for this holy mission.

This voyage will deliver us from the Turks' grip on the Mediterranean and we'll deal a blow to the heart of those infidels. Let it be so. Forget sleep. With the maps I've made, let our holy kingdom rule over all the land and put an end to domination by barbarians. The Bible and the books of the holy saints say that mankind's end and return to the kingdom of God will happen one thousand five hundred years after Christ walked the earth and we will again enter our lost paradise. This voyage I've set out on with only a few years until 1500 is doubtless the greatest sign of these prophesies coming to pass. It could also mean that we faithful servants of God will recreate this paradise on earth. My belief is that the true flag of victory will once again fly in Zion with the entrance of the armies of Christ to the holy lands just as the royal standards of Isabella and Ferdinand adorn the sky in Granada.

Ptolemy's Geographia, Strabo's Geographica, Pierre d'Ailly's Imago Mundi, The Travels of Marco Polo, and Toscanelli and Behaim's maps show me the way. The great ocean is revealed and the Santa Maria sails it thanks to the light provided by Catholic sailors and travelers. It would be impossible to overcome this ocean with these old ships—one carrack and two caravels—without our faith in Jesus Christ. The years of experience I've gained on the Mediterranean and my faith in God allow us to continue our voyage with heart.

I saw a swallow today, white and with a long tail. These birds don't stray far from land and, at the very least, I know they don't sleep on the ocean. This means we are very close to landfall.

I will award ten thousand maravedis to the first man to spot land. This prospect has excited the men a little. Even more, we've started to see seaweed on the ocean surface, which means land can't more than two or three days away at the most. The men, though, grow more impatient seeing these positive signs, and their confidence in me wanes if they don't see land after a short while. A large fireball fell over the ocean yesterday afternoon. Some of the men claimed it was the work of the Devil and that we should turn back. I explained to them that it was a meteor—something I've encountered many times—and that there was nothing to fear. This calmed them.

We will soon find land, by the grace of God, and no one will abandon my faith and persistence of fortune.

Red in the face with anger, Pinzon made up his mind that moment after coming face to face with this dishonor. The hardest part of carrying out his decision, however, would be to be able to tell Columbus before he wrapped his hands around the man's throat and strangled him. Columbus, however, was standing at the door looking on as Pinzon read his secret logbook.

99

"What is this shit, Admiral?" Pinzon shouted again, red faced.

Columbus grew more brazen once he realized Pinzon had read his secret logbook and tried to make the whole thing out to be unimportant. He walked around the table as he spoke.

"Come, man, what's the big deal? I mean, what should I have done? If I told the crew the truth about our course, we'd have been done for. Have you never heard of a white lie, man?"

"Which white lie are you talking about, Admiral? What you've written is plain deception, but I understand what you're really trying to do. You'll send these letters to the king and queen when we reach land, maybe your logbook full of lies, too, where you claim all success of the voyage for yourself with designs on becoming the one owner of the lands we find. All achievements are yours in this logbook with no mention of Niño or me. One would think you're the only victor of this voyage. How else should anyone interpret what you wrote?"

Columbus stood at the head of the table and poured wine from a jug into a cup decorated with gold and ivory.

"Don't exaggerate, Martin. I've only tried to maintain peace on the ship—"

Pinzon cut him off. "Stop this bullshit! We've long passed the time for this voyage's success. How can you lie to the ninety seamen who've given you their lives? I'm talking about the lives of the ninety men who signed on to your harebrained, vague plans with all they have. And don't look at me with that face. It's not just me and Niño—you making this voyage is only possible thanks to the crew, Admiral. Have you no shame?"

It seemed Columbus had grown bored from this talk. He refilled his glass and extended it to Pinzon.

"Let it go, Martin. Here look, have some of my personal wine."

Pinzon stood and looked at the cup, amazed.

"What happened? Why are you so angry?" Columbus continued. "Or is what's written in that logbook true? Should we not hand you over to Inquisition when we return for being a secret Muhammadan?"

Pinzon stood in silence with this implicit threat. He stepped forward, took the cup from Columbus' still outreached hand and brought it to his mouth. Columbus was about to smile in victory when Pinzon hurled the cup against the wall. The cup crashed against the stag head, knocking it to the ground and splattering red wine across the leopard pelt on the wall. Columbus was about to look back to Pinzon from the mess when Pinzon grabbed him by the throat and thrust him against the wall—his head now where the stag was less than a minute ago.

"If you threaten me even one more time, I'll slice off your damn head with my own sword and hang it on this wall!"

Pinzon was cutting off the blood to Columbus' head and his face began to go purple. He tried to speak, but nothing came out other than wheezing and spittle.

Pinzon shook Columbus against the wall again. "Listen to me well, Admiral. I'll finish out this voyage, not because of any promise I made you, but because of the one I made the ninety men on board. I'll continue with you until we find land, but know this—I'm gone after that."

Columbus' eyes opened wide as if he'd been punched in the gut.

"That's right, Admiral. You heard me. Everyone's on their own for the return journey. You'll have to fend for yourself for once."

Columbus was thinking about how he'd be able to return without him as Pinzon walked out and slammed the door. He looked at the stag head on the ground. Wine had soaked it and its eyes were glinting red.

100

Elif, mim, be.

Sheikh Hamdullah carefully picked up the collection of Prince Bayezid's various writings and began to read. It had *elif, mim, be,* written above the *basmala,* the three letters representing the spirit of the writing.

Bayezid sat across from his master and waited, excited and impatient.

The paper had an outer frame of dark beige and one of golden ink made from a mixture of saffron, tin and gum arabic inside it surrounding the writing. The golden ink sparkled and illuminated the white paper like sunshine over a field.

The page was divided into six main rectangles, each one an example of each of the six calligraphic styles.

Hamdullah carefully read the verse in the first frame.

And mention the story of Abraham in the Book. Indeed, he was a man of truth and a prophet.

There were squares in the empty space beside the writing on the left and right adorned with cypress motifs in green ink. Hamdullah smiled when he saw them—no doubt they were an elegant reference to the prince's first lesson with the sheikh in the cemetery so long ago. It made Hamdullah happy. This first line in *Thuluth* script got a passing mark.

He then looked to the next line down of a verse mentioning the prophet most-named in the Quran.

And We gave Moses the Scripture and made it a guide for the Children of Israel that you take no other than Me as Disposer of affairs.

Hamdullah carefully examined this second verse of the *al-Isra* surah. He looked over each of the letters' flourishes, forms, curves and dots. He looked at the color of the ink, its luster, the darkness of the black, the placement of the letters, their beginning and end points and a thousand other miniscule details. Empty space in a line should be filled with gold ink, and a Seal of Solomon was there— two overlapping triangles—bringing union to both text and design, and substance and meaning.

This second line also got a passing mark.

He began to read the third line, which was punctuated at the beginning with a little sun.

O Mary, indeed, God gives you good tidings of a word from Him, whose name will be the Messiah, Jesus, the son of Mary, distinguished in this world and the Hereafter and among those brought near.

The *Ali 'Imran* surah, verse forty-five. Hamdullah went over the letters filling the two lines with the same scrutiny. The letters were quite fluid and natural and he felt that the lines flowed with the spirit of the calligrapher. He reckoned this elegant writing couldn't have come from a surly, arrogant and impatient hand. This was certainly a script from the hand of a calligrapher who knows what he wrote and why.

The illumination around the verse fit with the serenity of the writing. The opaque, watercolor tones of the floral designs and wheat as a symbol of fertility were comforting to behold and the green leaves in places brought the composition together.

Hamdullah was expecting another verse in the *Reyhan* script in the next frame.

And if whatever trees on earth were pens and the seas were ink, replenished thereafter by seven more seas, the words of God would not be exhausted.

Hamdullah smiled again. He'd recited this verse to his student countless times. *A calligrapher's work never ends and words to write are never exhausted*, he would always say.

Praise God, he thought, the beautiful writing was worthy of truth the text cried out for. There was midnight blue dotted with little, golden-yellow stars to both sides of the writing, giving the effect of looking up at the stars of the night sky.

The last line was a verse from the Quran and a hadith qudsi, the words of Prophet Mohammad as revealed to him by God, in *Naskh* script—something for Hamdullah as the true master.

Muhammad is not the father of any one of your men, but he is the Messenger of God and last of the prophets. And ever is God, of all things, Knowing.

Were it not for you, I would not have created the universe.

The sheikh recited a *salavat*, asking God to bless the prophet and his descendants, as soon as he read these lines.

Bayezid had begun the line with *Halilullah*, continued with *Kalimullah* and *Kalimatullah*, and finished it with *Habibullah*—titles for Abraham as *friend of God*, Moses *who spoke with God*, Jesus as *the word of God*, and Muhammad as *the beloved of God*. He'd placed roses in pink ink on each side of the line, surrounded by palm fronds in an ornamented and segmented frame.

Handullah was satisfied that the page was complete in substance and meaning. He was proud of his pupil. This was a collection that showed respect and bowed before All-Knowing God. It joined together mathematics and esthetics as well as geometry and art on the page.

Handullah was sure of it now—Prince Bayezid had successfully passed all his lessons.

The master calligrapher took the pen, dipped it in the inkwell and drew a diamond on the paper. He said *bismillah* and started filling in the rectangle on the bottom with *Riqa'* script.

Thanks to God, who taught man what he knew not. Praise to the Prophet, who said teach your children to write, his family and his companions.

I have been entrusted by the pen of this paper and hereby grant ijazah. I, apprentice of Hayrettein of Marash in the line from Yaqut al-Musta'simi, sinner, poor of the poor, Hamdullah, give permission to Bayezid from hereon forth to sign his writings as the calligrapher. May God increase his wisdom and speed his search for the true path. May every word from his mouth and writing from his heart bring justice and prosperity to man. May the writing from his hand be exalted.

After he finished writing, Hamdullah rose to his feet and handed Bayezid, who followed suit, his certificate of *ijazah*—his calligrapher's license.

"May God make it beneficial and auspicious, Prince. But remember, the real lesson starts now. You wrote on the page what you felt in your soul. Now you will live it and work to sustain it. May the poor be fed by your pen, may the many afflicted benefit by your pen, may the world find peace by your pen. It's your duty to carry the principles of your writing to your life and your empire. Never forget the right of the pen."

Bayezid kissed his teacher's hand in thanks and praise.

BOOK SEVEN

The Gates of Heaven

101

Sitting on the southeastern coast of Spain, Malaga was the kingdom's largest port city. The ships carrying thousands of types of spices and fabrics from the east stopped at this port and all the Spanish ships setting sail for the Mediterranean and the Africa coasts left from this port. Malaga was the entrance to and exist from the kingdom. All customs procedures for incoming goods were handled there along with checking of where foreigners were subjects and the identities of people fleeing their lands. Malaga wasn't just this for Ferdinand and Isabella's kingdom—it had been the center for official business of the rulers of all the empires that had been on this land for over a thousand years. First the Phoenicians, then the Roman Empire and then the Caliphate of Cordoba all sailed the Mediterranean from here on the Iberian Peninsula in westernmost Europe. Phoenician walls stand next to the stones of an ancient Roman amphitheater in Malaga, along with magnificent Moorish buildings.

The intensity of all this bureaucracy frightened Davud. Bureaucracy meant more soldiers, more check points and greater risk. This was the main reason, after all, for keeping David and other important criminals imprisoned in this city.

The crowds of people living in the city for the past few weeks had maybe never been seen for centuries in the land's rich history. Many cultures had been instilled in every one of its stones.

That is, until this day.

August 3, 1492—the last day for non-Christians to flee and leave behind Ferdinand and Isabella's pure, Catholic kingdoms. Thousands of Jews who'd take their chances in different lands rather than convert and thousands of Muslims who'd come to understand recently that their time was up were moving on to an unknown future with the ships docked at the Malaga port.

These tens of thousands of people all had uncertain expectations for their fate. Word of those who set out from this port on the first ships in the previous weeks and months had already come back. These unfortunate people boarded the ships of Spanish and Portuguese pirates full of hope only to be brought to centers of the slave trade like Amsterdam and Venice and sold for exorbitant prices. They boarded with hopes of freedom, endured inhuman treatment and then disembarked as slaves. Mothers were separated from their children, wives from their husbands and young girls were sold to merchants as playthings. Not worth the cost, the elderly, both men and women, were thrown into the Mediterranean as soon as the ships set sail.

There were also sailors who turned to making a profit in quicker ways. First they loaded their ships with Jews and Muslims at Malaga, smiling and kind, and then stripped their passengers of whatever gold and silver they had as soon as they were out of sight of the wharf and savagely threw them into the sea, only to return on the hunt for more victims. The Spanish sailors had learned that some Jews had swallowed their gold before abandoning their houses and they tore open the stomachs of any they suspected while they were still alive.

Tens of thousands of Jews and Muslims were walking toward such a future that day. Some doubted what the future had in store for them while others held high hopes for a new, idyllic life. All the streets leading to the Malaga port—Calle Molina, Calle del Cister, Calle Mundo and many others—pulsed with throngs of people flowing to the sea.

The Catholics in service to Grand Inquisitor Torquemada, Queen Isabella and King Ferdinand couldn't remain silent to their escape. They surreptitiously collaborated with the sailors on the hunt for victims and royal knights looted what the fleeing Jews and Muslims had. More conscientious clergymen had been exerting much effort to convert them to Catholicism since the beginning of it all. The crowds these clergymen had incited were now yelling, *be Christian* and *you can't run from God* as they marched through the masses of Jews and Muslims and tried to turn them back. It being August escalated the situation even further. It's unknown if Torquemada had specially planned it this way, but a celebration of the capture of Malaga from the Muslims in August took place on the feast day of Saint Louis. As had happened for a few years, the procession carried statues of Jesus and paintings of the Virgin Mary in what looked like a taunt to the Jews and Muslims streaming past.

The people in the middle of a group of two hundred fifty Catholics were struggling to keep a throne aloft. There was a large crucifix with a masterfully carved figure of Jesus above the throne, all surrounded by gigantic candles. They were all dressed in white robes with pointed, conical *capirotes* on their heads and over their faces. The group behind was singing hymns with drums and shawms, creating an incredible din.

To add to all this, Torquemada had ordered a special *auto da fé* to be held in Malaga on this, the final day given in the decree for Jews and Muslims to leave. The final preparations were being made in the main square just up from the port. A platform was being erected in front of the piles of brush and stakes so the Grand Inquisitor, king, queen and other high officials could easily watch the condemned burn. There was also a mountain of banned books to the side of the platform. The book hunters had brought armloads of books to the square—books in Hebrew and Arabic, some from David's own printing press, and even Latin manuscripts they thought mentioned Judaism or Islam. Torquemada preferred to believe that the Catholicization of Iberia would be completed this day and that he'd be able to convince the king and queen not to stop at anything for this end.

Outside of this ruckus was a group on the ruins of the old Roman amphitheater facing out toward the two hills in the center of the city.

Davud and the others were uneasy.

He once again recognized the sheer impossibility of what he was about to enter in to.

102

Two galleys were spotted off the coast of southwestern Spain on August 3, 1492.

The high noon sun shone so brilliantly off their white sails as they streamed toward the far edge of the Mediterranean that those watching from the Malaga port couldn't tell if they were real or a vision. One was painted the blue of the sea and the other the red of the setting sun, and as they grew closer it became apparent they weren't alone.

Kemal Reis' Blue Lion and Burak Reis' Crescent of Victory were sailing straight for the Malaga port, each followed by one of the Gökes and two galiots in a triangle formation.

They were arriving at Malaga on the exact day and precise hour Piri had calculated. Neither Kemal Reis nor Burak Reis' crews had ever encountered such precise calculations before.

The two small squadrons left behind a stream of white foam as they sped along, and against the blue of the sea, they looked more like a flock of birds in the sky. Despite the heat, there was an unusual wind blowing from shore and the galleys sailed hard alee, their full sails billowing and oars up.

This worried Kemal Reis as he stood erect peering out from the bow above his ship's namesake figurehead of a blue lion just atop the spur. The wind was coming from shore, from the Malaga port.

"What gives, Captain?" Fingerless Shakir said. "You look all bothered again. We're here in Andalusia, aren't we? What's got you so twisted?"

"The wind," Kemal Reis said, not taking his blue eyes from the port about a mile away.

Shakir didn't understand. "Look at what you're worried about, Captain. What could be better? We've made it without tiring out the galley slaves."

"If the wind helps our ships, it'll help them a thousandfold. If it speeds us along, it'll make them fly."

Shakir looked at the captain, more puzzled than before. "Who're you talking about, Captain? What're you talking about? For the love of God."

Kemal Reis kept his eyes on the port. "Galleons. Spanish galleons."

They were close enough now to be able to pick out the ships offshore, and Shakir understood what Kemal Reis was getting at when he turned to look. His eyes shot open and he stood slack jawed. Like most of the rest of the crew, this was the first time he'd seen such ships.

Three galleons were anchored about a quarter mile off the port. Each was a beast—the smallest was one and a half times larger than the Göke and ten times more massive than Kemal Reis' smallest ship. The royal Spanish fleet was further behind them, anchored in the cove like sleeping giants.

Burak Reis' crewmen were also perched against the gunwale at the bow, staring out at the massive Spanish galleons growing larger as they neared.

"I'll be damned," Rattler howled. "Those aren't ships, they're each a damn island. What the hell did they make these for—are they actually going to sail the damn things or did they give up on the land to live on them?"

"What do you think, Rattler?" Big Ahmed said. "These aren't the galleys you're so used to. We'll see now, though, who's got what on who."

Rattler paid Big Ahmed no mind and kept on as if talking to himself.

"Mate, if they gave me one of these, I swear to God, I'd never set foot on dry land again—no more nagging wife, no more noisy little brats. Oh, then I'd be set and happy." He bent down and picked up his dog wagging its tail at his feet. "Come here, Qitmir, come. Look at these things—half island, half ship. One of them would be a whole world for you."

Everyone usually laughed at Rattler's nonsense. They were dead silent this time, though. Most of the men on deck stood swallowing the lumps in their throats and thinking what they would do if they had to go into battle against the galleons.

Burak Reis was calm and composed more than anyone. He leaned against the gunwale at the bow and set to planning how the Göke could run broadside. He exchanged glances with Kemal Reis, whose ship was sailing forty yards ahead of his bow, as if they were exchanging unspoken ideas. There was seemingly no need for these two master seamen to speak in order to come to an agreement after having fought side by side in so many skirmishes and battles large and small while sailing the seas. They were both mulling how they would approach the harbor, which galley would drop anchor where and the best path in the event of any attack—and it seemed they'd come to the same conclusion.

"Captain," Mute Yusuf said, coming up to Burak Reis, "do you see what I see?"

Yusuf had his eyes on the far left of the three galleons. Ludovico di Varthema's coat of arms was fluttering from one of its masts.

"How couldn't I?"

He'd seen on first glance that it was the famous pirate who'd slipped his grasp off Malta.

"I don't know if the Spanish fleet would want to get into all this mess, but lets pray that jackal doesn't recognize us. If he does, he'd attack us in the blink of an eye here in the comfort of familiar waters and also spur on the other Catholic pirates around to do the same."

"They'll get their answer if they attack, the lot of them," Yusuf said.

Burak Reis, however, was not so cavalier as his first mate. There was something out of the ordinary, but he couldn't give a name to it.

Kemal Reis and Yardman Jevher were having a similar conversation on the deck of the Blue Lion.

"I don't like the look of this port at all, Captain," Jevher said. "It's all a jumble and chaotic, it'd scare a man shitless. And then there's Ludovico's galleon anchored right there. That's no good at all."

"That tricky bastard doesn't scare me so much." Kemal Reis said. "The main problem is getting to port. There are weasels all over the place on the scent for gold. I see a lot of ships that'll take these poor wretches to the slave markets after telling them they'll deliver them to safety. I mean, look at the port—Venetians, Genoese, Portuguese—they're all there. And all with marauding crews. What a shame."

Kemal Reis and the rest of the men had seen a heart wrenching sight two days earlier off the coast of Ibiza, southwest of Barcelona. The crew of a Dutch carrack shrouded by fog was tossing all the elderly into the sea. They had finished by the time Kemal Reis and his fleet had gotten there and the ship had vanished into the fog. They rescued and old woman who was a stronger swimmer than the rest right as she started to go under. She explained the whole story through tears to the men on the ship. She said a captain from Amsterdam started from Toledo and then went on to Seville and Granada, picking up all the Jews he could for a price and saying he'd take them to Holland and Venice. He loaded as many people as he could and, then with them in the palm of his hand, took all their valuables, even their wedding rings. There were five hundred people on board, but the captain didn't want to carry the old people anymore and so tossed them overboard off Ibiza. Then he set course for Amsterdam to sell the rest as slaves. The thirty wild-eyed pirates on board did any number of unspeakable things to the completely harmless people on board.

Kemal Reis saw now that there were maybe more captains like this one at the port—he felt and heard them. He had taught some of them lessons in person in his pirating days and given others hell in battles after he became Captain of the Sea.

"It's going to be hard going if any of them recognize us, Captain," Jevher said.

Kemal Reis looked out anxiously at the Malaga port. He couldn't quite reckon why the galleons were there. And like Burak Reis, he also had an inkling something was wrong. Whatever it was, though, would be revealed in half an hour when the captain would find himself amid raining hellfire.

103

The feeling that he was getting into more madness rushed back to Davud after he looked out on the two stately citadels the city's previous Muslim rulers had strategically erected on top of the two highest points of the city.

"My God," said Abdullah. "The Alcazaba."

"And the Castle of Gibralfaro." Samuel added. "It's as great as they say."

It was frightening to even look on from the outskirts at the two fortresses rising skyward in the city they were about to enter. The city's then Muslim rulers had built the citadel on top of a hill in the center of the city in the eleventh century with all the architectural acumen and artistic sensibilities of the period. Five centuries later, it still looked as if it had just been built. A dozen square watchtowers jutted out from its countless, thick, stone walls. Amid the towers, only the roofs of dungeons could be seen in the middle of the citadel now.

"My brother's got to be there," Samuel said.

His voice reflected the trepidation in the group. Esther had so little hope that she didn't make a sound.

Malaga had been able to repel the Catholic armies' advances longer than other cities due to its strategic position and sturdy castles. The Catholics had begun their *Reconquista* from the north, advancing to the southern coast like a juggernaut, but they had to wait a few centuries longer before they could take Granada. Catholic armies had poured to the front over ten years, squeezing Ganada's jewel of Malaga until they were finally able to take it five years ago in 1487. Granada's fate had been sealed that day with the taking of Malaga.

Remembering what had happened to the city, Davud went back over the points of his plan in his head.

The first thing the Spanish did after they took Malaga was to turn part of the Alcazaba into a monastery. Torquemada had requested a fortification from Isabella for the bishops and priests who had won great enemies for themselves in the area's Muslims and Jews, and the queen gave him the Alcazaba. The citadel now nearly rivaled the Suprema in Seville with its own high Inquisition court and torture chambers. It was buzzing with hundreds of monks and dozens of bishops.

Davud looked from the Alcazaba to the Gibralfaro Castle—the center of the royal army.

Isabella had set aside most of the city's newest castle for herself. With the south of the city well protected, the castle on Gibralfaro hill was suited to protecting the rest of the city, and the kingdom's best knights were sent to be stationed there. Sultan Yusuf I of Granada had built the castle for the city only a century earlier. Its name came from the Phoenician for *Rock of Light.* The lighthouse on the hill had not only showed Muslim sailors safe passage, but also Phoenician and Roman sailors for the past thousand years, beckoning mariners on the Mediterranean. Yusuf I created a magnificent castle across from the Alcazaba by erecting walls and towers around the lighthouse.

Davud reckoned one didn't have to be a soothsayer to know that the castle was now full of hundreds of well-armed knights. Whatever happened while he was rescuing David, he'd have to be able to slip past the knights there without being noticed. He didn't even want to think of what would happen if he caught the attention of the Inquisition knights. There was nothing left to think about. The knights at the Castle of Gibralfaro meant certain death. It also housed at least a hundred knights of Santa Hermandad, as well.

Davud set his sights on the one thing that connected the two fortresses. There was a parapet, three hundred yards long, running between the Alcazaba and the Gibralfaro Castle—the only means of communication they had.

"This is worse than snatching food from the lion's mouth," Abdullah said.

"Not a lion, a dragon," said Samuel.

Davud put his monk's hood over his head and set off alone through the Roman amphitheater toward the gates of the Alcazaba.

Beatriz went running after him. She caught up and grabbed him by the arm, immediately taking his face in her hands and kissing him on the lips.

"Take care of yourself," she said to Davud's amazed look, and went back to join the others.

Davud's eyes seemed to thank her. Beatriz, Samuel, Abdullah, Esther, Zayd and the others dolefully watched him grow smaller as he descended the stairs, although with hope and prayers. A little while later they joined the flood of thousands of Jews and Muslims getting ready to flee Andalusia.

"Remember," Davud had said. "You'll find ships with three crescents on their flags. No others."

Santiago's Last Dream

God help me—I can't stand it any longer.

My spirit is no different than the ashes of the books we burned. It's as if it wasn't pages of Aristotle, ibn Rushd, ibn Arabi and Maimonides that burned, but my soul. Every letter of every book I burned was a part of me down to the hairs on my head.

I see a page in flames whenever I close my eyes at night. I writhe amid pages of Aristotle, a treatise by ibn Arabi or parts of the Talmud until morning. And not only while sleeping. I see an alif out of the darkness in the flames or an aleph in the embers every time I blink. Angry Arabic and Hebrew letters in iron sear my body one by one. I feel the curves of every red-hot letter—every waw, every sin—burn deep into my flesh. The glowing letters never cool, though, but rather burst into flames as they touch my skin, and as they flare they burn through my body completely.

Then the true pain begins. Man can maybe withstand physical pain for a while—he gets used to it, faints when it becomes too much and it passes. But what of pain of the spirit? When these flaming letters burn into me, it's as if they're falling through a bottomless pit, the flames fueled as they pick up speed and my whole spirit is scorched by thousands of fiery letters. Water quenches burning paper and ointment sooths the skin, but what is there for a soul on fire?

God help me—I can't stand this any more.

Years have passed since I was first assigned this work. I thought about my past as I caught my breath while sitting in the cloister of our monastery one day. I knew I was no longer content with the work I was doing and that I would question it more every time. While I questioned the work, however, as if I wanted to prove my obedience to the Church, sometimes it was me who found and burned more banned books than anyone else. Sometimes I was totally ashamed of what I was doing and would find an excuse to tell the other monks—a headache, sickness, nausea—and would go far from where we were. We were sometimes in a mosque, sometimes a synagogue and sometimes in a hidden library in a church that had been converted from one of them.

I thought that day, however, while I sat in the cloister of the monastery that I was disgusted with the work I'd done and I couldn't do it any longer. I didn't speak with anyone the rest of the day. I'd experienced such times before, but the tribulation and crisis of that day fell on me hard that evening. I hoped I'd be able to go back out with the light of morning and hunt books after lying down and resting to regain my energy. This is how it was most of the time. But when I closed my eyes that night, I dreamt of burning letters searing my body, appearing and vanishing in front of me, making me convulse as if pulling teeth and extracting all the hesitations of my soul. It was a hellish nightmare.

Lord, did I see heaven or hell?

A double door rose up in front of me the moment I closed my eyes—or opened them, as ibn Arabi would say. The wrought iron doors were gigantic and reflected the sunlight from behind me into my face, their silvery façade wrapped in golden sunlight. I pushed on the doors—perhaps three times as tall as me—and was surprised that these hulks of iron opened with such ease. I stepped through. The sunlight streamed in as the doors opened and glinted off every surface of the interior all made of metal. I'd never seen such a thing in all my life. I reckoned I was in some sort of house of God from the columns and wide-open floor, although I couldn't tell if the building was made of gold, silver or iron. The floor, walls, pillars, ceiling, the arches sprouting from the columns and even the windows shined with a metallic brilliance.

I felt heat under my feet, which I ascribed to the blazing sunlight on iron.

I saw Torah scrolls on the wall at the end of the long corridor in front of me and realized I was in a synagogue. The large cabinet that held the sacred Jewish books was on the eastern wall, also fashioned from metal like everything else. There were various stars embossed on the cabinet doors. There was a lamp hanging from gold chains attached to a curved overhang above the cabinet that reflected the light, further emblazoning every wall with brilliant incandescence. I had to shut me eyes for a moment from the intensity. The same impulse that urged me to open the doors drew me to open the scroll cabinet where I found the holy Jewish texts. The Ten Commandments were written in Hebrew on the parchment scroll, which were attached to metal rollers on each end. I wanted to reach out and pick up the text, but the metal rollers scorched my fingers as soon as I touched them and I recoiled.

That is when I realized what the heat under my feet was. The entire synagogue was iron beating in a raging fire. It was like the heat of the fire was rising with my consciousness. As I arrived at the recognition of the situation inside myself, so did the temple grow hotter, and as it did, the heat began to rise. First the columns, then the walls and finally the cabinet and vessel in front of it started to glow a burnt orange. Then the seven-lamp menorahs on both sides of me started spewing fire that fell to the floor like lava. The torches began melting down the walls. The columns, walls and the cabinet in front of me all started to slowly melt, the building turning into a lava flow and slowly collapsing on top of me.

I tried to escape as fast I could as my heart pounded and I got soaked in sweat. But how can one escape the center of a volcano? I noticed then that the parchment in the cabinet was untouched by all of this and I threw myself inside next to the holy scrolls. I pulled my knees to my chest and shut my eyes tight.

I don't know how long I waited in terror. When I opened my eyes, though, I found myself inside a wooden closet. The sweat was gone from my body, my forehead was dry and I felt relief. I kneeled in the small space, bowed my head and folded my hands.

The walls of the closet all had holes in them like some sort of lattice. The inside was dark, but the light coming through the holes allowed me to see the book above me. It was lying open and I started reading the lines on the page. It was the New Testament in Latin. I realized I was in a confessional.

I stood up, opened the door and went out. I was in a wooden church of unmatched beauty. Walking through the wooden pillars stretching from end to end was like strolling between the trees of a forest. The serenity I felt grew even more once I got to the center of the church. The pews to my right and left were empty and shined as if they'd just been newly varnished. I walked down the center walkway, running my hands along the backs of the pews as a gardener would to flowers.

I looked over the walls and saw paintings looking back at me, each more colorful than the next. There was the Immaculate Heart of Mary, the birth of Jesus, Joseph and the suffering of Saint Peter, all in vivid colors I'd never seen before, all so alive it seemed they could step out into the center of the church at any moment. There was also the three Magi, which I'd never seen so close, offering their gifts to the baby Jesus—Melchior bearing gold, Caspar frankincense and Balthazar myrrh—earthly matter, divine meaning and death.

I came to the altar just as I was about to be overwhelmed by the spell of the images. I raised my head over the hundreds of lit candles there. I couldn't wait to see the Lord in this beautiful church.

I looked up from the candles at the large cross on the wall, but alas, there was no Jesus, only an empty crucifix.

My astonishment still hadn't passed when beads of sweat started pouring from my brow and down my back. One of the candles on the altar all of a sudden lit the bottom of the cross on fire. I stepped back, trying to get away as the crucifix became engulfed in flames. The pews were also on fire in such a terrifying blaze it seemed people were sitting there and praying to the non-existent Jesus on the crucifix where now there were only flames. I don't know if there were actually people in the pews or if it was the playing of the flames.

Not long after, the paintings on the walls caught fire and began to melt. All I had seen with such clarity moments earlier—the Virgin Mary, Jesus, Saint Peter—were melting in their frames, their faces becoming monstrous, their beautiful, pure faces now full of anger and looking out in horror. These faces that I saw not long ago in heaven were now the beastly demons of hell.

I ran back into the confessional and tried to catch my breath as the pillars collapsed one after another and the wooden roof succumbed to the blaze. I was in a pit of despair. I held the Bible to my breast, fell to my knees and squeezed my eyes shut.

Not long passed when I felt a breeze on the back of my neck. I heard leaves rustling and the rippling of water. I opened my eyes and found myself in a small room barely large enough to lie down in. There was sunlight peeking through from under the door. I took the book I was holding and put it on the reading stand next to me. I was thinking about why this little stand the Muhammadans use when reading their holy scripture might be here when I noticed the Arabic verses in the book. It was a Quran.

I opened the door and went out into the courtyard of a stone mosque. Then I realized where I'd just left was a private room where Muhammadan scholars would seclude themselves for prayer. The courtyard I walked into was surrounded by continuous arches over pearly white marble. There was a hexagonal fountain in the center with all of its faucets spurting streams of water. The cool air on my face was relaxing. The masonry was so carefully set and fit together that sometimes when I looked at the massive mosque it looked more like a mountain than a building. The grand, towering minarets at each of the mosque's four corners seemed to have been built to be stairways to the heavens.

I went into the mosque feeling an odd sense of relief. The ceiling rose from four massive columns each made of a single piece of marble and ascending so high they seemed to be reaching for the sky. I craned my head back and saw a large dome that was like the sky itself. In the center of the dome were verses from the Muhammadans' book inscribed with great artistry—la 'ilaha 'illa'llah and Muhammadan 'abduhu wa rasulu—There is no god but God and Muhammad is His messenger.

Thousands of blues, greens and reds adorned the dome and stone walls, all set with a masterful hand. The sunlight from the windows dappled the walls like the sun shining through a cloud break.

One illuminated the marble mihrab on the southeastern wall and drew my eye. It was ornamented with emeralds, sapphires and many other precious stones. To the right on the same wall was the splendid, heavenly staircase of the marble minbar, its stone carved in the form of lace around exquisite, eight-pointed stars. I wondered if it had been men or angels who carved them. Then the nightmare returned.

First the hundreds of tall oil lamps suspended on chains from the ceiling flared and brimmed over, spilling flames onto the beautiful red carpets in balls of fire. They spread, glowing across the carpets and seemed to be burning through the floor.

Then one of these wells of flame burst, sending fireballs cascading to the floor. There were so many lamps that the dome looked to be raining fire. I put my hands to my head and started running for the door, but the burning holes in the carpets started growing into each other in twos and threes. I had to run around them in some places and jump over the flames rising from the floor in others. Fire had taken hold over the floor, and in some places the flames seemed to merge strangely with the flames falling from above. I couldn't tell any more whether the flames were rising or falling.

I got quite close to the door and could see the light and hear the gurgling of the fountain in the courtyard. I took a step past a flame, leapt over another smoldering pit and, after three steps, was at the door.

But I wasn't. I didn't have strength left to jump over one of the pits in front of me and fell in head over heels. I don't know how long I tumbled down the pit toward the angry fire below. What I do know is that I felt I was falling into the center of hell.

I ended up on hard ground and felt I my head crack along with a few ribs, my writing hand and my right arm. I couldn't feel my left leg, either. I saw myself surrounded by red flames and felt the heat as I was lying there half unconscious. I lost some of my sight from hitting the ground so hard and everything was blurred and bleeding into each other. I lifted my head from where I'd fallen and came face to face with the horrific scene. I started to slowly regain my sight, but everything was still indistinct and foggy.

A large stake rose from the middle of the fire.

The smell of burning human flesh then began to mix with the smoke and heat of the fire.

Then I started to hear a deafening scream. It was a woman's voice, screaming pierced by sobs and weeping, wailing and moaning, piercing my ears and echoing in my head.

I struggled to stand, and finally got to my feet, pushing myself up with my one good arm and leg. I turned around and saw the most horrendous part of the scene surrounding me.

My poor mother—who'd seen nothing but misery and suffering her entire life, and all for me—was tied to a stake and burning in the inferno. Her tears succumbed to the flames, steaming away as soon as they fell from her eyes. Her hands that had cradled me, hugged me and tickled my feet were already burned, and her breasts at which I'd nursed for hours were each a ball of fire. With terrible rage and pain I tried to jump over the flames to save her, but the fire grew taller and more intense whenever I got close, as if it could feel me, and in an instant there was a wall of flames in front of me.

I was utterly confused and fainted when I saw the flames take my mother's face.

I was dripping with sweat on my small bed when I opened my eyes in my room in the monastery. The pillow, sheets, blanket and mat were soaked and my heart was beating through my chest. There was an incredible summer downpour and large raindrops were pummeling the windows.

I now knew what I was going to do.

God help me.

105

Two monks met in a corner of a dark corridor of the Alcazaba. There wasn't even a single detail that seemed to separate one's appearance from the other. Both were in brown robes with hoods over their heads. Their faces were different, of course, but in the darkness and behind their hoods, that difference was lost.

"As we spoke of," Davud said.

"As we spoke of," said Santiago.

Davud and the book hunter were face to face. Santiago pulled the ring of keys he had off over his head and handed them over.

"The interrogation will start in half an hour. These keys will get you to the right room."

Then Santiago pulled out a folded and sealed paper from inside his robe.

"This is your scribe's certificate. You'll pass three checks in the corridor leading to the dungeons. Show it to the guards if they ask. And don't forget, it's all over if you lose it."

Davud hesitated when took the keys and paper.

"What about you, then? What're you going to do without the keys and this paper?"

It seemed Santiago had been expecting this question.

"Don't think about me. I'm doing something I've had to for a very long time. I'm ready to pay the price. If Father Paulo trusted you, that means you're the right person." He stopped there as if he didn't want to talk about it anymore. "There's not much time left. You know what to do. When you enter the interrogation room you'll see a table for one person in the left corner next to the table where the cardinals sit. Sit at the table and start writing down everything you hear and see in the book there. The rest is up to you. Act when you find the opportunity. There's a hidden tunnel when you get to the top of the citadel that leads directly to the port, but make sure you don't show yourself to anyone. If you do, the tunnel will be the death of you."

Davud nodded—he'd gone over the plans of the Alcazaba earlier. The determination in Santiago's eyes frightened him.

"Go already," Santiago said. "Remember, it's over if you lose the paper. And whatever you do, don't rouse the knights of Gibralfaro."

"I'll pray for you," Davud said.

Santiago smiled. "I'll need it. But now you'll need it much more than I do."

The two monks were determined as they parted to the separate ends of the corridor. They would complete what they set out to do, no matter the cost.

106

The prisoner was laid out over the wooden board of the *escalara*. Flickering candles faintly illuminated the faces of the priests in the dark room. The scribe off to the side was seated next to a candle that shined on the paper in front of him, but his face remained in darkness.

One of the most important parts of the process was to place the prisoner's head placed lower than his feet. Cardinal Cisneros was infamous for implementing Grand Inquisitor Torquemada's *Dictatorium* word for word. It seemed he'd memorized the book and the interrogation methods it prescribed in fine detail. Guards came to both sides of the prisoners and tied his wrists to the sloped, wooden apparatus. They then tightened the ropes around his ankles.

Cisneros checked over the binding of the man's wrists and ankles and was confident they were tight. He looked at the ink stains on the prisoner's fingers with disgust.

"This is the biggest sign of heresy."

He would've snapped the man's long, thin fingers then and there if it weren't contrary to the laws of the Inquisition. He looked over the man's face. He didn't know what to do with his lack of response. He figured this was another heretic *converso*. He saw the New Christian converts who'd reverted to their Jewish traditions as no different that a dog returning to eat its own vomit. He satisfied himself with the thought that the man had no strength left to move after being held for days in the dungeon. The man's face was ashen and his eyes were sunken and dark.

It wasn't out of hunger or exhaustion, however, that the prisoner didn't respond. He'd heard of this room many times and knew well enough that resistance was of no use—he had to focus on not confessing no matter what happened. He had to concentrate all his energy on it. He knew the day before that he would be taken to this room when he wasn't given the usual wet, moldy bread for his daily meal. A prisoner could vomit during the interrogation, after all, and foul the room.

He'd reckoned that the few days he'd spent in the dungeon amid the smells of excrement, dried blood and damp would've made his nose insusceptible to it all, although the thick smell of urine in the room proved he was mistaken, and so he relaxed when they blocked his nostrils. The guards didn't do this for the prisoner's benefit, but because by only being able to breath through his mouth, the soon-to-begin interrogation would be much more effective.

"Bring the prongs," Cisneros ordered.

The prisoner shuddered when he saw the iron prongs covered in the filth of all the previous prisoners' spittle. He tried to move but the ropes cut into his wrists and ankles.

One of the guards squeezed his chin and opened his mouth as wide as it would go, then another shoved in the prongs and fit them in place. Then they put a piece of cloth over his face.

Everything was ready now and the guards had their eyes on the water bucket on the ground.

There were four other men in the room—three high officials seated at the long table draped in a black cloth in addition to the scribe recording all the details of the interrogation off to the side. They were a monk who was an observer from Torquemada's Suprema, one of Cardinal Cisneros' priests and a doctor. Cisneros looked over at the doctor after all the preparations had been made for the interrogation.

Seeing that it was his time, the doctor rose nonchalantly and walked over to the prisoner strapped to the wooden plank. He gave a cursory look over the man, then turned to Cisneros and nodded. "You can continue."

According to Torquemada's codes for the Inquisition, accused heretics must confess their crimes firmly and consciously and of their own volition, they should be able to hear what is said and be of sound mind. A confession could be considered invalid otherwise.

The priest stood up and started speaking, periodically glancing at the documents on the table. The scribe was recording everything he said.

"We of the Tribunal of the Holy Inquisition of the Kingdoms of Castile and Aragon—Cardinal Ximenes de Cisneros Archbishop of Toledo for the Holy Catholic Church, doctor of canon law Father Francisco Sanchez de la Fuente and I, licentiate of holy theology, Pedro Diaz de la Costaña—with authority from the Kingdoms of Castile, Leon and Aragon and Grand Inquisitor Tomas de Torquemada—"

He stopped and picked up the papers detailing the man's information and crimes and continued.

"It is said the accused, David ibn Nahmias Marrano, jeweler, of the town of Montalban in Toledo, who was baptized a Christian at the age of nineteen in 1481, and despite being a Catholic for over tens years, has continued to practice Jewish traditions and live according to the laws of Moses.

"According to the testimony given against him by the witness to the Holy Church in confession, the accused, David ibn Nahmias Marrano, refrains from word on Saturdays, has been seen lighting candles in his house on Fridays in observance with the Sabbath and was found to have manuscripts and books in Hebrew and Arabic in his house—"

The hatred on Cardinal Cisneros' face grew as Father Pedro Diaz de la Costaña read out the accusations.

"In addition, the accused built a printing press, the device coming from the Germans, in a secret place in the town of Montalban with his brother, Samuel ibn Nahmias, and in collaboration with heretic adherents to the Muhammadan religion in the old Emirate of Granada, printed and disseminated hundreds of Hebrew and Arabic texts, the Quran, teachings of the Talmud and Gemara, the heretic Averroes and his Aristotelian exegeses, the philosophies of the old Hellenic philosophers and the heretic Maimonides' books both in Hebrew and Arabic, all of which are forbidden by our Holy Church—"

Cardinal Cisneros was growing impatient for the list of accusations to end.

"The accused has denied all of the accusations for days, insists that for many years he has been a good Christian walking the path of Jesus Christ, and asserts that the allegations directed against him are slander. For this reason, it was decided that the torture used for even the most unrepentant heretics will continue on the *escalara*."

Cisneros looked at the guards sitting next to Father Diaz de la Costaña. This was the moment he'd been waiting for.

One of them put the end of a metal funnel into the mouth of the accused and another took a bucket of water from the ground and was readying to empty it into the man's mouth.

The young man's eyes shot wide open in terror.

Cisneros gave a sign and the guard slowly tipped the bucket. The water soaking into the cloth in the young man's mouth and blocked his throat. He was trying to swallow since he couldn't breath through his nose, but he convulsed helplessly as the water filled his throat. Hoping for quick release, David felt as if he was drowning while the guard continued to pour the water into his mouth. But the most important feature of the *escalara*, like the Inquisition's other torture devices, was to keep the accused alive while inflicting the most pain and without spilling a drop of blood. It was strictly forbidden to spill blood in an interrogation, as it evoked Jesus Christ's self-sacrifice for humanity.

"Say it!" shouted Cisneros. "Do you accept that you are a believer of the religion of Moses?

"Say it! Have you celebrated the Sabbath on Friday evenings? Have you attended the Jewish circumcision ceremonies?"

The guards set the bucket aside and removed the metal prongs and cloth from David's mouth so he could answer.

He was coughing and lifted his head as much as possible from where it lay as he tried with great pain to empty his lungs of the water. His pallid face had become bright red.

Cisneros looked at David in the face, waiting for an answer. He was gasping for breath. He didn't say a word and laid his head back.

Cisneros gave the sign and the guards replaced the prongs and cloth and began to pour the water again, although much faster this time.

David was convulsing in panic, flailing his hands and feet forward and back against the ropes in a futile attempt to save himself. He felt as though he was under the sea, crushed under tons of water, or that he'd been buried alive with the shovels thrown over him.

The *escalara* was the least bloody yet cruelest of the methods of torture Torquemada had discovered.

The feeling of drowning and the panic it elicited created both physical and mental fatigue. Cisneros knew well from experience that the majority of even the most unrepentant heretics sang like nightingales after the second round. After all, he'd delivered full lists of the names of even the most tight-lipped criminals to the Church. He grabbed a printed page of Hebrew text from the table and returned to the David as he lay prone.

"Say it! Did you write this?"

David looked at the paper and a smile spread across on his face to the stunned looks of those around him. His eyes were on the letter *aleph* at the top of the page, in red and larger than the rest of the black text. This sudden smile vanished just as quickly and the young man began to weep.

He was thinking of Esther.

His memories came back as he looked at the page, and his sorrow and suffering grew as the remembered. He remembered two weeks before when everything started, picturing all the details of the day.

Cisneros signaled the guards for the third time. The doctor at his side, however, protested this time.

"Aren't you going too fast? The man may die."

"Then this is a risk we'll take under warrant of the Church," Cisneros shot back.

The physician was about to continue, but Cisneros interrupted with an insinuating threat, "I've heard you're grandmother was a Jew, doctor. I wonder if that could be partly true."

The doctor silently returned to his place knowing that Cisneros could very easily deem him a heretic. It wouldn't have been the first time.

David was thinking of Esther and Davud the Brave—the man who'd started everything, the Turk whom he couldn't figure from where he'd came. His brother Samuel, Beatriz, Abdullah of Xativa and Zayd ibn Uthman all passed through his mind.

The guards began to pour the water into his mouth again.

107

Davud knew he had to act when the second stage of the torture began. He'd been sitting at his table off to the side since the interrogation began, pretending to write and looking for his best chance. It would be easy to overpower the cardinal and priests in the room, but the two large torturers could make unwanted noise and the two guards at the door would have to be none the wiser until he and David walked out. Whatever Davud was going to do, he had to do it without making a sound. And still, David would become weaker with every minute of torture he endured.

Davud couldn't wait any longer.

"Sir, the ink's run out," the scribe said.

Cisneros didn't know what to say to this unusual interruption at first. The torturers also stopped pouring the water and looked at the scribe. The priests seated at the table also had their eyes on him, as they'd never seen such a thing before.

"The ink's run out, sir. I can't record the proceedings. You know this is a requirement we must obey."

Davud stood up as he finished speaking and approached a priest at the table as if to show him the empty inkwell. The guards were standing to the right and left. None of them, the guards included, had ever heard such an absurd reason for cutting off an interrogation half way through, and so were quite confused. Davud had to evaluate this confusion quickly.

Cisneros was supposed to make sure that all that transpired was done with full care. He approached the scribe and was about to tell him to go fetch more ink when Davud flung the ink from the pot into his face.

The ink covered Cisneros' eyes and face. Davud had already stepped behind him and had him by the throat before he had a chance to scream. The guards stood still, overwhelmed by surprise.

Davud's voice dropped. "Now listen to me well—even the slightest sound or mistake and I break the cardinal's neck. You do as I say and you'll stay silent."

Cisneros blinked a couple times and felt the arm squeeze around his neck. It felt more like a block of stone than any part of a man. Davud tightened his arm around Cisneros' throat so hard that the man's eyes were going dark, but he was still conscious. The cardinal would faint if he squeezed only a little more, and would have all the blood to his brain cut off if he held him like this for only five more seconds.

"Remove him from the *escalara* and bring him to his feet."

Cisneros had no intention of dying this day, and most of all, would not put his life in danger for a heretic and apostate Jew. He nodded feverishly to the torturers.

"Do as he says, you fools!"

The torturers had been standing with their mouths agape until then, and they reluctantly followed the order. One of them removed the cloth and prongs from David's face and mouth while the other untied his wrists and ankles.

David sat up on the *escalara* and tried to recover as he pounded on his chest and coughed. He saw Davud and smiled, shaking his head. He couldn't believe what was happening.

"I underestimated you every time," he said, smiling.

"I didn't think you'd want to drink that much water."

"And Esther?"

"Don't worry, she's safe. She's most likely waiting for you aboard one of the Turkish ships."

David recovered without losing any more time and jumped to his feet with newfound hope and power. After having water poured down his throat for the past half hour, the first thing he did when he regained his feet was punch one of his torturers. The man's head was thicker than he'd anticipated and he tried to shake the pain out of his hand. He'd never punched someone so hard and with such anger before in his life. He had, however, broken the torturer's nose. The man fell to his knees, his face bloody and holding his face.

Reckoning what would happen to him, the other torturer grabbed a knife from the table holding all the torture implements and threw it at David. Davud brought his foot to the man's stomach at the same time, sending the knife off its mark as he pushed him back into the wall where he fell to the ground. The torturer felt as though a sledgehammer had just hit him as he fell back, but was now lying unconscious after cracking his head against the wall.

About ten minutes later, opening the door just enough to squeeze through, a monk, a priest with his hood over his head and a prisoner with a cloth draped over his face exited the interrogation room.

The two guards at the door stepped aside.

"The man couldn't take anymore and fainted," said the monk. "The Father will get his confession in the dungeon. The cardinal and the tribunal want to discuss the results of the interrogation for a while without being disturbed. They'll call for you when they've finished."

The guards nodded, happy they could stand idle a bit longer, and took their places back in front of the door.

Davud and David hastily ascended the stairs at the end of a long corridor, leaving behind the two guards at the bottom. Davud could open all the doors with the keys he had and by showing his papers to any guards they came across.

Back in the interrogation room, the two torturers were on the ground and the clergymen's heads were lying on the table, all un-conscious. It didn't seem they would come to for quite a while. One of the priests was naked, his clothes now making an escape on Da-vid's body.

108

Captaining the Crescent of Victory, Burak Reis was in the lead of the Göke and Göke II as they were about to quietly sail into port. He had gone over all the fine points with Kemal Reis and the two had formulated their plan together. Burak Reis would enter the port first and make way for the two gigantic ships Sultan Bayezid had made to ferry back those suffering in Spain. Kemal Reis would escort them with two other galleys and keep an eye on the mouth of the harbor. If they were attacked or things went wrong, the two captains would be able to control the situation from in and outside of the harbor while the Göke and Göke II loaded as many people as they could hold as fast as possible and set off back to sea. In any event, they weren't to provoke or engage the Spanish fleet. If they did, it would mean the Ottomans going to war against the entire Catholic world.

Everything was going as planned as Burak Reis led the Göke and Göke II into the harbor. Even so, as he watched Burak Reis, Kemal Reis held back from telling Yardman Jevher that things didn't seem right and that there must be something going one that they didn't know.

Thousands of Jews and Muslims had filled the Malaga port and were trying to get on every ship there. They had to leave Spain that day if they were to keep their faiths. Those who remained would either have to convert to Catholicism or would be burned at the stake at the *auto da fé*, which were taking place across the relm.

Burak Reis was trying to land these two gigantic ships at port amid this chaos and confusion. Ludovico di Varthema's galleon was anchored a quarter mile from port, but then quickly pulled up anchor and headed straight for Kemal Reis' galley at the very back outside the harbor.

"God damn it!"

Burak Reis had seen the huge galleon's sails billow as it bore down on Kemal Reis. He was not one to lose his head or steadiness in even the most difficult situations, and he knew now they'd fallen into a well-planned trap—a second galleon was blocking the mouth of the harbor, cutting off the Crescent of Victory inside. It was clear di Varthema aimed to capture Kemal Reis when he was alone and had laid in wait until Burak Reis was cut off in the harbor with the Göke and Göke II.

Kemal Reis had recognized what was happening and had already ordered his crew to their battle positions. They had spread sand over the deck so they wouldn't slip in the blood and water that would soon wash across it and hung fenders of broadcloth, hemp, reed mats, straw and dirt over the broadsides to minimize any damage from cannon fire. They did this before every battle, but hanging the fenders with care carried much more importance considering they were going up against the cannons of a Spanish galleon.

"How many cannons does a galleon have?" Orion Orhan asked Gunner Mahmud the Kurd as he placed sacks of dirt along the broadside while watching the gigantic ship draw closer.

Mahmud was reluctant to answer. "Maybe a hundred. I'd say a hundred fifty. Port, starboard, bow and stern are all full of batteries on every deck, stacked on top of each other. They ready next volley on one deck when the ones on another deck fire."

Orhan swallowed the lump in his throat and went on putting the sacks in place. Mahmud and his gunners were hauling up cannon balls from the munitions stores below on the captain's order. Despite having lost an arm, Mahmud kept at work while his gunners carried up the cannonballs held in sailcloth, one at each end, and placing them at the ready next to the cannons. After sand had bean spread over the deck, another man poured water over it to keep any spark from the cannons from igniting the wood and pitch. Most important was to keep any fire and spark away from the powder stores, so they hung a curtain of sailcloth at the door. Doctor Ilyas opened up his bag of tools with a prayer, as he did before every battle, and laid out his gauze, alcohol, stitching thread and different size scalpels and knives for whoever would soon be brought to the corner of the ship set aside for him. Hard-Nose Ibrahim came out of the galley kitchen in his apron loading matchlock pistols while Fingerless Shakir sharpened his cutlass on a stone. Ibrahim handed the guns out to the soldiers—each of them only able to fire once. He didn't forget, either, to keep three for himself tucked into his waist.

Di Varthema's galleon was drawing nearer, the yellow and red banner of arms of the Catholic monarchs waving in the breeze.

"Those sons of bitches," Shakir said as he looked up from his blade. "Their flag's nearly as long as our galley."

The long, thin banner with a pointed end looked to be fifty yards long when fully stretched, flicking like a viper's tongue in the wind. And just as the reptile gets the scent of its prey, so was the galleon on the prowl for the Blue Lion, trying to figure out what it was before swallowing it whole.

The galleon's ten-yard spur jutted out from the bow of its three-deck hull. The lowest deck had ten cannons, the middle twenty-five and the upper deck had thirty. There were also twenty smaller cannons at the bow and stern. Three masts rose from the keel, each as thick and tall as a thirty-year pine. The mainmast in the middle towered nearly a hundred feet in the air. There was a crow's nest at the top of each mast along with pans that could easily hold twenty archers each. The crewmen on the Blue Lion were starting to be able to make out the more than a hundred pirates and fifty knights waiting to attack them from the galleon's deck.

Kemal Reis and his men thought it couldn't get much worse, but then Lookout Isa yelled out from the crows nest and they realized how wrong they were.

"Forty-five degrees starboard!"

The men looked up from their tasks to where Isa had yelled and saw another galleon approaching from starboard. Kemal Reis knew right away whose midnight black ship this was.

"The San Matteo."

The words fell from his lips. These were the Genoese pirates he'd taken on in the Adriatic three months before.

"Forty-five degrees port!" Isa called out this time.

Fingerless Shakir, Helmsman Musa, Doctor Ilyas and the others thought they'd heard him wrong, but he was pointing portside. When they looked, they all saw a galley heading for them flying a Portuguese banner.

"Due stern!" Isa yelled out for a third time.

Kemal Reis looked and saw another Spanish galleon a mile off and heading straight for them. This was another infamous pirate ship—the San Sebastian. It was an awe-inspiring scene.

The Blue Lion was about to be surround on all four of its sides— prow, stern, starboard and port.

"Seems you pissed off these buggers a little too much, Captain," Shakir said.

It seemed di Varthema had figured they were on their way to Spain and had enticed as many pirates, knights and enemies of the Ottomans as he could, and they were now closing in on Kemal Reis and Burak Reis' fleet from four sides in the waters off the Malaga port. As they'd agreed, the other ships waited for di Varthema to make his move, and taking the signal, they all started to descend on Kemal Reis' galley. Kemal Reis was in the middle of a nightmare. The galleons were all full sail, streaming toward him on different winds.

The enemy showed no sign of wasting any time, with di Varthema's galleon firing a salvo at the first galley to sail in front of it, making it erupt in flames. The galley was sinking below the surface before Kemal Reis could blink.

109

Davud and David found themselves on a rampart when they emerged into the light from the dark corridor of the Alcazaba. They were both in good spirits and the only thing left to do now was to get out from the citadel's walls without drawing attention and get to the port as fast as possible.

The two successive shocks they experienced, however, wiped the smiles from their faces and sank the hope in their hearts. Looking out from the highest point of the city to the harbor, they first saw the Ottoman ships surrounded. Davud immediately recognized Kemal Reis and Burak Reis' flags. He reckoned the two captains could handle the Spanish, Portuguese and pirates, but the sight of the galleons surrounding the Ottoman galleys was frightening to behold.

Davud, however, had to think about himself now and not his fellow countrymen aboard the ships, as there was a group of knights looking at him and David from the opening to the Castle of Gibralfaro at the other end of the rampart. Davud and David understood what was going on when they saw the person behind the knights preparing to attack three hundred yards away. If they'd been a little closer, they could've made out the rancor on Yehuda's face.

Yehuda had split off from the group on the way to the ships and run breathlessly to the command of the Gibralfaro Castle. Just a short time ago, he'd told the knights of what was happening and was granted a guarantee to be able to stay and live freely. Lucas, having long been on Davud and the others' trail, was at Yehuda's side. He stuck out from the rest with his pig-nosed visor, horned helmet and massive frame.

Davud thought at that moment that everything was over, that neither he nor David would make it to the Ottoman ships and that all his pursuits and struggles had been for nothing—everything was wasted. It would be impossible to overpower these knights and escape to the port. Boiling sweat was pouring down his back when he noticed a guard standing in a corner. He knocked him to the ground with one blow and took the man's bow and an arrow from his quiver. Fitting the arrow to the bowstring, he aimed at the other end of the rampart and let go.

The arrow flew through the air with a speed the knights hadn't expected. The knight standing in front of Lucas and Yehuda jumped to the side out of reflex as he saw the arrow come down. It kissed his neck and struck Yehuda through the throat.

"We should've done that a long time ago," David said.

Davud had always forgiven Yehuda, and Yehuda had betrayed him at every turn.

The knights had already started to advance as Yehuda fell down grunting and spurting blood. They had three hundred yards to go.

"Get the crossbow from under the guard's foot," Davud said as he hid behind the rampart's fortifications. "Load it as fast as you can and start shooting straight at the middle of the knights."

Learning the mechanisms of a crossbow took time, and it could shoot only two or three arrows a minute at most. David had never used any weapon before and could only do so much. Taking all of this into account and warning David of what he was going to do, Davud rained arrow after arrow down on the knights. He could shoot fifty to sixty arrows a minute—the only problem was he didn't have that many at hand.

"*Ya Haqq!*" he yelled, and began to shoot.

Each arrow struck a knight, but most of them were wearing full armor and they glanced off and fell to the ground. He nevertheless had succeeded in slowing the quickly approaching knights by aiming for the weak points at their joints and especially their necks.

He wished he had a Turkish bow. Unlike those of European armies, they were much tauter and had much greater force. A good archer could pierce a knight's armor from nearly half a mile away. David was working the crossbow, but it took him a long time to set it up and it wasn't helping them much.

Some of the knights had also grabbed their bows and were firing on Davud and David. They were stuck between two fortifications and were trying to protect themselves from the arrows from above while also attempting to stop the quickly advancing knights.

Davud saw that he had maybe twelve arrows left.

"Listen to me good!" He dodged the arrows flying at him and rolled to an iron hatch three steps away. The hatch clanged as he opened it and he put his back to the wall again. "You jump through here and go as fast as you can and don't look back. This tunnel will spit you out right in front of the port. Nobody will know what happened if you hurry and you'll be able to catch the ships."

David was worried and looked over at Davud. "What about you?"

"We can't both go at once. They'll chase after and it would only be a matter of time before they caught us. You'll have a chance to get away if I stall them, though."

"Forget it! I'm not going anywhere without you."

Davud grabbed David by the collar and angrily shoved his back to the wall. He was dead serious. "You're going to jump down there right now and run as fast as you can, damn it! Don't you get it? If you stay, then we both die! Don't worry, I'll see to myself."

David was scared and was going to objection again once he pulled himself together, but before he could, Davud had grabbed him by the waist and collar and chucked him into the tunnel. He tried to grab hold of the sides, but he'd fallen upside down and the hatch was three feet out of his reach.

Davud grabbed the iron hatch, but looked down at David just as he was about to close it. "Tell the sultan that God has made my prayers come true."

David was thinking about what this meant when the hatch shut with a clang and he yelled out, "No!"

When he stood back up, Davud saw that the knights had nearly crossed the rampart and were now only fifty yards away.

110

Kemal Reis was in a living nightmare with three galleons to three sides of him and a Portuguese galley to the other, and Burak Reis was trapped with a thousand-ton galleon blocking his exit from the harbor. Burak Reis ordered for the Göke and Göke II to land at port without delay and board the passengers. He had one eye searching for a way out of the harbor and the other on Kemal Reis' galley that was surrounded on the other side.

"Captain," Rattler said, "are we just going to sit here and watch with our thumbs up our asses?"

"Damn it, Rattler," Big Ahmed snapped. "You're still flapping your worthless gums! What? You know better than the captain, do you?"

Burak Reis had heard Rattler, and he didn't want to leave Kemal Reis on his own, either. The two captains had gone over this again and again—Burak Reis was not to leave the harbor without first completely loading the Göke and Göke II, no matter what. Even with the ships fully loaded though, there was still a leviathan in their way.

Di Varthema's galleon had already sunk one of the galleys in Kemal Reis' fleet that was right next to his own.

He turned to his men. "If it's out fate to die here today, then we die. No one can draw out or shorten by a minute the life God has given them. But if we're to die, let's die like men in battle! *Ya Allah, bismillah!*"

The men's excitement boiled over and they joined in their captain's zeal, chanting a battle prayer in unison.

Kemal Reis went to his head archer, Yardman Jevher, Chief Gunner Mahmud the Kurd and Helmsman Musa in turn and quickly explained to each of them what they needed to do. He reckoned di Varthema had to be stopped first since it was clear he was the one emboldening the other three ships. So, rather than dealing with the limbs, he intended to go straight for the head. He gave the order for his janissary archers to shoot on the pirates and knights on the deck of di Varthema's galleon. Helmsman Musa was then to turn the ship to port, Jevher would position the sails to the wind and Mahmud would prepare to fire without waiting for the sign from the captain. Overseer Jihan also got the order from the captain.

"All together, all together!" he yelled.

All the galley slaves on the starboard side began rowing at full speed along with ten at port to maintain balance.

The yardmen, helmsman, archers and overseer would have to fully employ all their individual skills in order to complete the complicated maneuver as fast as lighting. With all orders coming from Kemal Reis, it was most important he kept his full attention on every element of the ship. There would've been no way to make such a turn, most of all while enemy fire was raining down on three of their sides, if Kemal Reis and the crew of the Blue Lion hadn't already gone into and come out of dozens of battles together.

One of the first arrows the archers shot caught one man completely off guard, piercing di Varthema's helmsman through the eye. Di Varthema saw that Kemal Reis wouldn't surrender so easily as his helmsman collapsed screaming to the deck with an arrow sticking out of his eye socket and blood streaming over his face. More arrows followed. The archers were letting loose volleys by the second, striking the targets they only barely missed before. Some snatched arrows from their quivers and other from piles of eagle-feathered shafts at their feet. They took account of their ship's change in direction and pitch as they released their arrows at the deck of di Varthema's galleon.

Di Varthema was yelling and spitting orders at the hundred yardmen on the rigging and yards and cursing his men who where hit, even kicking one lying on the deck. The one thing di Varthema was trying to get his yardmen to do was run broadside the Blue Lion. If they could get into position, as was the galleon's primary power, it would be easy to target and fire off all three decks of cannons at once.

The maneuvers Kemal Reis had ordered, however, kept the Blue Lion off di Varthema's galleon's broadside as it passed between the galleon San Matteo and the others and evaded the cannon fire. He had in his mind that if he got stuck in the crossfire from the San Matteo and San Sebastian, it wouldn't only be the end of him, but also the end for Burak Reis and the hundreds of Jews and Muslims they came for. The smaller cannonballs from the bow of di Varthema's galleon and those from the San Matteo's broadside were falling short right next to the captain, sending foaming columns of water into the air.

Then there was a terrible crash at the Blue Lion's stern. A cannonball from the San Matteo had hit the back of the ship between the waterline and the gunwale in a weak spot unprotected by the fenders, crashing through the hull as if it were a sheet of paper and only stopped after striking the mizzenmast. The splintered wood from the broadside flew at the nearby crewmen, soldiers and deckhands, striking six of them through the necks, arms, legs and faces and killing two galley slaves below deck.

The galley's carpenters immediately went to work to close the hole, reinforcing it with sacks of dirt. The Blue Lion, though, had evaded the four attacking ships and was now behind di Varthema's galleon.

David, Esther, Beatriz and the other Jews and Muslims at the port nearly let out cries of joy when they saw the green flags fluttering with their white crescents. The river of people emptying onto the pier and everyone was pushing and shoving so they could get close and board the Göke and Göke II. David kept looking behind him. He was thinking about Davud and worried about whether he'd be able to get to the ships—if he'd be able to find a way to return to his lands—and so he was dragging his heels. But he also didn't want to waste all that Davud had endured and done for them. From this hour on he'd be living both for Esther and Davud. He had no doubt, though, that Davud would do what he had to in order to reach the ships. Beatriz was also scanning the crowds to try and catch sight of him.

Burak Reis had seen that that Göke and Göke II had filled up more than half way very quickly, but he was still growing impatient. They had to go as soon as the ships were full. Mute Yusuf was stationed at the gangplank to the Göke and Rattler and Big Ahmed at the Göke II, all of them quickly and orderly loading the people onto the ships. Rattler saw priests on some of the streets trying to dissuade the crowds from leaving and imploring them to embrace Catholicism.

He stared at them, angrily shaking his head. "Good God Almighty! Mate, what don't these bastard's get," he said to Big Ahmed. "These people are giving up the land where they were born and raised in and all they have. They set out for the sake of their beliefs and now these pricks are still yelling at them to be Catholic. These sons of bitches—these people've come this far and they still can't leave it alone. The Devil says rush in and draw your sword and take out their eyes with what power God gave you."

"Damn it, Rattler. If we make the smallest move we'll have the royal knights all over us. Don't forget—no matter what, we don't attack the royal knights or the priests!"

"I'll fuck their royal majesties' knights!"

"Save it a little longer for when we have a real fight on our hands. I mean look, that galleon's just sitting there blocking the way out the harbor. Let the ships fill up and the captain'll put it to those bastards."

"Well, if we wait any longer they'll be on Kemal Reis!"

Kemal Reis finally gave the order Gunner Mahmud had been waiting a half hour to here once they pulled behind di Varthema's ship.

"Alright—*bismillah!*" he yelled, bringing his linstock to the touchhole and stepping back.

The cannon let out a terrific blast as soon as he pulled away, sending a cannonball crashing into the galleon's broadside in between the main and mizzenmast. Twelve other gunners on the starboard side fired their cannons with him, nearly all of them striking the broadside toward the stern and toward the middle while others plunged into the sea and into the ship's hull.

With his wealth of experience at sea, Kemal Reis knew how to use his galley against such a hulking galleon. He had to get as close to di Varthema's galleon so he could use the galley's size to his advantage so that its high cannons wouldn't be able to aim at the Blue Lion. No matter how may cannons fired from the stern of the galleon, they would cruise over the galley and off into the sea. In addition to that, any cannons fired from the Blue Lion at the galleon, rising out of the water like a sea monster, were sure to hit its broadside somewhere and inflict massive casualties. The galleon was also dependent on the wind to move, with thousands of types of complex rigging for its sails and yards. While the galleon's crew slogged away at trying to maneuver its cumbersome bulk to get the galley in range, with its galley slaves at the oars, the Blue Lion could make five agile moves in the same time and evade the cannons poking out from the galleon's gun ports.

In the meantime, however, the Genoese pirates on the galleon San Matteo had again pulled close to the starboard side of the Blue Lion. The wind had picked up enough that it was coursing the galleon along faster than Kemal Reis had expected. The Spanish galleon San Sebastian was also about to squeeze the Blue Lion from the other side. Kemal Reis was getting blockaded again, and this time, having shaken off the shock of the first attack, the two galleons were more cautious, narrowing the area the Blue Lion could move in to prevent it from slipping through. The two galleons had drawn so near each other that their prows were nearly touching. The San Matteo and San Sebastian's gun ports snapped open and the gunners rolled the cannon barrels though. For the first time in his life, Kemal Reis thought he might not be able to get out of a blockade.

Burak Reis set to carrying out the plan he'd explained to his men for what they'd do as soon as the Göke and Göke II were full and they hauled anchor. The Crescent of Victory was leading the Göke and Göke II, but Burak Reis wasn't aboard. The captain had boarded the galiot leading his galley and was standing at its helm. There was no one else aboard save for him. The sails were billowing in the crosswind and the captain was streaming the galiot straight for the galleon. He had taken off his weapons and shoes and pulled off his shirt. The sun beat down on his well-muscled chest and his bronze shoulders shined in its rays. He stood steady as a boulder with his weather-beaten skin bared to the wind at the helm.

The men on the galleon at the mouth of the harbor thought the Ottoman sailors had gone mad again when they saw the galiot sailing straight for them. They flung open the gun ports and fired off a salvo. Streams of foaming sea rose up around Burak Reis' galiot like the columns of the Temple of Apollo. Some of the cannon fire tore through the galiot's bow, spur and sides of the main deck. The pirates on the galleon were rolling with laughter as they looked at Burak Reis, thinking he was taking himself to his own death.

The galiot started to take on water when it was sixty yards from the galleon. The shots from the cannon were quickly reducing the galiot to not much more than holes.

Rattler was watching from the deck of the Crescent of Victory. "I don't think the captain thought this plan through too good. I wouldn't be surprised if we never see him again."

"Shut that shit evil mouth of yours," Big Ahmed snapped back at him.

He was also well aware that Burak Reis was sailing to his death.

Two Spanish galleons were about to do in the two Ottoman captains.

111

Davud turned back after shutting the hatch to the tunnel on David and saw that the knights had gotten much closer—there was not much space left between them. He picked up the crossbow David had left behind and faced the knights in the middle of the rampart.

The first knight came in front of Davud, who lifted the crossbow with one hand and let the arrow fly when the man was only a few feet away. The knight was just about to swing his sword when the arrow pierced his armor and shredded his guts. Davud caught the knight's sword in the air and brought it down on another, slicing through his shoulder. This blow would've been rather powerless and the knight's nearly hundred pounds of armor would've protected him, but Davud wielding a sword was different.

The knights pulled up when they saw Davud cut down the two men in the lead, and they started approaching more cautiously. Davud had already retrieved the sword from the second knight he'd dispatched.

The knights pushed the three men in front forward, and by the looks of their simple helmets, they were the most unskilled among them.

Davud swung his swords, slicing through the arm of the man to his right and the leg of the knight to his left before he sent the third flying back with a kick, toppling into the two knights behind him.

The next two knights tried to take Davud out without getting close. One was slashing a poleax at him, its honed blade shining in the sunlight. Davud ducked under the strike and grabbed hold just down from of the flying ax head and plucked it from the knight's hands. The other knight whipped chains at his neck and their iron links wrapped around Davud's sword.

Davud found his feet and resigned his blade to the chains. When he looked up he launched this other sword directly at the knight's face as he was righting himself with his poleax. It flew through the air directly into the eye slit in the knight's visor and lodged into his face.

Davud now had the weapon he needed to hold the rampart. He stood steadfast in between the six-foot walls with the long poleax, swinging it back and forth and knocking down six more knights. He had no intention of letting anyone past him. It wouldn't only put his own life in danger if the knights got to the tunnel, but also those of all the Jews and Muslims boarding the Turkish ships at port. Maybe they'd declare total war on the Ottoman ships and then everything would be lost.

He cut two more knights down before another—this time more experienced—whipped a chain around his poleax and pulled it from his grip. He was unarmed and three of them rushed him. The one to his left swung his sword. Davud caught his arm mid strike before it could fall, twisted his wrist back and head butted his helmet. The knight's visor crumpled into his face and he fell to the ground unconscious. Davud immediately swung his elbow behind him into another knight's face and pulverized the man's nose. The knight in the middle swung his sword and hit Davud in the upper arm, leaving a gash as wide as a finger. All of Davud's old arrow wounds on his leg, shoulder and hand had also reopened as he fought and were bleeding.

He was detached from his growing pain, though, and was sending his foes to the ground with punches, kicks, knees and head butts to the face.

Another sword glinted at him, slicing his leg right where his old wound was, then another to his shoulder. Finally an armored fist to his face brought him to the ground and the knights piled on top of him.

"I want him alive!" Lucas bellowed from the opening to the Gibralfaro Castle.

Two knights had hold of his feet, two more had his arms and a fifth grabbed his head, all trying to hold him down. They struggled to keep him in place as he thrashed back at them like a raging bull.

As if all this weren't enough, Davud noticed more knights coming from the Alcazaba. He had his head craned back, looking at everything upside down, and saw the legs of a dozen soldiers running toward him. Drenched in sweat, he felt he was finally meeting his end.

He was caught on the rampart in between the two castles and the knights of Santa Hermandad were about to do him in.

112

The knight holding Davud's head pulled as if he were going to snap his neck when a spear came flying straight into his temple. He let out a deafening shriek and let loose of Davud's head as he fell down. No one knew what had happened. Davud was able to free his arms and there was no one left to hold him down. He didn't know where the spear had come from, though.

The knights still hadn't recovered from what had just happened before an arrow struck the one holding down his left leg. Then came a flurry of more arrows, each one striking a knight.

He lifted his head and saw the knights starting to flee down the rampart. Then he understood.

"The Almohads," he breathed.

Two-dozen Saharan archers were on the stairs of the Roman amphitheater at the foot of the castle walls raining arrows down on the rampart. They all were wearing Berber *litham* veils wrapped around their heads and faces of either black or deep indigo. They were the group that had run across Davud and the group on the road just a week before.

When Davud was lifting himself up, he realized the soldiers coming from behind him were actually fleeing the Almohad. They had managed to infiltrate the Alcazaba. The leader of the group drew his *Zulfiqar* scimitar and mercilessly stuck its double points in the ground. This was Ali. Davud remembered him well. His men were loosing arrows from two sides into the middle of the rampart and were pushing the knights back. How they'd found him, how they knew he'd be here and if they had come to save him all ran through Davud's mind.

He found the answers to all this when Abdullah of Xativa stepped out from behind Ali.

Ali came to Davud's side, reached out his hand and helped him to his feet. By this point, Davud had been well carved up.

"I thought you said you'd consider me an infidel if you ever came across me again," he said with a little suspicion.

"I changed my mind." Ali looked back at Abdullah. "They said you needed help, so we came. The enemy of my enemy is my friend." He then looked up at the groups of knights starting to fill the towers of the Gibralfaro Castle. "We don't have much time. All of the kingdom's knights will be here in only a few minutes."

Ali lifted the hatch that Davud had thrown David down a half hour earlier and looked over at Davud and Abdullah. "Now say a prayer and may the Ottoman ships be waiting for you at the end of the tunnel."

Davud was about to ask about him Ali and his men, but the Almohad cut him off.

"Don't even let it cross your mind. Our home is here. We were born in Andalusia and we'll die in Andalusia. The day will come when this land is ours again. Maybe not this year, and maybe not this century, but one day the banners of Islam will wave again on this land. That's when the witness we have bore will echo again in the mountains, valleys and over the plains."

He paused for a moment after speaking and then yelled, "*Wa la ghaliba illa 'llah!*"—*And there is no victor but God.*

"*Wa la ghaliba illa 'llah!*" Davud repeated, and turned to go.

Ali and his men were preparing their safe exit back to where they'd come from as Davud and Abdullah jumped down into the tunnel and started running as fast as they could.

Lucas had been watching all that had happened from a safe place with his men at the opening to the Gibralfaro Castle. He turned and ordered the six knights there to follow him. They all disappeared into the darkness as they descended the stairs of the castle and headed for the gates that opened to the coast.

113

Abdullah and Davud had been running for fifteen minutes and the white light at the end of the tunnel was getting bigger. Davud's arms and legs were still bleeding—he had lost a lot of blood as they went and couldn't run as fast as Abdullah, who took him under his arm and tried to help him along.

"We've made it. We're saved!" Abdullah yelled a couple yards from the mouth of the tunnel.

Davud didn't have time to tell him to stop and wait before he ran out. Abdullah took two steps out into the light of day and fell to his knees. A knight's ax was planted in his chest and he fell down limp, his eyes still open.

Davud collapsed at Abdullah's side in anguish and held his head, but it was far too late.

He looked up and saw that he was surrounded by half a dozen mounted knights. In the middle was Lucas with his telltale pig-nosed helmet and monstrous frame. He had a knight to each of his sides.

"This is it," Lucas said, more a rumble emanating from behind his ghastly helmet. His voice was guttural and hair-raising, grunting and wheezing, more roaring beast than man. "I'll finish you first, then go to the pier and order everyone to attack your ships."

He looked over at the Ottoman galleys going up against the Spanish galleons and then went on. "Of course, that is if your friends aren't already taken care of by then."

Davud held Abdullah's head to his chest as he reckoned how he could escape. He slowly grabbed a handful of sand from behind Abdullah's body. He made his move as soon as Lucas turned to look at the port and flung it in the face of the horse closest to him.

The horse reared back and stamped as the sand flew into its nose and eyes. Davud rolled under as its hooves flailed in the air and started running as fast as he could. He nearly had no strength left after the run through the tunnel and the blood he'd lost, but he'd stand a chance against the knights if he could at least get to a building and possibly find a weapon. All of the commotion on the streets from the festival and groups of Jews and Muslims fleeing to the port was to his favor.

Lucas and two of his men rode into and over the crowds with no care, but the noise and chaos frightened the horses and they wouldn't pick up their pace. One of Lucas' knights went off to gather more men while Lucas went searching for Davud accompanied by two other knights.

After running Malaga's streets for a short while, Davud came upon a mosque that was being converted into a church, half under construction and half a powder mill. He hauled himself inside. The walls inside were decorated with carved, Maghrebi type calligraphy and paintings of Catholic images. A wall was also covered in scaffolding in order to erect statues of Jesus and Mary. The interior had all the trappings of a worksite—hammers, mallets, piles of timber, nails, saws, chisels and dozens of other tools. It was obvious the workers had taken a break for the festival.

"He went into the old armory!" one knight shouted.

The building had been used as a storehouse for weapons during the battle to take Granada, and now that that battle had been won, it was becoming a church.

Davud bent down over the timbers first thing to find a thin tether to bind his broken hand. He wound it through his fingers and up his hand to his wrist twice over. It squeezed his hand into a hardened fist so he could use it. He was also trying to give himself a fighting chance for what he knew was coming. His strength had been sapped and he was exhausted.

114

Standing at the helm, Burak Reis was sailing his galiot straight at the thousand-ton Spanish galleon whose cannon fire was about to completely dismantle his ship. Outside the harbor, the galleons San Matteo and San Sebastian had blocked Kemal Reis as he was overpowering di Varthema's galleon.

Then something happened that changed the fate of the two Ottoman captains. Kemal Reis had said that let the servant of God strive and God will help. This was that day.

First, the wind that had been aiding the galleons suddenly died. The water's surface turned smooth as glass as the galleons' sails fell slack. Without wind, the behemoths were reduced to piles of wood floating on the water. Oars would've been of no use since the hulking ships' speed and direction were entirely dependent on wind. With this turn of luck, the Blue Lion would be able to use the power of its galley slaves to speed around and bombard the galleons.

The galleons still had an advantage with their number of men, however, and could've sunk the Blue Lion if they stayed where they were and simply fired their cannons from all sides.

Then the second godsend came. Kemal Reis' men had all ardently set to work so as not to miss their chance to escape as the wind abated, but now they all stopped. They heard cannon fire from somewhere. It wasn't from their ship or the galleons. The realized the sound was coming from the San Matteo, but the cannon fire was coming from somewhere else. The men on the Blue Lion could just make out the bow of a galley bombarding the galleon from the other side.

"It's the Chelebis!" Fingerless Shakir cried.

All the men whooped and cheered.

This old friend of Kemal Reis had come to their aid.

Another ship appeared behind the San Sebastian. Big Chelebi had brought his most faithful men, Chaka Bey and Kara Mürsel— the greatest and saltiest pirates there were off the southwestern coasts of Anatolia.

"You said come and we came, isn't it, Captain!" Big Chelebi hollered from the bow of his galley.

It had riled Big Chelebi having sent the captain off to enemy waters alone.

Chaka Bey began firing on the galleon near him both as a salutation to Kemal Reis and to get underway as soon as possible. Kara Mürsel had also set his sights on the Portuguese galley off port.

The Catholic pirates and knights hadn't expected to fall into a blockade of enemy ships themselves while they were trying to pinch the Blue Lion. Despite the galleons superior qualities, the tactical and mental superiority in the battle was with the Ottoman sailors, and the Catholic belligerents were falling prey to their own confusion.

Burak Reis was still heading straight for the galleon, The cannon fire had shredded over half the bow and broadsides of his galiot, but the captain had locked on his target and he'd reckoned its speed well so that his ship maintained pace toward the galleon. He dove off the stern right as his galiot got within thirty yards of the towering galleon.

Having gotten the signal he was waiting for, Blind Ali ignited the arrow he'd prepared, aimed at the point Burak Reis had shown him and released the bowstring. The arrow sailed over the sea and through a gun port at the stern, setting off a terrific explosion as the galiot rammed the galleon, lighting it into a furious blaze.

Burak Reis had earlier filled barrels with black powder at the stern where they'd be safe from the cannon fire he'd be taking. He'd explained to Blind Ali exactly where to aim. The timing and speed had to be perfect. If the galiot exploded too earlier, then it would sink without inflicting any damage on the galleon, and if Blind Ali missed his mark, then the barrels would be useless and the bow would simply crash into the galleon, which the massive ship could easily withstand with minimal damage. The starboard side of giant galleon, though, was now engulfed in flames and the all men on board were forced to leave their positions and fetch buckets of water to try to extinguish it.

The more than five hundred men on board the huge galleon were quick to haul up water from the sea and get the fire under control. Thick, black smoke was now rising from the broadside. Burak Reis had taken this into account, as well, and now the Ottoman pirates were emerging through the black smoke like phantoms. Rattler, Big Ahmed and the others were charging onto the galleon one after the other. The Crescent of Victory had sped behind the galiot while the men on the galleon were busy struggling to put out the flames. They had disabled its cannons and were now flooding aboard.

115

Lucas dismounted in front of the worksite and drew his sword.

"You wait here. Come in when the others arrive," he ordered his men.

His two-handed, double-edged sword was nearly five feet long and as wide as a man's hand. Unlike many in his company, he found the thin and pointed Spanish rapiers to be unmanly and effeminate. Most couldn't wield his sword with both hands if they tried, but Lucas sometimes swung it with only one.

He entered with slow, deliberate steps, his three-point shield emblazoned with the cross of Santa Hermandad in one hand and his sword raised and ready in the other. He'd learned not to make light of any enemy, but the abilities Davud had exhibited one after another made Lucas take him all the more seriously. He waited for his eyes to adjust to the darkness once inside. He slowly turned looked from side to side, peering through the eye slit in his visor. The wooden scaffolding, marble columns and statues, the old mihrab and the minbar next to it appeared as if he was looking through a curtain of fog in the darkness.

He was slowly trying to pick everything out when he felt a blow to his left shoulder.

Davud had been lying in wait with a large piece of timber and aimed for Lucas' head the first opportunity he saw. Far from bringing Lucas down, though, Davud missed his head and the timber cracked in half over his massive shoulder.

In a sudden reflex, Lucas slammed his shield into Davud, sending him stumbling back into the scaffolding and onto his back as the boards and poles fell on top of him. He felt he'd been hit by a boulder. Lucas hurried to the pile of splintered boards and furiously swung his sword down at Davud lying amid the collapsed scaffolding. Davud rolled to the side right as the sword was about to cleave his head in two, the blade instead splitting through a piece of wood.

Lucas was already back on the attack as Davud was standing back up, swinging his sword relentlessly. A strike glanced off Davud's shoulder into an iron piece of the scaffolding, sending sparks flying. Another came across his neck and collided into one of the old mosque's marble columns. Davud quickly sidestepped a third as it whistled through the air. The sword was coming so fast it was setting off sparks as it struck the metal and stone.

116

The Blue Lion had now pulled alongside di Varthema's galleon. Fingerless Shakir took hold of a hook on the end of a rope and launched himself across to the galleon, flying over to the main course sail on the mainmast with all his strength. He spun around a few times after the hook caught hold of the sail and then he came to a stop. He pulled on the rope to make sure it was firmly in place, grabbed hold and flung himself down with a battle cry, swinging like a pendulum over the galleon's deck. He swooped down onto the heads of two men before he'd reached the deck and started hacking away with his cutlass at everyone who came in front of him.

The men came swinging on ropes from the Blue Lion, rushing up ladders and over the gunwales, across gangplanks into the port-holes and jumping straight over. They had all descended on the galleon when Kemal Reis gave the order to board.

They were giving no quarter to di Varthema's pirates and knights. Yardman Jevher, Overseer Jihan and Helmsman Musa were flashing their yataghan sabers, Orion Orhan carefully took aim with his pistols, Hard-Nose Ibrahim was thrusting his spear and the rest of the warriors attacked with blades, maces and war hammers.

On the deck of the San Matteo, Big Chelebi smashed his club down on a Genoese knight's helmet, crumpling it and crunching the man's head inside. His son behind him struck down another pirate with every flick of his scimitar. Chelebi's men had swamped the galleon and were also out for blood.

The men on the Portuguese galley had fled after the initial shock, realizing the tide had turned against them, and so Chaka Bey and Kara Mürsel turned their attention to the San Sebastian. Their men streamed over the sides of the ship at once, kicking and hacking away with cleavers and axes. When the galleon's men saw the piled up bodies of their fellow pirates, they dropped their swords and began begging for mercy.

Another arm, ear or head went tumbling to the deck every time the sunlight flashed off Kemal Reis' sword as it flew though the air. He was no less as masterful a swordsman as he was a master of the Mediterranean. He set his back against the foremast with Yardman Jevher to his right and Overseer Jihan to his left and the three of them sliced through everyone who came at them as if they were reaping wheat.

The scimitar Burak Reis was wielding that day was the last thing many a pirate on the galleon ever saw. The knights' armor was no match for its Damascus steel blade and the pirates couldn't escape it no matter how they tried.

"Take that, you son of a bitch! Cross yourself with this, you shit!" Rattler was ranting as he took his silver-inlaid, matchlock pistols to their faces. He still had six more tucked into his waist.

Big Ahmed was busy slicing away with his scimitar next to his old friend "Shut your damn hole already, Rattler, and get to it!"

Right then a beast of a pirate leapt off a boom onto Rattler's head and plunged a knife into his heart.

"It's going dark! Oh God, there's a monkey on me!" Rattler slumped down, cracking jokes as he fell.

Big Ahmed heaved his sword and sliced off the pirate's head in one go. He knelt down where Rattler fell at the base of the jigger-mast. He could tell his friend had been mortally wounded.

"Rattler, mate! What're you doing to me?" Big Ahmed said as he started to cry.

He couldn't give a damn about the battle now.

"Qitmir," Rattler spat out through blood. "Take good care of Qitmir, Ahmed."

Big Ahmed fought back his tears as he hung his head for his friend of forty years

"Don't you worry," he said just as Rattler's blue eyes froze up at the sky.

Big Ahmed went mad with rage. He picked up his scimitar, his face pulsing red, and cleaved through everyone he found.

"Get off the ship—the powder room's about to blow!" Mute Yusuf shouted.

Everyone on board jumped into the sea. The Spanish pirates took off swimming in every direction while the heavily armored knights sank to the seafloor. The Ottoman pirates swam back to the Crescent of Victory and climbed back to deck. Big Ahmed couldn't bring himself to leave Rattler on the enemy ship. He threw his friend's body over his shoulder and plunged into the water. A short while later, the powder room caught light and the explosion sent a billowing cloud of smoke rising overhead. Not long after, the gigantic galleon was sinking below the surface as it was wrapped in flames. The mouth to the harbor was open now.

Kemal Reis, the Chelebis and their men had also taken control of the three galleons beyond the harbor. Everyone had turned and was waiting for Burak Reis to sail from the port with the Göke and Göke II.

There was little wind, though, which made the going all the more difficult. The Göke and Göke II were more similar to the galleons and had to rely on their sails when they were full of passengers. And now with more than two thousand people on each ship, it was impossible to weigh anchor.

Burak Reis quickly dispatched Mute Yusuf to the bow of the Göke and Yardman Jevher to the Göke II, where they strung a rope between the two ships with hooks.

"All together! Come on, all together!" Overseer Mikhail cried at the Crescent of Victory's slaves as they set to the oars. The strong men and sturdy youths on the Göke ran below deck and aided the galley slaves, latching onto the oars as the Ottoman sailors showed them.

The ships we so heavily loaded, though, that neither the oars of the lead galley or those on the other two gigantic ships could get them moving.

"All together, all together!" Overseer Mikhail kept calling, but after a while, he also went and joined the salves, grabbing an oar for himself.

Kemal Reis was worriedly watching it unfold from outside the harbor. The Göke and Göke II looked like they were rooted in place.

117

Davud was so focused on the flashing sword that he didn't see Lucas lift his leg and kick. The armored sole of Lucas's boot crushed his ribs and threw him back into the scaffolding that rose up to the ceiling. Three of his ribs were broken. The scaffolding's boards and poles began to fall apart and rattled and crashed to the floor from as high as the nearly hundred foot-high ceiling. The iron poles and boards piled on top of each other in a great cloud of dust. Lucas jumped back just in time to evade the falling debris.

Lucas climbed on top of the pile once the dust started to settle. There was no movement from under the pile of boards. There was no way Davud could've come out from under all of it alive. Lucas started kicking aside the wood and iron from where Davud had fallen with his armored feet—he had no intention of leaving without seeing the man dead. But after he'd removed a few of the boards, he saw there was nothing else there save for smears of Davud's blood.

Flaring his nostrils and breathing furiously, Lucas clenched his sword firmly and thrust it down to pierce any part of Davud he could find.

Davud had been able to escape from under the planks and crept behind Lucas in the clouds of dust. He hoisted himself up onto a chandelier hanging from the ceiling and swung himself down on Lucas. He wrapped his legs around the man's armor and an arm around his neck. He had grabbed a hammer earlier and was now striking Lucas over the head again and again. He beat at the knight's helmet, smashing away at its crown and visor. Lucas shook from side to side, but Davud clenched on tightly with his arm and legs and had no intention of letting go.

Lucas lost his balance and dropped his shield, but his sword stayed firmly in his hand. He shuffled back and brought Davud back into a marble column with such force that his arms and legs went limp and he fell from Lucas to the ground. Davud felt that his shoulder blade had broken and was waiting for Lucas to finish him off.

When he lifted his head, though, Lucas was staggering around with his arms outstretched and unable to see a thing. All the hammer blows had creased shut the sight hole and most of the air holes in his helmet. His head and face hadn't been harmed, but his helmet was a hindrance now. He grabbed it by the horns and started pulling it off.

Davud got to his feet before he lost the opportunity. He picked up a three-yard iron rod and swung it as hard as he could against Lucas' chest. It caved his armor into him and he fell back onto the pile of planks like a hunk of steel, pulverizing the wood as he landed. Davud rushed on top of Lucas and raised the rod to swing it back down on his head, but this time Lucas saw it coming through his helmet's still open air holes. He caught the rod with his gauntlet, pulled Davud off and belted him in the face with his other armored fist.

Davud's head went flying back and he ended up back on the ground. Lucas took the opportunity with Davud down to take his helmet by the horns and pull it off before he got to his feet.

It was the first time Davud had seen Lucas' grotesque face, and his hair stood on end as everyone's did the first time they laid eyes on him. The first sight of his jagged face, crooked nose and gigantic head was enough to scare anybody.

Not just his helmet, Lucas angrily tore off his chest plate that Davud had caved in with the iron rod, ripping it off as if it were a shirt rather than steel. His gauntlets and armor from the waist down were still untouched. Davud saw the scars on his chest from the whips and metal spikes that Lucas had tortured himself with for purification, and he realized that Lucas had come from amid deviant and perverted priests. Davud could now see how this man was resistant to all kinds of knives, punches and kicks, both bodily and spiritually. This was why swinging timbers and iron bars had nearly no affect on this man. A body exposed to such regular violence wouldn't easily suffer pain and, as long as the mind functioned, so too would the body.

Before Davud had a chance to recover, Lucas grabbed him by the neck and waist and flung him against a wall. He picked him back up and threw him against another wall, and then again as if he were a sack of grain, using the walls to do the beating for him. Tiles cracked and crumbled and the old mosque's worn, plastered and chiseled calligraphy and ornamental rose and pomegranate blossom motifs fell from the walls where Davud hit.

Lucas was about to pick Davud up for the fifth time, but Davud kicked up from the ground and caught him in the calf, sending him off balance and to the floor. Davud took his opportunity and grabbed a chisel with his good hand. He thrust it with all he had at Lucas as he was on the ground. Lucas rolled to the side, but the chisel ripped through his armor and stuck into his thigh, just above the knee, and sunk down to his bone. Davud gathered his strength again and stood back up while Lucas was screaming in pain and pulling himself to his feet.

Lucas' head came within Davud's reach as he tried to pull out the chisel from his leg. Davud pulled back his arm and punched Lucas straight in the nose with his wounded fist and then cuffed him over the ear. Davud knew he could produce the most force with his elbow due to the strength of the bone and its concentrated impact—enough to crush stone—and would be much more effective than trying to bang the man's head against the wall.

Lucas hadn't gotten the chisel all the way out before Davud planted his elbow into his temple with a terrific crack. He lost his balance and staggered around, but didn't fall down. Davud then punched him over and over, aiming straight for his heart. He had to punch up owing to the Lucas' great size and didn't quite find his mark, although he did manage to break a couple of the man's ribs. Davud's quick, successive punches left Lucas gasping for breath—he felt as if he had just had multiple boulders dropped on his chest.

Lucas stumbled back, but Davud followed, jumping up and kneeing him in the chin, sending him to the ground on his back. Davud's father had taught him the move he had once learned from an ancient warrior in Asia. Lucas had never known that a man could exert such terrible force with just a knee.

Davud was certain he'd broken the man's jaw. Lucas was nearly finished.

Davud jumped at Lucas for another attack, but realized his mistake as he got close. Lucas pushed himself back across the floor, which made Davud lose his footing, and the knight found time to get to his feet. He charged. Davud stood like a stone with his feet firmly planted. He grabbed Lucas as he charged and flung him to the ground. He'd known how to use an opponent's weight and bulk since he was a boy, being able to topple a fully equipped, two hundred-pound warrior. He had reckoned he'd be able to use it against the heavily armored knights in Europe, and he hadn't been mistaken. It was an incredible advantage when he found himself unarmed—it just took correct timing and balance.

Davud's vision was narrowing, however, and his head was spinning. He was starting to feel the effects of how much blood he'd lost from his many open wounds.

He didn't know how it happened, but Lucas took out his right leg and Davud dropped to his knee. It was broken.

With one knee on the ground, Davud resembled the constellation of *Hercules* that Beatriz had likened him to.

118

Lucas grabbed Davud by the head as he was knelt on the ground, pulling him up by his hair and dragging him to one of the few marble statues—one of the Virgin Mary that had been specially made for the conversion to give the old mosque a more Catholic appearance. He took Davud's head and smashed it into the statue's feet. The marble cracked and Davud collapsed with blood streaming from his forehead. Lucas grabbed him again and twisted his left arm back until it snapped. He was flat out on the ground and Lucas started relentlessly kicking him in the side with his armored boots.

Then knights of Santa Hermandad came panting through the door. The man Lucas had sent had come back with nearly five-dozen knights from the Castle of Gibralfaro, and they were all piling through the door into the old mosque, their weapons at the ready and fully armored. They surrounded Davud like ants to sugar.

Davud, soaked with blood, tried to get away from Lucas, pulling himself along the floor with his good arm, but with every movement, Lucas kicked him in the side again. He was starting to heave blood from his mouth.

Lucas kept kicking him and then picked him up again and hurled him at the partially removed minbar. Its finely carved wooden stars shattered as he collided into it. Davud ended up on his back, his eyes fixed at the old mosque's dome overhead. The scaffolding still reached up to the dome and the verses in its center had still not been completely removed. Davud saw an *alif* in the middle of the dome—half of it had been scraped away, but the other half and its head were still there. In between a dream and reality and half conscious, he reached out his good arm as if to take hold of the letter. Lucas gave him another kick and his arm dropped back to the floor.

He felt something like a pile of dust as his hand hit the floor. He came to and looked to his side. This wasn't dust. The old mosque had been used as an armory during the battles against the Muslims. It was black powder. He looked around and saw no less than six barrels of it inside the minbar and under the stairs.

Lucas had broken nearly every bone in his body, but when Davud saw him take his sword and turn to him to finish him off, he scratched his way across the floor until he was spread out lying over the black powder.

Lucas stepped up to Davud, took his sword in both hands and brought it down with all his strength right next to the minbar.

Davud had closed his eyes and was listening to the sound of the sword. He felt the wind from the blade and used all he had to roll to the side as the sword whistled down. Lucas' sword struck the stone and sent sparks flying and igniting the back powder.

Davud stared up at the *alif* on the dome and what else remained of the *shahada* as the old mosque exploded and sent the knights tumbling through the air.

His face lightened and a small smile spread across his face.

119

There was no wind from any direction and Burak Reis couldn't get the Göke and Göke II moving. He raised his head to the sky and closed his eyes.

"God, You are Great, Everlasting and Self-Subsisting. Do not shame us, o Lord. Do not leave us to waste away in an enemy land, o God. All-Knowing, All-Powerful, Lord of Glory and Generosity, help us."

He felt a breeze pass his nose before he could reopen his eyes. He looked up and saw the banner on the topgallant start clapping in the wind as it unfurled. He looked to the pier and saw the Göke's sails begin to move.

"Unfurl the sails!" he shouted.

The riggers and yardmen swung from mast to mast and set every sail the Göke had as they caught the wind.

The Crescent of Victory began sailing out of the harbor with the gigantic Göke and Göke II following behind.

David leaned his hands against the gunwale and looked out on Malaga from the back of the Göke. Next to his feet was the sack of books he'd been carrying since they first set out. He was still looking for Davud.

Big Chelebi came up to Kemal Reis on the deck of the Blue Lion. "I wouldn't be too pleased if I were you, Captain."

He turned to where Chelebi's eyes were looking and saw that two-dozen ships from the Spanish fleet had hauled anchor and were taking up battle positions. These powerful galleons, now with the wind, had set off for the Ottoman ships with full sails.

A deafening explosion came from shore just behind the pier. Pieces of an old mosque were hurtling through the air.

"Davud!" David said.

Tears started falling down Beatriz's cheeks.

The Spanish ships turned back to port after the explosion, thinking the city was being attacked from land.

The Ottoman fleet with the Blue Lion in the lead was disappearing over the horizon with more than four thousand Jews and Muslims loaded onto the Göke and Göke II while the Spanish sailors were still trying to figure out what had happened. The smoke from the explosion rose up over the pier and mixed with the smoke of books and bodies from the *auto da fé* underway in the city.

Sacrificium

I, the monk Santiago of Malaga, have found my due. This is where my story ends, ensuring the kindling at my feet is lit, my body tied to a stake and wearing a yellow sanbenito for all to see me as a heretic. They set light to the kindling long ago. My feet warmed quickly and are on fire.

My true pain, however, comes from the books burning a hundred yards from me. I had found most of them myself and delivered them to the Inquisition. Each of their covers is my face and their pages my limbs. Don't think of me, but extinguish these books if your power is enough to do so.

There's a crowd in front of me, a king and queen watching from behind and dozens of priests and monks to my sides. Some had been my friends until yesterday. I'm an enemy to them now, and some don't understand why I did what I did—questioning why I knowingly and wantingly aided a prisoner's escape from the dungeon and why I handed the keys to the Alcazaba and my papers over to a foreigner.

The flames have risen to my legs now. The hair is getting singed like a foul being prepared for supper. The smell is acerbic. The flesh on my feet has long melted away, leaving only the bone. I'm afraid to look down. Like one scared of heights who doesn't look down, maybe the pain from this fire that I'm struggling to endure will ease.

The smell, though. What am I to do with that? It's as if I'm frying and chewing my own flesh. There's an acrid smell when our flesh starts burning. It's nothing like the smell of cooking meat, of beef or mutton. Our flesh is different. As it burns it emits the smells of muscle, organs, blood, metals like iron and copper, and minerals. Our blood and juices slow the fire, making the smell and pain all the more unbearable.

And my ink-stained hands. My fingers, having written countless thousands of pages, my most beloved parts, are now torches.

These hands have tossed many books to the flame and recorded the torture of hundreds of innocent people. Let them burn.

I, the monk Santiago, am burning, but the embers of the fire inside me are dying down.

Water sprinkles over the cinders in my spirit as the fire consumes my body and the flames climb higher. My pain doesn't come from my own burning body, but from the thousands of pages I've set alight and the hundreds of people I watched burn in silence.

Maybe I could've saved one of them or found reason to save them. Maybe I'll be forgiven for my submission to this barbarism up until now. And maybe not.

But I know I've found peace. It gives me peace that these hands will no longer burn the works of Aristotle, ibn Rush, Maimonides or the Quran and Torah. Even though I don't forget my pain now that these eyes will no longer look upon burning bodies, it has lightened.

My hair is now on fire, too. Soon the flames will burn into my head. My mind and memories will go up in smoke and my eyes will melt from my skull as I roast like a slab of meat.

My spirit will be purified one day, though. Christianity will cast off this barbarism and regain its true message. This is my one want from God.

And now, I see my dear mother looking at me.

END
Elif

121

David felt an unusual sense of comfort take over him as he walked into the Audience Hall of Topkapi Palace. The spaciousness that had presented itself since he entered the palace only grew bigger. He was going for an audience with the sultan along with Esther, his brother Samuel and a few prominent Jews, accompanied by the chief rabbi of Constantinople. Beatriz was also with them. She'd since converted to Islam and changed her name to Billur Hanim. Like some of the Jews who'd come to the Ottoman Empire, she'd chosen to convert to Islam. Lace, which she had just learned how to make, ran along the edge of the scarf over her head. She also forgot her grief amid the magic of Topkapi Palace.

The first gate to the palace was the imperial gate—the *Bab-i Hümayun*. David wondered if it had come from the old Roman *Porta Augusta*. The walls of marble and concrete plaster around the gate, the calligraphy on its doors and two small mihrab led to an entrance with a large mihrab and high ceilings, leaving no doubt this was the center of the empire.

Behind this solemn gate lay a wide and spacious courtyard full of greenery. Behind this solemnity was confidence, and from that confidence, a deep sense of peace. David came upon two pointed towers a little further on—the *Bab-üs Selam*—the Gate of Salutation. There was more greenery here with janissaries on the move to both sides, palace officials and pages. David had never seen such regulation before. Smoke rose from the dozens of kitchen chimneys to the right and colonnades ran all around. To the left stood the Tower of Justice, which he'd first seen from the deck of the Göke as it sailed into port and had learned its name and meaning.

"This tower is the eye of the sultanate," Kemal Reis had said. "And not just of the capital city, but of the entire empire."

David felt his anxiety melt away as he passed through the Gate of Tranquility and saw the large fountain in the middle of the courtyard surrounded by thousands of flowers. This culture and its people to whom he was foreign welcomed him and he felt a great sense of warmth well in his chest as if even the land with its stones and buildings were smiling on him. Amid the gurgling water and multi-colored flowers, it seemed the towering, green porphyry marble columns had become one with the trees. It was as if they hadn't come from human hands, but had instead risen from the ground. Beyond this marble with white swirls though it was the door to the Audience Hall, which resembled the architecture of Andalusia. Its gate was surrounded by alternating green and white marble reminiscent of the red and white stones around the gates of the Alhambra. David thought this empire had collected in its buildings all the finest aspects of Rome, Andalusia and many other empires. Whatever richness people brought from east and west was all found here, brought together at the center. It had the magnificence of Rome and the grace of Andalusia.

Off to the side of the courtyard were guests who had just come from the Audience Hall or were waiting to enter. David couldn't help but smile at how adorable the sight was of a man in the group holding a small, white Maltese dog.

David thought for a moment that the sultan had sprung from the earth outside when Bayezid entered the Audience Hall. The sultan's dark blue caftan lined with fur, his quilted turban rising like a marble column, his loose robe with tight sleeves in a green like the trees in the courtyard and his brown leather boots made him look like a piece of Constantinople and the empire—or, that the empire emanated from him.

Kemal Reis and Burak Reis stood at the ready at the sides of the throne. Kemal Reis had risen in rank and gained more land after their success. Burak Reis and his men were given a large galley worth thousands of gold pieces and the governorship of Manisa was given to the Chelebis.

Billur Hanim kept catching a glimpse of the depths of the sea in Burak Reis' eyes. She couldn't help but think maybe he, too, could care for and take a foreign woman as a wife as Kemal Reis had with Mademoiselle Veronica.

"May God bless you and increase the power of your empire," Chief Rabbi Moshe Kapsali said. "Moses parted the sea and saved us from Pharaoh, and you, like him have crossed the sea and plucked us from the midst of flames and saved us from hell once again."

"We did nothing that Islam does not already order of us. Ferdinand and Isabella are fools, depriving their own land of such valuable treasures while enriching my own," Bayezid said.

This great compliment from the sultan, that he understood the wealth of a land with many cultures and that it was a source for boasting delighted the guests in the Audience Hall.

David and Samuel stepped in front of Bayezid, and David expressed his thanks.

"The chief rabbi mentioned that you're a good scholar and technician—that you produce books with a new contraption," Bayezid said.

"It's gracious of the chief rabbi to say those things about me. Yes, I print books on a printing press with movable type. If you would allow it, my brother and I would like to print the Hebrew books that we still have here in this land. It's our binding duty after the thousands of book that were burned and destroyed in Andalusia."

David realized he'd taken a great risk right after he finished speaking, as he reckoned Ottoman calligraphers wouldn't look kindly on printed pages, the same as those in Andalusia had done.

He'd also heard the sultan was a calligrapher himself, and so might be of the same mind as them. After all he'd experienced, he just couldn't hold back from telling his desires to this sultan who'd opened up the doors to a new life for him.

"I've examined that contraption," he told David with surprising interest. "It's still very new. True, it reproduces, but it loses the beauty. Writing is sacred to us. This sanctity should be written and reproduced with a worthy method."

David thought his hopes had been drowned and that the sultan wouldn't allow a printing press in Constantinople.

"But with this, as with every new development, its problems will be overcome with time. This doesn't happen by itself—someone must ensure the work continues. I say you and your brother open a printing house, reproduce the books that were burned and destroyed, and distribute them among your people." Bayezid then turned to Sheikh Hamdullah. "Our calligraphers do good work for now. Let them continue writing the Islamic verses with calligraphy."

Hamdullah acknowledged the sultan and nodded softly. Hamdullah was already developing a perfected form of the *Naskh* script on the sultan's orders. Since the printing press could not reflect the beauty and esthetics of the Quran, it was far from depicting the truth as writing does. Only a master calligrapher could do that.

David wanted to wrap his arms around the sultan with joy. He would be able to freely set up a printing house without having to answer to anybody and print Hebrew books as he pleased and distribute them among the Jewish community throughout the whole empire. He'd gotten consent from the highest authority. It was all like a dream.

There was something missing, though. Something was still burning him inside. He lowered his head.

"I wish your man you sent to save us could've been here with us today. We're forever in his debt. I wish he could be with his wife and daughter—he was always dreaming of them."

Sultan Bayezid was confused and he furrowed his brow. He looked over at Sheikh Hamdullah, Kemal Reis and Burak Reis as if to ask what David was talking about.

"Are you talking about Davud?"

David didn't know what to make of the sultan's confusion. "Yes. I wish he'd also been able also be with his family."

Bayezid stood up. As a rule, the sultan didn't stand in front of foreign guests in the Audience Hall unless there was something extraordinary. As he moved, it was as if waves from a stone dropped in water emanated from him, affecting everyone in the hall as they spread.

He took David by the shoulder and led him off to a secluded corner next to a window. The blue of the Marmara Sea stretched into the distance, its water sparkling gold with sunlight.

"I would've thought you and the others had learned by know. Although I suppose I may have forgotten just how tightlipped Davud is. So, I'm not surprised at all."

Now David was confused. He wondered why the sultan wasn't surprised and about whatever it was that he and the others hadn't learned.

Bayezid looked out over the blue sea as he remembered his old friend. "Davud lost his wife and daughter shortly after she was born." His voice grew heavier as he spoke. "I met him years ago in a small mosque in Amasya as I was turning from my youth. I heard the story of this man who appeared before me as I was irrevocably changing my life. It so affected me that I wanted to help him. For years he went from kingdom to kingdom and sent me information and intelligence. He always wanted to be far from Constantinople, as if he was running from his pain. Foreign lands were his salvation, although I recently heard that he wanted to return to his own land. This was going to be his final mission."

"But that's impossible," David said—his astonishment had made him forget he was in the presence of the sultan. "He was always saying his wife's name in his sleep and lived with the hope of one day being back with his family. He was always praying for it and dreaming of his family."

Then David remembered the last words Davud had said to him. *Tell the sultan my prayers have been answered.*

"For those who believe," Bayezid said, "death is not and end, but a beginning. No matter how much Davud questioned his fate, he never lashed out against it and always believed he would be in his family's embrace once again. He saw life as an exile from them—an exile he had to endure. He always prayed for this exile to end as soon as possible."

David would learn the details of Davud's story in the coming days—that the ship his wife and daughter were on succumbed to a fierce storm on the Mediterranean and sank, and that Davud couldn't set foot back in his house after their deaths—life had lost its meaning and he'd tried to find a remedy by going from one end of the empire to the other. Whenever David later heard these stories, he realized that a man whose life the waters had destroyed had saved him from the fire, and would think about the wisdom of the meaning of this over and over. He only understood much later that Davud was waiting to die every die, and David carried his pain with him for years as if it were his own.

"Fire or water—these are each only a means," Bayezid said. "God is the one who gives and takes life."

"He wanted me to tell you something," David said after the sultan had collected himself.

Bayezid turned from the window and looked at him.

"*My prayers have been answered.* Those are the last words he said to me."

Sultan Bayezid turned back to the sea with a faint smile. Tears were pooling in his eyes. "May his place be in heaven. Who knows, maybe he had a sense his moment was coming. Great men live through great ordeals, and his were particularly difficult." He turned back to David and tried to lighten the heavy mood. "But now you see to setting up your printing house and reproducing the burned books in Andalusia. You'll need to get started as soon as possible if what I've heard about the amount of books burned and libraries destroyed is true."

David, one of the last of the Sephardim of Spain, did as the sultan said. A knew life was waiting for Esther and him in Constantinople, in the Ottoman Empire.

122

A young man sat on his horse at it galloped through the stalks in a wheat field. His horse shined silver under the light of the sun and the wheat glimmered like gold. A river flowed next to the horse's path. The reflection from the sun wrapped its babbling water in a rainbow. This was more heaven than earth.

The man had never felt so alive, peaceful and light in all his life. The soft wind on his face calmed his pounding heart and excitement. He had longed for the smell of the wind for years. This warrior on horseback was locked on the figure ahead. There was a delicate woman holding a baby to her breast, waiting for him under the shade of a great plane tree.

It had been years since they'd seen each other. They had yearned for one another for all of those years.

The man was a Bedouin finding water in the desert—the woman was Penelope, waiting years for the return of Odysseus.

The man had seen this sight before and galloped through this valley of wheat toward his wife now waiting for him before. This time was different. Unlike before, he had no armbands, his shield wasn't hanging from his horse and his sword wasn't at his side. His white shirt was open at the collar and down past his chest, his muscles exposed to the wind. He felt as light as a bird.

Davud pulled back on the reins as he came to Elif and their baby, swung his leg over and jumped down. He looked into his wife's eyes, the color of garden soil under morning dew. With the smile on her face and the sun overhead, Davud felt he'd been reborn.

He hugged his wife and child and released his yearning.

This was more heaven than earth.

123

It was October 12, 1492 when land appeared on the horizon in front of Christopher Columbus' three ships captained by the Pinzon brothers, with Niño as the navigator and dozens of Muslim crewmen.

Columbus was certain they'd made it to Asia, but Martin Alonso Pinzon seemed to feel they somewhere else—an entirely different world with a turquoise sea and sandy shore that shined like a diamond. Niño was confident from his calculations this was a different continent in between Europe and Asia.

"Heaven!" Columbus cried.

After the ten-week journey across the ocean, Columbus was so overjoyed to see land it was as if he'd discovered long lost Eden. The king and queen in Spain would think the same on his return, as well, and send hundreds of ships to plunder the treasures of this lost paradise.

Neither Columbus nor Pinzon knew that day that they had cracked opened the doors to a new world.

124

Beyazit was on the edge of his seat in front of the counter of the Al-Andalus Jewelry shop a few blocks away from Times Square. His tea had long gone cold. With the excitement of the story, David Marrano, sitting across from him, had also forgotten about his tea. Neither of them cared.

David Marrano sighed. "Now let them see who and what it was they called barbaric Turks and the savage Orient for centuries."

Two large, framed texts were on the counter in front of Beyazit. They were the ones that had been hanging on the wall in the middle of the shop.

Marrano picked up the first one in Arabic. "So this one's in Sultan Bayezid's *Naskh* script."

Carefully framed and behind glass, the *alif*s and *waw*s passing through each other on brownish paper were mesmerizing.

"I paid a small fortune just to have this page. I would've pain ten times more, too."

They both looked over at the other frame—its text in Hebrew.

"And this is the first page David and Samuel produced in the printing house they set up in Constantinople. David got a printing press up and running in 1493, within a year after he came to Constantinople from Spain. It's the first text printed in Hebrew in the Ottoman Empire and one of the earliest examples from anywhere in the world."

He translated it for Beyazit—

God's wrath was on the people and the Jews of Spain were forced to leave their homeland with the barbaric edict of Ferdinand and Isabella, their names forever a dark stain in history. Both Jews and their centuries-old culture were burned. Hundreds of thousands of pages and tens of thousands of books were thrown to the fire, libraries ruined and synagogues were turned into stables. When we had said that it was all over, when hundreds of Jews were being burned at the stake and thousands other were forcefully baptized, the Great Turk Sultan called us to the gates of heaven and allowed me, David ibn Nahmias Marrano, along with my brother, Samuel ibn Nahmias Marrano, to produce Hebrew book on the printing press. May God empower Sultan Bayezid and preserve his protection, compassion and charity over us. May the rule of Bayezid's empire be victorious on land and sea.

125

Sultan Bayezid and Sheikh Hamdullah were strolling along the northwestern slope of a hill in Topkapi Palace that looked off to the Marmara Sea. The two thousand five hundred-acre palace grounds were surrounded by fortified walls and janissary guards—not even a rabbit could enter without the janissary agha knowing. There was no one else there that morning save for the sultan and sheikh.

They'd come for a breath of fresh air after the morning prayers at the Hagia Sofia. The oppressive humidity of Constantinople in August had not yet taken hold of the day. A refreshing breeze was blowing lightly through the garden as the sun's orangey blaze rose over the horizon. The blue sky was tinged with shades of yellow.

"Are you sure you want to do this? Hamdullah chuckled.

"I certainly am," Bayezid said. "And I've been waiting a long time for it."

It seemed he'd been waiting for this day for years.

Bayezid stopped under a tree. There was a quiver there waiting.

"What's that?" Hamdullah said. "It that a quiver?"

"Exactly. And a bow and two arrows."

"Where did you get these?"

"I never lost them." Bayezid pulled the bow from the red velvet quiver with gold brocade and held it out to Hamdullah. "You first this time."

Hamdullah took the bow, pulled an arrow from the quiver and took aim. He drew his lips and released the string. The arrow arced through the sky and fell to the ground nearly two thousand paces away.

"Looks like you haven't lost your old form."

Hamdullah laughed. "You're mistaken if you think I spend all my days writing. It's your turn."

Bayezid took the bow and the other arrow. He drew it back to his ear and took careful aim. He was trying to point the arrow up thirty degrees to get the longest arc. He squinted an eye.

"*Ya Haqq!*"

He released the string. He had pulled it so taut it looked as if it would snap, and the muscles in his arms had strained.

"I've waited years for a second shot."

The arrow flew though the air as if it were heading for the ends of the earth as it whistled between the blue sky and the green garden. It made a wide arc high in the sky and began falling back down. It was catching up with Hamdullah's arrow and could possibly pass it.

Bayezid's arrow kept flying swiftly though the air.

Sultan Bayezid saved one hundred fifty thousand Jews from Spain throughout 1492, and settled them in centers such as Constantinople, Amasya, Salonika and Safed.

He took many measures for these Jews to live openly and prosper and decreed laws with grave punishments for those who disturbed them.

Tens of thousands of Jews who had fled Portugal, Italy and Holland were forced to relive their ordeal years later in Spain, treated as third-class people in many places they went, forcefully baptized or thrown out. Many of those who first escaped to these lands later took refuge in the Ottoman Empire.

The road Bayezid opened was followed by later sultans, and the period's wealthiest Jewish families—the Nassis and Hamons first among them—moved to the empire. They brought much to the Ottoman Empire's political and scientific worlds, many as viziers and physicians.

The Nahmias brothers' printing press was the first in the Ottoman Empire and the greater Middle East.

The *Alhambra Decree* of 1492 was one the greatest man-made human tragedies in recorded history following the Holocaust during World War II and the decades of massacres and oppression in Palestine.

The same year as the Alhambra Decree, Columbus set foot in the New World, setting the stage for the Spanish to begin the centuries-long slave trade, carrying tens of thousands of Africans to the New World while also destroying the civilizations of the Aztec and Inca.

Despite the undeniable role Islamic scholarship had in aiding the exploration of the Americas, it is left out of history books the world over, and the cultural inquisition continues.

The rhetoric of there being a Christian Europe is unfortunately the greatest success—for lack of a better word—of the inquisitions of the late Middle Ages continuing in the twenty-first century.